BLOOD
WILL OUT

BLOOD WILL OUT

A Moretti and Falla Mystery

Jill Downie

DUNDURN
TORONTO

Editor: Dominic Farrell
Design: Jennifer Gallinger
Cover image: © Olga Ekaterincheva/Shutterstock
Cover design by Laura Boyle
Printer: Webcom

Library and Archives Canada Cataloguing in Publication

Downie, Jill, author
     Blood will out : a Moretti and Falla mystery / Jill Downie.

Issued in print and electronic formats.
ISBN 978-1-4597-2320-7 (pbk.).--ISBN 978-1-4597-2321-4 (pdf).--ISBN 978-1-4597-2322-1 (epub)

     I. Title.

PS8557.O848B56 2014   C813'.54   C2013-908357-X   C2013-908358-8

 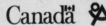

1 2 3 4 5   18 17 16 15 14

We acknowledge the support of the Canada Council for the Arts and the Ontario Arts Council for our publishing program. We also acknowledge the financial support of the Government of Canada through the Canada Book Fund and Livres Canada Books, and the Government of Ontario through the Ontario Book Publishing Tax Credit and the Ontario Media Development Corporation.

Care has been taken to trace the ownership of copyright material used in this book. The author and the publisher welcome any information enabling them to rectify any references or credits in subsequent editions.

J. Kirk Howard, President

The publisher is not responsible for websites or their content unless they are owned by the publisher.

Printed and bound in Canada.

Visit us at
Dundurn.com | @dundurnpress | Facebook.com/dundurnpress | Pinterest.com/Dundurnpress

Dundurn	Gazelle Book Services Limited	Dundurn
3 Church Street, Suite 500	White Cross Mills	2250 Military Road
Toronto, Ontario, Canada	High Town, Lancaster, England	Tonawanda, NY
M5E 1M2	LA1 4XS	U.S.A. 14150

For my brothers, Richard and Christopher.
Remembering our Guernsey years.

... night ghosts, and graves;
Blood cries for blood, and murder murder craves.
— John Marston
1576–1634

Prologue

Death of a Hermit

No horizon today. The mist gathered close to the land, touching the headland to the west of Rocquaine Bay and hiding the long sandy sweep of the western coastline from view. Certainly from his view. Of all the lost properties of youth, the one he most regretted was his marvellous vision. Cataracts, he supposed. Fixable, he knew that, but it would mean contact. He would think about it when the game became worth the candle and he could no longer read.

The tide was on the rise, but there was still an expanse of bare silver-grey sand, jotted with the red, brown and green of lichen-covered rocks, trails of seaweed, the *vraic* he had gathered with his father in the dim, distant past, when the world was young, at the first new moon after Candlemas, and then again in midsummer. He could still remember the sharpness of its smell in his nostrils, burning in the hearth, the ashes rich with potash to feed the soil.

He scrambled back from the beach over the rocks at the end of the high wall that protected the road against the high spring tides, something that became increasingly difficult with every passing day. Then he made his way past the Imperial Hotel and along the headland over Portelet Harbour, stopping briefly at the Table des Pions to pay his respects. A fairy ring long before it was used as a resting place by the soldiers of the local seigneurs on their *chevauchées* around the island parishes, it was a good place for him also to draw breath and courage before the hardest part of his climb, up towards Pleinmont Naval Observation Tower. Built by the Germans during the occupation of the island, deserted for years, it was now reconstructed for the tourists and, thankfully, open only two afternoons a week to disturb the quiet of the headland. Like the fairy ring, it too was haunted, and some of the presences were familiar to him.

After that, it was an easy walk across the Common, to the home he had built for himself. He was not the first solitary to have lived there, and he wondered if he would be the last. Probably so. Well-meaning and not so well-meaning individuals were constantly threatening his solitude and his peace of mind.

Home. He had built it like an Iron-Age round-house, and thatched the roof low over the only window. The walls had not been a problem, because he had learned about bricklaying from his father, who had built houses and worked in the granite quarries at St. Sampson. The roof had been a challenge, but he was determined not to use modern tiles. Finally, he had used a combination of turf and thatch, and compromised by lining the interior with batts of pink fibreglass insulation, covered in thick plastic as a moisture barrier. It gave a pleasant rosy glow to the place he called home, particularly in the light of his oil lamp, when the storms blew in across the Hanways and the Hanois Lighthouse wailed. Unlike the Iron-Age denizens of such a structure, he had not made a hole in the centre of the roof for the smoke to escape, but had added a chimney for his fireplace, keeping the thatch and turf well away from it.

He walked around to the door he had installed on the inland-facing wall, the one most protected from the prevailing wind. He never locked it, because less damage was done if the curious and the tearaways could get inside. Nothing of interest for the average thief, anyway: no stereos or televisions, no modern appliances. An intruder once made off with his camp stove, but had abandoned it in some bushes a few feet away. Not worth the effort, presumably. He raised the latch and let himself in.

This time, someone was waiting for him.

"I wondered when you would come," he said. "I knew you would come, eventually."

He felt a strange sense of relief, like a burden lifted. The other shoe finally dropping.

Part One

The Opening

Chapter One

Elodie Ashton bent down to pick up the secateurs she had dropped when she opened the door into the garden, and felt a twinge. The damp of approaching autumn was getting to her, and she had forgotten to put the nutmeg in the pocket of her gardening trousers.

Damn. She was far too young for this, she thought, both sore hips and superstitions. But better a nutmeg in her pocket than a needle in her trochanter, as had been suggested by Doctor Clarke.

"Too much sitting in front of a computer," he said.

"Is that your expert medical diagnosis?"

"Actually, yes. You're getting to an age where it's going to catch up with you, and you'll get fat."

"Don't beat around the bush, will you?"

The elderberry bush near the back door of the cottage was loaded with berries, and Elodie was determined to get to them before the wood pigeons and the blackbirds this year. The year before she had been on the mainland at a conference, and had missed the height of the season. As she reached up to cut a particularly luscious branch, she heard the sound of a car turning into her driveway.

Damn again. A voice calling out. Not damn. This voice was always welcome. Her goddaughter, Liz.

"I'm in the garden — come around!"

Detective Sergeant Liz Falla was off duty, wearing comfortable jeans and a black leather jacket. Her open-toed sandals revealed scarlet nails, and she was wearing large golden hoops in her ears. When she smiled, her resemblance to her father was striking, Elodie had often thought, but that was about all Liz had in common with her father — that, and a physical resemblance to those ancient Norman roots.

If, that is, the name Falla was indeed Norman, but it probably was. The theory that some poor Spanish wretch washed up in Guernsey when the Armada was blown off course in stormy waters, and stayed to reproduce, was unlikely, and the romantic possibility of being descended from fifteenth-century Jewish nobility fleeing Spain to escape persecution difficult to prove.

The rest of Liz was pure Ashton. She had her mother's singing voice, and the Ashton combination of an analytical mind and an intuitive grasp of circumstance and situation. Who knew what that big sister of hers could have done with her life, Elodie had often wondered, if she had not fallen in love with Dan Falla and had Liz when she was just out of her teens. But

Joan Falla seemed a happy woman, and had achieved what her little sister had not. Love and marriage. More precisely, a marriage that worked.

Elodie. Such a fancy name, an unlikely choice for her commonsense mother.

"Why?" she had asked.

"Your father's choice. Joan was *my* choice for your sister," was her mother's reply. And there the matter had rested.

"What are you doing around here?" Elodie asked, putting down the basket and hugging Liz.

"I'm on my way to work out at Beau Sejour Recreation Centre, and I left a little early so I could drop in and see you. Easy to do, now that I finally have wheels. Come out and let me show them off to you."

One of the unexpected bonuses of the last case Liz had worked on had been the gift of some vintage French couture. After checking with Chief Officer Hanley that accepting it was in order, about which he had been satisfactorily vague, she had promptly sold it on eBay and bought herself a car. Or at least made a substantial downpayment on a pretty little Figaro in pale aqua, a so-called "retro car," made by Nissan. Second-hand, but still … air-conditioning, leather interior in a soft cream colour — and a roof that opened. The stuff of dreams, now made reality.

Elodie's reaction was gratifyingly enthusiastic. "It's so … you, Liz. The perfect accessory!"

"I've always envied my Guvnor his Triumph, and I can't wait to show him." Together they walked back into the house.

"I thought I'd find you at the computer," Liz said, "working your magic for some verbally challenged mainland medico."

"Well, I'm working magic, but on my elderberry tree. Give me a hand. You can reach some of the higher branches for me before you go."

"Ah, come on, El. Not you too!" Liz protested. "Can't you just trust it to keep the witches away from your kitchen door without mumbling incantations over it?"

"It's doing a good job of that for me, all on its own. Haven't seen a witch in these parts, ever." Elodie chuckled and held out the secateurs to Liz. "I know how you feel about Aunt Becky, but this is Bacchic magic — sort of. My witches' brew is going to be a really potent elderberry-flavoured vodka. Come on, and I'll show you how to make a diabolically delicious potion," she said, pointing to a berry-laden branch near the top of the tree.

As they worked together, talking idly about this and that, Liz Falla thought to herself, not for the first time, what a puzzle this woman was. It was not so much that she had followed a different path from Liz's mother, Elodie's older sister — much older sister — but that she had opted for a career so far removed from people. She held the best parties, belonged to the Island Players and enjoyed appearing on stage from time to time, but spent her working career before a computer screen.

Elodie said little to her family about her professional life, largely because of the esoteric and special-ized nature of what she did, so Liz had looked her up and found her website. On it, she described herself as a medical researcher, editor and illustrator, and the examples she provided of her work were impressive. They varied from working with academic presses and editing specific research projects to composing speeches.

Elodie also said little about her personal life in London before she came back to Guernsey, but Joan Falla was sure there was heartbreak in her sister's past.

"She was divorced, Mum. That's heartbreak," Liz had responded.

"That's not what I mean," her mother had enigmatically replied.

If she had decided to hole up back home in Guernsey to escape from whatever troubles she'd experienced, Elodie could not hide her good looks. Even in her working gear of patched jeans and a loose-fitting green silk blouse that had seen better days, she was striking. From some distant Teutonic ancestor she had inherited curly red hair and the ivory skin of the redhead, but without freckles.

"I wish I'd inherited the tall gene that you and my sister got from somewhere."

"You are petite, Elodie."

"I am *short*. That's what I always say to your mother, and this is when I'd give a witch's incantation for a few extra inches."

Liz grinned. "I must say, it's useful in my job to have my mother's extra inches." She reached up and pulled down another branch. The basket was just about full.

"Why? Because you are as tall as the bad guys?

"Because I am just about as tall as the good guys. Great to look my fellow officers in the eye and say 'get lost' when necessary."

"Like that, is it?"

"Only sometimes. This looks like plenty — how much booze are you planning to make?"

"Liqueur, *please*. Yup, that's enough. Do you have time for a coffee?"

"And to see what you do with these little suckers. Time for both brews. It was a rough morning, which is why I'm on my way to Beau Sejour, to work it out of my system."

"Want to tell me? Or can you?"

Liz shrugged her shoulders. "I don't see why not. You know the old hermit who lives in that weird place near Rocquaine Bay? He topped himself."

The flippant tone did not surprise Elodie. She had heard it before in similar situations, or during family discussions. It drove her sister to distraction, but she knew it was her niece's way of coping — not just with her job — but with other people's anger, or pain. Or her own.

"Poor old fellow. Who found him?"

"The postman, believe it or not. Delivering magazines."

Elodie watched as Liz walked towards the kitchen door, then appeared to change her mind. She took a few steps down the path that led to the row of chestnut trees that separated her cottage from the garden behind her. The grass on each side of the path was scattered with windfalls from the apple trees, and soon the prickly cases of the chestnuts would join them.

"Looking for conkers? A bit early yet," she called out.

"There are going to be some beauts. Pity you weren't here when I was a kid."

"To me, you're still a kid." Elodie laughed. She paused, then asked, "So, no more about the hermit?"

Liz did not respond immediately, and when she did her voice was serious, flippancy gone.

"What do you know about your neighbour, the one who is renting Brenda Le Huray's place? The property that backs on to yours?"

Elodie came down the path and joined her niece. "Brenda moved in with her daughter, and I don't really miss her. She was always complaining about the chestnut trees. 'Messy,' she called them. His name is Hugo Shawcross and he's a folklorist, he tells me, a researcher, and certainly the Internet confirms that. He's the author of a number of books on the subject."

"You've met him?"

An early conker fell from one of the trees, and Liz picked it up. It lay in the palm of her hand still in its case, like a tiny hedgehog with greenish bristles.

"Yes." Elodie turned and looked at her niece. "This is not just idle curiosity, is it?"

"No." Liz gently returned the chestnut-hedgehog to the ground. "Let's have that coffee and make your potion." They started back towards the house.

"What do you think of him?" Liz had dropped her voice.

Elodie picked up the basket they had left by the door and shrugged her shoulders. "A bit too chatty for my liking. But he seems pleasant enough, certainly non-threatening."

Liz held the door as her aunt went in with the basket, and put it on the kitchen table. Elodie had made many changes in the early-eighteenth-century cottage, but, apart from its modern appliances, the kitchen was very much as it had been when its original owners roasted their beef and mutton on the spit over the giant fireplace. She knew how lucky she had been when the cottage had come onto the "open" market. Once you had left the island, it was difficult to get back as a homeowner, because of the protective property laws.

And the other piece of luck was a colossal divorce settlement. Every cloud, as they say. It had certainly helped when it came to putting in a bedroom and bathroom beneath the roof in what had been a loft, and taking out some of the interior walls downstairs to open up the space. She had replaced the white trim around the windows, put in a flagged driveway for her car, keeping the old limestone gateposts marking the edge of the property, and retiled the sloping roof in softly glazed coral-pink terra cotta tiles. Then, having taken care of the personal, she had had the whole place rewired to accommodate her professional working life.

"So, this is by way of being an official call?"

Liz laughed, took off her leather jacket and hung it over the back of a chair. "Not official, no. We've had a complaint about him, and since my boss has been off the island, I was asked to look into it. Discreetly."

"Discreetly?"

Elodie was transferring three large Mason jars to the worn pine surface of the sizeable table that stretched across the centre of the kitchen. She fetched a bottle of vodka from the equally sizeable sideboard, and some chopped-up lemon rind.

"Is he anything I should worry about? Here," Elodie pointed to a large crockery bowl high on a shelf near the fireplace, "get that down for me, would you?"

Liz obliged. "I don't think so, and the complaint is so bizarre it could be that we should be looking into the complainer rather than your new neighbour."

She pulled out a branch of berries from the basket, holding them up against the light, admiring their purple translucence in the sunlight streaming through the window. "Now what do we do?"

Elodie took another branch from the basket. "We'll need something for the stems and so on. They are mildly toxic. We'll use this." She pulled out a plastic pail from under the table, then a tall stool. "You'll be fine with a chair, but this suits me better.

"So, tell me — is he a flasher? A con artist?" She hopped up on to the stool, and started to pull off the berries, her fingers swiftly turning purple.

"Nothing so run-of-the-mill, El."

Liz hesitated. It had all sounded so ridiculous this morning, and she couldn't believe Chief Officer Hanley had asked her to look into it. But he had, and she knew why. Because the complainant was the wife of one of the major estate agents on the island, a man not to be trifled with. It was a familiar theme. She watched the juices trickle over her hands and thought of Lady

Macbeth, and blood, and said, "We have been told he is a vampire."

The shriek of laughter that burst out of Elodie shook the stool on which she was sitting, and she grasped the edge of the table to steady herself.

"Liz, Liz — which demented islander told you that? I cannot believe you are taking this seriously."

"I'm not, and it certainly added a little light relief to my morning. But Elton Maxwell's wife does."

"Ah. So the chief officer does." Elodie pulled out another branch of berries, and winked across the table at Liz.

"Got it in one. Mrs. Maxwell's a member of the Island Players. Do you know her?"

"Only as a fellow player. I don't socialize much with the Maxwells." Elodie leaned across the table. "Tell me more. Should I be avoiding the garden after dusk? Carrying garlic? Is she out of her tiny mind? If she has one at all?"

Liz shrugged her shoulders and went on picking berries from the stem in her hand. "She's not quite as wacky as that makes her sound, actually. She says he is writing a play for the group — do you know anything about that?'

"No. But then, I'm only just coming up for air after finishing a really tough project for a researcher at Great Ormond Street Hospital. What does playwriting have to do with vampires?"

"Everything. That's what the play is about, and what has upset Mrs. Maxwell is that Hugo Shawcross says it is an area of interest to him, because he is a vampire himself, descended from a long line of the undead. She says he is trying to create a splinter group within the Island Players, and has joked about secret oaths and blood sacrifices."

"Seriously?" Elodie had stopped working on her branch of elderberries, and now looked concerned. "I know they were hoping to get some new blood into the group — sorry, terrible choice of expression — and wanted to attract a younger crowd. But this doesn't sound like a good idea."

"No, and that was one of her complaints. That he is a bad influence on the island young. She also said he became threatening when challenged. Mind you, it could be that Mrs. Maxwell doesn't have much of a sense of humour. He told her to leave him alone or one dark night she'd wake up to find him chomping down on her. Or words to that effect."

"Yuk. Not nice." She caught Liz's eye, and giggled. "Sorry again, Liz, but this is just ridiculous. Does chomping down on someone's neck constitute a death threat?"

Liz grinned. "Don't feel the need to apologize. You should hear the jokes back at the office — well, you shouldn't. Some are just filthy. Even Chief Officer Hanley had difficulty keeping a straight face when he told me, and he's not a laugh-a-minute kind of feller."

"Were you planning on going round to talk to him? Do you need backup? We could take some of that." Elodie pointed to the string of garlic hanging near a thick rope of onions. "I don't have any crucifixes handy, I'm afraid."

"I sort of need backup — at least, that is what I was going to ask you." Liz was no longer looking amused. "But I am now rethinking that, in case this guy is —"

"Dangerous? Have you seen him? He's not much taller than me, looks more like Gandalf than a vampire, and I'm pretty sure I could take him if I had to." Elodie got up and went over to the sink to wash her hands. "See, Liz, I don't believe in fairies, or ghosts, or vampires. But I do think he could be trouble. The Island Players have always played second fiddle to GADOC, and I'm sure that's what this is about."

GADOC, the Guernsey Amateur Dramatic and Operatic Society, were the principal group on the island, with a history that went back close to a century. They performed at the well-equipped theatre in the Beau Sejour centre; the Island Players had come into being with a mandate to perform more challenging material. Their audiences, not surprisingly, were considerably smaller, and they were constantly in need of funds.

Elodie went on. "The Players may be hoping that something shocking will help membership. I can always just ask about the play — say I've heard about it. I often see him out in his garden, through the trees."

Elodie turned around and grabbed at a towel near the sink. "Let's get these beauties into the vodka with the lemon peel."

Liz went over to the sink, taking the towel from Elodie. Something fragrant was cooking in the oven, and the aroma drifted towards her as she washed her hands.

"There's a fantastic smell over here. What is it?"

"Lamb shanks, cooking *very* slowly, with red wine and herbs from the garden. And garlic, of *course*! Some time you must let me teach you how to cook, young woman. Living on omelettes, fish and chips, and Dwight's curries — delicious though they are, and I have some in the freezer — is not good. It'll catch up with you, sooner or later."

"Knock it off, El. You sound like my mother. Anyway, are lamb shanks a health food?"

"Kind of. They are good for the soul."

Together they filled the Mason jars, fastening down the lids, and Elodie put on the coffee. "How *is* Dwight?" she asked. "Still playing in that jazz group with your boss?"

"Yes. He's fine. We are not an item anymore, you know."

"I know." Elodie had her back to Liz, but could hear the subtle change in her voice. She took down two coffee mugs from the shelf near the fireplace and put them on the table. "Is that something you care about, or am I misinterpreting that change of key I hear?"

Liz grinned, and said, "Major to minor you mean? Actually, that's more about my Guvnor than about Dwight. Thanks." She took the filled coffee mug, sat down and took a sip. "He was going to come and hear me sing with my group, Jenemie. Then he had to go to London for a debriefing for this last caper — case — of ours and missed it. I was disappointed, don't know why."

Elodie looked at her niece, and felt a wave of tenderness. She was younger than her age in some ways, flitting from relationship to relationship, some of them from which she disentangled herself — or was disentangled. Her apparent insouciance about such things was not always genuine, her flippancy a useful cover for hurt.

"Have you heard him play? I have, once. He's good. Went with your Uncle Vern." She smiled. "Do you think your disappointment is artistic, or personal? Do you fancy him? He has a certain *je ne sais quoi*. Well, I do *sais quoi*. He's rather gorgeous."

Liz looked as shocked as if her aunt had made a deeply improper suggestion. "El, please, he's old enough to be my father. Besides, he's my boss." She took a deep draught of her coffee, pushing away the thought of an earlier attraction, a man old enough to be her grandfather.

"Artistic then, I'll take your word for it. Perhaps he doesn't want to blur the line between business and pleasure. It can be a dangerous one to cross," Elodie's voice hardened, but she did not elaborate, instead adding, "and your piano-playing Guv is not *that* old, kid. Have you been to the Grand Saracen, the club where he plays?"

"No, only to the restaurant upstairs. Emidio's. It used to be his father's. His mum was a Guernsey girl."

"A wartime romance with an Italian slave labourer, Vern told me. Tell you what, we'll go together some time. Looks like an ascetic, your Guvnor, but having watched him play, I doubt he is. A lot of smouldering going on beneath that detached exterior. Are you on duty after your workout? Why don't you come back here and share the lamb shanks with me? If you're free, that is."

"Love to. I'll eat and take notes. Are they easy to make?"

"A doddle. You can use that slow cooker I gave you and give your microwave a break. And I may have some info for you by then. Gandalf usually takes the air around the witching hour, and I'll stroll down in that direction and engage him in conversation."

"Okay, but be careful." Liz stood up and took her jacket off the back of the chair. "You may not believe in fairies or ghosts or vampires, El, but that doesn't mean Shawcross is a pussycat."

"He has one — a pussycat, I mean. I hear him calling it. Stoker." The two women looked at each other, and Elodie said, "First name probably Bram, don't you think?"

She laughed, but Liz didn't. Elodie went over to the sink and fetched a damp cloth, came back and started to wipe the jars. She looked across the table at her niece, her voice now deadly serious. "I may not believe in vampires, Liz, but that doesn't mean I don't believe in wickedness, and depravity and vice. I think there is as much evil in this world as good. Possibly more."

Liz looked at her aunt, startled at this sudden outpouring of hidden emotion, as if she had returned to some dark episode in her life, and Liz thought of her mother's enigmatic comment on her sister's past.

"But I don't have to tell you that, in your job," she added and changed the subject. "Is your boss still in London?"

"No, actually, he's taken a couple of days off." Liz pulled her car keys out of her pocket and added,

"At this moment he's probably messing about in his new boat."

Ed Moretti was thinking of his father. Not being a Guernseyman, Emidio Moretti had felt no particular desire to own a boat, although he had talked about it from time to time. So Moretti had got his knowledge and his experience from his mother's brother, who owned a boat and was only too happy to have a strong young boy as his crew. He looked across the deck of his new Westerly Centaur at his own crew, who was at that moment leaning rather perilously over the side of the boat.

Don Taylor was no young boy, but a man in his mid-forties with the string-bean build and the stamina of a long-distance runner. On an island measuring just over twenty-four square miles, he still managed to keep up his passion on the extensive network of cliff paths. He worked with the Financial Services Commission, one of the elements in the complex structure involved with the financial scene, now the island's main source of income. Moretti had worked together with Don once before, and Don had provided a key piece of information on Moretti's last case.

"Good decision to get a bilge-keeler with the tides around these parts." Don's voice drifted back on the wind to Moretti. "And you won't lose much except to windward. You'll not always be diesel-powered, I trust."

"I wouldn't dare, not with you on board, but I

wanted to give the motor another good outing while I was still able to get my money back."

Moretti looked up at the cliffs and felt happiness flooding him. Well, contentment anyway. The kind of escape and freedom he felt at the Grand Saracen, or playing the piano that had been his mother's, in the house that had been his childhood home. Beyond the treacherous rocks around Icart Point, he could see the coast beginning to curve inwards to Moulin Huet Bay, and out again to the Pea Stacks, three great rock masses on the southeast tip of the coastline, Le Petit Aiguillon, le Gros Aiguillon, and l'Aiguillon d'Andrelot, painted by Renoir when he visited the island. Midnight assassins, Victor Hugo had called them.

L'Aiguillon d'Andrelot was also known as Le Petit Bonhomme Andriou, and was supposed to resemble a monk in his cowl and gown. Passing fishermen tipped their caps to him, or offered small sacrifices — a libation, a biscuit, even a garment. Or so Moretti was told by Les De Putron, who had laughed at the old superstition and then doffed his cap as they sailed past.

"Better safe than sorry," he said. "Mind you do the same. Be on the safe side," he repeated.

Looking at the massive rocks, Moretti wondered at the power of superstition. An old observation post used by the Germans at Fort Grey, once in ruins, was now a shipwreck museum, a monument to the hundreds of lives lost along that hazardous coast. But perhaps they had not made an offering to *le petit bonhomme*.

The wind had come up, and Moretti concentrated on keeping the Centaur beyond the reefs and shoals of the promontory. Thank God he had done the sensible thing and taken lessons from Les, who ran a small private company running charters, renting boats and giving lessons out of St. Sampson's harbour.

He had thought at first of keeping the Centaur at Beaucette Marina, on the northeast coast of the island. At one time a granite quarry, blasted into being as a marina in the sixties by British army engineers, it had appealed because of its distance from where he worked, but in the end that told against it. He had a feeling that his boat would spend more time bobbing about with the seals who showed up at Beaucette from time to time, than with him at sea.

The obvious choice of mooring was the harbour in St. Peter Port, and marina rates were the same anywhere, but Moretti still liked the thought of getting outside the capital for a change. He finally settled on St. Sampson's as being closer to the small garage that looked after his Triumph; he could leave it in the safe hands of Bert Brehaut, the garage owner, when he was sailing. Security for the boats anchored there was good, with a punch-in code for berth holders and boat crews, but he didn't fancy leaving his roadster outside the solid chain-link fence.

Sometimes he stayed overnight on the boat, which came equipped below decks with a sleeping area that converted into a dinette, complete with small stove, storage, a sink and toilet. It had been a financial stretch, but would save him finding accommodation when he visited the other islands, or France.

"Tide's up. Want to pull in to Saints Bay and walk

over to that little Greek restaurant past Icart Point, near Le Gouffre? Les De Putron has a mooring and a dinghy he keeps there," he called over to Don.

"Great idea."

The winds calmed as they approached the small bay, and the choppy water settled into ripples, picture-postcard blue and beautiful. Moretti cut the engine, and they moved gently in to the mooring. A few minutes later, they had pulled the dinghy up on to the dock, and were climbing the steep path to the top of the cliffs, with the natural rock face on one side, and a man-made granite bulwark on the other. Somewhere, an invisible stream made its way to the coast, concealed by vegetation, its waters murmuring unseen.

It was tough going up the cliff path, steep and uneven, a track that had been there for centuries. Don leaped ahead, light and easy on his feet, and turned back to laugh at Moretti.

"Want a hand?"

"You're a bloody mountain goat, Taylor."

"That's what used to use these paths — goats, I mean. Goats and fishermen and smugglers. Watch the wall, my darling, when the gentlemen go by, as the poet says." Don gestured towards the wall's granite face.

"Not what I'm supposed to do when they're bringing in brandy for the parson, or marijuana for — whoever. Not in my job."

"True. Look at those, running down the side of the cliff. Even I wouldn't use those."

Don had reached the top, and was pointing at barely visible tracks down the sheer cliff face to their left.

"Goat tracks. Used to be all kinds. Goats, I mean. Falla, my partner, has an aunt who still keeps goats somewhere around here."

They turned left and headed towards Icart Point, with the sea and the cliff face close to the footpath. On the other side was St. Martin's Common, where sheep had roamed free for generations, but they were long gone, like most of the goats that had used the old tracks. Gone also were the *côtils*, the terraces where smallholders grew potatoes, or planted bulbs for the once-flourishing flower-growing industry.

There was little colour on the cliffs at this time of year, with the heather and gorse past their prime, but the sky was full of gulls wheeling and shrieking overhead in perpetual motion, and the wind carried the sound of the waves, crashing against the rocks, the familiar soundtrack of the coastline. Even up here, the air was flavoured with salt.

"You know what they say about gorse?" The wind was strong enough for Don to have to shout at Moretti. "When the gorse is not in flower, then kissing is out of fashion."

"And gorse is always in flower. More or less."

"So the kissing never has to stop. All one requires is the woman to kiss."

Moretti looked at Don's face, but he was not laughing. Was this just idle banter, or something more?

The little Greek restaurant was in a tree-filled valley above Le Gouffre, a small anchorage between towering cliffs. The waitress who served them sounded Australian, but the food was Greek. They ordered a range of appetizers and coffee and sat outside, watching a large marmalade cat luxuriate in the late summer sun in this protected valley.

"Sybarites, cats. They certainly know how to seize the day," said Don, popping an olive into his mouth and chewing with gusto. He had the voracious appetite of the long-distance runner, without a trace of body fat. "Speaking of which, is this your last day of freedom?"

The coffee was good. Hot, strong and black as — as the colour of his ex-lover's hair. Although Moretti was not sure you could call someone an ex-lover who had, in effect, been a one-night stand. Not that he'd planned it that way.

"It is, then it's back to the desk, I imagine. Break-ins and burglaries and little else. But maybe I'll have more time for the boat."

"And playing at the club with the Fénions? Means layabouts, doesn't it? Great name for a bunch of jazz musicians — or an outsider's perception of jazz musicians. Have you got a replacement for your horn player?"

"Nope. And no hopes of one on the horizon. So it'll be Dwight on drums, Lonnie on bass and me playing piano. Won't be quite the same."

"Still, let me know next time you are playing."

Moretti felt a damp little cloud of depression settle over him, and fingered the lighter he always carried in his pocket. Why a lighter should be the talisman that helped him keep off the noxious weed, he couldn't imagine. But it was at moments like this he still longed for a smoke.

Don dipped a *dolma* in tzatziki and swallowed it whole. "God, I love garlic. Just as well I don't have a woman in my life at the moment. I'll stink for twenty-four hours after this lot. How about you, Ed? Any new lady in your life?"

Women again. Moretti looked across the table at the man who knew about as much about his private life as anyone, which was virtually nothing. Idle chatter about women interested him about as much as discussing island politics, or what were now called "relationships." All three topics were minefields, as dangerous as these cliffs had been after the Germans left the island.

"No new lady, but a new man. Should take up about as much of my time as a new lady, and be far less rewarding. You've heard of fast-tracking?"

"Taking in graduates and speeding them to the top? Weren't you one?"

"Yes. APSG — the Police Accelerated Promotion Scheme for Graduates. I've got one arriving tomorrow, and my instructions are to take him under my wing."

"Don't see you as the mother-hen type." Don grinned. "Do you know anything about him?"

"Some. He is a Londoner, mid-twenties, has a science degree of some sort. I've spoken to him on the phone. Tells me he didn't want to be a teacher, so decided to be a policeman."

"Charming. Anything else he shared with you that's more endearing? What's his name?"

Moretti bent down to stroke the cat, who had come over to join them rubbing hopefully around his feet. "An interesting one," he replied, "Aloisio Brown. Mother's Portuguese. And no, I cannot think of a single aspect of this that's the least bit endearing."

He held out a piece of taramasalata to the cat, who took it from him with great delicacy, and ate it.

Chapter Two

It was coming along well. Hugo Shawcross leaned back in his chair and rubbed his hands. Beyond the study window, he could see the chestnut trees on his neighbour's property growing darker by the minute as the sun set. He must go out soon and call Stoker in, or he'd get into a fight to the death with Mudge, the small and surprisingly aggressive tortoiseshell female that lived two houses away. Fortunately, Stoker's life was ruled by greed rather than the need to assert his neutered-male superiority, and he could be relied on to leave the fray and return to his tidbit-carrying master.

Hugo saved the last speech he had composed, and contemplated it before turning off his laptop.

You have the dark gift. But this must be our secret. You must tell no one, do you hear me? No one. (Fade to black.)

Good. A strong ending to Act One. He already knew who he wanted to have as his Lilith, and that the difficulty would not be persuading her, but her family. Her mother reminded Hugo of Stoker's multicoloured *bête noire*, a small and surprisingly aggressive female whose genteel roots gave her an unshakeable belief in her own importance.

Carey, De Saumarez, Brock, Gastineau. The ancient aristocracy of Guernsey. *Les Messux*, as they had once been known. Of course, as Noel Coward had so inimitably put it, their stately homes were frequently mortgaged to the hilt, which had rather taken the gilt off the gingerbread. Or they didn't belong to them anymore, and had become hotels, or were broken up into elegant and desirable flats, which was the case for Mrs. Elton Maxwell, née Marie Gastineau. Island gossip said that Elton Maxwell had wooed and won Marie by making her an offer she couldn't refuse: the saving of her St. Peter Port family home. They now lived in one of the luxe apartments of the Gastineaus' former Georgian home on the Grange.

Hugo padded into the hall, removed his slippers and pulled on his boots. It could be quite wet at the back of the garden, and he hoped to find some mushrooms there, as he had before. He looked briefly in the hall mirror at his reflection with a tingle of satisfaction. *Not bad for a man of his age*, he thought. His occupation was sedentary, but the treadmill in his bedroom took care of that, and his nicely barbered beard conveniently hid the jowls that were beginning to form as he moved through his middle years. He must do something soon about replacing the weights he had left behind in his rather hasty departure from the mainland. His hair was thinning at the front now, but was still thick enough at the back to be worn on the long side, implying an artistic nature. He smiled at himself, then frowned.

"Bloody idiot," he told his reflection.

He shouldn't have done it, but he couldn't resist the temptation. Suggesting to Marie Maxwell that she could be the target of his undead affections had been foolish of him. If indeed he had any vampiric lusts, he would not have wasted his nightly visits on the undelicious Marie, but on her far more delectable daughter, Marla. Besides, from his research it seemed that vampires preferred virgins. Not that Marla Maxwell was the least bit virginal, exuding a sexuality so strong that the few young men who belonged to the group were in lust with her, rather more than with the theatre. Oh yes, the perfect Lilith.

Hugo went into the kitchen and selected a handful of fish-shaped morsels from a packet, then went to the back door, walked down the gravel path and started calling Stoker's name. As he did so, he heard a voice calling back from the garden beyond the chestnut trees.

"He's over here. Will he let me pick him up?"

Ah, his slightly standoffish neighbour with the pretty name. Elodie. A pretty name for a pretty woman.

"Not unless you are carrying food. Don't worry. I am, so he's likely to head in my direction."

There was a scuffling noise in the undergrowth, and Stoker appeared. Hugo picked him up and started back towards his house, calling "thank you" over his shoulder. To his surprise, he heard his neighbour say, "I am a member of the Island Players. Is it true you're writing something to open the new season?"

"Yes. Just let me put Stoker in the house, and I'll be back."

Hugo scampered back along the path, dropped Stoker unceremoniously inside the door, threw in a handful of fishy nibbles after him, and returned to the low fence near the chestnut trees. Elodie Ashton was standing there, holding a small basket.

"I was mushroom-hunting," she said, "and your cat joined me. But I don't think mushrooms are his thing."

"No, but they are mine. I was hoping to find some on my side. I have, before, and they're very good."

"As long as you know what you're doing," said his neighbour, and then added, "I'd love to hear about your play. Forgive me for not doing the neighbourly thing when you moved in, but I had a deadline. Now that's done, would you like to come over for a drink and tell me something about it?"

Would he like to? Elodie Ashton, so he was told by Brenda Le Huray, came from an old island family and knew everyone who was anyone. An ally on the Island Players would be a real stroke of luck.

"Love to! Just give me a moment to get out of these boots, and I'll join you." Hugo started to turn back to the house.

"Tell you what," said his now far from standoffish neighbour, "I've found some nice mushrooms over here, and I can see some beauties on your side. Why don't you pick them, bring them over and join me for dinner? They'll go very well with lamb shanks — or are you a vegetarian?"

"God no! Far from it! The bloodier the better!"

For a moment Elodie Ashton seemed startled by his facetious response, then she laughed. "Lamb shanks aren't bloody, of course."

"Just a figure of speech. I'll pick the mushrooms and join you in about an hour?"

"Perfect."

A shaft of sunlight sliced across the path and through the trees, making Elodie Ashton's red hair burst into flame.

More than perfect, he thought, as he hastened back to his house. *Lamb shanks, and a pretty woman who was an island insider! Marvellous. No. Bloody miraculous.*

They had needed the air-conditioning at the Beau Sejour Centre that summer, which had been hot and dry, right into September. Liz finished her exercise routine and made for the showers. Dinner with Elodie meant using the showers there, rather than waiting until she got home, her usual pattern.

As she got into the change room, Marla Maxwell was coming out of one of the shower stalls, towelling her hair and singing. Liz didn't recognize the song, but certainly the singer could have lured any red-blooded male onto the Pea Stacks in a matter of seconds, and he would have died happy. *Trouble on two nicely muscled legs*, thought Liz, as the girl surveyed herself with unabashed approval in one of the long mirrors. She was tanned without tan lines, which suggested frequent use of a tanning bed. When she saw Liz's reflection in the mirror, she turned round and fixed two startlingly blue eyes on her.

"Hiya. You're Detective Sergeant Falla, aren't you."

"And you're Marla Maxwell. Hi."

Liz was about to pull off her sweater when Marla Maxwell said, "I've got a problem. Can I talk to you?" The self-satisfaction was gone, and the girl now looked worried, a frown wrinkling her pristine forehead. Liz pulled her sweater back on.

"You can, but this is not the ideal place. Why don't you come and see me at the office? I'll be there tomorrow morning."

"I don't want to be seen at the police station, because someone will tell my mother. Why not now? No one's around."

Marla began to put on some clothes, which Liz found helpful. Although, God help her, she only fancied men, a naked Marla did nothing to establish a professional atmosphere in this already unbusinesslike setting.

"Okay. What's bothering you?" Resigned to her fate, Liz sat down on the bench in front of the lockers. Marla Maxwell threw her towel into her gym bag and started to tie her damp hair into a ponytail.

"Not what. Who. I'm being harassed."

"That's serious and we can help you. Who is doing this?"

"That's just it. I don't know. I'm getting these weird text messages, and they're not from the people who they say they're from. And someone's following me, I'm sure of it." Marla's low dramatic tones began to sound like something from one of the daytime soaps.

"That's all a bit garbled, Marla." Liz took the padlock off her locker and started to take out her belongings. "If these things are happening, surely your parents should be the first to know."

"No!" Marla Maxwell sounded as if she was about to burst into tears. "Because then they'd know about ... and I'll be sent to my horrid old aunt on the mainland, and if you say anything to them I'll deny everything!" The soap opera tone had returned.

"Marla, you still live at home, don't you? And your parents are friends of the chief officer's. I'd have to tell them."

"That's why I wanted to tell you here, not at the police station."

At this point, two women came in, chattering away, and Marla picked up her gym bag and ran past them, bumping into them in her hurry.

On her way back to Elodie and lamb shanks, Liz mulled over her change room encounter. Overly dramatic as the girl had sounded, there clearly was something bothering her, or why would she voluntarily open up a can of worms with a member of the police force? And a can of worms it was, since she was afraid of her parents finding out whatever it was she was doing — and it was easy enough to guess what that was. Sex, yes, and probably involving some youth the Gastineaus would consider undesirable. Or, rather, unacceptable.

It was a short drive to Elodie's cottage, but by the time she got there she had decided there was nothing she could do unless the girl laid a formal complaint. She could only guess at Marla Maxwell's age, but she suspected she was younger than she looked, still in her teens. Certainly she talked like a fifteen-year-old. She sighed, remembering herself at that age, hormones a-bubble, one minute melancholy and the next over the moon, secretive and sociable, a mass of contradictions. Come to think of it, had she really changed that much?

She was laughing as she drove up the gravel driveway alongside Elodie's cottage, but her laughter died when she realized she had forgotten to pick up a bottle of red, as she had intended. Thinking about Marla Maxwell's problems had driven it clean out of her mind. Ah well. Liz got out of her car, locked it, went up and knocked on the door before letting herself in. As she did so, she heard voices, Elodie's voice, and that of a man. The scent of something delectable hung in the air. Not lamb shanks. It smelled like mushrooms cooking.

"Liz! Come on through! Into the kitchen!"

She walked into a scene of cosy domesticity. At the kitchen table, her aunt was slicing up a baguette and, at the stove stood a small, bearded man in a striped apron cooking — yes — mushrooms.

Gandalf.

As she came in, he turned around. He was not looking particularly pleased at the intrusion.

"Liz, let me introduce my neighbour, Hugo Shawcross, who will be joining us for dinner. Hugo, this is my niece, Liz."

Gandalf nodded, managed a smile, said hello, then turned hastily back to his mushrooms. As he did so, Elodie mouthed something at Liz, shaking her head slightly. It looked as if she was saying, "Only Liz."

Ah, no job description.

Before Liz could make any response, Elodie said, with cheerful animation, "Hugo and I have been having the most fascinating conversation." She brandished the breadknife in the air like a cheerleader waving her pompoms. "Sit down, pour yourself a glass of wine."

"About —?"

"About vampires," she said. There was just a touch of hysteria in her voice, which seemed to Liz to be more about a wild desire to laugh, than fear. "Hugo can tell you all you might ever want to know about them."

Gandalf turned away from his pan of mushrooms, and chuckled. "The undead," he said, and held up his glass of wine, which stood close to the stove. From the colour of his cheeks, it was far from being his first, and he looked not in the least vampire-like. "Here's to the undead," he repeated.

Almost exactly an hour after their across-the-garden-fence conversation, Hugo Shawcross had arrived at

Elodie's front door carrying a very nice bottle of wine, a paper bag of mushrooms, and a buff-coloured folder. *The trouble-making play, presumably*, thought Elodie as she let him in, although it was not at all certain if he knew he was in Mrs. Maxwell's bad books. They exchanged the usual pleasantries, thank-yous for the invitation and the wine, idle chatter about mushrooms, appreciative comments from Hugo about Elodie's cottage, and an offer to do the mushroom-cooking.

"Lovely. I've already put out a suitable pan, and I'll make garlic bread — if you like garlic bread?"

"Love it."

"So," said Elodie, vigorously mashing crushed garlic cloves into the softened butter, "tell me about your play. I hear the subject matter is somewhat controversial?"

Hugo helped himself to a blue-and-white striped apron from a peg by the stove and put it over his immaculate white shirt. "Some have found it so, and, unfortunately, the some in this case is a Mrs. Maxwell, who has clout in the group."

So he knew that much. "Not just in the group, Hugo. She is island aristocracy."

"I know, and that's the other thing. I am, naturally, interested in the ancient Guernsey families — she's a Gastineau, isn't she? — but when I started asking questions about her family history she seemed quite put out, I can't think why."

"Not a good person to get on the wrong side of. You said 'the other thing.' What else is she upset about?"

Hugo stopped cleaning the mushrooms, and banged his fist on the wooden table. "It's my own fault," he said. "She got up my nose with her hoity-toityness and I made a stupid joke. The play, you see, involves vampires, and the Players are hopeful it will bring in a new, younger audience. She objected, and I — laughingly — claimed to have the inside track on vampires, because I am one."

"Gracious!" Elodie waited, but Hugo didn't go on to his neck-biting threat. "I wonder why she was so upset about vampires? It seems to me they are everywhere nowadays — in the entertainment world, I mean, and besides," she added, "you're not, are you?" She laughed and held up a clove of garlic, and Hugo playfully shrank away from her in jest. Hopefully in jest.

"Interestingly enough, they don't play a significant part in Guernsey folklore. Werewolves, yes, but no vampires. Of course, that could be why, because the werewolf is the sworn enemy of the vampire. But you're right. They are everywhere."

"Literally?"

The most troubling thing about Gandalf, thought Elodie, *is that he is absolutely straight-faced about this stuff*.

"Who knows. But he, or she, is an archetype, and we humans love archetypes. And we all know people who feed off the emotional energy of others." Hugo reached for the bottle of olive oil on the table and added some to the pan, which was already heating. He tossed the prepared mushrooms into the pan on the stove, then spread them out carefully. Faintly, they began to splutter. "But there is one overwhelming truth about vampires that has the Mrs. Maxwells of this world up in arms." Hugo poured himself another glass of wine and took a good swig.

"And that is —?"

"Sex. The vampire, above all, is an erotic metaphor. The vampire, Elodie, is always about sex."

Hugo Shawcross turned and fixed a piercing gaze on Elodie. Just at that moment, mercifully, she heard the sound of Liz's Figaro in the driveway.

They sat around the kitchen table to eat, and the meal was delicious. Liz was starving, so she ate and watched Hugo Shawcross, allowing her aunt to do the questioning. All she had to do was listen, and the wine had loosened Hugo's tongue, which probably didn't require much loosening in the first place.

"Are you a vampirologist? I believe that's what they're called — people who study the phenomenon?"

"Well, that is part of the project I am involved with right now, so maybe I am!" Hugo chuckled through a mouthful of garlic bread, and helped himself to more. "I was originally a university lecturer with a particular interest in European folklore, and I was able to devote myself to it after I took early retirement. I am now working with a group of researchers on a project dear to my heart."

Liz allowed herself a question. "About vampires?" she asked. It was all she asked, but Hugo Shawcross gave her an impatient glance as if she had interrupted some private moment, and turned back to Elodie.

"Have you heard of the *Malleus Maleficarum*?" Without waiting for a response, he continued, "Not many have, so let me explain. It is a fifteenth-century Latin text on the hunting of witches. In English, the title means 'The Hammer of Witches.' At one time, there was much heated discussion in the Catholic Church about its validity as a part of Catholic doctrine, but the twentieth century more or less threw it out the stained glass window." He chortled at his little *bon mot*. "We, a group of us, feel it's time to take another look at it."

Elodie got up, took Hugo's plate back to the stove for another helping of lamb. His back was to her and, above his head, she threw a glance at Liz and grimaced. "Sorry, Hugo, if I'm being a bit slow here, but does this book have anything to do with vampires?" She brought the plate back to the table and placed it in front of him, then reached out for Liz's plate.

"It's okay, El. I'll get my own, thanks. This is just delicious."

Cutting into her remark, Hugo went on. "Not directly, but the man who first translated it from the Latin was indeed a vampirologist. His name was Montague Summers. A much misunderstood man, in my opinion. I became interested in him, and thus interested in vampires."

"Hence the subject matter of the play."

"Oh yes! The perfect topic to bring in a younger audience, and to recruit new talent to the group. A dramatic theme." Hugo wiped a piece of bread around the last juices on his plate.

"A melodramatic theme."

Standing behind him, Liz could not see the expression on Hugo Shawcross's face at her observation, but she saw Elodie's eyes widen. She picked up her plate and walked back to her seat. As she passed him, he grasped her arm, nearly knocking the plate out of her hands.

"Wrong, little lady, wrong. *Serious* theatre. I will not allow it to be played any other way."

Looking down into his eyes, Liz saw malevolence — or was *she* now being melodramatic? She pulled her arm away.

"Sorry I spoke." She resumed her seat and her meal as if nothing much had happened.

"But there is the chance nothing will come of this, because of Mrs. Maxwell's opposition." Elodie poured herself the last of the wine from the bottle on the table. She could hear the wind getting up and starting a gentle moaning in the chimney, the defruited elderberry tap-tapping against the kitchen door. They were usually familiar, soothing sounds, but the conversation around the kitchen table gave them a disturbing quality.

"Exactly. I think I played my cards wrong there. Any advice as to how I can appease the lady?"

"Yes." Elodie got up and started clearing the dishes. "Write a part for her she cannot bear to refuse. There are always more women than men in community theatre, and more competition for roles. Is there a good role for her in the play?"

She laughed, and removed the empty wine bottle from the table. Hugo had demolished most of it, also the first, and was now at the stage where his tongue was having difficulties shaping itself around his words. He was looking thoughtful.

"Not yet, but I haven't started Act Two. " His face lit up. "But I have the perfect role for her daughter!"

Liz, who was beginning to wonder when she could take her departure, but also whether she should leave her aunt with this weirdo who clearly wanted nothing more than to be left on his own with her, started to pay attention.

"Marla Maxwell?" Elodie asked. "Stunning girl, and quite a handful, from what I hear. Marie Maxwell might be very happy to have her occupied where she can keep an eye on her. Coffee?"

Liz settled back in her chair.

"Wonderful!" Hugo Shawcross slumped back in his seat, rocking his chair perilously as he stretched his arms over his head. "Mama can be good, and the daughter can be ba-a-ad!" It came out as a bleating noise, sheeplike rather than sexy, which from the glance he gave Elodie was what was intended.

"And what is this perfect role?" Elodie began loading the dishwasher as the coffee brewed. Her guest swivelled his chair around to face her.

"Lilith," he said, with some difficulty. "Lilith, the greatest demoness of them all. Lilith!"

"Ah, Lilith." Liz's clear, resonant singer's voice floated over the heads of Elodie and Hugo Shawcross. "Just about the oldest-known demon in folklore."

Always nice to turn heads, thought Liz, and both Elodie and Hugo were now staring at her in surprise. She had her audience, so the little lady decided to hold forth.

"Of course, that is how men want to see her, as the betrayer of Adam left on his ownsome in the Garden of Eden, the baby-blood-sucking killer, seducer of men with her voracious sexual appetite, draining them dry. *I* think she got fed up with Adam pushing her around and got out from under. If you'll pardon the expression. I think she's great. In the gym change room I just chatted with Marla, fresh from the shower and in the altogether, and she'll fit the bill perfectly."

Liz smiled serenely and waited for a response. It came.

"Feminist claptrap." Hugo Shawcross got up from his chair with some difficulty. His voice was shaking, with anger or red wine, or both. "In Sumerian mythology —"

"I thought that was now disputed." Liz got up and went across to where Elodie was standing, holding the cafetière in stunned silence. She poured herself a cup of coffee, handed the pot back to Elodie and returned to her seat. "And after you've had great sex with an archangel, I doubt you'd want to go back to a mere mortal. *I* wouldn't."

"Coffee, Hugo?" The banality of Elodie's query landed on deaf ears. Hugo was weaving his way to the back door, stopping en route to pick up his play-script.

Liz got up and followed him. Given Mrs. Maxwell's enquiry and her recent conversation with Marla, it might be as well to make her peace with Hugo Shawcross. "I think a play about vampires will be a huge hit for the Island Players. Sorry I went on like that, but in my job you tend to question things all the time."

"You are an academic?" Hugo looked as if, suddenly, this explained everything.

"No, far from it." Liz laughed. "I'm a detective sergeant — I'm in the police force."

At her words, Hugo Shawcross seemed to sober up instantly. "The police force," he repeated. He mumbled a few words of thanks at Elodie, who rushed to open the door for him as he fumbled with the latch. On the threshold, he turned and said, "Not all about sex, vampirism, not all about sex." He pointed a quivering finger past her in Liz's direction. "In the end, in the beginning, it's always about the blood."

Behind him, an owl hooted with melodramatic timing.

"Was it something I said?" Liz was laughing.

"Where in the name of — Lucifer? — did all that come from?" Elodie sat down on the sofa in her little sitting-room, and surveyed her niece.

Liz held out the bottle of cognac Elodie had been planning to offer with the coffee. "Gandalf drank most of the wine, so I think I can risk a little of this in my coffee. Can I pour you some, El?"

"Please. No coffee for me. Are you taking some sort of university correspondence course in demonology?"

"God, no! I'm as ignorant as I ever was. Have you heard of Lilith Fair?"

"Can't say as I have. Enlighten me."

Liz poured them both cognac, came and sat down

opposite Elodie. "It happened in the nineties, an all-female concert series, started by a singer I like — a Canadian called Sarah McLachlan. There's a song of hers I came across when I was getting over — someone — so I looked it up, and got interested. But it was really about the music, nothing else. Shawcross said 'it's always about the blood,' didn't he. Outside of my job, for me it's always about the music."

"Apart from your — what did he call it? — your feminist claptrap, he seemed just as disturbed by that job of yours," said Elodie.

"Didn't he, though? Did he say anything before I came that might be useful?"

"It's more what he didn't say. He told me about his claim to be a vampire, but he didn't mention his threat. Other than that, there was just the fact that he quizzed Marie Maxwell about the Gastineau family history and she clammed up. Or so he said."

"Could just be he's nosy, and Mrs. Maxwell pushed him away. Wasn't there an old saying? The Brocks speak to the De Saumarez, the De Saumarez speak to the Careys, the Careys speak to the Gastineaus, but the Gastineaus speak only to God? That certainly doesn't include the undead."

"Speaking of the Gastineaus and God," said Elodie, "I did just that earlier this evening."

"You spoke to God?" Liz looked inquiringly at her godmother, whose religious scepticism was a source of some discomfort among certain family members.

"Almost. I spoke to a Gastineau, Marie actually, and put the cat among the theatrical pigeons. I'll let you know what happens."

"I'll look forward to hearing about it, but I should make a move now." Liz uncurled her legs from under her and started to get up.

"Stay and let that brandy go down a bit longer," said Elodie. "Let's talk of other things, anything else but vampires and demons. And blood. What was the song you liked? That had you researching Lilith?"

"It's called 'I will remember you.'" Liz grinned. "And you know what? I didn't."

After Liz had gone, Elodie went to her office and switched on her computer. "I don't remember," she said out loud at the screen. "I don't remember." She typed in "Lilith," and sat there into the small hours. When she finally went to bed, it was the reproduction of a painting that stayed in her head, of Lilith naked, tossing her long mane of hair, a snake wound around her legs, one of its massive coils hiding her pudenda.

Sex and blood. Sex and blood. The three words drummed over and over in her head until, finally, sleep came.

Chapter Three

The police station in St. Peter Port had at one time been the workhouse, "La Maison de Charité," a fine eighteenth-century building on Hospital Lane. Hospital Lane was formerly the Rue des Frères, which had led to the ancient friary, now Elizabeth College, the private boys' school on the island. Ed Moretti had been at school there, thanks to a scholarship. Certainly, his Italian father, who had survived slave-labour on the island during the occupation, and had come back to find and marry the girl who had saved him from starvation, could not have afforded the fees.

Class, he thought, as he got into his vintage Triumph roadster and looked back at his family home. *Like the poor, it is always with us, whatever they may say.* His own ancestral pile was a cottage, a two-storey building of island granite, that at one time had been the stable and coachman's quarters for a long-gone grand home. It was now worth more than any workingman could possibly afford. A coral-coloured climbing rose framed the curved stone archway of the traditional Guernsey cottage, with a window on each side and three above. From time to time, Moretti cut the rose back, but the fuchsia, honeysuckle and ivy on the old walls on each side of the property he left alone.

He turned the Triumph around in the cobbled courtyard and exited between the stone pillars of what had once been a gateway, and was now just a gap in the old walls, and made his way down the Grange, the road that led into the town past the old Regency and Victorian homes that had been built on the wealth acquired from privateering and smuggling. Some were divided into flats, one or two were hotels, and some were now in the hands of the new privateers, brought to the island by the billions created by the offshore business.

As he turned into the quadrangle outside the police station, he saw his partner, Liz Falla, getting out of a pretty little Figaro from the driver's side. Looked like Falla had transformed her Poirets and Delaunays and vintage feather boas into a pale aqua chariot. Not practical, perhaps, but who was he to criticize.

"Nice. Hope it doesn't turn back into a Paris-designed pumpkin at midnight!" Moretti called out of his car window.

"Hasn't so far. Hi, Guv. Hope all went well in London with the spooks."

Moretti watched Detective Sergeant Liz Falla walking towards him in her neat, conservative, dark blue suit, a white shirt open at the neck, her short dark hair feathered around a face once described to him as "Audrey Hepburnish," and smiled. He was remembering the first time he saw her, when he had wondered what on earth Chief Officer Hanley was playing at, partnering him with this inexperienced young woman with her easy, outgoing manner, so unlike his own approach to his profession. And to life in general, come to that.

"As well as could be expected — but I'm not allowed to tell you anything, of course."

"Of course."

Her grin showed the tiny gap between her two front teeth that made her look to his eyes even younger than she was. But, as she had shown on their two earlier cases, her intelligence and her perception outstripped her years and, whatever Hanley had been playing at, the partnership had worked out. He could only hope being saddled with Aloisio Brown was as smart a move by Hanley, because there were others who could have taken on the role quite as well.

As if she had read his mind, Falla said, "I hear you're babysitting some APSG brainiac. Right, Guv?" He could hear the laughter in her voice above the sound of her heels click-clacking on the stones.

"Watch it, Falla. I was one of those, once. You haven't met him yet?"

"He's arriving this morning. I hope that gives me time to fill you in on a couple of things."

"The death of the hermit? I saw the report in the paper this morning. Suicide, wasn't it?"

"That's what it looks like. Dr. Edwards says she'll get a report to us today."

"She?"

Moretti stood back and let Falla go through the doors first, and she grinned at him, as she always did at his gesture. "Would you rather I didn't?" he had once asked her, defensively, and her reply, "No. I quite like it, but don't tell anyone," had amused him, defusing the moment and turning it into a shared joke.

"Yes. Irene Edwards, just joined the staff at Princess Elizabeth Hospital. She was on duty when the call came in. Seemed to know what she was doing. I liked her."

"Good. A couple of things, you said? A rash of burglaries? An outbreak of graffiti? Someone important with ruffled feathers?"

Liz waited until they had signed in at the desk, and Moretti had exchanged a few words with the desk sergeant about his new Centaur. As they moved away she said, "Got it in three, Guv. Ruffled feathers."

Moretti groaned. "What now? Some constable not tugging his forelock when asking one of the *messux* or the moneymen to move an illegally parked car? What?"

They were now in Moretti's office. Liz Falla waited until he sat down and started to check his messages, the familiar pattern when they were not in the middle of an investigation and had anything immediate to discuss. She would have no problem guessing when he got to Chief Officer Hanley's message, so she pulled out a chair on the other side of the desk and watched his face.

Her Guvnor was looking rested, with a light tan, his usually sombre features more relaxed. The dark hair inherited from his Italian father was touched with grey, and there were lines around his eyes that showed even when he was not laughing. *No longer laugh-lines*, she thought, *but he wasn't much given to idle banter, which was probably why she hadn't noticed them before. Gorgeous, Elodie had called him. Not her type, which was just as well. Too much going on beneath the surface.* At one point he looked across the table at her and nodded.

"Dr. Edwards. Competent, like you said."

Then his expression changed. A series of emotions flitted across his face in rapid succession, moving from disbelief to laughter. Moretti switched off the machine and looked across the desk at Liz.

"Has Hanley developed a misplaced sense of humour, or has he lost his marbles?"

Liz replied, taking her voice down an octave. "This is serious stuff, Guv. We have been asked to investigate a report of a threat from a vampire, from the mouth of the undead himself."

"Who is this vampire? Does he exist? Or can you even *say* that about vampires?"

"Oh, he exists. I met him last night, as a matter of fact. I'll get us both a coffee and fill you in, shall I?"

"Let's start with the vampire and get him out of the way. You met him last night, Falla?"

"Hugo Shawcross. Bit of a coincidence here — I know you're not fond of coincidences — but he's rented a place near my godmother, and I dropped over to see if she'd met him, knew anything about him."

Swiftly, succinctly, Liz filled Moretti in on the details she considered relevant to Marie Gastineau's complaint: the play, the Island Players, the threat. Moretti listened without interrupting her, but his expression made his feelings quite clear.

"… and I feel myself, Guv, it's all a storm in a theatrical teacup. Volatile lot, these theatre people."

"Worse than musicians? Okay, don't answer that. I'll tell Hanley that we've looked into it, and — well, what you just said." Moretti finished his coffee with his usual grimace. "Terrible as ever, and yet I go on drinking it. Anything else before we move on to the hermit?"

"Only this." Falla told him about her conversation with Marla Gastineau in the Beau Sejour change room.

"So the girl is getting poison-pen letters — or the twenty-first century equivalent? You tell me she's a looker? Par for the course, surely. Lot of that going on in the social media, right?"

"Right."

"Tell me about the hermit."

"What did Dr. Edwards say?"

"You first. Not the gist, like your account about Hugo the undead. Everything, Falla. Everything."

* * *

"Poor old bugger! Just as I was bringing him one of his magazines, one of his favourites. *Archaeology Today.* I was expecting our usual little joke about the title. 'Boring,' I'd say and he'd say, 'Not a seller. I'm their only subscriber.' Which, of course, he wasn't. Then we'd laugh. Poor old bugger!"

"You're Gordon Martel, aren't you?"

"Gord, yes. I know your dad."

Liz Falla and the shaken postman stood outside the hermit's house, watching the SOC people going about their business, shrouded in their white overalls. Jimmy Le Poidevin, head of SOCO, shouted out from inside the police tapes in her direction.

"Take a suit from the van if you're coming in, Falla!"

As if she didn't know by now, but with Jimmy it wasn't sex discrimination. He'd have said the same thing to Moretti. Falla put a hand on the shoulder of the trembling letter carrier. He was wearing the lime-yellow shirt with reflecting bands that all postmen wore on delivery, and the shorts they all favoured, whatever the weather, so some of the shaking could have been from the chill air.

"Come on. We'll sit in the police car."

She escorted him over to the police Vauxhall, opened the passenger door, went around and got in herself. Outside the windows of the car, the mist was drifting in again from the sea, hiding the world from them as the glass started to fog up with their breath.

Liz pulled out her notebook, and said, "Go through it from the moment you parked the car."

She watched his face as he spoke. He would be about the same age as her father, probably close to retirement; a small man with a slight build, sparse sandy hair above a freckled face dominated by a luxuriant ginger moustache. He had been delivering letters as far back as Liz could remember, and the first question was the obvious one.

"Was the hermit's place part of your normal route? Doesn't look like he'd be on any route."

"Call him by his name. Gus Dorey." Gord Martel sounded angry and his face turned red. "I liked him, and I used to add him to my route when I was done, or when I was taking my lunch break."

"How did you meet him?"

"On the beach, not when I was working. I was out early, using my metal detector, and we got talking. He said he liked the beach before anyone else got there, but he was friendly enough. He wanted to know if I found anything interesting, and I said all kinds. He said he'd found stuff too, and would I like to see some. I could hardly refuse, could I? You never know, so I said 'yes.'"

"And had he? Found anything interesting?"

"Shards mostly. He had them put up where they caught the light. But he also had some old bottles, that kind of thing. Said he'd never found a message from a castaway in any of them. He liked to have a laugh, did Gus. Poor old bugger."

Gord Martel took out a large, pristine white handkerchief, unfolded it and blew his nose with vigour. Beneath the moustache his narrow lips trembled. Liz

Falla gave him a moment, then took out her notebook and pen.

"Let's go through what happened today. What time did you arrive?"

"Around my lunchtime, late morning. I parked the van ..."

"Did you see anyone? Anything unusual?"

"Nothing, not a sausage. So I walked up to the house shouting like I always, did, '*Wharro, mon viow*!'"

"You spoke patois together?"

"Not me, but I think he had some of the old language. He used to say '*Tcheerie*' to me when I left, so I started saying it back to him. Once or twice he said 'Cheerio' in a la-de-da kind of way, like a joke — you know, like the plum-in-the-mouth kind do. Gus was not fond of them arseholes, as he called them — sorry, miss, about the language."

"So you called out. Did he normally come to the door? Or did you have to knock? Get his attention?"

"Mostly he heard the van and was at the door by the time I got there. When he didn't this morning I didn't think much of it. But when I called out again and he didn't come, then I got worried. So I went in."

Gord Martel gulped, and held the handkerchief to his mouth.

"Went in? The door was unlocked?"

"That was usual. He never locked it, said it was for the best. Less damage than if the yobbos broke in."

"Had he had problems that way?"

"In the past. But not recently, from what he said."

"Then you saw him?"

"Right. I couldn't believe it. Swinging on that rope. I got out my mobile and got hold of you lot."

The postman was clearly in shock, his body trembling violently beside her on the seat.

"Had he said anything before this that gave you the impression he was depressed? Suicidal?"

"Nothing. He was his usual self."

"Which was …?"

"Cheerful. But he could get mad as a wet hen about some things. Like telephones, and tourists and the social services."

"Things that interfered with his life?"

"Right. The maddest I ever saw him was talking about some — 'girlie,' he called her — from the social services who came to talk to him about his 'lifestyle.' It wasn't so much at her as at that word. 'Lifestyle.' He did a whole speech about language and the death of it. I wish I'd written it down. He was a beautiful talker, Gus. I don't mean 'posh' — he hated that too — but all the words."

"Did he ever ask you inside?"

"If the weather was bad, yes. But mostly we talked outside."

"What sort of mail did he get, besides magazines?"

"Nothing much. I learned not to bring him junk mail. That was another thing he hated, and the closest he got to yelling at me."

"All those books he had — did you ever deliver books to him?"

"Some. He had a mailbox in the post office in town, on Smith Street, and once or twice he asked me to take the key and check it for him."

"Did you always hand the key back?"

"Of course. He'd stick it back in his pocket."

"We'll probably find it." Liz closed her notebook and put it away. "That'll be all for now, Mr. Martel, but we'll need a written statement from you. One other thing — did you notice anything different about Mr. Dorey's place when you went in today? Was it all as it usually was, when he asked you in? Did you touch anything? SOCO have not found a note, for instance."

"Touch anything?" Gord Martel sounded outraged at the suggestion. "I got the fright of my life seeing him hanging there, and I went straight back to the van. I didn't even check to see if he was still alive." At this, the postman burst into loud sobs. Liz put a hand on his shoulder, at which Gord Martel gave a loud gulp and turned to face her.

"There was nothing you could have done, Gord. The doctor said he died instantly. As it usually was, you said?"

"All I noticed was there was some stuff laying around on the floor and that, like he'd been looking for something, I thought. I'd forgotten about that."

"So he wasn't an untidy person?"

"Gus? No. Finicky, I used to call him, everything just so, 'specially his books. Meticulous was his word for it. Can't have been himself, because there they were, on the floor." Gord Martel put his handkerchief away and smiled tearfully as he looked out of the window towards the roundhouse of the hermit. "Poor old bugger," he repeated, "Poor old bugger."

* * *

Moretti had listened in silence to Falla's account, watching as she consulted her notes from time to time. When she finished, she closed her notebook and said, "Poor old bugger. That's what Gord Martel said, and that's how I feel. And Martel's right, Guv, about the tidiness. I was expecting to walk into a tip, but the place was all clean and tidy. He'd strung himself up from a girder that connected to the chimney, kicked the chair away, and there were books on the ground around that area. I've asked to have them left there, where they are, until you have a chance to take a look. But it seems pretty straightforward, doesn't it?"

"Lonely old hermit does away with himself, yes. But listen to this." Moretti handed the phone over to Liz. "Not the chief officer and the voodoo, Falla, but Dr. Edwards."

Dr. Edwards's voice came as a surprise to Liz. In person, she was an imposing woman, tall and big-boned, with striking features. Although she had long, dark hair she always wore it coiled up into a chignon, which probably made it easier to fit under the hoody-like protective headgear. On the phone, though, detached from her appearance, her voice was light, almost girlish.

"Hello, DS Falla. This is Dr. Edwards. Here is my first impression, as promised. Mr. Dorey probably died the morning he was found — I'll be more precise, I hope, after the post mortem. He was an old, frail man, and the drop caused a cervical fracture from the look of it — in other words, he broke his neck. Doesn't always happen, and the PM will tell me if he was asphyxiated, or died from occlusion of the blood vessels, or the fracture did him in. But there is something else that's a bit of a bother." A moment of silence and then the girlish voice added, "He still had quite strong leg muscles, perhaps from doing a lot of walking, but his upper body on the other hand — it was skinny and weak to the point of emaciation, which is why his neck snapped like a twig." Another pause. "So, what I'm saying is — how did he manage that humungous knot on that massive rope? Thought I'd throw that at you." A silvery laugh and then a click.

Moretti and Falla looked at each other. Liz spoke first.

"Is she saying what I think she's saying?"

Moretti looked across the table at his partner. "If you think she's saying the hermit had a helper. then, yes. I think that's exactly what the observant Dr. Edwards is saying."

Chapter Four

The drive out to Pleinmont, on the southwestern tip of the island, was one of the longer journeys on Guernsey, and gave Liz Falla time to regale Moretti with an account of her evening with the vampire. Once or twice he threw his head back and laughed with a lack of restraint that took Liz by surprise. In the short time they had been together as partners, she rarely remembered him behaving in such an extroverted way.

What had changed in his life, she wondered. She knew he had originally come back to the island after the breakup of a long-term relationship, and since his return had been involved with a couple of women, neither of them islanders. As far as she knew, those were love affairs, not life affairs — a big difference, in her book. He was an ascetic, according to Elodie, with hidden fires. Maybe the hidden fires part only showed when he was playing jazz piano.

She had looked up "ascetic." It was one of those words she thought she knew, but really didn't. Someone who had been briefly in her life, flaring up and self-destructing, brilliant as a shooting star, had encouraged her to do this. "Severely self-disciplined," her dictionary said; the word "abstinent" was also used. Well, that bit wasn't accurate.

"I was sailing around this part of the coastline yesterday, with Don Taylor — remember him? It was a great day. Reminded me of when I was a kid, risking my life climbing the cliffs at Le Gouffre with Andy Duquemin." Moretti was laughing again. "There really is a god who looks after small boys, Falla."

So it was a boat, not a babe. "Not small girls, Guv? It's okay, you don't have to answer that. That's just some of my feminist claptrap. I know what you mean."

"Don't you have an aunt who lives around here? The one you'd rather not talk about?"

Liz Falla made an unnecessarily brisk twist of the wheel to the left as they turned on to the coast road.

"She's actually my great-aunt and yes, she does. With her simples, and her goats and her ouija board — sorry, planchette. She considers the ouija board newfangled. Here we are, Guv."

Ahead of him Moretti saw the hermit's round-house, surrounded by police tape. The strange building had been there for well over a decade, as far as he knew, but certainly had not been there when he and Andy Duquemin had roamed the cliffs and the Common. He remembered asking his father about it, when he came home on his first vacation from London

University. It was his mother, the island girl, who had answered him.

"Gus Dorey. Came back with his mother after the war to find his family home in ruins. Reprisals, I imagine. He built that himself, when he came back again, years later. His parents were long gone by then."

"Gus Dorey," said Moretti. That visit was the last time he saw her, and he heard again the echo of his mother's voice, saying the name. When he got out of the car the brisk wind of autumn made his eyes water. "Is there anyone watching the place, Falla?"

As he asked the question, a uniformed constable came out of the house.

"Yes, Guv. Looks like it's PC Mauger. I think he came on duty this morning."

PC Mauger walked briskly towards them across the rough scrub that surrounded the house, his arms folded across his body against the wind.

"'morning, DI Moretti, DS Falla. You didn't bring any hot coffee with you, by any chance?"

"Sorry, no," Falla replied. "Anything to report?"

"Nothing, but PC Bichard, who was here last night, thought there was someone hanging about outside. When he went out to check, he could see nothing, wondered if it was his imagination playing tricks."

"He's a policeman, he's not supposed to have an imagination playing tricks." Moretti's voice sounded sharp, and both officers looked at him with surprise. "I'll speak to him when we get back to the station. Let's take a look at Gus Dorey's hideaway. I'm assuming SOCO are done here?"

"Yes, sir. I was told not to move anything, but no need to wear gloves. There's not much to see, sir. Is there, DC Falla?"

"Not much."

Falla watched Moretti go ahead of them into the roundhouse, and turned to PC Mauger. "Did Pete Bichard say what he meant by 'hanging about'?"

"Blimey, he's in a mood, isn't he? What's got up *his* nose?" One look at Falla's expression quelled any further comments about Moretti's mood, and he went on, "He thought he heard a vehicle on the road, then he thought he heard it stop. Then he thought he heard someone moving around. That's all."

"Did he go outside and take a look?"

"Yes. It was pitch-black and he saw nothing. Then he heard a vehicle again on the road, but he saw no headlights, which was weird. Should have seen them from here."

Falla looked back towards the road. There were few trees, and Pete Bichard was right. He should have seen headlights.

"Go and sit in the car for a bit, Bernie, get warmed up."

Bernie Mauger trundled happily off towards the road, and Liz went into the roundhouse. Moretti was kneeling on the wooden floor surrounded by books. Behind him lay the chair, still on its side. He looked up as she came in.

"Interesting," he said.

It was Moretti's default word, and could mean mildly interesting, or extremely interesting, depending on the circumstance. She waited for him to elaborate, which was usually best and, given his sudden hissy fit with PC Mauger, probably advisable right now. If she wasn't a copper, the laughing Guv of a few minutes before would seem like *her* imagination playing tricks.

"Some of these are quite valuable." Moretti held up a nondescript-looking book bound in a faded green, brushing the silvery-white dust left by SOCO off the cloth cover. "First edition of *Nicholas Nickleby*, 1839, with the original etchings and frontispiece. Probably worth a bob or two."

"A bob or two?" Liz crouched down beside him.

"A thousand pounds or two," Moretti replied. "Until the place is cleared, we'll have to keep a police guard on it. Word will get around."

"Wow!" Liz looked at the books around them and picked up a leather-bound volume. "What's this?" Moretti took it from her.

"Looks like a book about James Gillray, with some very nice steel engravings — he drew satirical cartoons, Falla. He had eclectic tastes, our hermit." Moretti gestured at a scattering of ancient Penguin paperbacks with their distinctive orange, black and white covers, the little penguin standing in a white oval alongside the titles. "Do we know if he left a will?"

"Jimmy didn't mention it, but I don't think that was a priority. Everything was left in place, except the rope. Jimmy took it back to Hospital Lane. He'd been cut down — the hermit, I mean — by the time I got here." They both looked up at the exposed beam, surrounded by the pink batts of insulation.

"We'll need to find out if there's a will. The death will soon be reported in the *Guernsey Press*, and possibly some lawyer in town will come forward. Though he doesn't seem to have been a lawyer type of person.

"Let me tear myself away from these," Moretti swept a hand over the books on the floor, "and take a look around. Not that there's much else to look at." He stood up, brushing the dust from his hands.

There was indeed little else in the hermit's hideaway. The place was lined with sturdily constructed bookcases that looked homemade, and the only attempt at decoration were the shards, bottles and pieces of driftwood placed on top of them. Some of the shards were arranged on the narrow ledge beneath the one small window in the roundhouse. On the floorboards were a couple of woven wool rugs that also looked homemade, the colours faded to a blur. There were blankets and a threadbare quilt on the truckle bed that could have been easily moved closer to the fire when necessary. An ancient hipbath stood close to the fireplace, a towel draped over the higher end. A camp stove, a kettle, a few pots and pans and pieces of cutlery on a trestle table alongside a loaf of bread and some cheese, an overripe banana and an orange, some canned goods, a packet of tea. Another table was loaded with magazines, and there was a battered armchair covered in a threadbare fabric Moretti remembered from his childhood, called moquette. There was a space left on one of the bookshelves for a small pile of neatly folded clothes, and there was a well-worn pair of felt slippers near the armchair.

"Was he wearing boots, Falla, did you notice?"

"Yes, Guv, and an overcoat. One of the boots had fallen off."

"As if he'd just come in. Hmmm." Moretti looked up at the pink surface above him. "Interesting choice of ceiling material. Makes the place feel quite —" He paused.

"Cosy," Falla supplied for him.

"Almost." Moretti stood up. "I need to talk to the postman. Did you ask him to come in to the station to make a statement?"

"Yes, Guv. I told him it could wait until today, but he may have been in this morning. Want me to check if he's been?"

"Go ahead."

While Falla used her mobile, Moretti walked around the hermit's hideaway. Cosy, yes, almost: a refuge for a man of some education and learning, and ample means, apparently, for the books that were his passion. For Moretti, sanctuary was in the sound of Sidney Bechet playing "Petite Fleur," Miles Davis playing "Tempus Fugit," Oscar Peterson playing anything.

Why had Gus Dorey chosen to live this way? Had the world been for him too much, late and soon? Had he found the getting and spending laid waste his powers? Not hard to understand, thought Moretti. Drifting down the years the words came back to him.

So might I, standing on this pleasant lea, have glimpses that would make me less forlorn …

"Guv." He realized Falla was speaking to him, holding out her mobile. "It's Sergeant Jones. He's interviewing Gord Martel right now."

"Sorry, Falla. I was thinking of Wordsworth."

He took the mobile from her. "Sergeant Jones, Moretti here. I have a question for you to ask Mr. Martel about Gus Dorey. Did he smell?" He heard the question posed, and the postman's indignant reaction. "I take it that's a no? Thanks, Sergeant — yes, that's all."

He handed the mobile back to Falla, who was looking at him quizzically. "You have a question yourself, I think?"

"I was going to ask you where Wordsworth came in, but that'll keep. Did he *smell*, Guv?"

In answer Moretti walked across to the shelf with the small pile of clothing, and picked up a shirt.

"There's no public laundry for miles, and this stuff is impeccably laundered. There's no way that was washed under the coldwater pump outside, near what looks like his vegetable patch, and any iron would have had to be an old-fashioned non-electric one. I don't see one, so I doubt he used the hipbath. Therefore —?"

"Either he went into town with his washing or —"

"Someone was doing it for him. And something else. If Dr. Edwards's suggestion that this is an aided suicide is accurate, then whoever helped Gus Dorey was not after his worldly goods." Moretti bent down and picked up the Dickens. "They had some entirely different motive."

"Maybe he asked his laundry person to help him end his life."

"And maybe his laundry person gave him no choice in the matter. Because, Falla, whoever threw these books around, it wasn't Gus Dorey, who loved them. It was the mysterious other person who was in this room with him. And they were looking for something, probably while he hung above on a rope he couldn't have tied by himself."

At that moment, Moretti's mobile rang. He answered it briefly, then looked at Liz Falla, who was staring up at the crossbeam by the fireplace.

"Duty calls. That was Chief Officer Hanley. We're needed at the station. Aloisio Brown has arrived."

"*Who*, Guv?"

"The brainiac, Falla. Let's go and face the music, shall we?"

Chapter Five

Hugo Shawcross's back was killing him. The phone call from Marie Gastineau had come as a complete surprise, sending him rushing to his laptop to put in an all-nighter. He couldn't remember doing that since his student days. *Mind you*, he thought, *if I am indeed one of the undead, last night should have been a walk in the park for me*. Or perhaps a stroll in St. Martin's Churchyard among the gravestones, hand in hand with La Gran'mère du Cimetière, the ancient menhir that kept watch at the gate. Over the thousands of years she had stood there, she must have seen a vampire or two, he thought.

He giggled and stood up abruptly, instantly regretting both actions. Not only did his back hurt, but so did his head. However, the euphoria of the wine had lasted through the night until dawn, and now he just had to survive the hangover. He thought back to the

message he had found on his answerphone when he
got back from Elodie Ashton's.

"Hello, Hugo. This is Marie Maxwell."

The tone of voice was the first surprise. Light,
almost flirtatious, harpy turned seductress. Very different from the unearthly shrieks and howls, reminiscent of Stoker's encounters with Mudge, that had
greeted his little joke. He sat down at his desk and
listened in disbelief.

"I realize you will get this message after your evening with Elodie Ashton, and I apologize for intrud-
ing so late, but I just couldn't leave it until tomorrow
morning, because I have put the wheels in motion."

Wheels in motion? Was he to be expelled from
the island? To be burned at the stake at the foot of
Fountain or Berthelot Street, like they did in the old
days? Disbelief turned into apprehension. What game
was this woman playing?

"Elodie, bless her, phoned me earlier this evening
and explained, and it all sounds quite *thrilling*. A part
for *me*!"

Aha. The cooing voice continued.

"As Elodie said, the academic sense of humour is
often — *esoteric*, was her word for it, and I completely
misunderstood, didn't I! So, I have arranged a little
get-together at my house for tomorrow evening. I have
managed to get hold of most of the Island Players who
really *matter* and I very much look forward to having a first read-through of your play." The timbre of
her voice deepened, vibrating with emotion as Marie
Gastineau moved into "actress" mode. "From what

Elodie says, you have seen past my façade of society hostess and sensed hidden depths. Evil is certainly within my range, and will make a welcome change from my usual roles."

Evil? Not at all the reaction envisaged by his neighbour. Or was she the one who had suggested it?

A trill of laughter bubbled up from the answerphone, then the message concluded on a note of command, the familiar, imperious Marie Gastineau firmly back in control. "Call me in the morning to confirm — won't you?"

"Bloody hell," said Hugo Shawcross.

He had been regretting his abrupt departure, earlier than he had planned, thanks to that chit of a policewoman. But, it turned out it was just as well. He sat down at his desk and turned on his laptop.

Aloisio Brown sat in Moretti's office, reading a pamphlet on the desk. He was tanned, dark-haired, probably very much like his Portuguese mother, thought Moretti. He stood up as they came in, turning a pair of large brown eyes in their direction, smiling as he did so. Next to him, Moretti heard Falla's intake of breath. Moretti extended his hand.

"Aloisio Brown — have I said your name right?"

"Call me Al. Everyone does, except my mother."

The smile turned into a grin, and the brown eyes turned towards Liz Falla.

"Detective Sergeant Falla, I presume?" It was

clear what those brown eyes thought of what they were surveying.

"Call me Falla. Everyone does, except *my* mother. Well, almost everyone. Hi."

Moretti could almost hear the violins playing.

"You have just got back from the scene of the suicide, I'm informed. Sergeant Jones let me sit on the interview with the postman. I heard your question to him, sir."

"What did you make of it?"

"I'm not sure, but I presumed it was unexpected, given the way the deceased was living. That he didn't smell, I mean."

"Yes." Quite the brainiac. "Falla, play the message from Dr. Edwards for — Al."

Dr. Edwards's light voice filled the office. When the message was finished, Al Brown looked at Moretti.

"Liquid sunshine," he said.

"Liquid sunshine?"

"The sound of the pathologist's voice." Al Brown smiled at Liz Falla, who smiled back.

"We don't have a pathologist on the island," said Moretti. He could hear his own voice sounding somewhat metallic. "Dr. Edwards was the duty doctor." There was a silence, then Moretti continued. "And doesn't liquid sunshine mean rain?"

Before anyone could add anything to the absurd dialogue, the phone rang. Moretti picked it up.

"Moretti."

"Hello, Detective Inspector Moretti. DS Falla told me you were the officer in charge. This is Irene Edwards."

Moretti put her on speakerphone, and sunshine or rain filled the office, depending on the listener's point of view.

"I will be at the hospital this afternoon, if you are free."

"Of course. Three o'clock suit you?"

"Perfect. See you then."

As he hung up the phone, Moretti said. "I want to take a look at the rope first, and then get something to eat. How about you, Al?"

"Great! I just had time to check in at my digs, and I'm starving. Also, I don't know where's good — and cheap — to eat in St. Peter Port."

He stood up and took his jacket from the back of the chair, put it on. *Looks like he works out*, thought Moretti.

"How about La Crêperie, Guv? It's close and we can walk there, come back for the car." Falla gave Al Brown another smile.

As he walked past him, Moretti realized he was taller than Al Brown, and that the brainiac's dark curly hair was receding slightly at the temples.

His inner child rejoiced.

The rope lay in front of them on the table in the incident room. It had been cut close to the knot to release the hermit's body, and the strands revealed were considerably cleaner and lighter than the rest of the rope.

"Tar, or oil. Seaweed or algae stains. He must have found this on the beach." Moretti touched one of the dark patches with his gloved hand.

"He supplied his own rope, that's what I thought," said Falla. "But at the time I saw him, I thought it was straightforward, a suicide."

"It may be, but looking at the thickness of the rope, I tend to agree with Dr. Edwards — that he had help."

"Assisted suicide." Al Brown bent over the rope, then straightened up. "But who helps a hermit? From what the postman said, he didn't have friends."

"Exactly. And who in their right mind would drop in out of the blue and casually offer to give a complete stranger a hand in his death? You saw the postman's reaction right after his discovery of the body, Falla. Do you think he might have had anything to do with this?"

"Not unless he's a brilliant actor, Guv."

"But who helps a hermit?" Al Brown asked again. "By definition, a hermit's someone who avoids human contact?" He looked at Moretti.

"Let's go eat, and we'll fill you in on the business of the books," said Moretti.

The Crêperie was on Smith Street, a narrow, winding road close to the centre of the town, now closed to traffic and for pedestrians only. On their way, they passed a bookstore, its name on a board above the door decorated to look like a mediaeval manuscript: WORDS.

Al Brown stopped to look in the window, and said, "Unimaginative perhaps, but the name says it all, doesn't it. Always good to see people are still reading the old-fashioned way."

Falla, walking ahead of them, turned and grinned. "Thought you'd be all gadgets and iPods and e-books, you being from the big city," she said.

Al Brown looked hurt. "How can you say that to a bloke who plays a Portuguese guitar?" he said.

"A Portuguese guitar?" Moretti and Falla spoke in unison.

"Yes, but you wouldn't know that. I learned it at my mother's knee." Al Brown turned to Moretti. "I know you play jazz piano, sir," he said. "Chief Officer Hanley told me this morning. It seemed to — puzzle him."

Al Brown smiled. Moretti's inner child was beginning to feel better.

"I play guitar," Falla said. She was looking delighted. "And sing," she added. "With a group. We call ourselves Jenemie."

Suddenly, she stopped. "Here we are." She pushed open the door and they were greeted by a gust of warm air laden with delicious cooking smells.

"God, that smells good! Do you play together at all?" Al Brown stood to one side of the banquette for Liz Falla to go past him, and waited for her and for Moretti to sit down.

It was Moretti who answered.

"We don't."

Liz Falla gave him one of the unfathomable looks he was getting to know quite well — unfathomable because he couldn't read from it whether it was reproach, or disapproval. His mother's generation would have called it an old-fashioned look, which covered a multitude of sins.

Over seafood crêpes for Moretti and Al Brown, and a caramelized onion crêpe for Falla, Al Brown and Liz Falla discussed the merits and differences of the acoustic and the Coimbra Portuguese guitar, which was Al Brown's instrument. Ad nauseam, in Moretti's unspoken opinion, but clearly not in theirs. Ignoring their conversation, his mind drifted to thoughts of yesterday's trip with Don Taylor. Through the mist of pleasant recollection, he realized he was being asked a question.

"Books, you said, sir. The hermit was a reader?"

"More than that. A collector of rare and beautiful books that he, or someone, threw around on the floor in among his Penguin paperbacks."

"Then that wouldn't be him. Someone was looking for something?"

"Could be. And whoever it was did not recognize — or wasn't interested in — a two-thousand pound Dickens first edition — give or take a pound or two."

"My God! The postman — Gord Martel? — said the fact Gus Dorey had done that to his books showed his suicidal state of mind. But I thought he meant the untidiness, rather than anything more complicated."

"And he might be right." There was a framed maxim on the wall close to the bar, that had caught Moretti's eye when they came in.

Heaven is where the police are British, the cooks French, the mechanics German, the lovers Italian, and it is all organized by the Swiss. Hell is where the cooks are British, the mechanics French, the lovers Swiss, the police German, and it is all organized by the Italians.

He looked across the table at Falla and said, "I am tempted at this point to say that my gut tells me this was not a disordered frame of mind, but perhaps that's my Italian blood speaking, and not my British police training. Falla has strong views about that kind of thing."

Falla snorted with derision. "So would you, if you came from my family. I believe in fingerprints, and forensics, and DNA, not hunches."

"Does that rule out the gut? Instinct? Intuition?" asked Al Brown, turning to Falla. "You surprise me."

"I thought intuition was now a dirty word in our business," she replied. "I thought deduction was drawing conclusions from known facts, like alibis, motives, that kind of thing."

"Deduction," said Al Brown, "is also, sometimes, a blinding moment of insight into another human being. Isn't it?"

"I think we're back to intuition," said Moretti. He saw that Falla was looking irritated, and felt annoyed with himself for winding her up. He was about to attract the attention of the waitress, when Al Brown said, "I should tell you why I asked to be posted here."

"I wondered," said Moretti, settling back on the banquette. "With your qualifications, most of the U.K. was at your disposal."

"Did your gut tell you?" Falla stood up and motioned to Al Brown to let her out. She was still looking annoyed. "I'm off to the ladies, in that case." She extracted herself from the banquette and left them. Al Brown looked after her and said, "Did I tread on her toes?"

"In a way. Liz Falla's ancestral roots are linked to one of the ancient Guernsey families called Becquet, many of whose female members were burned as witches. They died out long ago — not surprisingly — so it's not proven, but she has an aunt and a grand-mother who believe otherwise, and they feel this gives her a real advantage in police work. It drives her to distraction, being told by granny and admiring Auntie Becky that she has 'the gift.'"

"And has she?"

"I'll leave you to decide that." Moretti paid the bill and, after the waitress had left, said, "Let's talk about you. Why *are* you here?" Focusing his gaze on him, he noticed that one of the braniac's ears was pierced. Did he wear an earring when off-duty? That would give Hanley something else to puzzle over.

"I'm here," said Aloisio Brown, rebuttoning his smart navy blazer, "because I believe in magical thinking."

"Magical thinking?" Falla rejoined them, sling-ing the small black bag she carried on to her shoul-der. "Sounds like my Aunt Becky's been talking to you

— did she fly over and visit you on her broomstick?" She still sounded annoyed, only this time it was with both of them. Moretti, who was checking his messages, looked up at her jibe.

"Magical thinking's serious stuff, Falla. It has been known to kill geniuses — so even graduates of the APSG program need to watch their backs. Don't we, DC Brown?"

Chapter Six

Princess Elizabeth Hospital was near the centre of the island, west of St. Peter Port and just outside the parish of St. Andrews, in an area called the Vauquiédor. It had started life as a mental hospital, but after the Second World War was renamed for twenty-two-year-old Princess Elizabeth, and reopened by her. A major extension in the nineties had added a radiology department, a new maternity unit and children's ward. A new clinical block was in the works. It was also the site of the principal mortuary on the island and, when necessary, whoever was the surgeon on duty served as pathologist.

Dr. Edwards was waiting for them in the mortuary.

"Hello, DS Falla. Greetings, gentlemen."

Shrouded in her pale blue protective gear, her hair hidden by a cap, the doctor was an androgynous figure, the divergence between her appearance and voice less marked.

Liz Falla did the introductions and, as they put on protective clothing, Moretti got straight to the point. "You think this could be an assisted suicide, Dr. Edwards."

His voice echoed back, the sound magnified off the bare walls. Somewhere a tap was dripping.

"I do." Irene Edwards went over to one of the tables and pulled back the sheet. "I got him out when I heard you had arrived. Take a look."

Gus Dorey was white as the sheet he was under, frail as a one-dimensional sketch of a human being, a line drawing in death. His strong nose jutted out on his sunken face, which was otherwise wiped clean otherwise of individuality. He lay there still, unable any longer to escape the peering eyes and human contact he had avoided in life.

"There's nothing much to him," said Moretti. He looked at the hermit's veined hands, the bones stark against the transparent skin. "If he had tied the knot on that rope, he should have marks, even rope burns."

"I agree." Irene Edwards turned the hands over, laid them back down by the side of the body. "Nothing there. I already checked. And he probably would have had trouble seeing to tie a knot. He had cataracts that would soon have needed attention. Is there anything else you want to see?"

"No."

Gently, Irene Edwards pulled the stiff sheet up over Gus Dorey's face, pulled off her gloves and looked at Moretti.

"What happens next? Procedures are different here, aren't they?"

"Yes. Outside, I think."

Liz Falla looked at Moretti. It was not the first cadaver they had looked at together. They didn't seem to affect him. She had never sensed repugnance or discomfort in him when they looked at the recently dead; his familiar air of detachment always remained firmly in place. It was more, she thought, as if he was respecting the feelings of the dead man by taking the discussion outside.

Breaking the silence, Irene Edwards said something to the mortuary technician, who stood waiting at a discreet distance, and they left the room.

In the corridor outside, Moretti said, "The magistrates court becomes the coroners court when necessary, and they will take care of this. But I'll have to inform my chief officer first."

"I leave it in your hands," said Irene Edwards. "And you'll let me know?"

With one swift movement she pulled the cap off her head, the gesture loosening the chignon from the large comb that held it, and a mass of dark hair cascaded around her shoulders. She smiled, and both men blinked, Aloisio Brown smiling back at her. The comb clattered to the floor and she picked it up without comment and put in her overalls pocket.

"We will," said Moretti. He turned to Al Brown and Liz Falla. "Right now, we need to head back to the office. I'll need to write a report and speak to Chief Officer Hanley."

They said their goodbyes to Irene Edwards, and she disappeared back into her echoing world with its inescapable smell of human mortality and decay hanging in the air beneath the antiseptic.

As the door closed behind her, Moretti said, "I want you both to go back out to Pleinmont and search Dorey's roundhouse thoroughly, and I want you both to do the search. No one else. I want to keep this as quiet as possible."

"Peculiar," said Liz Falla, and both men turned to look at her. She was looking back at the mortuary.

"An odd choice of word," said Moretti, "even in the circumstances. What is it, Falla?"

"He reminded me of someone. Even in death, white and cold like that. That's why I said 'peculiar.'"

"Who did he remind you of?"

"I have no idea." Liz looked at Moretti and smiled, sweetly. "But maybe it was my imagination playing tricks, Guv," she said.

It was chilly in Gus Dorey's roundhouse. Constable Bury had been only too happy to go and sit outside in the police car and leave Al Brown and Liz to the task in hand. He helped them carry in the boxes they had brought with them and then asked, "So how long do we have to do this? There's not much here except about a million books."

Al Brown picked up the Dickens first edition from the floor, where it still lay.

"A million books, full of magical thinking — the sort of magical thinking that matters to me, at any rate."

"So, tell me about magical thinking."

They had divided the room in half and had agreed that the books came first, if only so they could be removed to a safer place. Constable Bury might not have the slightest idea of their value, but others might not be so uninformed.

"Oh, here's his glasses. Remember, Dr. Edwards said he had cataracts." Al Brown picked up a case on the floor, which had been hidden by some of the books. "Not prescription by the look of it. The kind you can get in Boots the Chemist. What do you want to know?"

"You were saying you came here because of it. You asked to be posted here. Was it because you thought we still worshipped pagan gods and danced in the light of the moon?"

Al Brown pulled himself back from Nicholas Nickleby's world and shrugged his shoulders.

"You don't? What a disappointment." His tone changed. "Let's get a few things straight, Liz. Yes, DI Moretti told me about your aunt and your grandmother. Yes, I can understand your being pissed off. No, I don't believe you're all a bunch of primitive pagans. What I meant was that I wanted to work somewhere where there was some flexibility of structure, and I hoped to find it on Guernsey. I attended a lecture given by a retired superintendent from the Met, and he talked about your Guvnor's handling of a complex case here. He said he didn't go by the book."

Al Brown slapped the Dickens he held in his hands. "I wanted to have that chance."

"So not going by the book is magical thinking?" Liz was piling up a heap of Penguin paperbacks, checking inside each one as she did so. "And it can destroy geniuses? Sounds like dangerous stuff to me."

Reluctantly, Al Brown put down the Dickens. "If I keep reading these we'll get nowhere. I think DI Moretti was referring to the death of Steve Jobs, the founder of Apple, a genius who believed that magical thinking could cure him of pancreatic cancer."

"Sorry, but I don't get it. What has that to do with my Guv not going by the book, and you coming here?"

Al put the first edition in one of the boxes and picked up the Gillray bibliography. "You've started on the Penguins, so I'll keep going with the hardcovers. It has to do with MI Teams — Murder Investigation Teams — and Action Managers, and all that crap. It was supposed to simplify and to accelerate the process, but like anything else, it depends who's in charge. I felt — trapped."

Liz Falla looked over at Al Brown, who was lovingly examining the Gillray page by page. "DI Moretti answers to Chief Officer Hanley, which can be frustrating, but mostly our supreme leader worries about not offending the powers-that-be. That'll be what the Guvnor's talking about right now with him — paperwork and vampires."

"*What*?"

A few Penguins and a complete Gillray later, they were both rocking with laughter. Al Brown selected a handful of small faux-leather-bound volumes. "Nelson,

Collins, nice but not of great value. Does anyone read *Barlasch of the Guard* anymore?"

He looked across at Liz, but she was apparently engrossed in the paperback she was holding, her attention held by something on the page.

"Anything interesting? What's the book?"

"It's not the book. It's this." Liz was holding out a tiny, yellowed scrap of paper. "It's an address."

"In Guernsey?"

"No. In the U.K. A street address, somewhere in London, I think. Looks like Gus Dorey's writing. He's put his name in some of the paperbacks."

"Does he identify whose address it is?"

"Yes. He does." Liz smoothed the fragile piece of paper with one finger, and held it out to Al Brown.

"'My darling,'" she said.

Chief Officer Hanley was looking remarkably cheerful for a man whose face leant itself more readily to melancholy than merriment. Moretti handed him the report on Gus Dorey and he laid it to one side without looking at it.

"What are your first impressions of DC Brown?"

"Pleasant, intelligent, as one might expect. What was your impression, sir?"

"Much the same. We'll see. Possibly a little light-weight, perhaps?"

Moretti had no idea what the Chief Officer meant and decided not to pursue it. Maybe he had noticed the pierced ear.

"About this vampire nonsense," he began, "DS Falla knows some of the members of the Island Players, and feels it is a storm in a theatrical teacup."

The chief officer positively beamed. "Oh absolutely. Mrs. Maxwell phoned me this morning and explained."

"Explained?"

"Yes. Seems to have been a misunderstanding. Mind you, I didn't quite follow her clarification, which had more to do with something she called dramatic licence, than common sense. Anyway, we're off the hook, thank heaven. I don't mind telling you, Moretti, it's a great relief."

"I can imagine, sir. A waste of police time."

"Quite. We have other fish to fry. Organizational fish."

The chief officer's metaphoric clarification seemed quite as cryptic as Marie Maxwell's, and left Moretti feeling apprehensive. He picked up the Gus Dorey case notes.

"These are my notes on the apparent suicide of Gus Dorey, the hermit at Pleinmont."

"*Apparent* suicide?"

The chief officer's expression returned to its default downcast disposition.

"There is a possibility, according to Dr. Edwards, who did the initial examination, that someone helped him. And I agree with her, sir."

One of Hanley's best qualities was his ability to listen, which he did in silence until Moretti had finished.

"So," he replied after a moment's thought, "Assisted

suicide, not murder. Were there signs of anyone else being there?"

"There were books on the floor, some of them valuable. It looked as if someone had been searching for something. Either they found it, or were scared off by activity outside. I've read the postman's statement and he says that Dorey had a mailbox in town. We'll be looking for a key, but someone else may have got to it first. DS Falla thinks the postie is not involved. Her instincts are good, sir."

"No argument here. That's why I promoted her so fast, and put her with you. Where is she now, by the way?"

"Out at Pleinmont with DC Brown, doing a more detailed search, and packing up the books. They'll have to be put in storage here until we can track down next of kin. I'll put PC Mauger on to that, but if Gord Martel didn't know of any relative, I think we'll find no one."

"If the intruder handled the books, we may get fingerprints. One thing about a hermit, I suppose — less chance of being swamped with hundreds of them. Did you say you thought he had been helped by someone? We may get their identification that way."

"Only if the intruder forgot to wipe off their own prints, which is unlikely. The general public may not understand the forensic study of blood spatters or PCR analysis, but even kindergarten kids know about fingerprints. We are, of course, fingerprinting Gord Martel so we can rule him out. Or in. At this stage I am not closing any doors."

Moretti thought of the open door in Gus Dorey's roundhouse, unlocked and unguarded. Had he, perhaps, been waiting for whoever it was to come in? There were no signs of a struggle, and even an old, frail man would surely have fought back. If only to protect his precious books.

"Wise move. Could just be common or garden theft, couldn't it?"

"Then why go to the trouble of faking a suicide, sir? That took some doing, and a lot of risk. The intruder could have taken anything while Dorey was out for what seems to have been his customary walk."

"So you think someone wanted him out of the way?"

"I do."

"Dear, dear." Hanley pulled Moretti's notes towards him. "Perhaps this is a good time to have DC Brown here," he said.

Moretti tried a little humour. "And fortunately, Mrs. Maxwell has dealt with her vampire situation, so we have more manpower available than if we were tracking down the undead."

"Oh *that*." Hanley waved a dismissive hand in the air. "The reason I was keen to get DC Brown here is because he is familiar with the Met's approach to murder investigation — MI Teams, Action Managers and so on. It is time we looked at reorganization, DI Moretti. We must keep up with the times."

Moretti suspected his own face had fallen into the familiar lines of his boss's countenance.

"And," the chief officer went on, "here we have

an apparent murder, don't we? At least, that is what I would call helping to hang an old man. Wouldn't you, DI Moretti?"

Chapter Seven

So, thought Hugo Shawcross, *these are the Island Players that really matter, according to Marie Maxwell,* née *Gastineau.* At his first introduction to the group, answering the queen bee's call, he had met only some of those now assembled, and the meeting had been in the flat belonging to Jim Landers, the owner of the bookstore on Smith Street, and current president of the Island Players. His minimalist one-bedroom, book-lined flat opposite Elizabeth College, the boys' private school on the island, was a very different setting from the elegant high-ceilinged sitting room in the former Gastineau townhouse. It was Jim Landers who had invited Hugo to join the group after he visited the store, and they had got into conversation about books both current and rare.

The eleven Island Players were perched on ornate upholstered chairs with gilt backs, or sunk into the brocaded cushions of Empire-style sofas with curved, carved legs. The paintings in heavy gilt frames around the walls looked to be of the *Monarch of the Glen* variety; if there were family portraits they must be elsewhere, which was a pity. The Persian carpet beneath their feet was huge and in poor shape, worn thin in places, which probably meant it was an antique, thought Hugo, and worth a ton of money. He surveyed the chosen few assembled for the reading.

First, Jim Landers. Probably in his mid-fifties, with a neat grey beard and closely and carefully barbered hair. He was well-read, and modest enough about his erudition to make Hugo feel vaguely uncomfortable. There was a restrained and distant quality about him — not so much all passion spent, thought Hugo, as most passions not released.

Next to him sat Ginnie Purvis, who taught English in the private girls' school in St. Peter Port. She did little to hide her adoration of Jim Landers, though he appeared not to notice. Taller and bigger-boned than Hugo, she made him feel vaguely uncomfortable, because she appeared not to notice him at all. But then, from the way she was peering at the script he had handed around, she was probably short-sighted and reluctant to put on her glasses. Hugo put her in her late forties and, as she bent her head over the script, he could see the grey roots of her expensively bronzed and highlighted hair.

Next to her sat Douglas Lorrimer, who was in partnership with Elton Maxwell, heading the leading estate agency on the island, and his wife, Lana.

Lorrimer was a small man physically, but he made up for his lack of size with a booming voice and bombastic manner. From their introduction at Jim Landers's, Hugo gathered he was the financial advisor to the group, which put him squarely in the pro-vampire camp, and in Hugo's corner. "Creative concerns," he told Hugo, "are not in my bailiwick. I leave that to the artsy crowd," pointing at Marie and chortling. Marie, Hugo noticed, did not seem in the least offended — but then, this was her husband's business partner, and taking offence was probably inadvisable.

From the condescension shown to Lana Lorrimer by Marie, however, it looked as if Lana had only made the cut by virtue of her marriage. But some of the condescension could be because Lana was a well-endowed blonde in her forties who could curl her lip quite as effectively as the queen bee. She was in the process of reading his script, and Hugo could not tell from her expression whether she liked it or not. As if feeling his eyes upon her, she looked across at him and, suddenly, winked. It was so swift he wondered if he had imagined it. But he bore it in mind.

Sitting in the centre of the circle were Marie and her daughter, Marla. Hugo had never yet set eyes on Elton Maxwell but, if his daughter had combined the genes of both parents, it seemed likely he was handsome, fair-haired and tall. When not spitting blue murder at him, Marie was a striking woman, somewhere in her forties, with dark hair and eyes, unlike her blonde, blue-eyed daughter. But they still looked very much alike.

Elodie Ashton was sitting next to Raymond Morris, who had introduced himself as part-time artist and director of Hugo's "*oeuvre*," as he called it. Sporting a pencil-line moustache above very white teeth, he was dressed all in black, from his beret to his boots and, when asked by Hugo about his painting, described it as "a blend of Dali with a dash of the Douanier, but all my own." Hugo said he couldn't wait to see it. Well, what else does one say to someone who was going to direct one's own "*oeuvre*"?

Elodie was in animated conversation with the man sitting on the other side of her, who had arrived late. Hugo had been trapped in small talk with the Lorrimers about the intricacies of the open and closed housing market, and had watched with annoyance as a tall, grey-haired man with strong features, who looked to be in his fifties, took the seat he had planned to make his own. From what he could hear, Elodie and the man were talking about finances, and there was something about his beautifully cut tweed jacket and air of self-possession that suggested money. As Hugo took one of the three remaining seats, Elodie called out to him.

"Hello, Hugo. I don't think you've met Aaron Gaskell."

Aaron Gaskell nodded, smiled and raised his hand, revealing a magnificent Rolex on his wrist. Hugo had recently checked a similar timepiece out and backed off at the astronomical price. He disliked him immediately.

"Hello. I know who you are. This looks like a lot of fun."

A pretty young woman with bouncing blonde curls sat down next to him, and her dazzling smile smoothed over Hugo's ruffled feelings. Unlike the other Island Players in the room, who had come dressed in the *de rigueur* shreds and patches as seen on professionals shown rehearsing on TV, she was dressed simply, but formally. Her short-sleeved blouse revealed just a hint of cleavage, and her pencil-skirt showed off long legs that were either tanned or stockinged above stiletto heels. On her ring finger was one of the largest diamonds Hugo had ever seen, so big he couldn't see if it concealed a wedding ring.

"I know who I am, but I don't know who you are," Hugo replied, echoing, he hoped, the conversational tone, and was gratified to hear her trill of laughter.

"You Hugo Shawcross and me Tanya." She giggled and pointed across the room to a man who was coming back from some other area of the house, carrying what looked like a double Scotch. "And that," she said, "is Tarzan. Well, he's my husband." Which settled the wedding-ring question.

Tarzan was large, heavy-jowled, his elephantine build accentuated by the baggy pachyderm-coloured corduroys he was wearing. He looked considerably older than his Marilyn Monroe look-alike wife. He glanced across at her and shambled over to sit by Jim Landers, displacing Ginnie Purvis, who scowled and moved down next to Marie Maxwell.

Recovering from the disappointment of not himself being Tarzan, Hugo asked, "What is Tarzan's name?"

Tanya appeared to find this exquisitely funny. She leaned across the circle of chairs and called out, "Hey, Rory, there's someone here who doesn't know who you are! Imagine that!"

She turned to Hugo and pursed up her scarlet lips in mock-disapproval, then, with a sweeping gesture in the direction of her husband she said, "Let me introduce you to island royalty, Hugo. Marie, Ginnie and Rory. The oh-so-elite, blue-ribbon members of the Gastineau clan. Taa-daa!"

The reactions of the assembled Island Players varied from amusement on Elodie's part, to annoyance from Marie and Ginnie. Marla gave a nervous giggle, and the Lorrimers looked bored.

"Shut up, Tanya," Lana said.

There was very little reaction from either Raymond Morris, Aaron Gaskell or Jim Landers, and Hugo got the feeling this was predictable behaviour from Tanya.

"Gastineau?"

His own reaction was one of surprise. He could see now a family resemblance between Rory and Ginnie, but a very different mix of Gastineau genes had swum in Marie's direction.

"I know about Marie, but I didn't realize ..."

"Then you're one of the very few. Rory's the oldest, and Marie's the youngest. Ginnie is in between, in more ways than one."

"But her name is Purvis."

"Married and divorced. Years ago. He came out of the closet once it was no longer terribly terrible to be gay."

"Poor woman."

"Poor ex-Mr. Purvis in my opinion." Tanya snorted, giving an oblique character assessment of Ginnie Purvis. "Ginnie's ex was a sweetie, they tell me. But she chucked him out."

Hugo looked around the room. Things were turning out better than he could have dared hope. The group was beginning to look quite promising, and the island was the perfect place to work on his script while he lay low for a bit, until his mainland problems died down. Besides, he needed time to pursue his other reason for being here, and he had made a promising start with that, quite inadvertently, as it turned out.

Marie Maxwell was tapping her pencil against her script, and making clucking noises, but there was one more question Hugo wanted to ask.

"So, if your husband's the oldest, why don't you live here?"

Tanya giggled and patted Hugo's hand. "Heavens, Rory live in a ground-floor flat? Over his dead body, darling. We live in the family pile out in Forest. That's where the Island Players perform."

So there was another Gastineau mansion. Probably where the family portraits hung. But Marie was catching his eye and calling the group to order.

"Attention, everyone. Let's go around the circle introducing ourselves for our newest member, Hugo, and then we'll take turns reading his *marvellous* play. But first, Hugo, would you say a few words to the *uninitiated* among us about —" Marie gave a theatrical shudder, "*vampires*."

There was an uneasy ripple of laughter around the circle and Hugo got to his feet.

"Count Dracula," he said, surveying the group, "said it best. *The blood is the life*. He was quoting the Bible, actually. Deuteronomy. The vampire is a once-human creature who chooses his victims carefully for great beauty or intelligence, a thirst for power, an appetite for cruelty, the ability to influence others. They are the chosen ones, the embodiment of one of the most powerful forces in life." Hugo paused. "Sex," he said and surveyed the room, realizing with a thrill they were hanging on his every word. "And of all our worst fears." He paused again.

"Death."

Some, including Marie, began to look uneasy, and Hugo was torn between annoyance and relief when Tanya gave a wriggle and squealed, "Ooh, scary!"

He gave her what he hoped was a reassuring smile. "Don't worry, Tanya. The vampire can only cross the threshold if he is invited into your home and your life. It is only when you allow evil in that it can enter."

To the manifest irritation of the assembled Island Players, Tanya had more to say.

"That's a tricky one, isn't it? I mean, how do you know? Some of the ones in the shows look quite — normal."

Hugo decided to be facetious. "When in doubt you must avoid the gaze of the vampire. Do not look into his violet eyes."

With a dramatic timing so perfect it could have been staged, the door flew open and a young man stood there.

He was tall, slender, fair-haired and pale-skinned, his bloodless colouring accentuated by his dark clothing. He rested his hand on the door frame as his beautiful eyes swept the room. Whether they were violet or not, Hugo couldn't make out from where he stood, transfixed.

"Sorry to be late," he said. "May I come in?"

His voice was musical, the inflexion studied, slightly affected, an expensive private school education resonating through the vowels. Beside him, Hugo felt some sort of physical reaction from Tanya Gastineau. It seemed like a recoil, rather than a wriggle, but that was unlikely. Bedazzled, both of them, he was sure.

The young man's arrival was greeted by an outburst of nervous laughter from most of the group. Marla Maxwell was the first to speak.

"Oh, Charlie," she said, breaking into giggles, "You're such an idiot. You're always late."

Marie Maxwell looked from the young man to her daughter.

"Who is this?"

Marla smiled with an unfeigned innocence that was totally suspect and completely unconvincing.

"He's a friend I invited to come along to the reading, Mother. Charles Priestley."

Raymond Morris interrupted what looked to be turning into a mother-daughter fight to the death.

"Sit down, young man. We need some more young males, so you may come in useful. Let's get on with the reading."

Charlie Priestley ran weightlessly across the room and squeezed himself in on the sofa between mother and daughter. The assembled thespians held their breath and waited for one of Marie's explosions. Most of them had witnessed the outburst with Hugo, and were still mildly surprised they were planning to perform what had been described as a depravity. But only mildly. Most of them also knew the reason for her *volte-face*.

Visibly simmering, but valiantly keeping her emotions under control, Marie gave Raymond one of her hostess-with-the-mostest smiles.

"Raymond already has a good idea of what he is looking for, haven't you, Raymond?"

Raymond smiled inscrutably, and they began.

It went surprisingly well. As he listened to them read, Hugo wished he could have a say in the casting, but felt reasonably sure that the black-clad Raymond would have the last word, heavily influenced by Marie Maxwell. He had already had his mind changed for him about his Lilith, and prayed that Morris had the intelligence and the backbone to cast the right person as the vampire. When it came to the men, he wasn't sure the power necessarily lay with Rory Gastineau.

No, now there was the beautiful Charles Priestley. A gift from the gods, a fallen angel if ever he saw one. He could almost hear the beating of his wings. *Back to the drawing-board*, thought Hugo. *Can't pass up a chance like this.*

"Fade to black. Curtain!"

Raymond Morris closed his script with a flourish and surveyed the group. Rory Gastineau turned to Hugo.

"One thing missing," he said. There was a slight slur as he spoke. "There is no title page. What's it called?"

Hugo smiled. "I wasn't sure until now," he said, "but I have settled on the obvious."

"Which is ...?"

"*Blood Play*. That's actually a technical term, as we vampirologists know, but I'll explain later."

Ginnie Purvis was looking worried. "I'd like to ask Hugo —" she gave an unsure glance at Raymond Morris, who had been on the verge of standing up. He remained standing, and waved an impatient hand at Ginnie to continue. "What are we going to do about this chorus of maidens? Are we going to have them? I mean, there's no one here who ..." Her voice trailed off.

It was Raymond who answered. "Of course we're going to have them, Ginnie. Absolutely vital in a play about vampires. And, with Hugo's permission, of course, I see you, Tanya, as their leader!"

Hugo was sure the "permission" was hollow, but he certainly had no problem with inserting Rory's luscious wife into the script.

"Wonderful!" he said, and beside him Tanya wriggled like a happy puppy.

"Oooh — I am going to be the boss maiden!" she squealed.

Across the table, Ginnie Purvis gave a massive snort. "Talk about casting against type," she said to no one in particular. She stood up and added, wearily, "If anyone would *like* to give me a hand with the refreshments, it *would* be appreciated."

She left the table, followed by Marla, and Charles Priestley. Beside him, Hugo again felt that movement of recoil Tanya had made earlier, and remembered her comments about this particular Gastineau.

Marie Maxwell looked about to say something, her expression heralding another oncoming storm, but was interrupted by Raymond Morris, script in hand and a placatory smile on his face. A few minutes later, Marie's expression reverted to annoyance as her daughter and Charles Priestley reappeared with the refreshments.

Raymond turned from Marie and addressed Marla. "This is where you will come in useful, Marla. You can recruit some of your friends for us! To play the part of maidens in the play, that is."

"Good idea!" Hugo decided to avoid witticisms about vampires and virgins, for fear of re-offending Marie. Besides, looking at Marla, sitting there shimmering sexuality next to Charlie, the fallen angel, if her friends resembled her, finding actual virgins might limit the field. "So, Marla, can we rely on you to find us some fresh blood?"

He laughed, Marla laughed, and as everyone else smiled, the lights went out, fading the room into black.

Then Marla started to scream.

Moretti held up the fragile scrap of paper against the light on his desk. It was nearly dark outside, and he could hear the sound of the foghorn in the Little Russel. Attempts to get rid of foghorns, suggesting they were no longer needed, had been strenuously resisted by the harbourmaster, and certainly Moretti would have missed their doleful call through the season of mists and the fogs of winter. He must get back to his Centaur, soon. Some time, he supposed, he must give his boat a name.

"There's a piece of a watermark on it, and I think I can guess what it is. Basildon Bond," he said. "Long time since they made writing paper quite like this. Not sure if it has any significance, but what book did you find it in?"

Liz Falla smiled. "I wondered about that. It was in a collection of plays by Oscar Wilde — *The Importance of Being Ernest*. I saw it once, and as far as I remember, it was sort of fluffy. Not a great love story or anything."

Liz groaned, rubbed her eyes, and stretched her legs out in front of her. It had been a long day, with a lot of kneeling and crouching. She had left Al Brown to see to the storage of the books in the station, and come up to report to Moretti. They had divided the hermit's collection into two groups of boxes: books opened and checked, and books yet to be examined. There were many more of the latter.

"We'll have to look into every book, and I'm going to get Al to do that," said Moretti. "I want you to be free to talk to anyone who comes forward about Gus Dorey. Local people are more likely to open up to you. The paper will carry the story of his death tomorrow, and I want you here at the station to field any calls. Someone is going to come forward, if only to have a chat and a gossip. We need all the information we can get, and gossip may be where the truth lies, in this case."

"Words, words, words, I'm so sick of words," said Liz. "Isn't there a song about that?"

Moretti laid the tiny scrap of paper down. "You should know, Falla. Aren't show tunes up your alley?"

She was giving him that look again, and this time he realized what it was about. Of course, he had passed up a chance to hear her sing. Best that way, staying out of each other's private lives.

"Tin Pan Alley's not the alley I'm up, Guv. Closer to your turf, I'd say." She hesitated, as if about to say something else, then, to Moretti's relief, there was a knock on the door and Al Brown appeared.

"All safely stowed," he said. "What next, sir?"

Moretti told him and the brainiac appeared delighted.

"A pleasure."

"A solitary pleasure, Al. You sat in on the interview with Gord Martel, so you heard what he said about a mailbox. We can get it opened, but it would be interesting to see if the key is missing. Tomorrow, Falla is going to be taking any phone calls here in my office. I'm going to take a look at births, marriages and deaths at the Priaulx Library, and PC Mauger will look through the newspaper archives. Gus Dorey wasn't always a hermit. At some point he had a life."

"Is there any chance of my getting the loan of one of the police Hondas?" Al suggested. "I have a licence, and it would save the use of a car."

"Good idea. I'll arrange it before I leave tonight."

Solitary pleasures, thought Moretti. Dwight and Lonnie won't be there, but I'll go to the club and play a little.

Liz stood up and stretched, yawning. "I'm off to the gym. How about you, Al? Do you want to come?"

Whether out of cussedness or kindness, Moretti heard himself saying, "I'm going to get something to eat at Emidio's and then I'm going to the Grand Saracen. That's the club where I play, Al. If you're interested."

About twenty minutes later, they were picking up Al Brown's Portuguese guitar and heading for Emidio's, and Moretti was kicking himself for the suggestion.

Chapter Eight

"Hey, Ed, good to see you. Who's your friend?"
Deb Duchemin, co-manager of Emidio's,
the restaurant opened by Moretti's father, surveyed
Aloisio Brown with interest. She was a striking
woman, close to six feet tall, her appearance flamboyant, her hair colour chosen to attract attention. At the
moment, it was red, with a broad streak of white near
her face. Although she had the demeanour and discretion needed for her position at Emidio's, with her
height and large frame, Deb also had strength enough
to handle the drunks, drug-dealers and other unattractive types she sometimes had to deal with running the Grand Saracen, which occupied the massive,
vaulted cellar of the large eighteenth-century house on
St. Peter Port's waterfront, that had belonged to the
kind of smuggler and buccaneer for which the club
was named.

The Grand Saracen had started life as a bar beneath the restaurant, with a small stage that was rented out to the occasional singer or group, and Moretti still retained a part interest in the business. When he returned to the island, he decided to use the space, and put together his own jazz ensemble. Deb had introduced him to his bass player, Lonnie Duggan, whom she had known in what she called "the bad old days," without specifying what exactly she meant. Lonnie drove one of the town buses — "occasionally" — was talented, lazy, but energetic enough to play from time to time with the Fénions. Then one day Dwight Ellis had walked in for a drink, and become their drummer. Thus the band came into being.

"Colleague, Deb." Moretti did the introductions. "What's on the menu tonight?"

Deb indicated the board on the wall. "*Involtini alla Cacciatore*. And, as per usual, osso buco. You play guitar? Man, does Ed need you, Al, since his sax player was arrested!"

She roared with laughter at Moretti's expression, her heavy earrings swinging, and pointed to Al Brown's guitar. "Here, let me take care of that, and you can pick it up on your way downstairs. I'll bring you some wine and leave you to decide. The house red okay?"

Both men agreed and, when Deb left the table carrying the guitar in its case, Al Brown said, "Two questions, sir ..."

"I'll guess the first," Moretti interrupted. "My sax player was a local financier who got himself in out of his depth with career criminals. He was good with the sax and hopeless at international conspiracies."

"Pity. Good sax players are hard to come by."

The wine arrived, brought to the table by Deb's partner in the business and in life, who introduced herself in her husky, damaged voice as she poured the wine.

"I am Ronnie, short for Veronica, Bedini, and I'm glad Ed's got himself someone else for the club. Business is down in the bar since Garth was arrested, so you'd better be good."

Deb had had a string of relationships since Ed had known her, but Ronnie Bedini appeared to have staying power. Ronnie was not an island girl, but was also not one of the current wave of Latvians, sometimes Hungarians, who waited tables or worked at the hotels. When Moretti was growing up, the wave that washed ashore was Italian, like his father, then came the Austrians and, later, the Portuguese. Many of the girls, chosen for their looks to wait tables, serve drinks and bring in the customers, were also selected as brides by Guernseymen for much the same reason, and stayed on the island.

Ronnie was one of Deb's strays, and she was looking considerably less waiflike since she had kicked her drug habit. She was a tiny brunette, with various body-piercings and highly decorated arms, and she was responsible for some of the abstracts and collages on the walls of the restaurant. They were outside Moretti's field of expertise, so the only opinion he had offered when asked about them by Deb was that they certainly added colour and interest to the room.

"DC Brown's a colleague," Moretti repeated.

This assumption that Al Brown would be a regular player was disturbing. From what he had overheard of the conversation between Falla and the brainiac, much of the music played by Portuguese guitarists was of the gypsy jazz or *fado* variety, which was not his style. The last thing he needed was to lose his bass player and drummer in a fit of pique about a *manouche* player imported into the Fénions.

"So what's it to be?" Ronnie held her pad at the ready.

"That," said Al Brown, "was going to be my second question. What is *involtini alla cacciatore*?"

"Veal scallops stuffed with chicken livers and prosciuttto, rolled up and cooked with Marsala. Out of this world," Ronnie replied.

Both men ordered the veal scallops, Ronnie departed, and Al Brown raised his glass.

"Here's to magical thinking, and freedom of self-expression," he said.

"Don't you Met-trained guys believe in structure?" asked Moretti. "That's what Chief Officer Hanley believes. He's hoping you'll teach me about MI Teams and Action Managers."

"Shit," said Aloisio Brown.

"The lights came back on and the screaming stopped."

Elodie sat on the edge of the sofa in her sitting room, hands clasped, leaning forward towards Liz. It was about ten o'clock when Liz received Elodie's text, and she had been on her way home from Beau Sejour. If she had not had her recent conversation with Marla

Maxwell in the change room, she would probably just have talked it over with Elodie on the phone.

"Screaming? Just Marla, or anyone else?"

Elodie shrugged her shoulders. "Someone else did, but by the time the lights came on he or she had stopped. Could have been a man or a woman. Just a high-pitched sound, so I don't know. But thanks for dropping by."

"You seemed worried, and I was at Beau Sejour. Besides, wine with risotto sounded good." Liz took another mouthful of *risotto frutti di mare*. "And it is."

"I should come with you some time," said Elodie. "I'll admit, it was scary, particularly after reading Gandalf's play, but it was what Marla was howling that really bothered me."

"Which was ...?"

"'Leave me alone! Stop trying to frighten me! What have I done to you?' — That kind of thing. It sounded like it was not the first time something disturbing had happened, and I started to worry about what I had done."

"Putting the cat among the theatrical pigeons, you said. What did you do?"

Elodie shrugged her shoulders. "I rang Marie and told her that Shawcross saw her as an evil seductress. I laid it on with a trowel and she was thrilled. Then this happens, and I wonder whether I opened some can of worms with my trowel, although I don't see why or how."

Liz put her plate down on the table beside her, and picked up her glass of wine. "Neither do I, but it's a coincidence of a kind, and my Guvnor doesn't believe in coincidences." She hesitated, and then continued. "I told you about Mrs. Maxwell's complaint, and I don't suppose it matters if I tell you about my encounter with Marla at Beau Sejour, since she refused to make it official. She says someone is pestering her with what she called 'weird text messages,' but she doesn't want her parents to know. I haven't looked into it yet, but can you make a text message anonymous? I think you can, but I'm going to double-check."

"You can." Elodie got up from her chair, went over to the sideboard and brought back the bottle of wine to the table. Her face was sombre. "If the texter has an unlisted number, it would not come up on the display, and it would be very hard to trace. And you cannot return a message left from a private caller, not surprisingly."

Liz looked at Elodie. She had poured herself another glass of wine, then curled up in her chair, the position suggesting vulnerability, fragility. Not her usual body language at all, and Liz remembered her mother's cryptic response to her observation about her aunt's divorce.

"It'll be interesting to see if Mrs. Maxwell gets on to us about this tomorrow. Did you see anyone enter or leave the room around about the time the lights went off?"

"I've been thinking about that. There was quite a bit of coming and going, because of the refreshments. There were twelve of us in the room —" Elodie stopped. "Hold on, there were thirteen of us, because of the late arrival."

"Late arrival?"

"Yes, a friend of Marla's. A young chap. Charlie, she called him. Charles Priestley. Central casting for a beautiful — is there such a thing as an *homme fatale*? From Hugo's face, I think he'll be doing a rewrite, and we'll find a new character added. I thought Marie was going to blow a gasket, but she held on."

"She said something to me about someone she didn't want her parents to know about. Maybe it's this feller. Was this before or after the lights went off?"

"Well before."

"Did the late arrival just walk in? Or did he have to be let in?"

"Walked in. I don't know who else was in the house, but Elton Maxwell didn't make an appearance and no explanation was given. But we all know he is not a fan of the theatre. Marie just left the front door unlocked and we let ourselves in."

"After Charlie Priestley arrived, did anyone leave?"

"No, I am sure no one left during the reading. We didn't break, but went straight through."

"So someone else came in and switched off the lights — unless it was a power failure. But that would be another coincidence." Liz got up and carried her plate through to the kitchen. She called back, "So how was the vampire's play? Any good?"

There was silence from the other room. Then Elodie replied, so quietly Liz could hardly hear her words.

"Yes, unfortunately," she said.

When Liz came back from the kitchen, Elodie was pouring herself another glass of wine. Next to her on the sofa lay her copy of the play, and she picked it up and put it on the table between them. Liz pulled it towards her.

"Isn't there usually a title page? This looks like the cast of characters."

"Yes. I think Gandalf had a rush job on his hands last night, and he gave us the title in the meeting. *Blood Play*."

"Bit obvious, isn't it?"

"It is, as he said, a technical term. There are actually organized groups who get together and cut themselves and others, and drink each other's blood."

"Revolting!" Liz put down her glass of red wine with a shudder.

"That's the whole point, really, that it is taboo, and that heightens the mythical quality of blood. Sadomasochism, pleasure and pain, but supposedly performed by consenting adults on each other."

"So when you said 'unfortunately,' you meant what I said. Revolting."

"I wish I did. I cope better with disgusting than — desolate. Gandalf's creation took me by surprise, I'll admit."

Elodie kicked off her slippers and put her feet up in the chair. In profile, away from the table lamp, her face and her expressions were hidden from Liz.

"Apart from Lilith, what do you know, Liz, about vampire legends and the present craze for them in film and on TV?"

"Not much. Not my thing, fangs and open graves and dead people walking. In my job I see too much blood to find it sexy — and that's what it's all about, isn't it? Oh, and death, I suppose. Sex and death."

"Primal fears in a nutshell, these days usually sugar-coated with sweet young things falling for glamorous male figures who are mad, bad and dangerous to know; dead as doornails, but immortal, with immortality achieved by drinking the blood of virgins."

"Yuk, in my opinion. How can you call that sugar-coated, El?"

"Because on TV and in books and movies they have corrupted corruption. They dodge the issue of death, turn what is terrifying into highjinks in the dorm, scary pyjama parties, that kind of dreck."

"And Gandalf didn't."

"No. In his play, he returns again and again to the most terrifying theme of all. Loneliness. Right up there with death, in my opinion." Elodie swung around, facing Liz. "I cannot believe I am saying this, but I felt sorry for the vampire."

Liz decided to lighten the moment. "And which of our island farceurs is going to play the bad guy? Do I know him?"

"You know both the person who will probably play him, and the man who should. Raymond, with his usual unerring lack of vision and backbone, will choose the wrong one. He should choose Rory Gastineau, and he will choose Jim Landers."

"That's a surprise. Doesn't it take guts to turn down a Gastineau?"

"Not this one. Rory's boozing has never stopped him learning lines, and there was such angst when he read. Jim is all intellect and not a shred of true emotion.

But there is no love lost between Marie and her big brother, and Raymond knows it."

"Angst? Didn't he recently marry gorgeous Tanya — whoever she was before she met Rory?"

"After shilly-shallying around for years, Rory found himself one beautiful brood mare. Or, rather, she found him. She came here to find herself an off-shore millionaire, so they say, and found herself island royalty instead. But there you have the problem for Marie, Liz. If Rory and Tanya have a boy, Marla no longer is the heiress apparent. And Ginnie will never be a threat, as long as all she wants for Christmas is the bookshop owner. Jim just isn't interested."

"Is he gay?"

Elodie laughed. "Not if his behaviour towards me is anything to go by. I went out to dinner with him a couple of times. I enjoyed his company, because the conversation was interesting. But he wanted more, and I don't want anyone in my life, just at the moment."

"I've never really met Jim Landers, but he doesn't strike me as the type to have much small talk. What did he talk about?"

"Books, of course!" Elodie laughed. "His passion. But I learned something about his background, which was army. He spent most of his childhood on the move in places like Kenya and Zanzibar, with spells at boarding school, depending on how dangerous his father's postings were. Seems to have seen little of his mother, and was not very fond of his father, from what I gathered. But he's not one to express emotion. It was more what wasn't said than what was."

Liz thought briefly about asking how Elodie knew Jim Landers wanted more, since he wasn't one to express emotion. But only briefly. She got up, and started to pull on her fleece jacket. "I've got to go. We're still dealing with the suicide, and the trouble with hermits is they don't socialize with anyone. Talk about loneliness!"

"Is loneliness the same as aloneness, I wonder. No next of kin, I suppose. Is that the problem?"

"Yes." Liz paused, then said, "I lost my train of thought back there, but I remember it now. I thought there wasn't much Gastineau moolah left to fight over. Is there?"

"Quite a bit in what the Americans call real estate. As well as piracy, it is how the family originally made themselves rich and powerful, with houses and land here, in France and in England. But they have sold off most of what they had over the years and kept only the town and the country house. The house out in Forest is worth a few million, because it is open market, apart from a small cottage in the grounds — and there are acres of grounds. There would be any number of potential buyers for the land alone. There have already been heavy hints dropped by Maxwell and Lorrimer, but so far Rory isn't budging. And as long as he was unmarried, Marie was happy. Any heir has to be legit, apparently, to inherit, and males always take precedence."

"Wow. Quite Jane Austen, isn't it."

"With more than a touch of one of the Brontë sisters — *Tenant of Wildfell Hall*, perhaps. Baroque and Gothic, rather than *Buffy the Vampire Slayer*-ish."

"Oooh, *heavy*."

Just as both women started to laugh, an unearthly howl rose outside somewhere in the garden.

"Oh my God." Liz clasped her throat, an instinctive gesture she would think about afterwards. "What the —?"

"Relax." Elodie got up and leaned over the sofa to pull one of the curtains slightly aside. The night garden was lit by a full moon in a cloudless sky, as beautiful and unreal as a stage set. "I'd know that sound anywhere. Gandalf must have let Stoker out when he got home, and he has sought out his mortal enemy, Mudge."

"Ill met by moonlight," said Liz, coming over to join Elodie at the window. "That was Titania meeting Oberon, wasn't it, and holding on to the little boy."

"Yes. An orphan. The son of someone dear to her, but she, being mortal, died." The sadness in Elodie's expression filled the room. *Maybe*, thought Liz, *she has opened a can of worms, but for herself as much as for anyone else*.

"What role are you auditioning for in *Blood Play*, El?"

"None," her aunt replied. "I've already told Raymond I will be script assistant, but that I want no part in this." Elodie turned back to Liz. "There's an old German saying I once heard, and I've thought about it quite a bit over the past few hours. Can't remember the German, but it goes something like this: *Don't paint the Devil on the wall*."

Elodie pulled the curtains together, shutting out the moonshine.

The bloodcurdling screams faded and died away.

* * *

"Just One of Those Things." "From This Moment On." Slowing into "All the Things You Are" and "You Go to My Head." Behind, alongside, echoing sometimes, Al Brown gradually unfolding and developing the melody as Moretti began to like what he heard, to trust what he heard, and to give him space. *It's hard to play slow* drifted into his mind. The words of Miles Davis, master of slow tempo magic. Even playing "Tempus Fugit" he could make time stand still.

They took the tempo up before they finished the set. "Lady Be Good," "I'm Beginning to See the Light," "Lover." The small crowd in the Grand Saracen whooped and begged for more. They gave them "You Rascal You."

People began to filter downstairs from the restaurant, and Ronnie Bedini came down to help serve the drinks. Whenever he turned to look beyond the edge of the small stage, Moretti could see her dark eyes fixed on the tall, beautiful Latvian girl who served the drinks in the downstairs bar. Trouble? He hoped he was wrong. Deb seemed happy with her current lover.

"You've done this before," Moretti said to Al Brown as they walked back through the quiet streets to the Triumph.

"I have. How did you get into playing jazz piano?"

"I learned to play the piano at my mother's knee. Then, when I was about fifteen I picked up a record of

Thelonius Monk. It was scratched and damaged but that was it."

"For me, it was Django, of course. You have a drummer?"

"And a bass. They're good."

"Great," said Al Brown.

Chapter Nine

Just on the outskirts of St. Peter Port, the Priaulx Library began life in much the same way as so many splendid homes in Guernsey; it was built in the eighteenth century on the profits of brandy running and contraband. The Priaulx family bought it from Peter Mourant, the smuggler, and Osmond Priaulx bequeathed it and his vast library to his beloved island. It stands just above the statue of Queen Victoria, who would probably not have been amused by its history, and close to Victor Hugo on his massive plinth, granite cloak blowing perpetually in the wind, whose sympathies would certainly have been with those law-breaking toilers of the sea.

Ed Moretti and Police Constable Bernie Mauger walked the short distance from Hospital Lane to the library, cutting through Candie Gardens, which had originally belonged to the house and which were part of Osmond Priaulx's gift. It was a beautiful morning, and PC Mauger was humming to himself as he walked, happy to be part of Moretti's investigation. He wasn't sure why they were going to all this trouble about an old hermit's suicide, but his was not to reason why. He was just chuffed to be along for the ride, unlike both plainclothes and uniform back at the station, who were grumbling about Hanley allowing Moretti so much leeway.

"'The solace of my life,' Osmond Priaulx called his books," said Moretti, as much for himself as for PC Mauger.

"Didn't know that, sir, but I remember my dad telling me that, when they renovated the roof a few years back, they found all kinds of weird stuff left there by the roofers who'd done the job a hundred years before. Supposed to stop evil happening, or something."

"Interesting. Did they leave them there?"

"Don't know, sir, but most likely. Could have been unlucky to move them, right?"

Moretti looked at the constable to see if he was being ironic, but there was no sign of levity on his broad, placid face.

"What is it we're looking for, sir?"

"I don't know." PC Mauger looked at Moretti, puzzled. "But I can tell you where to make a start. Ask for the records in the archive between about 1950 and the present day. Concentrate on the fifties, sixties and seventies, and on any news item with the name 'Dorey.' And don't forget the classifieds."

PC Mauger's frown deepened on his wall of a forehead and he shook his head in dismay. "Dorey," he repeated. "You've been off the island a while, haven't you, sir. Had you forgotten it's one of the commonest surnames here?"

"No, and I wish he was called something else, but he isn't. What I want you to look for is family stuff — scandals, feuds, any unlikely news items about court cases, legal disputes, that kind of thing. Meanwhile, I'll be getting a copy of his family tree, birth certificate, and so on. Oh, and look out for anything to do with marriages either here or on the mainland."

"Right, sir. Is it about wills and such? Who gets what's left? Wouldn't have thought there was much, not with him living out there in that shack."

Those were Moretti's thoughts also. What could Gus Dorey still have in his life that had brought about his death? As far as they knew, only some pricey books, and they had been left untouched. Irene Edwards said he had cataracts, and since reading was unmistakably his passion, probably the only joy left in his life, losing that passion might be cause enough for suicide. The solace of his life, as it had been to Osmond Priaulx.

Passion. All passion spent perhaps, but once there had been a passion in his life.

My darling.

Moretti realized PC Mauger was speaking to him.

"Do you want me to come and tell you whenever I find anything that might be something, sir?"

"Only if something comes up that strikes you as really unusual. Otherwise, make a note of anything and everything Dorey-related in that time period."

PC Mauger's puzzlement turned into resignation. Still, it was better than traffic duty.

Moretti and Bernie Mauger were greeted at the Priaulx by the head librarian, Lydia Machon.

"Your sergeant told me you were coming, and why," she said. "That poor old man. It was in the paper this morning."

It was the first time Moretti had met Lydia Machon, the head librarian. Slim, tall, with silver-white hair framing her face and dark eyes, she looked to be in her late fifties, and there was an air of quiet intelligence about her.

"Did you know him, or any of his family, Mrs. Machon?"

"No, I'm afraid not. I am between generations, as you might say. He was considerably older than me, and I think he lived off the island for many years. And there is no younger generation, I imagine. I used to pass his place, of course, when I was out there, walking my dogs, but I never saw him."

"Did you ever see anyone around, anyone going in or out?"

"No, never. It always looked deserted, but I assumed he was inside."

"PC Mauger will be looking at the newspaper archives and I will take a look at your records of births, marriages and deaths."

"Come this way, Constable Mauger. The newspaper archives are upstairs, in the Harris Room."

   Bernie Mauger followed the head librarian up the curving staircase with its polished banisters, his hefty frame swallowing her up from view, and Moretti took a look around.

   He must have been in here as a child, he supposed, but he had no recollection of doing so. He only knew the remark about the solace of books because he had looked up something about the library on the computer that morning. There it was, in Latin, inscribed on a brass plaque above the fireplace in what had later been the dining room of one of the island's bailiffs — Peter Carey, scion of one of the great island families. The bailiff is the head of the island parliament, the States of Guernsey, one of the most powerful figures on the island, but since Peter Carey's day, the position occupied a much reduced legislative role. His death was noted with uncommonly grim immediacy on another brass plaque: *Peter Carey died in this room.*

   Over the fireplace was a portrait of Osmond Priaulx, his likeness still present in the house with his books, as was the urn with his ashes. There were some nice pieces of furniture in the room, but the dominant feature was the bookshelving that lined the walls from floor to ceiling. In spite of the dark wood of the panelling, the rooms were not sombre, with huge windows letting in the sunlight.

   Words, words, words, as Falla had said. Now they needed some deeds. Bernie Mauger was no great intellect, but he was thorough and conscientious, good with computers, and could be relied upon to keep his mouth shut. At the moment, only the chief officer, Falla, Al

Brown and Irene Edwards knew about the possibly assisted suicide, and Moretti hoped to keep it that way until Falla had had a chance to talk to a few people. He had asked the *Guernsey Press* to add something to the announcement of the hermit's death: *The police are asking for information about Mr. Dorey's heirs or descendants.*

"Detective Inspector." Lydia Machon had returned. "Our births, marriages and deaths archives are over here." She looked at him questioningly. "Knowing why you were coming, I looked up his birth certificate, but were you hoping for more? A will, perhaps?"

"Anything that would help us resolve the property question, that kind of thing. Do you hold wills?"

"Not current ones, no, but it will certainly be interesting to see if anyone comes forward to claim the land."

"Any particular reason?"

Moretti felt his heart beat faster, the reaction of the hunter seeing the spoor on the trail ahead, where before there had been not a track in sight. Lydia Machon's expression was difficult to interpret, but she appeared to be wavering about continuing with her observation.

"My husband, Cyril Machon, was a lawyer. He was quite a bit older than me and he died a few years ago. He and his family stayed on the island during the war, and once, when I asked about the shack near the Common, he told me that the house that had been there was burned down toward the end of the war. He was still a child when it happened, but he remembered his father saying, 'Dorey got what was coming to him.' No one rebuilt there or laid claim to the land until Gus Dorey put up his shack." Lydia Machon hesitated, then added, "Inspector Moretti, I have learned in this job to keep my counsel, but I see no harm in telling you what my husband told me some years ago."

"Did he say anything else you can remember? Anything about the son?"

"I only remember he was surprised at the son's return after so many years."

"What year was this, do you remember?"

"I will never forget. It was 1995. By then my husband was a sick man and did not make it through the year."

Lydia Machon suddenly became brisk and businesslike. "I took the liberty of printing up the birth certificate for you, and you can take it with you, Inspector. Here it is." She handed Moretti a piece of paper from a desk near the fireplace.

"You are sure this is the right Gus Dorey?" Moretti asked, taking it from her. "I imagine your records are full of Doreys."

Lydia Machon laughed. "Chock full of them, yes, but the address is the correct one for the property. I made sure of that. Oh, by the way, I checked and he was the only child. I'll leave you to it. The microfiches are on this floor."

Moretti looked at the piece of paper he held in his hand, on which was recorded the birth of Gus Dorey who came back to be a hermit on his father's land, only to hang, or be hanged, on a rope at the age of eighty-one. *Born June 21st, 1931.* Born at the summer solstice. Mother, Agnes Mahy; father, Augustus Dorey. Did he, like his father, get what was coming to him?

Moretti sat down and started to look at the microfiches Lydia Machon had left for him. It didn't take long to find what he was looking for, the year of the death of Augustus Dorey, Senior. Nineteen-ninety-five, the year his son came back and built himself a home near Pleinmont Common on his family's land. So, no return of the prodigal son, no fatted calf, but the passing of the prodigal father.

It took a little longer to find the death certificate of Agnes Dorey, because Moretti didn't have Lydia Machon's memory of grief to narrow the gap and pinpoint a year, but Agnes had predeceased her husband by twenty years.

"Sir." It was Bernie Mauger, beaming, jolting him out of the past. "Found something interesting, sir. Come and take a look."

Moretti followed in Bernie Mauger's substantial wake upstairs to where the newspaper archives were housed. The constable pulled out the chair for Moretti and brought over another chair. In this part of the library there were one or two people working at tables, and they looked up briefly as Moretti arrived. Up on the screen was an issue of the *Guernsey Press*, somewhat the worse for wear, the printing faded. Moretti scrolled up and found the date. Sunday, April 12, 1953. Just over sixty years ago. He moved the article back on to the centre of the screen. It was quite brief.

*Police were called to an altercation in Forest
during the evening hours of Saturday, April
11. General Roland Gastineau reported
an unprovoked attack on his son, Roland
Gastineau, by Gus Dorey, a student. There
were no serious injuries, and the general
declined to press charges.*

"Well done, PC Mauger, good hunting." Moretti
could feel his heartbeat accelerate again. "Copy it, and
be sure to move on to another screen. Don't leave it
up, okay?"

"Right, sir. Doesn't do to mess around with this
lot, does it?"

"No. I'm going back to take another look at the
births, marriages and deaths around this date. Then
I'm leaving you to it. See if you can find if there was
any follow-up to the story."

Bernie Mauger was right. It didn't do to mess
around with *les messux*, but it looked as if he was going
to have to do just that. And the longer PC Mauger
thought that was the reason for discretion, the better.

Besides, he really didn't know if Gus Dorey's fisti-
cuffs with the General's son had anything to do with
anything. But, for some reason, Gus Dorey had come
back to the island and got into a fight with a member of
a family with clout. And that, in itself, was interesting.

* * *

Liz Falla was having a busy morning. She had set herself up in Moretti's office and had told the desk sergeant to send up anyone who wanted to give information about the death of Gus Dorey. Sergeant Bennett looked disbelieving.

"Even all the usual old farts and crones who come in to waste our time?"

"Especially all the usual old farts and crones who come in to waste our time."

"I'm splitting my sides, DS Falla."

The sergeant's laughter followed her up the stairs.

An hour or so later, she was seriously thinking of rescinding her request. The outpouring of aimless reminiscing and fabricated nonsense purporting to be the truth from the handful of people who came in, and from a couple of phone calls, was making it difficult for her to keep her cool. Some of the vituperation about Gus Dorey, Senior, was unpleasant and, in many cases, self-righteous and self-serving.

But the vituperation was, possibly, useful. It was the repeated story, the hopefully factual version embedded in the overblown oratory and purple prose that Liz recorded in her notebook after the storyteller had left the office or put down the phone. Just about every person who came in was middle-aged and beyond, but too young to have been directly involved in the incidents they recalled, which had generally been passed on by another generation. If the stories were to be believed, Gus Dorey, Senior, had collaborated in every possible way with the Nazis, from informing about wireless sets to selling goods on the black market, to handing over escaped prisoners. There was enough of an overlap between stories to give credence to some of it, at least.

However, to Liz's follow-up question after she had let them have their say, "Yes, but what do you know about his son?" her informants had little to add. The only useful information was that he and his mother had not been on the island during the war, but had left when so many were evacuated.

Then the silver fox walked into the office, unannounced.

Reginald Hamelin was a senior member of one of the most prestigious law firms on the island. His nickname referred to his magnificent and carefully maintained head of hair, his cunning in his chosen fields of law — property and matrimony — and his unpleasant behaviour when cornered. More or less retired for some time, he was brought out of mothballs for certain clients. He was still a powerful man, because he knew everyone who was anyone and, more significantly, what was hidden behind closed doors, in the back of family closets and, if there were bodies, where they were buried.

"Ah, it's the very attractive Detective Constable Falla."

An elegantly manicured hand was extended across Moretti's desk.

"Detective Sergeant. Good morning, advocate Hamelin." Liz Falla took the proffered hand briefly and indicated the chair on the other side of the desk. "How can I help you?"

Reginald Hamelin surveyed the seat offered as though it might need sterilizing, then sat down, slowly.

He gave Liz the warm, charming smile she had seen in court just before he skewered a witness on the stand, or challenged opposing counsel.

"You have been elevated, Detective Sergeant. Felicitations. Well-deserved, I am sure. I am not sure *you* can help me, but I happened to be in town on other business and, after seeing the news of Dorey's death in this morning's paper, I thought I'd drop in. Where is your superior officer?"

Well, well, well, as her superior officer liked to say.

"Not available at the moment, sir — or did you mean Chief Officer Hanley?" Liz made as if to pick up the phone, and out came the well-tended hand, swiftly.

It was an open secret that Hamelin and Hanley disliked each other. The chief officer had unexpectedly resisted an attempt by Hamelin to get rid of an inexperienced young constable, still on probation, who had misguidedly given the silver fox a traffic ticket, and then added insult to injury by declaring that he did not care who Hamelin was, he had mounted the pavement with excessive speed, and was driving dangerously.

"Moretti. Detective Inspector Moretti." Hamelin bared his teeth, straining for charm, and failing. "But you will have to do."

Liz Falla bared her own teeth in response, and waited.

Chapter Ten

"The war again?" said Liz.

Al Brown looked at Liz Falla and raised his eyebrows.

"The war again?" he echoed.

Liz was sitting next to Moretti on the other side of the table at Emidio's. It was eleven o'clock at night, and Deb had opened the doors to them and produced lasagna, and red wine, along with a large loaf of crusty bread. At this hour of the night, with the place to themselves, the feeling was of the tumultuous past of the building, rather than its mundane present. Beyond the huge plate-glass window installed in the opening to the harbour, where the privateers had hauled up their casks of brandy from the sailing ships below, the foghorn wailed softly, persistently, guiding present-day buccaneers through the mists and fog of a September night.

"I'll leave you to it. You know where the dishwasher is. And the till. Clean up and lock up," she told Moretti.

She turned off most of the lights, leaving their booth in its own pool of light, and disappeared into the kitchen. A moment later they heard the heavy back door bang shut behind her. Moretti pulled out his mobile and turned it off, and Liz and Al followed suit.

"Not the war, this time," said Moretti.

Back at the office, he and Falla had to wait for Al to spring himself free from the enthusiastic clutches of Chief Officer Hanley, who was anxious to hear how he would be applying his Met training to the case. It gave them both a chance to compare notes about the wartime offences of Gus Dorey, Senior, and share the information with Al Brown on the way to the restaurant. Al confined himself to comments about Moretti's Triumph, the model, the year, its four seats as compared to other Triumphs, but his comparative silence spoke volumes.

Moretti topped up Al Brown's glass.

"You look like you need this," he said. "What Falla means is the occupation of the island in the last war, and what was said about the hermit's father. But this time I don't think so."

"That's what advocate Hamelin wants us to believe," said Liz. "All he basically said was to let sleeping dogs lie, to leave well alone, because the father is long gone, and why sully the son's memory?"

"Since when did Hamelin ever care about sullying?" Briefly, Moretti explained the silver fox for Al's benefit, and then told Al and Falla what he and Bernie

Mauger had found at the Priaulx. "Besides, nothing was said about the suicide in the report."

"Hamelin still has an ear to the ground, Guv, and I doubt Gord Martel has kept quiet," Liz reminded Moretti. "I'm sure all kinds of people know by now the hermit hanged himself."

"Come on, Falla. The silver fox doesn't slink in to Hospital Lane just because a poor old man takes his own life. I hoped a lawyer might come forward with information, but this is something else. No one risked helping Gus Dorey to hang himself because of what his father did in the war."

"Not revenge?" Liz took another helping of lasagna and tore off a chunk of bread. "You once said that war casts long shadows."

"True, but Gus Dorey had been in his hideaway many years, and no one had touched him. It doesn't make sense. Something more recent triggered this. Did you find anything helpful, or unusual, Al?"

"All kinds of stuff that was unusual, perhaps. For instance, he liked writing out passages from books, sometimes just quotations, and putting them back in one of the books." Al Brown took a mouthful of wine, and closed his eyes. "Nothing like chianti with lasagna in my opinion, and this is a nice one." He picked up the bottle and looked at the label as he spoke. "And he did a lot of underlining. I'm trying to put his jottings in some sort of order, see if there's any pattern."

"Pattern?"

"I haven't shared this with the chief officer yet, but I'm not a big fan of some modern police methods."

In his position as superior officer, Moretti resisted smiling, but Falla did not feel the need.

"Still, there was some interesting research about patterns of behaviour in one of my courses that might come in useful. Dorey seems to have been a compulsive note-taker, but only if he cared passionately about something — language, class prejudice, for instance — but what really grabs my attention is that most of his notes have to do with love. Not disappointed love, or love betrayed, which you might expect from a recluse, but love shared, love returned. Sometimes he underlined, not in the valuable books, and sometimes he wrote the same quotation out more than once, and those are the ones I'm most interested in."

Al Brown smiled across the table at Liz, who smiled back at him.

"For instance?" For some reason Moretti suddenly felt the need of a cigarette. He touched the lighter he always carried in his pocket, his talisman. His pattern.

"There is only one quotation in French, and so far I have found it three times." Al pulled out his notebook. "My French is pretty rusty, but it translates something like this, 'A happy memory is perhaps on this earth closer to real happiness than happiness itself.'"

"I think that's from a poem by Alfred de Musset," Moretti said. "Interesting."

Liz's thoughts turned to her late-night conversation with Elodie. *Three primal elements*, she thought, *not two. Sex, death and love.*

"So this is more likely to be about love than about revenge?" She was looking unconvinced.

"I don't know, Falla, but someone is anxious to cover up something. Hamelin's visit to Hospital Lane makes me even more curious about the report Bernie Mauger found about the fight between Gus Dorey and General Gastineau's son. Now, *that* is the sort of family for whom Hamelin comes out of the woodwork. He doesn't usually offer himself as an emissary, uninvited."

Liz put down her glass of wine and pulled out her notebook, riffling back through the pages. "I didn't bring this to your attention, Guv, but perhaps now I should. Remember all that vampire hooey and Marla Maxwell's text messages? Something else has happened, this time at one of their meetings about the play. I took some notes, in case."

Moretti looked across the table at Al Brown. "You know about this vampire stuff, Al?" Al Brown nodded, smiling at Liz again. "Fill us in, Falla."

As Liz read the notes she had taken after leaving Elodie's, Moretti tried to concentrate on the content, and not the sound of her voice by his side filling the empty room with its music. In the dim light, Ronnie Bedini's paintings took on a soft sheen, a glow and a subtle vibrancy far removed from their brash and brazen, more brightly-lit selves, and Moretti thought of her looking at the Latvian girl.

"That's it, Guv."

Bringing himself back to the matter in hand, Moretti asked, "Which member of the group gave you all this?"

Across the table, Al Brown was looking surprised, and Moretti could hear the mild reproach in Falla's voice.

"My godmother, Guv, as I said. Her name is Elodie Ashton," adding for further clarification, "She's my mother's sister."

"Sorry. I got distracted by Ronnie's artwork. Maybe I should talk to your aunt, although the place to start should be with the Maxwells. But I don't think we'd learn anything by the direct approach, and Hamelin's visit only confirms that. What are your aunt's working hours? Can you fix this up?"

"Of course. She works from home, but she keeps pretty much to normal working hours — non-members of the police force working hours, that is."

Moretti and Al laughed, and Liz pulled out her phone and turned it on.

"I might as well text her now. Oh my God …"

"What is it?" Both men spoke in unison.

"Talk of the — it's my aunt, she's been trying to reach me. Something else has happened. The police are at her place."

Moretti stood up. "Must be more than threatening texts or someone putting out the lights to scare people if uniform is out at this time of night," he said.

He felt Liz Falla's elbow brushing against him in the narrow space of the booth as she texted back, then she closed her phone, and turned to him. Even in the dim light he could see the shock on her face, which was unusual. One of his partner's best qualities was that she kept calm in most circumstances, her emotions under control.

"It is, Guv. Much more. Someone has tried to kill Hugo Shawcross."

* * *

Moretti parked the Triumph as close as possible to the cottage. Falla had directed him, but the flashing lights of the ambulance and the police car had marked out their destination like beacons in the dark long before they turned into the lane.

As he jumped out from the back seat of the Triumph, Al Brown asked, "Did they live together, the playwright and your aunt? Is this her house?"

"Yes it is, but, God, no, they didn't! She hardly knew him. He rents the place that backs on to this."

Liz raced ahead of the two men along the path to the cottage, pushing past the ambulance driver as she did so, and in through the open door.

"Hey, wait, miss!" The driver started to go after her.

"It's all right, she's a police officer and a family friend." Moretti pulled out his identification, as did Al Brown. "You haven't moved the victim yet?"

"Any minute now, they tell me, sir. Nasty business. There was a lot of bleeding and they had to stabilize him first."

Moretti hurried ahead of Al up the narrow path Falla had taken, between two old limestone gateposts that must have been the original entry before the driveway was put in at the side of the cottage. He glanced up at the roof as it gleamed in the flashing lights of the police car and ambulance. Terra cotta from the look of it, which must have cost a bundle.

Perhaps Falla's aunt was in the offshore financial

business, Moretti thought as he went in through the front door, followed by Al. He knew what that kind of renovation cost, having looked into doing something similar for his own place, and reluctantly rejecting the idea. Some interior walls had been removed when the cottage was renovated, making it more open than it would have been in whatever century it was built, and to his right he could see a kitchen, where two ambulance men were picking up the stretcher from the floor. Moretti recognized Police Constable Le Marchant, who was hauling a heavy kitchen table to one side to clear their path. Moretti and Al Brown hurried to give him a hand, then went over to the stretcher. The playwright was on it, moaning, which was a good sign, a sign of life.

"We're out of here," one of the stretcher-bearers called out as they ran past them. Moretti got a brief glimpse of a small man with a blood-stained beard, his neck swathed in bandages. As he passed, his eyes met Moretti's and he gurgled something. At least it sounded to Moretti as if he were trying to put together a sentence, sounds with meaning, rather than a vocalization of agony.

"Didn't expect you here, Guv. Nasty business," said a shaken PC Le Marchant, echoing the driver's words.

"Were you the first on the scene?"

"Yes. Jimmy Le Poidevin and his team are out in the garden. They just arrived."

"Not smelling the roses, I imagine. Is that where it happened?"

"Looks like it. Not that the victim is saying much, not with his throat cut."

"Good God. Was it the homeowner who found him?"

"Yes, and he was lucky — well, if you can call getting your throat cut lucky. She has some first aid training, and kept a cool head, what's more. Saved his life, the ambulance blokes say. I've got a statement from her, but just about where she found him and how she found him."

"She must be in shock," said Al Brown. "Does she need medical help?"

"The ambulance people have talked to her. They wanted to take her to the hospital, but she says she's okay. That's her through there with DS Falla."

Through the archway between the kitchen and what presumably was the sitting room, Moretti could see Liz Falla sitting beside a woman on a sofa. She had her arms around her, and all Moretti could see was a mass of titian-red hair falling over the dark blue sleeve of Falla's suit.

Her aunt? He supposed he must at some point have imagined Falla's aunt as a grey-haired middle-aged woman, like Falla's mother, whom he had once met in town with her daughter, because this was a surprise. A flamboyant middle-aged woman, apparently, who kept her hair long and dyed it red.

"Falla?"

Liz Falla and her aunt looked up as he spoke. Behind him he heard Al Brown murmur.

"Va-va-voom."

"We don't have to do this now. It's late, and you've had a shock."

Elodie put a hand on Liz's arm, and looked at Moretti. Al Brown had left them and gone to talk to Jimmy le Poidevin and the SOC team outside.

"I'm all right. I know how important it is to do this as soon as possible, and besides, I really don't see myself getting into bed for a good night's sleep." She gave a shaky laugh.

Sitting next to her niece on the sofa, Elodie Ashton struck Moretti as being completely unlike her niece, and it was not just in colouring. Even seated, Falla was considerably taller than her godmother. Not his type, but Al Brown was right. Va-va-voom indeed.

"Okay. I know you've already spoken to PC Le Marchant, but just start at the beginning, and Falla can take notes. Where were you — in here?"

"Yes. I was reading. I had music on, but very low, background-type music." At this, Elodie turned and said to her niece, "And in case you're wondering, it was Chopin."

"Poor Chopin, reduced to mood music," said Liz. She hugged her aunt and grinned at Moretti, and the atmosphere in the room lightened somewhat. "Go on, El."

"Then I heard what sounded like a Mudge and Stoker confrontation outside."

"Sorry?"

This time both Liz and Elodie smiled at Moretti's bewilderment, and Liz said, "I've heard one of those, Guv. Stoker is Hugo Shawcross's cat, and Mudge is his bitter rival. It's a truly god-awful howling." She turned to her aunt. "But this time, it wasn't."

"No. It seemed to be getting closer and went on and on and on. Finally, I couldn't stand it anymore, so I decided to go and take a look outside."

Elodie gently extricated herself from her niece's arms, and stood up. Moretti could see rust-red streaks and smears on the pale yellow sweater she was wearing; the wristband of the sleeves were heavily encrusted with the playwright's blood. There was a smudge of blood on her cheek, and her long hair was probably smeared also, but with that colour it was difficult to tell. She staggered slightly as she stood, and he got up and took hold of her arm. She was tiny, nearly a head shorter than his six feet.

"No." She shook him off, almost angrily, and Moretti returned to the chair he had pulled over opposite the sofa. The lady was not for touching, apparently, or only by Falla. "I've got some adrenalin to get rid of. Don't worry, it takes a lot to make me faint, and I've already done that with the emergency crew."

She started to pace up and down between Liz and Moretti, talking as she did so, her sentences short and clipped, but her voice under control.

"I opened the door. The motion light outside had come on. Hugo was lying just beyond the back door in a pool of blood. I could see the trail he had taken to get there. He looked up at me and made this terrible gurgling sound, and I could see his neck."

Elodie stopped pacing and turned to Liz.

"I knew he was in serious trouble, so I grabbed anything that came to hand, which happened to be the fleece jacket I keep near the back door, and I started applying pressure. Thank God he's such a little fellow, and thank God for adrenalin, because I was able to get him into the house — well, enough to close the door. You see, I didn't have to be a medical expert to know that kind of injury doesn't happen when you trip over something in the dark. That kind of damage is — man-made."

Elodie returned to sit by Liz, who took her hand. She didn't pull away from her niece, Moretti noticed, but leaned against her, closing her eyes.

"Before you shut the door, did you see anything at all?" Moretti asked.

"No. But I think he'd travelled quite a long way."

"Why do you say that, El?"

Elodie looked up at Liz's question, and her reply was soft, quiet, chilling. "Because of the trail that shone in the moonlight behind him. Like a bloody flare-path."

There was a pause and, as Moretti started to get up, Elodie Ashton started to speak again.

"Who would have thought little Gandalf would have so much blood in him?"

Her words grew into a crescendo of sound as she started to laugh, helplessly, shock overwhelming her once more.

Part Two

The Run

Chapter Eleven

It was unusually quiet in the incident room. Woken in the small hours of the morning by Moretti's phone call informing him of the attempted murder of Hugo Shawcross, Chief Officer Hanley's instinct for self-preservation and desire for a peaceful life surfaced rapidly.

"Let's keep this first meeting to a need-to-know group, Ed. Who would that be?"

"Al Brown, PC Le Marchant, PC Mauger, Jimmy Le Poidevin. I have told DS Falla to come as soon as she feels she can."

"Her aunt must be in shock. Shouldn't she have been in hospital overnight?"

"She's coping well. But there's quite a cleanup to be done, and DS Falla is taking care of that."

Who would have thought Gandalf would have that much blood in him?

Gandalf?

"Blood everywhere, sir."

"Horrible. Poor old lady."

Moretti thought of correcting Hanley, but refrained. No point at this hour of the night going into descriptive specifics that were unnecessary.

Jimmy Le Poidevin, head of forensics, was unusually subdued. He and his team had barely slept, and his first remarks were addressed to Al Brown, who was looking his usual dapper and well-turned-out self.

"Seen anything like that before, back in the centre of the universe?"

"London, you mean?" Al Brown smiled serenely, unperturbed by the forensic chief's adversarial tone, which he had heard more than once the night before. "Yes. Garrotting was a favourite technique used by one of the street gangs while I was doing my training."

"Well, it certainly isn't *here*," said Chief Officer Hanley, looking in irritation at Jimmy Le Poidevin. "This is — unprecedented. Do we have any reports yet from the hospital, Moretti?"

"Not yet. I told them we want to hear from whoever examined Hugo Shawcross as soon as possible."

Chief Officer Hanley turned to Al Brown. "This is where your expertise and Met training will come in useful, DC Brown. Perhaps you could tell us how you would set up a team at the outset of a similar investigation."

Jimmy Le Poidevin made a little puffing sound like a steam engine under pressure, and Al Brown looked at

Moretti. Knowing how Al felt about Hanley's expectations, and seeing the effect this had on the head of forensics gave Moretti a mildly euphoric sensation that cleared his head, rapidly compensating for his lack of sleep.

Then his mobile rang.

"It's DS Falla, sir. She's on her way from the hospital, and she's bringing Dr. Edwards with her, to give us a report. We're in luck. Dr. Edwards performed the autopsy on Gus Dorey, and she's perceptive."

Moretti looked at Al Brown. "If DC Brown doesn't object," he said, "I would like to fill you in on some details of the Dorey suicide."

Chief Officer Hanley turned his irritated attention from Le Poidevin to Moretti as Al Brown sank back in his chair.

"The Dorey suicide?" he repeated. "This is hardly the time or place, Moretti. What on earth has *that* got to do with *this*?"

"I'm not sure, sir. But before Dr. Edwards arrives, perhaps I could go over a few things, including the visit of advocate Hamelin, and his conversation with DS Falla."

"Hamelin?"

Moretti now had Hanley's undivided attention. He gave the chief officer a succinct account of what little they had unearthed at the hermit's shack, moving on to Marie Gastineau's original complaint and the events at the reading, culminating with the strange coincidence of the news item found by PC Mauger and the unlikely appearance of the silver fox at Hospital Lane. By the end, the chief officer was looking bemused.

Not surprising, thought Moretti. *So am I.*

"Are you suggesting, Ed, there's a link between the Gastineaus and this — this horrific attack? Good God!"

"Good *grief*." Jimmy Le Poidevin stirred in his seat and stood up, turning to Chief Officer Hanley. "Before we explore Ed's flight of fancy, sir, may I go over more factual aspects of the crime? SOCO's report, for instance?"

"Of course," Hanley looked at some papers he held in his hand. "I have already looked at what you have to say, Jimmy, and it seems you didn't find much. Apart from blood, that is."

"Well, true, sir." Jimmy went on, bloodied but unbowed. "But from the evidence of where the blood trail begins, the victim was originally attacked at the end of his own property, and somehow made his way up the path of Ms. Ashton's property to her back door. I'll be curious to hear from the doctor how he managed *that* with his throat slashed. We erected lights, of course, but I have a crew back there today to check if we missed anything. The ground is littered with leaves, chestnuts, all that kind of shit, and it'll be easier in daylight. We are hoping, of course, to find whatever was used to do this."

"May I interrupt, sir?"

Al Brown looked cautiously at the head of forensics and then at the chief officer. Hanley gave an authoritative wave of the hand, and a warning glance at Jimmy Le Poidevin, who protected his own fiefdom and field of expertise against all comers with the ferocity of a junkyard dog.

"I noticed last night that Shawcross must have put up quite a struggle when the attack began. At the back of the property there is damage to undergrowth and bushes. Then, of course, as his throat was cut, he lost his strength, but possibly his initial defence took the assailant by surprise — he's a very small man — and whoever it was took off when Mr. Shawcross started to make a racket, not staying around to see if he had completed the job."

"And —?" The head of forensics interrupted. "That's stating the obvious, isn't it?"

Al Brown gave Jimmy one of his charming smiles. "So it would seem, and it's also stating the obvious that there may be evidence at the spot, apart from blood. Clothing fragments, a button. Among the leaves, chestnuts, that kind of shit. Just thought I'd say."

Jimmy Le Poidevin went red in the face. "Are you suggesting —?"

Whatever he was going to say was interrupted by the arrival of Liz Falla and Irene Edwards.

Moretti rarely noticed the effects of strain or lack of sleep on his partner's face, but this time he did. She looked at him and smiled, and he wanted to go over and say something about the events of the night that were personal rather than professional. But even as he registered his unfamiliar reaction, Falla had started to introduce Irene Edwards to the chief officer. And by the time introductions had been made, Hanley had moved the discussion on to Dr. Edwards's report, and Irene Edwards's silvery voice was filling the incident room.

Dr. Edwards would have had their undivided attention even if she had not been dressed in a well-cut suit in a pearl-grey shade that followed the contours of her figure, but it didn't hurt to look at her, Moretti thought. Clearly, Al Brown, PC Mauger, PC Le Marchant and the chief officer felt the same way. Difficult to say with Jimmy, who had closed his eyes, as if to resist the siren's song and remain his usual confrontational self.

"First of all, Hugo Shawcross is doing quite well." Dr. Edwards looked at Moretti. "He is out of surgery, heavily sedated, and will not be able to talk for a while, but he has already asked for pencil and paper. However, he has not written down whodunit, I'm afraid; rather, he's asked for someone to look after his cat. That seems to be his main concern at the moment, and Liz has already taken care of that."

"Yes." Liz Falla grinned at the assembled officers, and Moretti felt himself smiling back, relieved at his partner's return to her usual easy-going self. "I stayed overnight with my aunt and let him — Stoker — in to Mr. Shawcross's house this morning. There was a key near the back door and I fed him and locked the house. It had been unlocked all night." Liz turned to the head of forensics. "No signs of a disturbance of any kind, but might be best to take a look. I left the key with the desk sergeant. I'll be needing it again for the cat."

"Will do." After opening his eyes and looking at Hanley's face, Jimmy restrained himself from further comment, and Irene Edwards continued.

"I imagine I'm not the first to say that Mr. Shawcross was lucky, but he was. First of all, the attacker did not quite cut the carotid artery, and second of all, Ms. Ashton kept her cool. Forgive me if you already know —" quick glance at the forensics chief, "but the common carotid artery carries blood from the heart to the brain, and divides into internal and external branches. Mr. Shawcross's right external carotid artery was partially severed. If it had been completely cut, surgery would have been far more difficult, because it would have recessed into the neck by the time we got him into the operating room. Any questions so far?"

"Was that why he was able to crawl as far as he did?" Hanley asked.

"Yes. Also, he may be a small man, but he is very fit. Quite muscular, which will have helped him when he was forced to defend himself. And there, at the end of his trail, was Ms. Ashton, waiting to apply a tourniquet." Irene Edwards looked at Liz, and smiled, and then at Moretti.

"You had a question, Detective Inspector?"

"Yes. If Mr. Shawcross had the misfortune to be a cadaver at this point in time, I would be asking this question of our head of forensics." Jimmy Le Poidevin looked sceptical. "From the wound on Shawcross's neck, did you get any idea of what might have been used?"

"I know what was *not* used, and I'm fairly certain of this. A knife. It looks like a ligature of some kind, and not something soft, like a scarf. Obviously, we were working fast, but it also seemed to me that it was some sort of a double loop. There were two parallel lines. And there's something else."

Irene Edwards looked again at Liz Falla, but this time she was not smiling.

"I've already mentioned this to DS Falla. Mr. Shawcross's neck is a mess, but it seemed to me there was evidence of — bite marks."

"*Bite marks?*" Hanley, PCs Le Marchant and Mauger, and Jimmy Le Poidevin spoke in unison.

Moretti looked at Liz Falla and Al Brown, then at Chief Officer Hanley.

"Well, well, well," he said.

"Why did you mention so specifically the damage to the undergrowth and bushes?" Moretti asked Al Brown. "Seems to me you had a reason."

Moretti, Liz Falla, Al Brown and Irene Edwards were in a booth at Emidio's eating pizza and salad. Not much of substance had been added after the doctor's dramatic statement, and Moretti had gone over his plan of attack with his MI Team. It seemed to soothe the chief officer when he used the term, and gave the impression he was using Al Brown's expertise, thus taking both himself and Al off the hook.

"I did." Al refilled his coffee cup from the vacuum flask Deb had put on the table, and did the same for Irene Edwards who was sitting opposite him. "But it may be too late. Jimmy had put up tapes, et cetera, last night, but I watched a fair number of boots stomping around the area. Is he always so confrontational?"

"Always," said Liz.

Moretti watched her pick at her salad, leaving the pizza untouched. *Not like her. Must still be in shock,* he thought. He turned to Irene Edwards.

"Bite marks?" It was said as a question. "I didn't want to appear to be doubting your judgment in the incident room, but ..."

"You wonder if I am off my rocker? It's okay, so did I, but I've seen bite marks before, and these are bite marks. No doubt about it. Whoever tried to kill Shawcross took the time to bite the back of his neck as he was holding the — whatever it was."

"Which suggests the ligature was held and force used, but no stick, for instance, to twist it at the back. Do you think a woman would be strong enough to do this? I'm assuming not."

"If she was built like me, possibly. I am about a head taller than Shawcross, and that would give me an advantage, pulling whatever it was around his neck. May I make a suggestion?" It was directed as a query at Moretti, but it was made assertively, the higher register of the doctor's voice intriguingly at odds with her physical presence.

"Please do."

"Perhaps Hugo Shawcross was not an unwilling victim. Perhaps this was a game that got out of control. After what Liz told me about the play, I wondered."

"Possibly," said Moretti. "Pity he can only write his answers, because it will be easier for him to conceal clues from facial expression, body language. I've got PC Le Marchant on guard duty at the hospital, and no one else is allowed near him. I'm going to leave seeing him another day, because I'm hoping time for reflection will make him see sense and confess. If there's anything to confess, that is."

"Can't bite marks be identified?" Liz asked. "Mind you, we'd have to narrow the field a bit before trying to do that."

"They can, but there are a high number of false positives," said Al. "And something else I remember from one of my courses. About game-playing and fantasy. The modus operandi may differ, but the fantasy is always the same. Whoever did this will not be able to resist trying again."

He took a slice of pizza off the serving-plate and put it on Liz's plate. "Eat up," he said, "It's going to be a long day, DS Falla, and when it's all over you'll still have to feed the — *what* did you say he's called?"

"Stoker. Bram Stoker."

No one laughed.

Chapter Twelve

"Gandalf?"

Beside him in the Triumph, Liz chuckled. It was good to hear.

"When Elodie first told me about Shawcross, I was worried. Not for any real reason, but because he sounded creepy, and she lives on her own. She said he looked like Gandalf and she could take him on if she had to."

"After what Dr. Edwards said, that seems less likely. But the creepy part holds up."

"Doesn't it, though. Is that why you've got Bernie Mauger looking for satanic rituals, and all that stuff?"

"That's why. And it's why I've got Al Brown out at the hermit's place again."

Moretti thought of telling Falla about his last conversation with Al.

"How do you feel about hanging around overnight? Take the Honda in with you, out of sight. Someone

came back the night after Dorey died. It could have been the murderer, or it could have been his laundryperson. Interesting, either way."

He decided to leave it for the time being.

"That's a nice place your aunt has," he continued. "Is she in the offshore business?"

"Not in the way you mean, Guv, but in a way she is. She's a medical researcher, editor and illustrator, and she handles it all through the Internet. But that fab cottage comes courtesy of a divorce settlement, she told me. More than that I don't know. Why?"

"Just curious." Moretti changed the subject. "Do you think you can handle Marie Maxwell?"

Moretti felt, rather than saw, the look Falla gave him.

"If you don't think I can, Guv, why aren't you doing the interview?"

"Because I want her to feel reasonably superior and reasonably comfortable with someone she thinks she can push around."

Beside him, Liz snorted.

"Chances are that Marla is in school right now, and I leave you to use your judgment about whether to tell her about her daughter's Beau Sejour revelation. She might open up to another woman, particularly if she's worried about her daughter. But don't let her know you've heard about the play-reading incident, or that your aunt talked to you. See if she volunteers the information first."

"Will do. Anything you want me to concentrate on?"

"Any possible link between Gus Dorey's death, Hamelin's social call and the Gastineau family. But tread carefully. We don't want to be warned off by Hanley."

Moretti turned into the paved courtyard outside the erstwhile Gastineau town mansion, and brought the Triumph to a halt in front of a splendid front entrance between two pillars.

"Don't worry, Guv. I'll play it just as I did with her silver-haired messenger-boy."

"God help her, Falla."

She laughed as she walked away from him, the spring back in her step.

Moretti waited until he saw the front door open, and Falla go in, then turned the Triumph around in the courtyard and headed back up the Grange in the direction of St. Martin. No need to tell her he was going to interview her godmother, and put Falla on the horns of a professional and personal dilemma.

In the few hours between returning home late at night, and the meeting with Chief Officer Hanley that morning, Moretti had done little sleeping and much thinking, and most of his thought processes involved Liz Falla's aunt. Her presence of mind and her relationship with Falla had impeded impartiality of thought, and it had taken a while before objectivity replaced sympathy.

Had she met the blood-stained Shawcross at her door, as she said? Or had they been together at his house after the play-reading? Her godmother had openly admitted to Falla that she had encouraged both him and Marie Maxwell, and it was clear from what Falla had said of the evening spent with her and the self-professed vampire that he fancied Elodie Ashton. Which was not such a surprise, but perhaps they had more in common than an academic interest in theatre. After all, Elodie Ashton had found him too pushy, according to Falla, when he first moved in, and then had asked him to dinner. And the dinner invitation had come after Falla had told her about Marie Maxwell's complaint to the chief officer.

The coral-pink roof of Elodie Ashton's cottage glowed in the autumn sunshine as Moretti pulled up in the driveway. It was isolated enough in the peaceful bucolic setting of St. Martin not to have attracted a curious crowd of onlookers when emergency services had arrived the night before, and in this neck of the woods the well-heeled householders who were Elodie Ashton's neighbours would have wanted nothing to do with domestic disturbances in the small hours.

SOCO were back at the cottage, and Moretti had specifically asked them to look out for any other footprints besides Hugo Shawcross's on the bloodied path, and not just at the site of the initial struggle. It should have been an unnecessary request, but Al Brown's observations were worrying.

From the front of the property, the only sign of anything unusual was the incident van, parked ahead of Moretti's Triumph; its occupants were presumably all at work in the back garden, from where Moretti could hear the sound of voices. He decided to walk around and make it appear as if that were the purpose of his visit. As he started to follow the path around the side of the cottage, the front door opened.

"Detective Inspector."

Elodie Ashton came out to meet him.

She had tied her spectacular hair back into a ponytail, and was wearing glasses, which did something to lessen the impact of both hair and eyes. Her dress was decidedly casual — she was enveloped in a baggy sweater and track pants that had seen better days. The oversize clothes made her seem even smaller, more vulnerable, and Moretti reminded himself that it was not always good things that came in small packages.

"Ms. Ashton, good morning. I was just on my way round to talk to the forensics people. I hope they have not been too much of an inconvenience. DS Falla tells me you work from home."

"Not much of that this morning, Detective Inspector." She gave a ragged laugh. "Might just as well not have bothered to put on my specs. Would I be right in thinking you need to talk to me as well as the forensics crew?"

"You would."

No point in beating around the bush with this lady, so Moretti followed her into the cottage.

The afternoon sun filled the interior with light, unimpeded by walls. As they passed the kitchen area, Moretti saw exposed brickwork, a magnificent fireplace, copper pans catching the light. A bowl of bronze and yellow chrysanthemums stood on the kitchen table, and on the back of the large kitchen range something savoury was simmering in a sizeable stockpot.

"That smells good."

"Making stock is a more productive way to spend the morning than pretending to work. I find cooking as soothing as —" She hesitated.

"Chopin?"

She didn't laugh, but answered seriously. "That's a difficult one to answer. Depends on the stress, perhaps. I was about to have a coffee, which is also good for stress. Would you like one, Detective Inspector?"

"Please."

Elodie Ashton indicated the sofa on which she had sat the night before with Falla, and returned to the kitchen. The living area and the kitchen extended down the right side of the cottage, and what must have been smaller windows at the back had been replaced by a large picture window looking onto the garden. The staircase had been left where it originally was, but was now open, its polished boards curving into space to the upper floor. Presumably at one time the kitchen had been at the back of the cottage, because what would have been the original kitchen door remained, alongside the long, curved window, through which Moretti could see Jimmy Le Poidevin and his merry men, working away.

"Here we are."

Elodie Ashton handed Moretti a boldly decorated pottery mug of coffee, and sat down opposite him, removing her glasses. Her eyes were blue, not green, as he had thought.

Once enquiries about cream and sugar were over, Moretti said, indicating the garden, "You'll be glad when that's finished."

"Actually, I don't mind having them there for a while. They are rather a cheerful bunch, whistling away. Company beyond a pane of glass, but minimal contact. Quite nice."

Moretti had no problem agreeing with that.

"Good coffee," he said. "DS Falla tells me you work from home, in the field of medical research."

"Yes. But I'm not one of those geniuses who make great discoveries in labs. My job is to put those discoveries and theses and reports into plain English. Well, as plain as possible in what is often really obscure and esoteric subject matter."

"So you must have a good grasp of a wide range of medical disciplines to do that."

"I have." Elodie Ashton did not elaborate, but pointed to a door to their left. "When the renovations were done, I had the original interior wall on that side left in place, and set up my office in there. It looks on to a little copse of trees, which is pleasant, but private."

"I understand you started your career on the mainland. Had you ever run into Hugo Shawcross before? I know you told my partner you introduced yourself after hearing about the complaint over the play, but I thought I'd just get that question out of the way."

The blue eyes were now flashing fire, which Moretti had not previously thought possible for blue eyes, even if you had red hair.

"Are you suggesting I might have lied to Liz? She was the one who brought up the subject of vampirism, I did this to help her, and walked into an attempted murder. Now I wonder if I will ever be able to look out on to my garden again without seeing him. Let alone thinking about who might be waiting out there for me, in the dark. I think you're suggesting, Detective Inspector, I tried to kill poor little Gandalf."

Moretti kept his voice level. "So the first time you heard about the play and Mrs. Maxwell's complaint was when your goddaughter told you."

"Yes." The blue eyes were now looking sceptically at him. "You are wondering, aren't you, if this was some kind of sick game that went wrong. Right?"

"Right."

A waste of time prevaricating with this woman. She was as sharp as — well, her godchild.

"Look." Elodie Ashton put her coffee mug down on the table between them. "You don't know me, but if you did, you'd know that introducing myself to Hugo Shawcross and inviting him into my home was out of character. It was a spur of the moment thing, done for Liz. I like my own company and the company of others in groups — like the Island Players, for instance. I'm good at parties and bad at tête-à-têtes. For me, there is safety in numbers. I like — distance."

"Company beyond a pane of glass." In many ways, she was describing him, thought Moretti. Not that he was good at parties either. "Believe it or not, I understand."

"I believe you."

She seemed about to add something, but stopped, which made Moretti wonder what Falla might have said about him to her godmother.

"So you went out of character for your goddaughter. Was it as entirely altruistic as that? Or did your invitation have just a little to do with the challenge of taking on a Gastineau?"

"Just a little." Elodie Ashton smiled, relaxing back into her chair, and Moretti found himself smiling back. "Quite a lot, actually. I enjoy being part of the Island Players, and Marie Maxwell is gradually taking over. It is turning from a comradeship, if there is such a word, into a dictatorship. I couldn't resist it, and look what happened."

Elodie picked up her coffee mug from the table, and looked into it, as though she were reading the coffee grinds. The smile had gone, and Moretti could no longer see the expression in her eyes. "I am, Detective Inspector, the last person to involve myself with anything to do with blood play or the undead."

"Care to explain?"

"No. It's — personal. Nothing to do with all this. I was going to help with the play, but I'd opted out of performing. Still, I imagine the whole project is now kaput." She looked up at him, her feelings under control again. "How *is* Hugo Shawcross? I should have asked before, but I don't want to think about last night anymore than I can help."

"He's doing remarkably well, thanks to you, not talking yet, but has already requested paper to write down what he wants." *Leave it at that,* he thought. *No need to tell her it's just about the cat.*

"Good to hear." She turned away and looked out of the window. "I wonder if they've found anything."

Moretti stood up. Looking out of the window clearly signalled the end of Elodie Ashton's co-operation, but there was little more to gain by continuing now, and best to leave her to mull over what he had suggested. *Not much mulling to do, though,* he thought. Still, he didn't see her as a game-player. Not this type of game, but there was definitely something she was holding back.

"Thank you for the coffee. I'll go and talk to them." He indicated the door that led into the back garden. "Is it all right to go that way?"

"Of course. Mr. Le Poidevin told me I could use it now. Sorry I yelled at you."

She didn't sound very sorry.

"It comes with the job. I've heard worse."

She walked over to the door and unlocked it. "Liz enjoys working with you — her Guvnor, she calls you. One thing —" Elodie Ashton turned back to Moretti, looking up into his face. Seen from above, she had quite an arrogant curve to her nose. "I gather you haven't heard her sing? She's good, you know."

"So I've been told." *Time for a swift exit,* he thought.

"In her own way, as good as you."

Taken by surprise, and before Moretti had time to respond, Elodie stood back in the doorway, and indicated the path along which she had seen Hugo Shawcross struggling towards her, drenched in his own blood.

"I'll leave you to it," she said, "I'm locking myself in again."

Moretti found himself standing alongside an elderberry tree, planted close to the former kitchen door. If he remembered rightly, it was supposed to keep the witches away.

Only time would tell if the redhead in the house was a heroine, or a harpy, or a bit of both. So many women were.

Chapter Thirteen

"Ah yes."

Marie Maxwell's unfocused greeting seemed out of character, and almost as if she was expecting to see Liz Falla on her doorstep. She was wearing light slippers over bare feet, and what looked like diamond studs in her ears flashed expensively in the light from the open door.

"Come in. I know who you are. Terrible, terrible."

Above the bare feet and slippers were slim-fitting black slacks and a heavy white sweater that looked hand-knitted, but expertly hand-knitted, and Liz immediately coveted it.

"Detective Sergeant Falla, Mrs. Maxwell. You have heard about the attack on Mr. Shawcross?"

"Certainly I have. My cousin's daughter is on the nursing staff at Princess Elizabeth Hospital, and she phoned me this morning. I imagine that's why you're here. Terrible, terrible."

"Yes, but he is making a good recovery. Thanks to Ms. Ashton's prompt action."

They were still standing in the hallway. Marie Maxwell suddenly came to her senses as if awakened from a trance, clicking into hostess mode with offers of coffee, tea, water, and choices of rooms for the interview.

"Wherever is best for you, Mrs. Maxwell. This shouldn't take long."

Liz Falla followed her into a small room that looked like a private sitting room, feminine in décor and design. Over a fireplace blooming with baskets of silk flowers hung a large painting of a dainty lady on a swing. Liz recognized it as the reproduction of a well-known painting by Fragonard. She had once been given a box of chocolates with the same image on the lid by a suitor as hopeful as the two gallants in the painting. She wondered if they had been equally as unlucky.

Liz took the seat indicated by Marie Maxwell, a pretty little tub chair upholstered in ivory velvet, and her hostess sat down opposite her in a matching chair. As she took out her notebook and opened it, Marie Maxwell said, "You're the officer who knows about what has been happening to my daughter, aren't you? The text messages and so on?"

Good. The decision to let Marie Maxwell know had been taken out of her hands.

"She told you about our conversation at the gym?"

"Yes. I have a mobile, of course, but I really don't understand how to do anything with it except make or receive a call, so all this is beyond me. And now I have to worry it all has something to do with this *terrible* attack."

"Let's start with when Mr. Shawcross first became a member of the group, and when the harassment of your daughter began. Has she told you when that was?"

Marie Maxwell jumped up eagerly from her chair and crossed over to a charming little escritoire by the fireplace. She opened it and took out a small notebook.

"I thought of that myself. Marla tells me the trouble began weeks before Hugo Shawcross first joined the Island Players, almost certainly before he was even on the island."

"Did Marla tell you anything specific about the text messages? What they said. Or threatened?"

Marie Maxwell shrugged her shoulders. "The usual things these teenagers do, or say. You know. About her being pretty and a Gastineau mainly. That kind of thing."

Marie had suddenly become vague, and it was difficult to tell if the vagueness was genuine, or assumed. And if assumed, Liz asked herself, why?

"Did Marla open up to you because she heard about the attack on Hugo Shawcross?"

"Yes. She was in the room when my cousin phoned. But I already knew there was something going on because of her hysterics when the lights went out at the reading."

"The lights went out at the reading?" Liz repeated.

"Yes. The power had been switched off all over the house — well, our part of it."

Liz waited for Marie Maxwell to continue, ready to prompt her if necessary. But prompting was the last thing Marie needed. The information poured from her, and it differed very little from what Elodie had said. Apart from her final statement.

"I couldn't get Marla to give me any real explanation, and I am sure this all has something to do with that very strange young man she met at a party."

"Met at a party?"

So far, hushed regurgitation of Marie Maxwell's final utterance seemed to be all that was necessary.

"Yes, at the lieutenant-governor's son's birthday party. I mean, I couldn't really refuse to let her attend — you understand, I'm sure."

Of course Liz understood. This was an invitation to be treasured, trumpeted from the rooftops.

"What made you concerned about this young man?"

Marie Maxwell leaned towards Liz Falla, and put out a hand, almost as though she were about to touch her, then withdrew, pulling herself together.

"The fact that I knew nothing about him until he was in my house. Marla knows we have a shortage of young men, and that it was very unlikely Raymond would turn him away."

"Raymond?"

"The director. I can usually persuade him to go along with my ideas, but in this case Hugo was in Raymond's corner."

"The name of this — strange young man, you called him."

"Charles Priestley. I understand he was educated in Britain and is now staying here with his uncle before attending university. He is certainly charismatic, but in a way I find … iffy."

"Iffy?" echoed Liz. "In what way?"

Marie Maxwell waved her hands in the air, at a loss for words for the first time since the interview began. Liz dived into the momentary silence.

"We'll check him," she said. Then, swiftly changing direction before Marie Maxwell had a chance to dilate further upon her maternal concerns, she asked, "Is advocate Hamelin the Gastineau-Maxwell family lawyer, Mrs. Maxwell?"

The change in Marie Maxwell's body language was immediate, her expression and her body frozen into stillness, her jaw slightly dropped.

Liz Falla waited. Over the past two cases she had been on with her Guvnor, she had learned that silence at such moments is often golden.

"He is. Why do you ask?" Marie Maxwell's voice wavered as she finally spoke, and Liz decided to dive even deeper, and not worry about the chief officer.

"Because he came to talk to me about two days ago, about the suicide of the hermit on Pleinmont Common, Gus Dorey. From what he felt free to tell me, there are concerns about certain past issues resurfacing. I understand there was at one time bad blood between your two families?"

Not that advocate Hamelin had been the one to say that, but no harm in giving that impression.

"Bad blood?"

Now it was Marie who was the echo in the room.

"What on earth has that pathetic old man's death got to do with *this*?"

"I was wondering if you could help us with that, Mrs. Maxwell. Clearly, advocate Hamelin did not feel free in his professional capacity to say more than he did, but the disturbing messages and the harassment of your daughter just might have a connection with the suicide. Of course, we would not have come to that conclusion without advocate Hamelin's visit."

It would be worth being raked over the coals by Hanley to land the silver fox in deep doo-doo.

Marie Maxwell drew herself up in her chair and leaned forward, speaking in a voice vibrating with emotion.

"There's something I must tell you, Detective Sergeant."

"Yes?" Liz waited expectantly, pen in hand.

"I *refuse* to be intimidated by whoever has done this *terrible* thing. The attempted murder of Hugo Shawcross alters *nothing*. We have the play, we have the players. The show must go on!"

Before Liz Falla had the chance to make any kind of response to Marie Maxwell's swerve in direction, there came a roar from the half-open doorway.

"Over my dead body!"

Elton Maxwell was standing there.

At least, that was who Liz presumed it was, not having ever met Marie Maxwell's husband. Although Marla looked facially very much like her mother, she had also inherited much of her father. He was tall, fair-haired, with a slender build, and fine features, which were temporarily distorted in rage. He strode across the room and, ignoring his wife, addressed Liz.

"Who, pray, are you? Another of my wife's so-called artistic friends?"

These kinds of moments held their own satisfaction. Liz pulled out her police identity card and held it up close to the engorged face of Elton Maxwell.

"And you are ... sir?" she asked, soft as a cooing dove in a Fragonard painting.

"Good God, the police! I'm Elton Maxwell, of course."

Elton Maxwell spluttered to a halt and sat down abruptly in a frail-looking chair that matched the little escritoire by the fireplace. It creaked as he did so, and Liz saw that the slender build was deceptive. Elton Maxwell had an incipient paunch.

"That's right, sir. Detective Sergeant Falla. I am investigating the attack on Hugo Shawcross, and the threats to your daughter."

"The threats to my daughter?"

With Elton Maxwell now sounding like Little Sir Echo — a song her grandfather in his cups used to sing unasked and unendingly at family gatherings — Liz Falla asserted herself, and forgot about Moretti's caveat.

"Phone and text threats that may have some connection with the attempted murder of Hugo Shawcross and the suicide of Gus Dorey, and the visit by advocate Hamelin to Hospital Lane after the announcement of the hermit's death in the *Guernsey Press*."

She expected a verbal onslaught from Elton Maxwell, and a verbal onslaught there was, but it was directed at his wife, not at her. Swerving around in the tiny chair, he shouted at Marie Maxwell, "I told you that was a blockheaded idea, but what else could I expect from that dunderhead of a brother of yours! Both of you boneheads, and Ginnie the only one with a sensible head on her shoulders!"

In anger, Elton Maxwell's northern accent became more noticeable, his attempt at being posh slipping disastrously.

Certainly not a Channel-Islander, thought Liz. *The Gastineaus may be dunderheads, boneheads and blockheads, but hot-headed Mr. Maxwell has just given me information I might never have extracted from his wife.*

Marie Maxwell's cool calm and collected response suggested she was used to her husband's outbursts. But she was too smart not to realize the damage her husband had done.

"Get off that chair, Elton, before it collapses under you. You've enough trouble with your back since you put on that weight, and you fussed enough about what I paid for it without turning it into a heap of matchwood. Which was how you described it, as I recall."

Elton Maxwell did what he was told. Without comment he transferred himself to an upholstered stool that looked uncomfortable, but serviceable. In spite of the explosion, Liz Falla felt that the balance of power lay with Marie, and not Elton, so she continued to question the weaker vessel.

"So you are saying, sir, that your brother-in-law suggested advocate Hamelin's visit?"

"I am suggesting nothing, and this interview is terminated." Elton Maxwell stood up. "With an attempted murder and my daughter under threat, we need to have a lawyer present in future." His anger returned, but again it was not directed at Liz Falla. "And I don't mean that antediluvian ponce your family keeps trotting out!"

"Very well, dear."

Marie smiled serenely. She got up like a queen from her ivory velvet throne and addressed Liz, her poise more intact than it had been at the start of the interview. "Let me see you to the door. As you can see, my husband must have his way, I'm afraid."

Have his way my eye, thought Liz. *I would bet next months' salary the show will go on.*

Over his dead body, if necessary.

Outside, in the small courtyard where Gastineau ancestors would have mounted their horses and pulled up in their carriages to unload their ill-gotten contraband, Liz took out her mobile to text Bernie Mauger at the Priaulx, but decided to check her messages first. There was nothing of importance, but one that was cheering, from Dwight Ellis. They still kept in touch, and from time to time he came to hear her sing. She had yet to hear him perform with the Fénions, only with a pick-up band at the restaurant where he worked part-time.

Everything Dwight did was part-time, including bouts of cooking and spells of house-painting.

"Hey, Liz. I've got a new bike, a Piaggio Xevo. Sexy name, huh? Want a ride some time?"

The message had been sent only about thirty minutes earlier. Liz texted him right back.

"Right now. Bring extra helmet, pick me up Gastineau place, the Grange."

She texted Bernie Mauger, and then Moretti.

"Interview over. Getting something to eat. Where and when do we meet?"

The reply was immediate.

"Hospital Lane about an hour. Bernie Mauger's come up with something."

They had loved and laughed their way through about one year together, before either of them were interested in commitment. That's what they told each other. But what had finished them was Liz's parents' discomfort with her Trinidadian boyfriend. At the time, neither had said that, but instead had harped on incessantly about his only steady job being as a drummer. Which hadn't helped his cause. So she and Dwight had parted company and drifted into other, part-time relationships quite as transient as Dwight's career path. Or lack of it.

It felt good to have her arms around Dwight again, to peer around his shoulders at that beautiful profile of his. Dwight had cheekbones to die for. She had asked him once, "Where did you get your pretty face?

Your mum or your dad?" And he had replied, "From all those Moors and white sons of bitches who helped themselves to my beautiful black female ancestors." Then he had laughed and moved on to something else.

"Where we going?" His voice lilted back to her on the breeze.

"My place. Glategny Esplanade. Remember?"

"How long we got?"

"An hour. A lifetime?"

"Man, that's scary, woman." He had the warmest of laughs, rich and resonant.

"A lifetime's no time at all."

Chapter Fourteen

Bernie Mauger was beaming. In front of him on the desk in Moretti's office lay two or three sheets of paper. From the look on her Guvnor's face, their value was bigger than their bulk.

"Sorry I'm a bit late, Guv. I still mistime getting here by car."

Liar.

"Never mind, Falla." Her Guvnor, fortunately, seemed in as sunny a mood as Bernie Mauger. "Bernie's come up with a couple of possible leads, one about where Gus Dorey went to university, and the other is about the daughter of General Gastineau. Lucy Gastineau."

"Daughter? I thought there was just a son, Roland, the one who got into the argy-bargy with Gus Dorey. He'd be Marie's father, wouldn't he, and I thought he was dead."

"He is, more's the pity, and so is his wife. Bernie and Lydia Machon, the head librarian, found the death notice for the sister."

Moretti held out one of the pieces of paper across the desk to Liz. It came from the *Times,* and was dated June 12, 1971.

> *In London, after a brief illness, in her fif-tieth year, the death is announced of Lucy Gastineau, daughter of Roland Gastineau (deceased). Cremation has already taken place. If wished, donations may be made to the char-ity of your choice.*

Liz looked at the scrap of paper in her hands, with its swift dispatching of Lucy Gastineau's life.

"Cold."

"And not entirely accurate. Bernie found the birth announcement."

Moretti handed Liz another sheet from the small pile. It came from the *Guernsey Press,* and it too, was brief.

> *The Gastineau family are pleased to announce the birth of a daughter, Lucy Marie. A sister for Roland.*

"Look at the date, Falla."

"November, 'thirty-one. That would make her ..."

"In her fortieth year when she died. Could be an error by the newspaper — fortieth, fiftieth — but it could also be that someone was muddying the waters, trying to put who knows who off the scent."

"But there's no link with Gus Dorey, is there?"

"Not directly. But they are the same age, and they could possibly have met at university." Moretti picked up another of the sheets of paper from the desk. "According to this *Guernsey Press* announcement, Gus Dorey was awarded a scholarship to Bristol University, to study history in 1949. Bernie is going to check the archive for the Ladies' School for Girls, since we are reasonably safe in assuming that's where she went. Only problem is, the school was evacuated during the war, and those records are not complete, so Lydia Machon says."

"We could ask Rory or Marie Gastineau about their aunt, couldn't we? Or the other sister, Ginnie. From what I heard this morning, it was Rory who sent Reggie out on the warpath." Liz hesitated before adding, "I pushed things a bit, Guv."

At this, Moretti looked at Bernie Mauger who, reluctantly, got up from his chair.

"I'll get right on to the Ladies' School archive," he said.

Liz waited until the door was closed, then took out her notes.

"Pushed things a bit, Falla? Did the pushing get results?"

"Yes."

Liz went through her notes, adding the soundtrack

of Elton Maxwell in full cry about the silver fox and the stupidity of the Gastineau clan.

"And I'm sorry if I bring Hamelin down on our necks, but it was worth it," she concluded.

"You know what, Falla? I don't think that's likely to happen. I suspect they'll call their attack-dog off. Or, should I say, their antediluvian ponce."

They both laughed.

"I'll just check my messages, Guv." Liz pulled her mobile out of her pocket. "Where's Al? Still out at Pleinmont?"

"Yes, and he'll be there a while. Overnight, in fact. Remember, PC Bichard thought he heard something the night after Dorey's death."

"Wow." Liz looked up. "You think whoever tied that rope for the hermit will return to the scene of the crime?"

Moretti shook his head, and gathered up the papers on the desk, putting them in a drawer, which he then locked.

"That would be far too easy. No, Falla, not the — do we call him, or her, a murderer? We don't know yet if Dorey asked for his death. I'm hoping Al will get a visit from someone else."

There was no response from Liz Falla.

"The launderer, Falla, the launderer," Moretti added.

But his partner was looking at the screen of her mobile, and Moretti didn't need see her expression to guess who had texted her. When she looked up, it wasn't anger he saw on her face. It was more like stunned disbelief.

"You think Elodie was playing sick party-games with Gandalf?"

"There was that possibility." Moretti stood up, breaking, he hoped, the mood of the moment. How he hated the personal intersecting with the professional, and it had been unrealistic of him to think he could avoid it in this instance.

"And have you ruled it out?"

Falla's voice was dispassionate, cool.

"Not her style, I think."

"Good. What next?"

Falla was moving on, and he could only hope the detachment he heard in her voice was just that, a reflection of her professionalism. Moretti felt a wave of relief. He would be saddened if she was hiding hostility to him, and he noted his own reaction with some surprise.

"The hospital. Time we tried to talk to Hugo Shawcross. About vampires, and *Blood Play*, and why he's here on the island in the first place."

"*I have unleashed powers of evil.*"

Hugo Shawcross was not allowing the partial severing of his carotid artery and heavy doses of morphine to tamp down his orotund style. The unleashing of powers of evil had come as the answer to Moretti's question as to why he thought this might have happened.

"Can you be a bit more specific, sir? You are suggesting you have some responsibility for this attack. What might you have done to cause it?"

The response was swiftly scribbled, and equally unhelpful.

"*Evil exists.*"

Moretti restrained himself. "In my job, I have no problem agreeing with you, but an attack out of the blue of this nature is unusual, to say the least. Let's go back over the evening. You came home after the read-through at the Maxwells, went into the house, then went out to call your cat in for the night. Am I right so far?"

Notebook in hand, Liz Falla intervened. "To save yourself too much effort, sir, why don't you tap once for 'yes,' and twice for 'no,' if that's all the answer required."

One tap.

"When you were outside, did you notice anything different?"

Two taps.

"Did you hear any unusual sound or noise?"

Two taps.

"You had to walk to the fence between the two houses, because there was no response from your cat?"

One tap.

"From what SOCO tells us, you went across into your neighbour's garden, beyond the fence."

Two taps, agitatedly.

"So the attack occurred on your property, and you were pulled, or forced into Ms. Ashton's garden?"

One tap.

"Did you at any time get a chance to look at your attacker?"

Two taps.

Falla's practical suggestion was proving almost as unproductive as the earlier pronouncements about the existence of evil. Moretti decided to change direction.

"Why are you here on the island, sir? What led to that decision?"

Hugo Shawcross's hand holding the pencil suddenly moved as frenziedly as the indicator on a lie detector charting extreme emotion, causing various responses along a web of tubes to the screen above the bed, triggering the instant appearance of a nurse at the door.

"That was some reaction. Do you want me to check whether he has a record? He seemed less than thrilled when he found out I was a cop, and I don't think it was just that three was a crowd."

"That'll keep for tomorrow. Hugo isn't going anywhere for a while."

They were in the police Skoda, which was now the car of choice of the island force instead of the BMW. Whenever he could, Moretti avoided using it, or the police Vauxhalls, but, as they left the Hospital Lane police station for the hospital, he had decided against the Triumph.

"So — where are we going, and why the Skoda?"

Moretti looked at Liz. She was putting the key in the ignition, and from what he could see of her profile, it was difficult to tell if she was angry, but everything in her manner suggested she was.

"For the next interview, I want to look as official as possible, not give the impression of friendly local sleuth, deferentially impressed by island aristocracy. Though I don't think a Skoda is going to excite them into subservience." It was heavy-handed, but normally it would get at least a glance and a grin. "You're annoyed with me, aren't you?"

"Pretty pissed off, yes. Since you ask, but it's not my place to …"

She shrugged her shoulders and started the engine. "Where to?"

"The Gastineau family pile in Forest."

At least this got a glance from her.

"I'll need to use the GPS. I don't drop my calling card off at too many mansions. Will they be there?"

"They'd better be. I arranged it before our hospital visit." Moretti paused. "Can we talk about it?"

Not his style, talking about it. Not his style professionally or personally, and this was the worst of all possible worlds, because it was both. His partner was programming the GPS and did not respond.

"You first, Falla. This is too damned uncomfortable, with your aunt sitting between us in a bloody Skoda."

"I may say something I regret, that's all."

"Carte blanche. Feel free to piss me off."

The police car turned out of the courtyard to head south out of St. Peter Port along the Esplanade. Falla said nothing until they started negotiating the hairpin bends of Val des Terres, her voice swerving like the Skoda.

"Elodie got dragged into this by me. She did this for me. She did this to get Hanley off my back while you were messing about in your boat. Now she herself could be a target. That's why I'm pissed off."

They were now heading west towards the Forest Road, the inhuman female voice of the GPS punctuating the silence in the car.

"Fair enough. Is it possible you could move in with your aunt for a while?"

He had no intention of discussing his reasons for interviewing Elodie Ashton, because Falla, pissed with him though she might be, knew why he had done so. Not that it was making her feel any better.

"I've offered, and she refused. But I'll be going over regularly to feed that wretched cat. I don't want my aunt anywhere near Shawcross's place."

"I thought you liked cats."

"Not funny, Guv."

"Arriving at destination," announced the disembodied voice.

At least she was calling him Guv again.

Chapter Fifteen

The island of Guernsey is divided into ten parishes, whose roots go back hundreds of years to the even more ancient feudal fiefdoms. Only one of them, St. Andrew, has no coastline. The parish of Forest, on the south coast, has one of the most spectacular of all. The cliffs are so high that there are few bays and coves easily accessible by land, and Moretti remembered sailing with his uncle to La Bette and Le Jaonnet bays, diving from the side of the boat and swimming in their deserted waters. He would do that again, he promised himself, soon.

He remembered now seeing the house, high on the cliffs, a dark, forbidding outline against the sky, and wondering how the sea and the rocks might look from up there, but at that time had no curiosity about who might be living in it. Seen now from the front, it had a very different appearance, displaying the charm of the old Guernsey farmhouse combined with Georgian elegance, as a later generation of Gastineaus had added to their home. It was cleverly done, an architectural marriage that worked. Around the house was a stretch of lawn extending behind the house to the cliff edge, and as they drove closer to the house they passed huge beds of multi-coloured roses.

"There's the lady of the manor."

Liz Falla pointed out of the car window at a distant figure on horseback, riding towards them through a small copse of trees. Another figure followed close behind.

"Do you know anything about her?" Moretti asked.

From this distance, it looked as if Tanya Gastineau's riding skills went further back than her recent marriage and newly elevated income.

"What's the local gossip, you mean?" Liz took the Skoda around the circular driveway and brought it to a halt by a massive set of steps leading to an equally massive door. "Not much, apart from the fact she came looking for a rich husband, and most likely got more than she bargained for. The lord of the manor drinks, apparently. Not that he's been thrown out of many local watering-holes, because he's more of a crier, than a fighter. Someone usually comes and takes him away."

"Interesting. And here comes the lord of the manor, down the steps to meet us in person."

Rory Gastineau was shambling down the steps, looking beyond the car at his wife, who had dismounted from a very pretty bay, and was in the process of handing her over to the young man with her. The sound of their laughter reached Moretti and Falla through the closed car window.

"Hmmm," said Falla. Moretti glanced at her before opening the car door, but she said no more, and Rory Gastineau was already by his side.

"I fetched her back," he said. He was holding a mobile in his hand, so presumably he was referring to his wife.

"Thank you, sir." Moretti waited until Tanya Gastineau had joined her husband, before introducing himself and Liz Falla.

In her impeccably cut jodhpurs and tweed jacket, Tanya Gastineau looked like something out of a novel by Georgette Heyer or, possibly, Scott Fitzgerald. Certainly, she looked the part, whatever her origins. She pulled off her riding helmet, and a mass of blonde curls tumbled into the sunlight. The colour in her cheeks was as rosy as the flowers in the beds behind her.

"Hiya," she said. "I'll come quietly." She threw back her head and laughed at her own joke, and the young man did the same.

Rory Gastineau looked dourly in his direction and said, "That's enough for the day. Put those animals away, and do whatever it is I pay you to do."

The young man flinched, turned on his heel and led both horses away. Tanya Gastineau went over to her husband and took his arm.

"I'm here, my sweet, safe and sound. Isn't that part of what you pay Roddy for?"

Then she kissed him, and Moretti watched Rory Gastineau transformed into a doting, besotted, helpless slave to the beauty and life force of his young wife. It was all on his face, because his words were plain and unadorned.

"Of course."

Hast thou not dropped from heaven? drifted into Moretti's mind as they walked up the granite steps into the house.

Where did that come from, Moretti wondered. Caliban, of course. *I'll kiss thy foot, prithee be my god ... I'll swear myself thy subject.*

It was a role that had intrigued Moretti at school, and in his police work he had encountered many Calibans. Ugly, needy, pathetic, but rarely tragic, figures. They aroused conflicting emotions, including sympathy, and in his experience it was wisest not to trust them. They were often masters at manipulating the good instincts of others to their own ends. A bit harsh, comparing Rory Gastineau to Shakespeare's island monster, but he would do well to remember that overwhelming passion led people to do desperate things.

Not that he could connect any dots between what had happened to Hugo Shawcross, and Rory Gastineau. The connection, if there was one, was through the death of the Pleinmont hermit.

Inside the house, Rory Gastineau trundled ahead of them, with Tanya by his side, caressing his arm, stroking her monster. Moretti noticed he didn't touch her himself, and he found himself wondering at the nature of their love life. If Rory Gastineau was unable to show affection or sexual imagination, then he could be in real trouble. Simply manufacturing an heir to the Gastineau throne would not hold this young woman. Or was he being naïve? Was that all Rory required, and was the blonde goddess disposable?

And I will kiss thy foot ...

Probably not.

"We can talk here."

They were in a room on the back of the mansion overlooking the cliffs. Most of whatever back wall there had been previously was gone, replaced by huge windows. Beyond a wide terrace, the lawn stretched to the cliff edge, an oasis of controlled cultivation between massive rocks, clumps of gorse and heather. Around the edges of the lawn, Moretti could see spikes of little white flowers. Lady's Tresses, his mother called them. They had survived the lawnmower this year, which had been hardly used because of the hot, dry summer.

"Breathtaking," said Moretti. Through an open window came the sound of the sea, crashing onto the rocks below.

"Yes. Difficult this year for the gardener. Salt and sea air and sun. Damaged everything but the weeds."

Rory Gastineau swept his hand over the land and seascape, his view extending no further than the edge of his property.

"That's where we were going to do the play, if the weather was nice."

Tanya Gastineau had joined them.

"Boo hoo," she added, but her disappointment sounded genuine.

Behind them, Liz Falla said, "I understand from speaking to Mrs. Maxwell this morning that she intends to proceed."

This drew a squeak of delight from Tanya and, to Moretti's surprise, a broad smile from her husband.

"Put that in your pipe and smoke it, Elton," he said.

So, whatever the tensions between sister and brother, thought Liz, *Elton is the real enemy. When their backs were to the wall, the Gastineaus stood together.*

Moretti turned back from the window, and addressed Rory Gastineau.

"You have obviously heard about the attack on Hugo Shawcross. We have now interviewed Ms. Ashton, whose actions saved Mr. Shawcross's life, and Mrs. Maxwell."

"See —" Rory sat down, pulling his wife down beside him on one of the sofas by the window, and waved his hand at Moretti and Liz to do the same. "I don't know why my sister had to be brought into this. We only know the man through the group."

"That is what we thought too, sir, until my partner, DS Falla, had a visit at the station from advocate Hamelin."

There was a swift exchange of glances between husband and wife.

"I see you know about that," Moretti added. This was all taking too long to get to the point, and he decided to take a leaf out of Falla's book and force the issue. "Advocate Hamelin suggested there is some connection between the apparent suicide of the Pleinmont hermit, Gus Dorey, and past events in your family. Then we have the inexplicable attack on Mr. Shawcross soon afterwards. Whether or not these two events are associated remains to be seen, but, since we need to talk to you about both, killing two birds with one stone seemed best."

On cue, a seagull shrieked and swept close against the glass, startling Rory, who had his back to the window. He jumped, and his wife put her hand on his arm again, soothing him.

"The recluse with that place out at Pleinmont?" Moretti had the feeling Rory Gastineau was playing for time. "If advocate Hamelin suggested our family had anything to do with the man, then advocate Hamelin is off his rocker."

"Very possible, sir." Moretti couldn't resist the response, and saw Falla swiftly lower her eyes to her notepad. "So you are saying you know of no connection between the Gastineau family and Augustus Dorey?"

Rory Gastineau had an ungainly bearing, an unattractive manner, and an ill-matched assortment of nose, mouth and oversized eyebrows jutting over slightly protuberant dark eyes, but he had a wonderful voice. It reverberated through the room, reaching every corner.

"That is what I am saying."

Moretti pressed on.

"There is a newspaper report of a fight between your father and Gus Dorey to which the police were called. This would be before you were born, but it is such an unusual occurrence I wonder if you were ever told anything about why that happened."

Rory kept his eyes fixed on Moretti's face, but his wife's reaction, though slight, was more revealing. The pretty blonde curls bounced as, lips parted, she glanced swiftly at her husband, then back again at Moretti.

"I can only imagine it was something to do with the war. I heard once that the hermit's father was a collaborator. But no, I wasn't told about it." Suddenly, Rory Gastineau went on the attack. "Why in God's name are we being bothered with all this? The poor old sod killed himself, you said. Suicide, you said, right?"

"Apparent suicide. There are circumstances that need further investigation."

Words, words, words. Smokescreens sometimes, and sometimes bombshells. He had hidden behind jargon, but had scored a direct hit. Moretti watched Rory Gastineau's large face turn scarlet, his chest heave.

"God," he said.

Moretti struck while the iron was hot.

"Then we have the cyber-threats and attacks on your niece, the strange business of the power being turned off during the play-reading, followed shortly after by the attempted murder of Hugo Shawcross. This may all be coincidence, and we may have more than one would-be murderer on this island, sir, but this is a small island and I don't believe in coincidence."

At which Tanya Gastineau flung her arms around her husband and started to cry.

"Tell them why you hired Roddy," she sobbed. "Tell them. You said not to say anything to anyone, but tell them, or I will."

Above the tousled curls of his wife, who was weeping helplessly against his chest, Rory Gastineau did what he was told, and the story was similar to the one Liz Falla had heard from Marla Gastineau in the change room at Beau Sejour, except that one or more of the messages had been verbal, not texted. This time, however, there was more detail in the telling, and what struck Moretti was the implication that this was about revenge for something that remained unspecified. More disturbingly, whoever was doing this was suggesting the verbal attacks would not remain verbal attacks.

That they intended to go further, and to kill Tanya Gastineau.

Neither Moretti nor Falla interrupted until Rory said, "And that's the big difference between what this bastard said to Marla and to Tanya. He didn't threaten to kill Marla. It was more like bullying, the kind of thing young people do to each other. More normal."

This drew an incredulous response from Liz Falla. "More normal, sir?"

"You know what I mean."

Moretti leaned towards Tanya. "Mrs. Gastineau, did you get any idea of who this might be? On the phoned-in threats, did you recognize the voice? Your husband said 'bastard,' so I am assuming it was a man."

From the depths of her husband's Fair Isle sweater, Tanya glanced up at Moretti.

"I've no idea," she said in her little-girl voice.

Rory Gastineau detached himself from his wife and stood up. A long strand of his wife's fair hair caught on Rory Gastineau's sweater, curling against a scarlet diamond shape in the Fair Isle design. "I think that's enough for now," he said.

Moretti got to his feet, taking a last look at the view. Beyond the windows, the tiny white flowers of the Lady's Tresses fluttered in the breeze, and Moretti remembered that the lady they were named for was the Virgin Mary.

Tanya had made a quick recovery. She sprinted ahead of them, leading the way, clearly anxious to be rid of them. Liz caught up with her, and Moretti heard her ask, "Did you learn to ride here, Mrs. Gastineau, or in England?"

"Oh, I've loved horses since I was a little girl." A trill of laughter. "One of the promises Rory made me, when he persuaded me to come and live here, was a beautiful horse, and Rory always keeps his promises — don't you, Rory?"

Tanya glanced back over her shoulder at her husband, who was walking beside Moretti.

"Yes."

The look Rory gave his wife was now not so much adoring Caliban as uneasy soothsayer, with an upcoming warning about the Ides of March.

At the top of the steps, Liz extended her hand.

"Thank you, Mrs. Gastineau. So you didn't meet on the island?"

"Oh no. We met in my hometown, not Rory's. Bristol," she added. Then her hand went up to her mouth as she saw her husband's face.

* * *

"Well, well, well. So Rory Gastineau paid a visit to Bristol. Congratulations, Falla."

"She's lying, Guv. Not about Bristol, I mean."

"Not about Bristol, but she's in on some or all of whatever is going on in that family. And she could well have edited the messages she was getting for her husband's ears. We'd need a warrant to get Tanya's phone, I'm sure, and she may well have disposed of it by now."

"I think she recognized the voice," said Falla.

"That was my feeling. There'll be a record of the marriage, and we need to know Tanya's maiden name. She may have married for money, but there's money in her past. Horse-riding as a hobby is not cheap, and she looks like an accomplished rider." Moretti looked at Falla, who was turning the Skoda out of the driveway and onto the road. "There's something going on she doesn't want her husband to know about. That was quite a 'hmmm' you gave when you saw her and her so-called bodyguard. Did you recognize him?"

"No, but then I don't hang out with the huntin', shootin', fishin' set. Still, that's the thing — there's not many of them on the island. I bet he's from the mainland, and I wonder if she knew him before. I'll ask around. What did you think of her, Guv?"

"She's sharp — I don't buy the dumb blonde act — and manipulative. She's a pretty woman used to getting her own way, and I hope she hasn't overestimated her power. There's something nasty going on, and someone dangerous behind it. What do *you* think, Falla?"

"I think I'd like to know what mascara she uses. All that weeping and wailing and not a smudge in sight."

Moretti laughed. Falla's insights were always valuable, sometimes in surprising ways.

"Interesting. You don't plan to do too much weeping and wailing in the near future, I hope."

Next to him in the car she was smiling, but she didn't answer. They were now on the Forest road. "Back to the station, Guv?" Liz asked, pausing for directions.

"You hungry, Falla?"

"Starving."

"Come on, I'll buy you dinner. Or do you have plans?"

Afterwards, Moretti would recall his partner's sideways look and her smile.

"Not till later. Thanks, Guv."

"There's a nice little pub in Forest, with a great cook. The best crab cakes on the island. Is all forgiven?"

"You got me with the crab cakes, Guv. Lead the way."

Chapter Sixteen

It had been an interminable day. Al Brown looked at his watch and yawned, then glanced longingly at the police Honda, propped beneath the window, draped in one of the blankets from the hermit's bed. It had been impossible to conceal it from the view of anyone coming in the door, but at least he had managed to get it inside the roundhouse without anyone seeing him. He was sure of that. It was a tempting thought: he could just skive off right now, and no one would know.

Besides, how often do you get the chance to catch a murderer single-handed? Or maybe a washerwoman.

Outside the window, night was finally falling, and if anything were going to happen, it would be under cover of darkness. The difficult task ahead of him was to stay awake and alert. He drank the last of the coffee in the thermos he had brought with him, ate the last cheese and chutney sandwich, purchased at Marks and Spencer's on the Esplanade, got out his emergency rations, and put them in his pocket: a packet of chocolate-covered coffee beans. Chocolate-covered coffee beans had the same effect as a shot of nitro for the heart — if what his father said was anything to go by. He had used them before on stakeouts, much to the amusement of his former colleagues, who used other, sometimes riskier, substances. Not to mention illegal. Some relied on alcohol, which was always a temptation.

It was dark in the roundhouse now, and the flashlight he had with him was for emergency use only. He put the book he had brought back in the carrier on the Honda without too much regret. He was trying to read a Portuguese Nobel Prize winner in Portuguese, and was finding it heavy going, requiring his total concentration. It was a poor choice for a stakeout. Particularly one where you were on your own.

Al took a look through the window, with its sad little lineup of coloured shards on the narrow sill. They caught the last, faint gleam of the setting sun beyond the outline of the German Naval Observation Tower, its futuristic shape looming against the darkening sky. When he had some time to himself, he would explore this other island reality that was not only present in the structures left behind, but also in the island psyche. At least, so it seemed to him, although he had been here no time at all. Then he sat down in the rickety armchair, which he had pulled against the wall close to the window, away from the door, and waited.

One hour, two hours. There was no longer the sound of even the occasional car on the unpaved road that crossed the Common close to the roundhouse. In the silence, he could hear the waves crashing far below on the rocks and, now and then, the cry of some sea-bird overhead. Al was aware of his breathing changing, felt his eyelids closing.

Chocolate coffee bean time.

He was taking the packet of coffee beans out of his pocket when there was a sound from the direction of the window, almost above his head. Then a narrow beam of light cut through the darkness of the room.

Thank God he had moved the chair, he thought, crouching lower in the seat. The way his heart was beating, it was as well he hadn't got to the coffee beans, or he would have needed defibrillation, and he doubted whoever was outside the window holding a flashlight would have obliged.

The light circled the room for a minute, illuminating the rose-pink ceiling, then disappeared. Al shot up out of the chair, crept across the room, and stationed himself behind the door just before it started opening, very slowly. A gloved hand appeared, holding the edge of the door and Al grabbed it. The strength of the intruder's response took him by surprise, as whoever it was — certainly male — fought him off, attempting to slam the door between them. Al wrenched the door open, only to have it shut on his hand. He gave a yell of rage and pain.

"You son of a bitch!"

The hinges on the door finally gave in to the pressure and succumbed, leaving the door half-hanging in his damaged hand. He thrust it away from him and started off down the path, but the intruder was fleet of foot as well as strong, and was now nowhere in sight, swallowed up in the darkness. Reminding himself that whoever it was would know the unlit Common better than he did, Al started back towards the roundhouse, pulling out his mobile.

As he did so, there was a slight movement to his right near some gorse bushes on the edge of what he assumed had been the original boundaries of the Dorey property.

When he had first arrived, he had taken a look around, and discovered the remains of what once must have been a wall around the property, now just rubble. He wasn't good at identifying plants, being a city boy, but it looked as if the Doreys had grown quite a kitchen garden there. There were brambles that looked like old raspberry bushes, and mint everywhere, the scent rising as he crushed the leaves beneath his trainers.

So the bastard hadn't taken off, but had gone to ground. Al crept in the direction the noise had come from, hoping his throbbing hand would be able to hold on to the creep who had damaged it. Christ, hoping his throbbing hand would be able to hold on to his guitar again. Play it again.

As he did so, there was another sound, the sound of someone crashing through the undergrowth, risking exposure and making a bid for escape. Anger and pain gave him wings, an adrenalin rush that propelled him from the path into the abandoned kitchen garden. Ahead of him there was a cry as the would-be intruder tripped over one of the tangled canes, and Al was upon him.

"Got you, you bastard."

Only whoever it was crushed beneath him was neither bastard nor son of a bitch, but a woman. An elderly woman, from the face that looked up at him, terrified.

"What the hell —"

Al pulled himself up off a skinny body that clearly had not been attached to the hand that slammed the door on him, then pulled her up, wincing as he did so.

"This is a police investigation area — see the tapes? What are you doing here?"

"You've hurt your hand."

The face framed by a mass of wild grey hair was striking, regaining some of its long-lost beauty in the moonlight, the high cheekbones accentuated by the loss of youthful flesh, the eyes that looked up at him dark as sloes in a maze of wrinkles. She took his hand in hers, gently, her roughened skin rubbing against the swelling, making him wince again.

"I need to ask you some questions. Someone else was here."

"Yes. He hurt you. He got away."

"Did you see him?"

"Yes. And no. Come."

She was leading him to the pump that stood close by the kitchen garden, and he allowed himself to be led, marvelling at her swift recovery from the shock of being tackled and thrown to the ground. And at himself, docilely following her. On the way, she bent down and picked a large leaf of some kind from one of the tangle of plants around them, and tucked it into her thick frieze of grey hair.

The water from the pump was ice-cold against the swelling, and his captive, become benefactor, turned his hand this way and that beneath the flow. Then she picked up a corner of her long woollen skirt, dried his hand, and pulled out the leaf from her hair.

"Hold this around your hand. Tight. Long as you can."

Al did as he was told. Of necessity he had let go of her, and so far she was making no attempt to get away.

"You know who I am?" he asked her.

"Police. If you let me go back into there," she pointed at the roundhouse, "I'll talk to you."

"Okay. You lead the way."

"Stay close," she said. "I'm not afraid of you, but the other one."

"Other one?"

She did not reply, but walked ahead of him, glancing around as she did so. Al pulled the damaged door to one side with his left hand, taking care to stay clear of the section held by the intruder, and she walked in ahead of him.

"You moved things." She sounded angry.

"You know this place well? You knew Gus Dorey?"

"You're not Guernsey," was her answer.

"No."

Al repeated his question. She was smiling now, stroking the chair in which he had held vigil.

"He's dead," she said. "I'm going to sit in his chair. He used to let me."

She sat down, and Al took out his small flashlight, transferred it to his left hand and shone it in her direction, avoiding her face. She was slender, thin as a wraith in her smoke-grey dress. The most substantial thing about her was her footwear, a pair of heavy boots.

"I think I know who you are. You're his laundry lady, aren't you?"

"His laundry lady." She seemed delighted by this. "That's me."

"Did he pay you?"

She gave this some thought, then replied. "He gave me money for my teeth."

At this, she whipped out a set of false teeth, waved them at Al, gave him a toothless grin, then put them back in her mouth.

"You helped him, he helped you."

"The Golden Rule. Isn't it. His mother called it that. I read stuff for him when his eyes got bad."

"Books?"

"Not books. He said not to say."

Gently now, he thought. *Gently.*

"But he's gone now. Someone hurt him. The man who hurt me. No Golden Rule for him, the one you're afraid of. What — stuff?"

"Papers." Suddenly, she changed direction, and whether it was adroitness or dementia Al couldn't tell. "What's your name?"

"Aloisio Brown. You can call me Al. What's yours?"

"Meg. You can call me Meg. That's what Gus called me." Then she burst into alarmingly vigorous and tuneless song.

"*Old Meg, she was a gypsy and lived upon the moors. Her bed it was the brown heath turf, her house was out of doors.*"

Unlikely, Al thought, *for a laundry lady.*

"Keats," he said. "Was he one of Gus's favourite poets?"

A shrug of her thin shoulders. Poetry again, but this time thankfully not set to music.

"*Footsteps echo in the memory, down the passage which we did not take, towards the door we never opened, into the rose garden.*"

"T.S. Eliot." Al looked at her, trying to estimate the age gap between Gus Dorey and Meg the gypsy. Gus Dorey was eighty when he died and, in spite of her unkempt appearance and weather-worn skin, this woman seemed younger. "Did you know Gus a long time?"

"A long time." She got up from the chair, and Al, who was sitting on the edge of the truckle bed, got up and followed her to the window.

"See that?" She was pointing into the darkness at the outline of the observation tower, silhouetted against the night sky. "He found me there one day, when it was all over. When the bad guys were gone."

"Bad guys?" The slang sounded bizarre, coming from her. "The Germans, you mean."

"Only they weren't my bad guys. Rudi, and Werner, and Herman. They were my *freunde*. They played card games with me, and I used to win, and then they'd give me sweeties. Except when it was nearly over, and there were no sweeties left."

"You'd have been very little. What were you doing out here, on your own?"

"That's what they said. 'Where is your *mutti*?' they asked, and I said, 'Sleeping. Better than when she's awake.'" Meg the gypsy put a thin hand to her cheek, and Al had no difficulty interpreting the gesture.

"Did they — hurt you, in any way?"

He asked it hesitantly, but she didn't seem put out by the underlying implication.

"Gus asked me that. No, not the bad guys. They were missing their *kinder* — Rosa, and Friedrich and *lieber kleiner Frechdachs*, Heinrich." She laughed, shaking her head over naughty little Heinrich, remembering those much-loved children of the bad guys. "Then it was over, and they went home."

She turned from the window and looked at him. Meg the gypsy was crying.

"I'm sorry."

It wasn't hard to imagine, or to believe, the lonely, abused child wandering around the Common and finding refuge amid the weapons of war with bored, frightened, homesick soldiers.

"Then Gus came back, and he came to the tower and saw me, inside. After, when they'd all gone. I got stuck, climbing up to the roof, and he heard me yelling and got me down. But he went away again."

"And then he came back and built his house. This house."

"Yes." Her face lit up, beautiful again. "Werner said to me, when I was crying, 'God will look after you, *liebschen*.' God didn't, but Gus did."

"I am glad." Al took out the packet of coffee beans and held it out. "Want some?"

"What is it?" Meg the gypsy looked at him suspiciously.

"A kind of sweetie. I'm going to have one." Al did so.

"Just one," she said. Then, thrusting her hand into the bag, she took a large handful, and popped one in her mouth. As they crunched companionably together, Al asked her, "The man who hurt me, he's been here before?"

"Yes. Looking for secrets. So Gus said not to tell."

"I can keep a secret. Who is he? "

She gave him a disbelieving look. "I wasn't born yesterday," she said.

With a speed that took him by surprise, she was up out of the chair, across the room and out the door, scattering coffee beans as she went.

"Jesus!"

Like ball bearings beneath his shoes, the chocolate-covered beans brought Al crashing to the slick floorboards, as Meg the gypsy sprinted through the door into the darkness.

Chapter Seventeen

Detective Inspector Ed Moretti was feeling restless. Crab cakes with his sergeant had had that effect on him — sitting outside in some pleasantly warm autumn sunshine with a beer for them both, since they could now consider themselves off-duty. And the crab cakes were just as good as he remembered, as was the company.

Not that they had discussed anything personal. They had gone over the interview with Rory and Tanya Gastineau, and the pros and cons of bringing them down to the station, to see if that might dislodge more information. Moretti was reluctant, feeling they needed more direct evidence of a link between the Gastineau family and Gus Dorey. Falla's next task was to check out the newspaper reports of the wedding and to find out Tanya's last name and any other family details she could; Moretti's first job was to set up a proper incident room the next morning and to arrange for the "MI Team" to meet at Hospital Lane. It was time to share some of the information beyond the "need-to-know" group approved of by the chief officer, and to go over what they had so far.

Not that they had very much. He was hoping Al out at the roundhouse had got lucky. Nothing had been heard from him yet, but it was unlikely anyone would turn up until later, and he didn't want to risk contacting him, in case he interrupted anything.

The more he thought about it, the more doubtful he was becoming about a link between the assisted suicide and the attack on Hugo Shawcross. There was unquestionably something going on in the Gastineau family, but it could be there was also a random psychopath on the island who had been triggered by talk of vampires.

Not bloody likely.

He sat down at his mother's piano and started to play — a tango for some reason. Not "Jealousy," a tune he disliked, but something he'd heard in a film some time ago that was all about the tango. He had gone with Val, he remembered, when he was living and working on the mainland, when they were still in love and planning a life together. She had enjoyed every minute, so he had not shared his personal opinion about two hours of nothing but the tango. Still, one or two of the melodies had stayed with him, even if Val had not. In his experience, music was always easier to stick with, and to remember.

But then, he was the one who had done the leaving. He picked up his personal mobile, phoned Lonnie.

"Lonnie — how do you feel about doing a set tonight? I've got something new for us. Are you free?"

Lonnie's lazy, always cheerful, voice rumbled into Moretti's ear.

"I'm always free!"

Which was usually true. He, Moretti, was the only member of the Fénions with a steady job. At least that's how it was in the off-season, when Lonnie made a few shekels playing at the club with Dwight, and whichever local guitarist or harmonica player was available, when Moretti was not. On those occasions, the Fénions became Lonnie and the Layabouts. In the summer, Lonnie was a bus driver, one of the few Guernseymen still employed by the company.

"Great. I'll get hold of Dwight."

Dwight, too, was always free, usually freer than Lonnie, but tonight he sounded reluctant.

"Come on, Dwight. Can't the dishes wait? Or whatever you're doing at the moment?"

There was a pause, and Moretti heard whispering. Ah, a woman.

"Bring her," Moretti said. Then he phoned Don Taylor, as promised.

"So what's new?"

Lonnie was already on the little stage, his bass between his knees, softly plucking the strings, the sound reverberating in the almost-empty space. It was earlier than their usual hour to play, and only a few people had wandered down when they saw Moretti arrive. Lonnie played a riff, spun the bass and rested it carefully against the piano. Lonnie was the only Fénion who had to bring his instrument, and his instrument case lay at the back of the stage behind Dwight's drums, with his familiar, battered panama hat on top of it.

"Dwight coming?"

"On his way."

Moretti sat down, took off his jacket and tie, and looked sorrowfully at the empty ashtray on top of the piano. He kept it there for the same deeply buried and quixotic reason he kept his old lighter in his pocket.

God, how he missed smoking, particularly in the club. His father, he was sure, had dwindled and died of grief, but the process had also been hastened by cigarettes. Since it didn't look like he was going to die for love, Moretti decided to rule out nicotine, and had finally won the battle. Only it was a battle that was never over, something he always reminded himself of when dealing with some screaming, writhing piece of humanity, stuck fast in the arms of morphine. Or whatever was their particular poison.

"This is what's new."

Slowly the opening notes of the tango drifted across the space, and Lonnie began to play along, picking up the rhythm and the mood with his usual intuitive swiftness, so markedly at odds with his lemur-like movements in everyday life. Moretti remembered the first time he had heard Lonnie play, how amazed he had been by the speed of those powerful sausage-fingers in contrast to the physical lethargy he otherwise displayed.

The sounds of the tango drifted up the stairs into Emidio's, and the space began to fill up. Moretti saw Don Taylor arrive, on his own, as he usually was. Don waved at him, and took a seat close to the stage. Then Dwight arrived.

Only this time, Dwight was not on his own, as he too usually was. Not that he often left on his own. Moretti watched him walk in with two women, kiss one of them, leave them at a table near the back of the room, and walk towards the stage, greeting Don Taylor as he passed. Then he saw Don gesture towards the two women, who then made their way to the front of the room to join him.

Liz Falla and her godmother, Elodie Ashton.

Moretti realized he had stopped playing, and he and Dwight waited for Lonnie's final grace note. A ripple of applause as Dwight joined them on the stage. He grinned at Moretti.

"I brought her," he said.

Nothing to say really, thought Moretti. *Always easier for him to let the music do the talking*. He watched Falla introduce Elodie Ashton to Don, waited for Dwight to settle himself, and started.

Sammy Cahn's "I Fall in Love Too Easily."

Behind him he heard Dwight make a sound that could have been either amusement or indignation, as he and Lonnie followed his lead.

They were just through the first set when a group of three women came down the curving staircase into the Grand Saracen. The Fénions never had a reliable timetable for their audience to follow, but Deb had a sign made up that she put outside when the three of them turned up together. As she grudgingly said, the enhanced cash receipts at the bar made it worth her while, but an actual schedule would be appreciated — something, she knew, would never happen. Although he didn't know them, Moretti recognized two of the women as regulars, who were often in the club when the Fénions were playing. He also recognized the third woman with them. It was Irene Edwards, dressed in black, her dark hair falling free on her shoulders.

They finished the set with a club favourite, "I Get a Kick Out of You," and the three Fénions left the stage. Lonnie did his usual amble to the bar for a beer, and to chat up whichever beautiful girl was working that night. Normally, Dwight would go outside for a cigarette, but tonight he went to the table by the stage, and Moretti followed him.

"Hello," he said. Well, it was a start.

Falla gave him one of her wide smiles that made her look about — well, even younger than she was, although what she was wearing did not, and Moretti realized he rarely, if ever, saw her in something other than her sensible dark suit. Whatever she was wearing bared her shoulders, revealing eye-catching evidence of her gym workouts.

Don stood up. "I don't think you know —" He indicated Elodie Ashton.

"Yes, we've met."

Don, blissfully unaware of any underlying currents, was about to carry on when there was an interruption, as Irene Edwards came up to the table, and Falla made the introductions, swiftly acknowledged by the doctor. After appreciative remarks about the music, Irene Edwards turned her heavy-lidded Mona Lisa eyes and her silvery voice on Don Taylor.

"You're the runner, aren't you? The chap I see out in all weathers on the cliff paths?"

With pleasure and satisfaction, Moretti watched as a gobsmacked Don was courted by one of the most striking women in the room, who was, apparently, desperate to find a running partner who knew the island well.

"… unless, of course, you prefer running on your own? So many do."

"God, no! I get tired of my own company. May I buy you a drink?"

It looked like the loneliness of the long-distance Don was over.

Moretti took the chair vacated by Don, which happened to be next to Elodie Ashton. No glasses tonight, and her extraordinary mane of hair was on full display. She was wearing something in a vivid cobalt blue that did nothing to diminish the impact of her eyes.

"Liz brought me to keep her company while Dwight's on stage," she said, "and to give me a ride in her new car."

Talk about Figaros and Triumphs and Piaggios kept the conversation going in safe directions until it was time to play again. Whether it was the Scotch he always had in the first break, or whether it was the shared laughter about the unimportant, all-important, trivia of everyday life — something he didn't indulge in too often — Moretti heard himself saying, "Sing for us, Falla. I know you've sung with Dwight in the past. He told me."

As she got up on the stage with Dwight, he recovered his sanity, and started to worry about their shared worlds of work, and now play.

What door have I opened?

Then he stopped thinking as she sang, with the soft-shoe shuffle of Dwight's ghost-notes on the snare-drums behind the voice a former lover of his described as a blend of Enya with echoes of Marianne Faithfull. A voice he now heard as entirely her own.

"What's it all about, Alfie?"

What indeed.

The Fénions, Liz, Elodie, Don and Irene were the last people to leave the Grand Saracen. Upstairs, Emidio's was closed, and it was Ronnie who saw them out. She wanted to talk to Liz about her singing.

"I'll be singing with my group next Saturday, at a pub in Castel. Unless I'm working, that is."

Liz looked at Moretti, who was watching Irene Edwards and Don. She was thinking of something to say about his music that didn't come out sounding feeble. She had never thought she knew the policeman, but now she felt she knew him better through the piano player. And that she would never say.

Irene Edwards and Don were laughing, apparently over the fact that the glamorous doctor had lost her ride home, and Don had come, as usual, on his bicycle.

"Put your bike in the back, Don," Moretti called out. "Thank God it's not mud-covered. I'll give you both a lift."

"It's okay, all taken care of."

Don waved and he and his new running partner left, heading for the taxi rank on the Esplanade, wheeling Don's bicycle between them.

It looked like the gorse was going to be in full bloom.

"Good night, Guv." Moretti realized Liz was talking to him.

"See you at the office tomorrow."

Something about Don's situation must have got to him, warming the cockles of his heart, whatever that meant. As Liz turned to leave with Dwight and her godmother, Moretti heard himself saying, "Can I give you a lift?"

All three turned around.

"I've got a car now, Guv," said Liz helpfully.

"No. Your godmother."

The two women laughed, and the godmother said, "That'd be nice."

"Why are you doing this?"

Her directness made him smile. "I'm not entirely sure."

"Perhaps you are a neatness freak — you know, two and two and two."

"God, no." Pity it wasn't a warm summer night, and he could have watched all that red hair blowing in the breeze. "Falla was really — to use her word — pissed with me. I think that's it."

Oh, what a charmer I am, Moretti thought. They had moved out of St. Peter Port and were heading south, out from Sausmarez Road to the Route des Blanches, in completely the wrong direction for his cottage.

"So nothing to do with me. That's a relief."

She didn't sound sarcastic, or ironic. She sounded serious.

"I suppose what I'm trying to say in my own silver-tongued way is that, if I have to consider you a suspect again, I will. Just so there's no misunderstanding."

"I'm not at the moment a suspect? Good for me." She turned towards him, and he glanced in her direction. It was a relief to see she was smiling. "And, just so there's no misunderstanding, I'm going to ask you in when we arrive. To check for bogeymen, as Liz would have done. I'm still spooked."

"Not surprising. If it's any comfort, this has nothing to do with you, I'm sure. You had the misfortune to be Shawcross's neighbour, and he had the good fortune to be yours."

"What in God's name is going on?"

"I wish I knew."

The memory of the horrific attack on Hugo Shawcross hovered between them in the enclosed space of the Triumph, and they were silent for a while.

* * *

Moretti did what she asked, and checked over the house, including the two bedrooms and the bathroom upstairs. Again, there had been considerable revamping on the second floor, with the bathroom made into an en suite with the main bedroom. He found her choice of decoration as much to his taste as he did downstairs. The only sign of disorder was a pair of jeans and a shirt thrown across the bed in the main bedroom. Obviously, Falla had given her aunt short notice. Then he took a brief walk around the garden behind the house, with the help of a large flashlight.

"No sign of anything out of the ordinary. Should I have met the cat?"

She laughed, taking the flashlight back from him. "No. Liz let him into the house when she came to pick me up. The sound of him fighting at night gives me the shivers." She paused, and then said, "Thank you. Poor Liz has to be here every morning to deal with Stoker, and this gave her a break — if not from looking after the cat, from looking out for me."

"Not a problem." A cliché at the ready for every occasion, Moretti made his way to the front door, re-establishing the policeman as he did so. "That's a good lock, I'm glad to see."

"It is." As she opened the door, she said, "By the way, I'm Elodie when you're off-duty. Not the aunt or the godmother or the suspect. Good night, Ed."

"Good night, Elodie."

Smiling to himself as he walked back to the car. Elodie, rhymes with melody. Nothing to worry about, not his type.

Not a problem.

Which left him plenty of time on the drive home to think about the renewed liaison between Dwight and Falla. He knew they had been involved before because, when Hanley first made Falla his partner, he had been bewailing his fate one night at the Grand Saracen.

"So I've got to share my car with some gum-chewing, comic-reading female. Hanley has saddled me with some bright-eyed, bushy-tailed, just-out-of-school-girl called Liz Falla."

And easy-going, laid-back Dwight had slapped him down. Hard.

Moretti checked his messages when he got home on his police mobile. Nothing from Al.

Damn.

The mobile rang in the small hours, the very small hours. Groggy with the sleep he had just fallen into, Moretti asked, "Al? What's up?"

The message was brief and to the point.

"I've fucked up, that's what's up."

Chapter Eighteen

In the incident room, Liz Falla, Bernie Mauger, Rick Le Marchant, and two constables added to the team that morning, plus Jimmy Le Poidevin, were awaiting the arrival of Moretti and Chief Officer Hanley. As yet, there was no sign of Al Brown, but it was clear from the information up on the board that Moretti had already been in. Liz went over and took a look at what he had posted.

"He's put bloody arrows between what I consider two completely separate enquiries." The head of forensics jabbed an irritated fist at the board. "What in God's name does he think there is to tie the assisted suicide of a vagrant and the attempted murder of this playwright or whoever he is. They simply don't move in the same circles."

"I thought vagrants were, like, tramps. Didn't Gus Dorey have a house?" asked Le Marchant. This got him an irritated glance from Le Poidevin, and a grin from Liz Falla. Before this could go anywhere, the door opened, and in came Chief Officer Hanley, followed by Moretti and Al Brown.

"Good morning."

Like obedient schoolchildren, those already in the room chorused their response to their supreme leader's greeting, sitting down after he had taken his seat. Moretti remained standing by the chief officer's side, and Al went round to join his fellow officers. He looked washed out, forlorn, thought Liz, no longer his dapper, well-groomed self. There was an almost hangdog look about him, which she would not have thought was part of his emotional makeup.

A rough night in the roundhouse? She was looking forward to hearing what had happened, because clearly something had, and she too was beginning to wonder if they should be running two separate lines of enquiry. Maybe whatever had happened to make Al look like death warmed up would clarify things.

"I'm going to hand the floor over to DI Moretti." Hanley gestured in Moretti's direction. Then he added, brows knitted in warning, "This does not necessarily mean I am in agreement with some of his decisions about how to proceed, and the facts of the two enquiries as he has interpreted them. But I have agreed to let him put his case to you."

This is being set up more like a court of law than a debriefing, Liz thought. *As if my DI is on trial. What happens if the Guvnor doesn't make his case? Will they give one or t'other to another DI? Sounds like it.*

Liz studied Moretti. If her Guvnor was feeling any signs of anxiety, he wasn't showing it. Of course, he was good at that. He simply pointed to the head of forensics.

"Jimmy, I want you to start us off with what you've got."

The forensics head looked at the chief officer and then at Moretti, ponderously making his point. "*Both* crime scenes?"

"Both crime scenes. Start with the Dorey murder."

"Assisted suicide, and *that* is still moot."

Moretti smiled at Jimmy, which was, thought Liz, strange in the circumstances. She had not spoken to Elodie since her aunt's departure in the Guvnor's car, so there was no way of knowing whether his air of tranquillity was connected in any way. However, one thing she'd make book on was that the evening had not continued as it had for her.

Jimmy proceeded in his familiar, autocratic way, going over the appearance of the crime scene — not that he called it that — and the body, referring to the photos on the board and his notes, talking about fingerprints identified — the victim's, and the postman's — and unidentified. Which was where it became interesting.

"There is one set of prints that we found on chair, table, fireplace, window, and door. And on things like food containers, shelving, et cetera. Dorey had a regular visitor, who unfortunately does not have a record, so at the moment we have no idea who this is." Jimmy paused for dramatic effect and turned to the chief officer. "But in my humble opinion, sir, when we have identified those prints we will have found the person who helped to hang Gus Dorey. *If* that is what happened."

With the air of one who has solved the mystery of the big bang theory, Jimmy sat down, closed his folder, and waited for the murmurs of excitement to subside, all of which came from the four constables and the chief officer. Liz Falla was looking at Al Brown, who was looking at Moretti.

"Go ahead, Al," said Moretti. "After what we have just heard from Jimmy, we should hear your report next." He sat back again in his chair, relaxed as if he were listening to music, which he probably was.

Al stood up. His body language could not have been more different, but was just as easy to read.

"I was on surveillance at the roundhouse last night, and there were a series of events which, unfortunately, I mishandled."

More murmurs of excitement, and Moretti sat forward.

"Don't editorialize, Al. Just tell it."

As Al went through his catastrophic night at the hermit's hideaway, the proverbial pin could have dropped in the incident room. His account of the two intruders had them on the edge of their seats. All except Moretti. He now seemed not just at ease with the world, but positively cheerful, surveying his colleagues with what looked to Liz like — well, triumph. He had taken his lighter-talisman out of his pocket and was turning it round and round in his fingers. Or was she now seeing him in a different light? Looking at him now, she could hear fragments of music, his music, in her head. Right now, it was "Sometimes I'm Happy."

"And you didn't even get her real name, this — Meg the gypsy?"

Chief Officer Hanley's shocked response was followed by Jimmy Le Poidevin's incredulous snort.

"No, sir."

Hanley addressed Moretti, his voice quivering with indignation. "You set up a one-man surveillance? We'll have to put out an all-points bulletin of some kind to pick up this woman."

"Not necessary, sir." Moretti put his lighter back in his pocket and pulled out a piece of paper. From where Liz was sitting it looked like an email. "I know who she is." He smiled across the room at Liz, whose strong dark eyebrows had almost disappeared beneath the jagged line of her bangs. "She won't be going far, and I think I know how I can find her."

Hanley held out his hand for the email Moretti was holding.

"This about her? You've made enquiries?"

"This?" Moretti looked at the paper as if surprised to see it there, shook his head. "No. This came in from Dr. Edwards just before I arrived. Knowing that there was some reluctance on the part of some people to accept Dorey's death as suspicious, she took another look at the body this morning."

"And?" Jimmy Le Poidevin interjected. "We already know what she thinks about the knot."

"Not the knot, Jimmy. What happened *beneath* the knot. Best I read to you what the doctor's new findings are." Moretti stood up and started to read.

"'DI Moretti, I owe you an apology.'" Moretti looked over at Al. "So you see, Al, even this smart professional overlooked something." Al was now looking both crushed and relieved, thought Liz, if that was possible.

"Can you cut to the chase? We've still got one more crime scene to go," Jimmy protested.

"Here's the chase, Jimmy," said Moretti. He sounded angry now, all trace of contentment or triumph gone from his manner. "Not just Gus Dorey's neck, but his hyoid bone was fractured." Moretti looked down at the email. "It's a horseshoe-shaped bone in the front of the neck between the chin and the thyroid. And, let me quote Dr. Edwards again: 'It is very difficult for the hyoid bone to be broken in an adult, because of its inflexible ossification. It strongly indicates to me that the victim was strangled, and then hanged.' End of quote."

Moretti folded up the email. "So, Jimmy, not suicide. Not even assisted suicide, but murder." He looked around him. "And I want that kept to just the nine people in this room. If it goes any further, I'll have someone's guts for garters."

For a moment there was a stunned silence. Hanley was the first person to speak.

"Good God. Has she any more surprises about the other victim?"

"Not that I know of, and Mr. Shawcross is to be released from the hospital today. But I am convinced, sir, that we have one person doing this."

"One raving lunatic out there is, I suppose, better than two." Hanley gave a sardonic little laugh at his observation. "But still, there's no apparent rhyme nor reason, is there? Which will make finding this maniac all the more difficult."

"I'll not deny it's going to be difficult, but I think, sir, you've hit the nail on the head," said Moretti.

Everyone looked surprised, including the chief officer.

"Yes," continued Moretti. "No apparent rhyme and reason, so all we have to do is to find out what *that* is, and then we'll have him. Or her," he added.

"Her?"

"Possibly."

Chief Officer Hanley now looked despondent, a facial expression that came naturally to him, on learning that the one half of the human race he had thought excluded, now must be included.

"However," Moretti went on, "Al's pretty sure the first intruder was a man, and chances are he nearly came face to face with the raving lunatic." Moretti was smiling again, and before the chief officer could say anything about Al or raving lunatics or the failure to catch them, Moretti turned to Al and asked, "How's your hand?"

Al Brown held it out in front of him, and everyone looked for signs of contusions, bruises, broken bones. Apart from a faint redness on his olive skin, there was nothing to see.

"Amazing,' said Moretti. "Quite amazing. And now if we could have SOCO's report on the *second* crime scene. Jimmy, over to you."

* * *

"You rubbed his nose in it a bit, Guv. All that about the coming and going between the two gardens."

"Didn't I, and with reason. We can rule out the button that was found, since there's a button missing from Shawcross's jacket, and we can eliminate various boot-prints by comparing them with SOCO's, but using anything as evidence in a court case will be impossible. I'd hoped the ligature might have been dropped, since the strangler took off in such a hurry, but no sign of it. I'm thinking of going and taking another look myself."

Moretti, Falla and Al were sitting in Moretti's office. PC Le Marchant had been dispatched to oversee the boarding up of the roundhouse, and PC Mauger was on his way to escort Hugo Shawcross home. Moretti had deliberately chosen Bernie Mauger, because he hoped his simple country manner and his comforting bulk might — just might — encourage confidences. Gandalf needed someone in his corner, and that someone must not be Elodie Ashton. Now that he was back home again, both Falla and her godmother were at greater risk.

The two other constables, Perkins and McMullin, had been assigned tasks they found puzzling, but theirs was not to reason why when duty called and took them away from the trivial round and the common task.

Constable Perkins, however, had asked one question. "Billie the Bus Bum is a really unreliable witness, sir. Well, he's nutty, isn't he?"

"Yes, and no," was the unhelpful answer. "You get on every bus route on the island if necessary, and when you find him, just ask him what I told you. Okay?" The tone of voice was not chummy, and PC Perkins took the hint and left for the bus terminal on the Esplanade.

"Billie the Bus Bum?"

Al had recovered some of his self-possession, the self-confidence back in the tone of his voice. "Although," he added, "I hesitate to ask, after —"

"The flea in Constable Perkins's ear?" Moretti pulled his papers together in front of him, and smiled at his colleagues. "Falla will tell you I'm not fond of widening the number of officers involved on a case, because on this island everyone knows everyone and is related to half of them. So, for Perkins and McMullin, it's on a need to know basis. Billie is one of our island fixtures. He carries everything he owns in a knapsack and uses his welfare money to ride the buses. Nutty though he is, he's a wealth of information."

"About Meg the escape artist?"

"The escape artist who healed your hand, yes. I'll fill you in on the details later, but first I want Falla to give us the news from the society columns. Over to you, Falla."

Liz took out her notebook. When she had opened it during the meeting, Moretti had moved swiftly on to the need to protect the roundhouse from further intruders. She had worked with him long enough to know the reason why, and to close it again. At least it was just her notebook this time, not her mouth.

"The wedding dress was spectacular, Princesses Grace and Di rolled into one pricey package, but I'll spare you the frills and the furbelows, whatever *they* are, and cut to the chase." For a moment, Moretti heard Jimmy Le Poidevin's exasperated voice floating on the office air, and smiled. "Tanya's maiden name is Finlay, and her father is Duncan Finlay, the owner of Finlay Holdings, who operate a bunch of shopping plazas in the southwest. But his empire is falling apart, and he declared bankruptcy about a year before the marriage."

"Looks like Tanya was used to living well, and decided to use her own God-given talents when daddy's money started to dry up," said Moretti. "Anything more, Falla?"

"Not much of any use. But the wedding-guest list is interesting, if it's complete."

"Who's on it?"

"Not so much who's on it, Guv, as who's not. Ginnie Purvis, née Gastineau."

"Interesting." Moretti stood up. "Falla, you and I are going to talk to Ginnie Purvis, and Al, I want you to go and do some shopping at WORDS. Use your charm on the owner, Jim Landers. It'll be hard-going, because the owner of WORDS is a man of few words unless they come in books. We need to talk to everyone associated with Shawcross's play."

Liz flipped to an earlier page in her notebook. "Douglas and Lana Lorrimer, Raymond Morris, Aaron Gaskell. Oh, and Charles Priestley. The beautiful boy. According to my aunt, central casting for an *homme fatale*."

Moretti was humming to himself, and Liz caught the melody.

You do something to me.

But his words were sombre.

"A fatal man, or a fatal woman. Take care. Remember, whoever this is — bites." Then he added, "'*His biting is immortal; those that do die of it seldom or never recover.*' Or her, perhaps, in this case."

"Wordsworth again?" said Liz, raising an eyebrow, and Moretti laughed.

"*Anthony and Cleopatra.* Remember what you found on that scrap of paper, Falla. It is the rhyme and the reason for all of this."

"*My darling,*" she said.

Chapter Nineteen

The address for Ginnie Purvis prised out of a reluctant school secretary was on Candie Road, near the Priaulx Library and the Candie Gardens. Liz Falla had to call the school because the old phone number was now out of service. The school secretary had informed Liz she could not hand out a new number, but would pass on the message.

"How soon will you be able to do that?"

"Ms. Purvis is now in class and cannot be disturbed unless this is a family emergency."

Liz asked when Ms. Purvis took her lunch hour, then said, "Tell Ms. Purvis we will meet her at her house at that time."

"But Ms. Purvis will not be happy if she is late for the afternoon classes. She has two."

"Ms. Purvis will not be happy if we turn up at school to interview her, I am sure."

"Very well," was the response, although it was clear that it was not very well.

"I wonder if Ms. Purvis gets special treatment, as a Gastineau?"

"Probably, but I doubt the kids she teaches care one way or another. They'll only care if she's magic."

"Magic, Guv?"

They were in the Skoda, heading up towards Candie Road from Hospital Lane, with Liz watching out the car window for the address they had been given. This time, the Skoda was the car of choice, because Moretti knew they would have to leave it on the road, parked up on the pavement in the area in which Ginnie Purvis was living.

"I believe she teaches English, and I had the good fortune to have an English teacher who was magic. Even if he had committed murder, I would still remember him as magic. You never forget."

"Lucky you. This is it, Guv."

They were outside a terrace of simple, semi-detached two-storey houses in varying degrees of upkeep, alteration and renovation. Each one was enclosed by a stone wall around a small patch of ground at the front, and Ginnie Purvis's house had an additional hedge somewhat higher than the wall. The house on one side of her was immaculate, with a professionally landscaped small front garden of topiaried little trees and a mini-fountain amidst colour-coordinated flowers. The house attached to hers was in the throes of renovation. An old bathtub stood on a pile of rubble in front of it, and inside the open front door two men in overalls were hammering away at a wall.

"What is a Gastineau doing here, Guv? No way I could afford one of these, even if it was one of the grotty ones, but still."

"Great minds, Falla. Just what I'm thinking — and here she comes. A Gastineau peddling like merry hell, approaching from the south."

Ginnie Purvis on a bicycle was making her way towards them, skidding up on to the pavement and screeching to a halt. As Moretti and Falla got out of the car, she too was screeching, and puffing in between.

"Is this really necessary? In the middle of a school day? Mrs. Bonner said some very bossy young lady simply would not take no for an answer."

Various responses came to mind, but Moretti decided to keep his mouth shut. He gave a warning look to the bossy young lady, who appeared to be on the verge of opening hers.

"Perhaps we could take this inside?"

Ginnie Purvis opened a rickety iron gate and wheeled her bike through into the front garden and propped it against a wall. She removed her helmet, took a lunch bag from the carrier on the bicycle, and unlocked the front door.

"Come in."

They were in a narrow hallway that led directly into a front room, with a wall, and an archway in place of a door. Most of the furniture in the room was huddled towards the centre, making the space seem even smaller. There was a strong smell of paint and turpentine in the air. Liz Falla sneezed.

"Sorry."

She sneezed again.

"Careful. Don't touch anything. I'm having it all repainted, and then I'll decide what I'm doing about further renovation."

Moretti introduced himself and his sergeant, both of them showing their police badges.

"Obviously you have just moved in, Ms. Purvis. It was necessary to make the phone call, because the only phone number we have for you was out of service."

"Yes. Do you mind if we do this in the kitchen? This is, after all, my *lunch* hour."

The kitchen, which overlooked a tiny back garden in a state of neglect, looked like it had not yet been touched. A depressing dun colour dominated the space, highlighted by dark brown cupboards above tatty countertops, with a similarly coloured floor underfoot. Ginnie Purvis gestured towards two chairs and a table. All three were of elegant design, possibly Italian, and certainly had cost a Euro or two.

"Sit down, and let's get on with this."

Moretti sat down, and Liz moved over to the window. Ginnie Purvis opened a top-of-the-line stainless steel fridge and removed a bottle of juice of some kind. Then she unpacked the lunch bag she had put on the counter and removed a sandwich. The thickly cut bread smelled good, and Falla heard her stomach growl in response.

Ginnie Purvis removed her heavy anorak, revealing a well-fed and sturdy body in a lime-green sweater and trousers of a colour not unlike the kitchen walls, sat herself down opposite Moretti, took a large bite of her sandwich and said through her mouthful, "Let's get on with it. This year's Upper Three are trouble enough if I'm on time, not that I'm ever late. What was so urgent you had to drag me out of school?"

"The attempted murder of Hugo Shawcross after returning from the play-reading at the Maxwells' house. You have, I am sure, heard about it."

At the window, Liz Falla watched Ginnie Purvis's reaction. She put down her sandwich and exclaimed in exasperation, as if someone in Upper Three had mislaid her textbook, "Good *grief*. Of course I've heard about it. I'm sorry, Detective Inspector, but for this you took me out of school? Not that I'm not horrified, but I really don't see how I can help."

"We are speaking to everyone who was at the reading, Ms. Purvis. Where were you after the meeting? Did you come straight back here?"

"Yes."

"Can anyone verify that?"

"You mean, do I have an alibi?" Ginnie Purvis picked up her sandwich again and took another hearty bite out of it. She demolished part of her mouthful and said, "Not unless one of my neighbours saw me come back, no. Sometimes one of the group gives me a lift, but this place is so close to the Grange I took my bicycle last night. That is one convenience of being here, as opposed to where I was living before, and it's also close to the school. So much easier when the girls want me to participate in one of their clubs, or we are putting on a play, or something."

The sandwich now gone, Ginnie Purvis got up to fetch a glass from the counter, and poured herself some juice.

As she returned to the table, Moretti said, "Always nice for children when they have a teacher who plays a role in their lives outside the classroom."

The heavy features of the middle Gastineau, so like her older brother's face, lightened into something approaching comeliness.

"So important. To them and to me. Yes."

A burst of hammering came through the wall and the momentary transformation disappeared, returning Ginnie Purvis's face to exasperation.

"Thank God I'm out during the day. I've had to speak to them about weekends, and they promise me it'll all be over well before the Christmas holidays. Now I'm in town, I am hoping to have the Sixth Form's Christmas party here, when my own renovations will be close to complete." She brightened again at the thought, finished her glass of juice, and looked at her watch.

"I've got to go. Unless there's anything else?"

As Moretti and Ginnie Purvis stood up, Liz Falla put away her notebook in which she had written virtually nothing, and picked up a paper bookmark from the windowsill.

"Did you get this from the station, Ms. Purvis?"

Ginnie Purvis pulled her right arm through the anorak sleeve and took the bookmark in her hand.

"Yes. I keep a few of them handy in the staff room. It's not enough to teach the wonders of Shakespeare and the wit of Shaw. The wherewithal to be at a private school does not protect some of my girls, or their mothers, from hard home lives. They need to know there is help." She turned the bookmark over in her hand, and looked at Falla, not Moretti. "You know the most important thing on the good side, Detective Sergeant? The last one on the list: *Accepts me as I am.* When that happens, everything else falls into place."

"And on the bad side?"

Ginnie Purvis turned the small scrap of paper over, and paused a moment. Then she said, "There are a few on this side, but I'd have to say, *Always blames me.* Right up there with *Embarrasses me in front of others.* Yes, I know what that's like."

Moretti's chic Italian-designed chair made a scraping noise on the floor as he put it back, and Ginnie Purvis seemed to return to the present. She put the juice bottle back in the fridge and, as she turned to face him, Moretti asked, "Where were you living before the move to Candie Road, Ms. Purvis?"

"I'm surprised you don't know, Detective Inspector, since you were in Forest yesterday, interviewing the happy couple. Did you also meet Roddy the Body?"

It was said with heavy sarcasm.

"Roddy the — do you mean the gentleman who takes care of Mrs. Gastineau's horse? The groom?"

Moretti felt, rather than saw, the expression in Falla's eyes behind him, and he knew she would be remembering that first impression of hers. He had already decided to say nothing about Gus Dorey, and only had a second in which to decide to say nothing about the threats against Tanya Gastineau. For the first time since they had arrived, there was real anger in Ginnie Purvis's face and voice, a depth of emotion unstirred by the attempted garrotting of Hugo Shawcross.

"'Gentleman' seems particularly inappropriate, and it all depends what you mean by 'groom,' but that's who I mean. There is a nice little cottage on the grounds that I used to call my own, and I was turfed out when Roddy the Body arrived. My brother Rory is a complete and utter fool."

"For marrying? Surely he had waited long enough?"

They had all reached the front door at the end of the narrow hallway. Ginnie Purvis turned back to them and, to Moretti's surprise, started to laugh. It reminded him of the way men laugh when insulting each other in pubs or at football matches. He could almost see her lip curl in mock derision.

"Not for marrying, Detective Inspector. But for marrying the kind of little floosie who is usually seen jumping out of a *cake*!"

"Well, well, well. Enough hatred there for poison-pen letters, or texts. Or phone calls."

"Whatever else she's hiding, I don't think Tanya would have kept quiet if she'd recognized Ginnie Purvis's voice, Guv."

Falla's voice was sombre, but her expression was

hidden from Moretti as she checked the intersection.

"The bookmarks. Tell me about them."

"One side depicts a good relationship, the other an abusive one. What was really interesting to me was what she chose from each side. Compared with some of the other stuff, Guv, being blamed or embarrassed was pretty harmless."

"Other stuff?"

"Bullying, hitting, violence — that other stuff."

"And the good side? Being accepted, if I remember rightly, for what you are."

"Yes." Falla turned the Skoda into the Hospital Lane car park beneath the ancient gateway from the old Maison de Charité, with the stone depiction of a pelican feeding its young from the blood dropping from her breast. She pulled in alongside the other police cars and switched off the engine. "Sometimes life is very unfair to women."

Moretti looked at his detective sergeant, surprised.

"Why do I have the feeling you are not talking about abuse, or glass ceilings, or doing all the housework?"

"I am, and I'm not. I'm talking about something really petty and trivial and frivolous. The luck of the draw, the sheer bloody luck of being born — a *babe*."

Nothing clever or trivial or frivolous to say about cakes or babes came to mind, so Moretti got out of the car, and waited for Falla to do the same.

"Come on, Falla. That sandwich made me hungry. We'll get one of our own, some decent coffee, and go talk to Aaron Gaskell," he said.

* * *

"I'm not surprised to see you."

Aaron Gaskell got up, shook hands with Moretti and Falla, and indicated the two seats by his desk. Tall, good-looking, dressed in an understated and expensive way, he was the perfect accessory for the understated and expensive offshore company in St. Peter Port for which he worked.

He turned a charming smile in Liz Falla's direction. "I think our paths crossed, did they not, a few weeks ago?"

"That's right, sir. I'd forgotten." Falla turned to Moretti. "Mr. Gaskell had a problem with where he was allowed to park close to his office. We got it sorted out."

"Most satisfactorily." The charming smile again. "But I'm not sure how I can help you, in any practical or constructive way, because I am so new to the island," he said.

"It's quite straightforward, sir," said Moretti. "Where were you when Mr. Shawcross was attacked? I imagine you know when that was."

"I was actually here, for my sins. Only the cleaning staff were in, and I can get them to confirm that, because they were not thrilled at being denied access to my office."

"Falla will take the names from you, sir, and we'll check."

A few notes taken down by Falla, a shrug of the shoulders and a shake of the head from Aaron

Gaskell as to why anyone would have attacked Hugo Shawcross, and then the phone on his desk rang. He picked it up, saying, "I apologize, Detective Inspector, but I really should answer this."

"Of course."

Moretti stood up and, as Liz Falla put away her notebook, she asked, "Just one more question, sir." Aaron Gaskell put his hand over the mouthpiece of the phone. "Why did you join the Island Players? As a newcomer to the island, I wonder how you heard about them."

"When I arrived they were performing a favourite of mine, that's why."

"Which was?"

The charming smile again. "Ionesco. *The Lesson*, it's called. I am very partial to the theatre of the absurd."

"What did you make of Gaskell when you sorted out his parking problem?"

"Too good to be true was what I made of him, then and today. I'll check that alibi."

"Way of life for us, isn't it, Falla?"

"What is, Guv?"

"The theatre of the absurd, Falla. The theatre of the absurd."

Chapter Twenty

Al Brown liked bookstores, but the ones he really liked were the tucked-away shops in corners of back streets, where the rents were low and where you could sift through out-of-print hardcovers by long-gone publishers and dog-eared paperbacks that looked as if they had already been read more than once from cover to cover.

WORDS was not like that. There were books in the window, but none outside, and certainly the width of the street would have made that difficult. The current display in the window was centred around graphic novels, a marketing term Al found vaguely amusing, since it had nothing to do with porn or sex, necessarily, but referred to illustrations and dialogue that could have come out of a comic book. He took a look at some of the titles. *Quite a mix*, he thought, from twentieth-century superheros to the Arthurian legends to the horrors of modern warfare.

On one side of the display was a selection of books with wizards and magicians on the cover, à la Harry Potter. He opened the door to the pleasant sound of a lightly jingling bell, rather than an electric buzzer. There was an agreeable smell of freshly brewed coffee in the air.

"Good morning."

Jim Landers was standing by a display of books by local authors, ranging from small, illustrated collections of the local flora, to accounts of the island's wartime years and its history of witchcraft. He had a duster in his hand, which he returned to the counter near the back of the store.

"Can I help you, or do you just want to browse?"

The voice was neutral, detached, repeating what he must have said a hundred times or more without either discernible enthusiasm or the lack of it. He had what Al thought of as a distinguished look about him: tall, no sign of middle-aged spread, good bones, good posture, an air of good breeding.

"A bit of both, actually. I've only just arrived on the island, and it's nice to find a bookstore like this. Some of them nowadays carry more novelties than novels." Al gave a light laugh, without response, as a pair of calm grey eyes surveyed him, somehow managing to do so without curiosity. "Do you have the latest Martin Amis? I believe it's just out."

"It is. Over here, with our new arrivals."

Al followed Jim Landers to a table close to the door.

"Great." He picked it up. "I'll take this. Not to everyone's taste, I know, but I am a fan, as my father was of his father. Amis, I mean."

"Certainly the apple didn't fall far from the tree."

It was impossible to tell from Jim Landers's face or voice if this was a compliment or a criticism, but perhaps the owner of a bookstore had to be circumspect about his tastes for the sake of good customer relations.

As he took out his wallet to pay for the book, Al said, "I've just joined the Guernsey police force, and I'm involved in the investigation into the death of Gus Dorey — you may have read about it in the newspaper — and also the attack on Mr. Shawcross. DI Moretti is leading the investigation. Do you know him?"

This time there was a reaction in the calm grey eyes. A new alertness, as if his attention was focused on Al for the first time since he came into the shop.

"Ed Moretti, do you mean? Yes, he comes in here from time to time, buys books."

"That's how I found out about the shop, and I believe you are a member of the Island Players. Mr. Shawcross was writing a new play for the group, wasn't he?"

"He was."

Blood from a stone, thought Al Brown. *But at least this one is a captive audience, and can't just run out the door, scattering coffee beans beneath my feet.*

"I understand you were at the play-reading. Are you directly involved with the production?"

Jim Landers smiled again.

"Are you just buying a book, or are you here to question me?"

"A bit of both." Al Brown laughed. "I should introduce myself — Detective Sergeant Al Brown. Aloisio Brown, actually."

They shook hands. Jim Landers's handshake was not too soft, not too hard, but just right.

"Yes, I am involved with the play. Since Hugo is in no position to speak, Marie Maxwell and Raymond Morris have asked me to play the lead."

"Doesn't this mean you will be playing the vampire? Scary stuff — but actors like to be stretched, challenged, I believe."

"This is not a horror-comic vampire, or one of those teenage heartthrob types." A touch of distaste now in the measured voice. "Hugo has taken an intellectual approach to his anti-hero."

"Brains rather than blood and gore? Sounds interesting."

"It will be."

The doorbell jingled, and a tall, cadaverous man came into the bookshop. He was wearing a black beret, black clothes, and sported a pencil-thin black moustache. The Daliesque persona was not lost on Al Brown, who was brushed aside as though he were invisible.

"Jim! I come bearing glad tidings. Rory has given the go-ahead and we'll start rehearsing out at Château Gastineau at the weekend. Hugo will be rising from his sickbed to join us. Marie has appointed herself his guardian, though I doubt whether even a Gastineau should feel safe in these circumstances."

Salvador Dali laughed, heartily, and Jim Landers did not. He indicated Al and said, "This is one of the policemen involved with the case. Detective Sergeant Brown. I understand we are all to be interviewed.

Raymond has saved you a trip, Sergeant. He's the director of *Blood Play*. Raymond Morris."

Raymond Morris looked startled.

"Good Lord. I suppose we are all suspects. What do you want to know, Sergeant? Where we all were, I imagine. I've directed enough whodunits in my time to know *that*." Raymond Morris gave a let's-share-the-joke smile in Jim Landers's direction, which was not returned.

"And where *were* you, sir?"

The director turned again to Landers.

"Have you seen any ID, Jim? This could be anybody — I know *that* cliché, as well."

Al produced his badge and held it up, slightly closer to Morris's face than was necessary. He was beginning to feel annoyed at being treated as a mildly amusing peasant.

"I'll repeat my question, sir. Where were you when Mr. Shawcross was attacked, which was right after the read-through at the Maxwells'. Did you go straight home? Did you go on anywhere else? Was anyone with you? Or must I just take your word?"

Al watched with interest an exchange of glances between the two men. Raymond Morris looked shaken, and even Jim Landers's calm surface was ruffled.

"We'll have to ask you to come into the station, of course, and make statements."

Raymond Morris spoke first.

"This is a bit awkward, Sergeant. As a matter of fact, Jim had a brief meeting with our treasurer, Douglas Lorrimer, and I had a brief meeting with his wife."

Al couldn't resist.

"Business or pleasure, sir?"

Raymond Morris had regained some of his composure, trying out his light laugh again.

"My only business with Lana is pleasure, and I hope we can keep that between these four walls. Douglas knows I gave Lana a lift while he had his meeting with Jim. Case closed?"

Al ignored the attempted witticism, and turned to Jim Landers, who had withdrawn behind the counter.

"You confirm this, sir? Did you have a meeting with the treasurer?"

"I can. Douglas and I talked budget, and had a drink."

Al turned back to Raymond Morris, who made as if to leave the shop.

"Just before you go, sir, to answer your question. No, the case is far from closed, but what is going on between you and Mrs. Lorrimer is not my business. Not at the moment. All we need is a signed statement from both of you, and that we need between the four walls of Hospital Lane in the next few hours. Okay?"

"Perfect! Will do! Thank you!"

A set of impossibly white teeth gleamed beneath the pencil-thin moustache, the bell jingled and, with a whirling gesture of farewell, Raymond Morris was gone. Behind the bulwark of his counter, Jim Landers was picking up his duster, his face averted. Al Brown held out his purchase.

"Glad you had this." Was it possible, he wondered, to shake that sense of calm withdrawal about this man? Worth a try. "Did you know, Mr. Landers, that you were acting as a kind of a decoy for Mr. Morris?"

Jim Landers looked up from his duster.

"As you yourself said, Sergeant, what is going on between those two is none of my business. I'll be at the station after the shop closes. My assistant cannot be here today. Enjoy your Amis. Good day."

Constable McMullin had a sheaf of papers in his hand and a tentative look on his face, a face so young and unmarked it seemed to Moretti to be a tabula rasa for a life yet to be lived. Even his hair had not yet decided what colour it was going to be when it grew up.

"It's unbelievable, sir, seemed at first like a real stroke of bad luck."

"Tell me about it."

"In the seventies, when the university was changing over from paper records and putting everything onto the computer, there was a massive screw-up. Dozens, possibly hundreds — they're not sure — of student names from the late fifties and into the sixties were either missed or erased, and the paperwork destroyed before the error was found. They made an effort to track down as many as possible, through newsletters and so on, but they still have many missing. They have no record of a Lucy Gastineau, which means nothing, but they do have an Augustus Dorey. He was there, studying history, between 1949 and 1953, graduating with an Upper Second. But not in history. He changed courses and ended up with a law degree."

"So our hermit was probably a lawyer. That should make it easier to trace his career. Anything else?"

"That was about it, but then I thought about clubs."

"Clubs as in stamp collecting, sports?"

"Yes." PC McMullin rustled through his papers and pulled one out. "I thought, people at colleges and things join clubs a lot, don't they, so I asked about club records. Some keep good records, depending on how keen the president and the treasurer and so on were, because sometimes they kept in touch afterwards. Gus Dorey was a member of the Debating Society, and they gave me the name of a couple of members from the time he was there. Of course, they'd be pretty old now."

"Seventies, yes, or more. Go on."

"Well, then it was something the admissions lady said. She said it might be worth trying the Drama Department. They had good records of past productions and that kind of thing. It was important history for them, because Bristol was the first university to open a Drama Department and offer it as a degree course. She said there were all kinds of pictures and photos in the archive. And I got on to this really helpful lady, who did some checking around the same years Gus Dorey was there." PC McMullin gave a little laugh. "She's a bit of a mystery buff and she said it was like looking into a missing persons file. Like a cold case, and she just kept at it. That's why I took so long."

"You haven't taken long, Constable." Moretti could feel his heartbeat accelerate as he saw footprints

on the track ahead of him. "PC Perkins is still out riding the buses. Tell me you found her."

"I found her." PC McMullin was beaming now.
"Well, *we* found her, and she's even emailed me a photo."

Liz Falla walked into Moretti's office to the sound of
laughter. Her Guvnor looked up as she came in, and
gestured towards Police Constable McMullin like a
ringmaster introducing a brand new act.

"Come on in, Falla, and see what McMullin has
dug up from the mists of time."

Liz walked over to the desk and looked down
at a faded photograph, downloaded from an email
attachment. Two men and one woman in what looked
mediaeval costume stood in a semi-circle. The woman
appeared to be addressing the men, and she was laughing as she did so. A very young woman, almost as tall
as the men, slender, laughing. In the faded black-and-
white photo, her long hair, which was coiled up in a
braid around her head, looked dark black against the
whiteness of her skin.

"There she is, Falla, rehearsing in Christopher Fry's
The Lady's Not For Burning. Someone, God bless them,
has written all three names and the name of the play
beneath the photo. "

"Lucy?" Liz ran around the desk to join them, just
as Al Brown came into the office.

"Lucy Gastineau. Gus Dorey's darling."

Chapter Twenty-One

"**H**e's got that."

Al Brown gestured towards the play title written under the image. "Funny how I speak of him in the present, but to me he's very much alive, since I've been living with his library the past few days. I'll go down to storage and take a look through again to see if there's anything of interest. There were so many books I ended up just giving each one a shake for loose papers."

Moretti looked at Falla, and then turned his attention to a still-beaming PC McMullin.

"Well done, Constable. And now I'm going to ask you to do something difficult." McMullin sat forward in his chair. "You are not going to say a single word about your triumph. Delete the email from the computer you used, and keep your mouth shut. No bragging. If the name Lucy Gastineau in conjunction with Bristol University and Gus Dorey gets outside this room, I'll know how."

"Yes, sir." McMullin stood up, clearly disappointed. "Will there be anything else?"

"I'll let you know."

Taking a last look at the photograph as he turned to leave the room, PC McMullin said, "I used to do some acting at school. I really liked it, especially the musicals. Only chorus, but … "

"Did you now? Sit down, Constable."

Moretti was looking at the photo as he spoke, and when he looked up it was at Liz Falla.

"Can you ask your aunt to get PC McMullin into the play, Falla?"

"Ask, Guv?" Liz smiled at the startled constable, who had returned to his seat. "They'd jump at the chance. Always short of men they are."

McMullin was now looking as if he'd just made a killing on the football pools.

"I'd be your mole, sir?"

"Got it in one, Constable. DS Falla will let you know as soon as she hears it's a go."

"Do I pretend not to be on the force, sir?"

"Absolutely not. Keep the acting onstage. You will be exactly who you are, a stage-struck copper called — Bob, isn't it?"

"Yessir!"

Moretti waited until the Island Players newest thespian had left the room, then turned back to Falla.

"He used his initiative about the Bristol enquiries, thought for himself, so it's worth a try. When you brief him, Falla, talk to him about Charles Priestley. He's not that much older than the golden boy, and might be able to strike up some sort of friendship with him. But stress the fact that he's there to observe, and to listen, not to ask leading questions. I don't want PC McMullin ending up like Shawcross. He might not be so lucky."

Moretti looked at Al. "So how did you get along with the man of few words at WORDS?"

Al Brown grinned. "I'll start off with the juicy stuff, shall I? Jim Landers's alibi is the treasurer, Douglas Lorrimer, and the director's alibi is the treasurer's wife."

Al Brown filled in the details, interrupted only by the tapping sound of Moretti's pen against the black-and-white photo on the desk.

"So there's hanky-panky. Par for the course, I'd say, and probably nothing to do with anything relevant to the case. Falla, I'm sending you to interview Lana Lorrimer, and to handle it with your usual tact and delicacy. In other words, play it by ear."

"I'll try girls-together first, see what happens, Guv."

"And now let's talk about Meg the gypsy."

"And Billie the Bus Bum?" Al asked. Moretti nodded.

"Billie knows everything about the island's gypsies — and I don't mean the Roma, but the roamers, because he's one himself. But, unlike Meg, Billie has a set pattern, taking a specific route one day, and another the next. Meg drifts, but if anyone knows where she is at the moment, Billie will."

Moretti got up and crossed to the window. No fog-horns today, but a light rain was beginning to fall, and he would probably hear them during the night. Music drifted into his mind, nothing unusual about that. *Someone to watch over me.* His back was towards the room as he started to speak.

"My mother knew Meg the gypsy. Margie, she called her. But she only knew her after the war, when she was involved in some children's welfare outfit. Margie needed help of all kinds, and resisted most. She ran away from home and was taken back, only to run away again. She usually turned up around the Pleinmont Common area, and her home was on the road that runs behind the Imperial Hotel. At that time, it was a farm, with outhouses and some greenhouses, and was falling to bits. Her father was a drunkard, and her mother kept the family's income going by sleeping with the enemy. Or so they said. I'm a bit vague over the details, but both parents died when Meg was in her late teens, which would be around about the mid-fifties, and left Meg a property owner. She lived in squalor in the place, visited from time to time by social services. Then, when the island started to make money with money, the property became valuable, and parts of it were sold off, including the eighteenth-century farmhouse."

Moretti came back into the room and sat down again.

"I remember my mother saying to my father, 'How did little Margie do it?' And I think we now know how. Gus Dorey the lawyer did it, set it all up for her. I'll put

Bernie Mauger on to that. I've got him checking out Hugo Shawcross at the moment."

"That would be when Dorey came back in the nineties?" Al interjected.

"Couldn't have been. Had to be earlier than that. My mother died in the early eighties."

It was Moretti who broke the silence that followed.

"So there was contact between Meg the gypsy and Gus the hermit before he built his roundhouse. We already knew that from what she told Al about being rescued from the tower, but that must have been before he went away to university. There seems to have been another, quite lengthy period of contact, if it involved setting up the farm sale, and Meg kept quiet about that. And there would have been a bond between them. Both had a parent who consorted with the enemy."

Moretti stood up, stretching his arms above his head.

"I don't know about the two of you, but I'm more than ready for a very late lunch. Then, Al, I want you to visit Doug Lorrimer, and check out both his and Jim Landers's alibi."

Liz picked up her jacket and slung her small purse across her shoulders. The expression in her eyes took Moretti by surprise, and disconcerted him. Not humour, or anger, or even that insouciance with which his partner so often handled life's difficult moments. It looked uncomfortably like tenderness.

But all she said was, "What will you be doing, Guv?"

Relieved, he replied, "Later I'm going to talk to someone from the *Guernsey Press*, but right now,

Falla, I am going to look for a little lamb who's lost in the wood."

Moretti took the Triumph for this trip, because he was sure to get parking near the Imperial Hotel at this time of the year, after the departure of the summer visitors. The light rain had stopped, the morning mist had lifted, and the sky was clearing as he drove out to the southwest coast of the island.

He parked the car by the curved sea wall opposite the hundred-year-old hotel, got out, and felt the sea air against his face, filling his lungs with its freshness and lifting his spirits. He took a moment to look out over the curve of coastline stretching towards Rocquaine Bay, the occasional wayward wave hitting his face. The tide was high, the water slapping against the wall, and in the distance a shaft of sunlight caught the bright white cylindrical top of Fort Grey on its promontory. Originally known as the Château de Rocquaine, and now called the cup and saucer by the locals, not all of the site's incarnations had been military. According to one island history, it had in the past been associated with "the unholy revels of the witches."

Unholy revels. Meg the gypsy had, in the past, run into some unpleasantness with creeps who branded her a witch for their own amusement, but the intimations of unholy revels in this case had nothing to do with her, and everything to do with someone in the Island Players' coterie.

Moretti reluctantly turned away from the sea and the shore and started up the hill beside the hotel. To his left was a terrace of houses and beyond them more homes scattered along the coastline. To his right, the road was bordered with thick undergrowth, hedges and trees, and not far to the south was Pleinmont Common, much of it now owned by the Société Guernesiaise, and maintained as the island's largest nature reserve. When Meg the gypsy wandered from her home to return to the place where she had found happiness, she was unlikely to run into too many people, particularly at night, even in the height of the season.

But that was only when she was at the farm and, from her conversation with Al at the roundhouse, Moretti had the feeling she was aware of the danger to her of "the other one." Like most wild creatures, she had a well-developed sixth sense, and a strong instinct for self-preservation. Al Brown could attest to that.

"Farm" was an inaccurate description of the collection of buildings that came into view around the next corner. To the left of a wide, curving driveway between four-foot high white-painted brick walls stood the original farmhouse, its ancient stone walls lovingly preserved, but other than that, very few changes had been made to the exterior. To the right of the driveway stood a building that must have once served as the barn for the livestock, or as a place of storage for crops. Around this solid brick structure, the wall rose abruptly to about six feet in height, with a set of steps leading down to the lower level. Moretti walked around the outside of the building, which had no windows facing the road.

"Can I help you?"

At the bottom of the driveway stood a woman holding on to the collar of a large dog of uncertain breed, but of far from uncertain ill-humour. As Moretti turned back and made as if to move toward them, it showed an impressive set of teeth and growled, deep in its ample throat. Moretti stood still and slowly removed his police badge from his pocket.

"Detective Inspector Moretti. I wanted to either have a few words with Meg or speak to someone about her. It might affect her safety."

"You're here about Meg. Eduardo, right? Relax, Darcy."

Darcy relaxed, thumping heavily to the ground by his mistress's feet with a groan, as if the effort to be ferocious had exhausted him.

"You know me?" No surprise on this island, but the woman's use of his Italian name was. He couldn't quite place her accent. English, yes, sounds of a privileged upbringing in it, but there was something different in the lilt, a softening of the "t" when she said "about" and "right."

"I know your mother's old friend, Gwen. She lives not very far from here."

"Of course. But she always calls me Edward."

"Nonetheless, I know the story."

Darcy's owner was above average height, and looked to be in her sixties, although Moretti found judging age more difficult the older he got, for some reason. Her salt and pepper hair surrounded a strong-featured face and a pair of sharp blue eyes behind heavy-framed glasses. She was dressed in loose garments that flowed around her and looked handwoven rather than mass-produced, and something about them reminded Moretti of Al's description of Meg's clothing. Around her neck was a heavy silver chain with a chunk of amber hanging from it the size of a hen's egg. She too was wearing heavy boots, unlaced, as if she had pulled them on when seeing him outside.

"I think you'd better come in. I haven't seen Meg for a day or two. Not too unusual before. But now that Gus Dorey is gone, a bit worrying."

As he followed her, Moretti looked around the yard. There was nothing much in it, no decorative display of plants in pots, or flowerbeds. A tractor was parked at the far end of the property.

"Is this still a working farm?" Moretti indicated the tractor.

"No, hasn't been for years. I let Roland Le Tissier park that back there. He's sold off so much land he's not much room left, and he clings to that tractor as if maybe one day the greenhouses will rise again."

"Not likely."

She didn't respond, but opened the door and let him and Darcy inside.

Moretti walked into a large high-ceilinged room, in the centre of which was a loom, surrounded by baskets of wool, giant skeins of all colours. A half-finished piece hung suspended on the loom in colours of the autumn, golds, browns, some red. There was the smell of sandalwood in the air, and alongside the loom was a round table with sticks of incense burning in a brass censor. The working area was brightly lit by two standard lamps of industrial rather than ornamental design.

"Sit down, Inspector." She indicated a couple of teak chairs near the table. "I had just made chai tea when I saw you outside from my kitchen window. Like some?"

"I'd love some."

His hostess kicked off her boots by the door and Darcy lay down beside them. She disappeared beyond one of two doors on the side of the room furthest from the road, and was soon back holding two glasses in handled silver holders, the scent of cinnamon now joining the sandalwood in the air. She sat herself down and raised her glass to Moretti.

"Cheers," she said. "Let's get down to business, shall we? That —" indicating the work on the loom, "is a commission piece and time is a-wasting. For you too, I imagine."

"Yes." The tea was delicious. "Let's start with your name."

"I didn't introduce myself? Goodness, my mother must be turning in her grave. Maud Cole. How do you do."

She extended her hand. She had a strong grip.

"How long have you known Meg? Is that what you call her?"

"It's what she likes to be called. She was here before I was, of course, and we took to each other from the beginning."

"How long have you been here and, forgive my asking, but do you own or rent the farm?"

"I own it. I got a good price on it, because few people wanted it with Meg on the premises."

"Do you know if Gus Dorey was involved in any way in arranging legal matters for Meg?"

Maud Cole looked surprised. "Didn't you know that? Yes, he was, originally. I didn't deal with him, because by the time I came here, he had withdrawn into his hermit-crab existence, and everything was done through the law firm of Allan and Le Page."

"Did Meg ever talk about her friendship with Gus Dorey? About anything he owned that was private, or precious, or about signing papers for him — anything?"

Maud Cole appeared irritated at Moretti's question. "The secret of our successful relationship was that we never asked leading questions, and we never exchanged confidences. I am somewhat of a loner and so is she. I come from a family of eccentrics, which, in the case of some of them, is a polite way of saying they were barmpots. Meg, by the way, is not."

"Certainly she appears to have her wits about her, and I know something of her history. I'll fill you in on the events that brought me here looking for her."

Take a chance, tell her.

Maud Cole listened in silence, leaning forward, cradling her glass in her strong hands.

"So she could be in real trouble. I wish I could help you more. What do you want me to do?"

"Do you have a mobile?"

Maud Cole was amused at the implication in his question. "Yes, of necessity, because of my clientele, but not by choice."

"Let me know anything that happens, day or night, however slight it may seem — someone around you don't normally see, sounds in the night, that kind of thing. And, of course, let me know if and when Meg turns up again. Perhaps you could lend her Darcy at night."

Maud Cole was amused again. "He's an old dog, but his bite can be just as bad as his bark. Meg loves him, and that's a possibility. She's not very good about locking her door at night."

"Might I take a look at her place?"

"If Darcy and I are with you, I don't think she'd mind."

Darcy led the way across the yard, and bounded into the door of Meg the gypsy's home. Inside, he sniffed around, then sank to the floor, watching his owner.

"Would he react if anyone else had been here?"

"Pretty sure he would. It all looks in order."

In order it was. The place was neat and tidy, and it looked as if Meg used this room for everything other than sleeping. There was a large, comfortable sofa, a table and a chair, a small fridge, a stove and a sink. In one corner was a sizeable laundry tub and ironing board, with an iron on it. The laundry lady's accoutrements.

"She used to live in squalor, I believe. What happened?"

"I happened. People tried to tidy her up, corral her, fit her into some acceptable frame — for them. I accepted her eccentricities and the rest fell into place."

Outside, the light was dimming as evening approached. Darcy rolled on to his back and started to snore lightly. Moretti thought, *How my mother would have liked this woman.*

"Forgive my asking, but your accent, I can't place it."

"Irish Ascendancy, that's what you hear, Inspector. The sound of privilege and oppression, inbreeding and entitlement." Maud Cole laid a hand gently on the arm of Meg the gypsy's sofa and stroked it. "I think part of my desire to help Meg is a sort of atonement for the sins of my forefathers. War reparations, if you like."

"I'm glad she has you in her life, Ms. Cole."

Ms. Cole started to laugh.

"Miss, please. Miss I will always be. By choice. I named Darcy for my favourite literary hero, and he is the only male being who will ever live under the same roof as me. He is unsexed, you see."

Not just atonement. Meg and Maud share other miseries in their very different pasts.

Maud Cole opened the door to leave, and Darcy and Moretti followed her.

Chapter Twenty-Two

Lana Lorrimer was available for interview, but could the detective sergeant come out to see her, because coming into town was inconvenient that afternoon. Or she could come in to the station tomorrow. The detective sergeant didn't mind in the least, because she could give her Figaro a run in the autumn sunshine out to St. Martin — one of her favourite parishes on the island, and where she intended to live when she won the lottery.

Following the directions given her by Lana Lorrimer, Liz's journey took her past Sausmarez Manor, the stately home of one of the great island families, now open to the public and turned into a stately pleasure dome. There were manor and garden tours, radio-controlled boats on the lake, tea rooms, trains, and you could pitch and putt, or take a ghost tour. So far, the Gastineau family had been spared becoming a three-ring circus, but for how long?

The light rain had now cleared, so Liz risked putting down the roof, and enjoyed herself so much it was with regret she found herself at Lana Lorrimer's front door. Or, rather, at the front of the Lorrimers' property, an elegant limestone house set far back from the road behind a lawn showing signs of the summer drought. There was no front door visible from the road, only four windows on the upper and lower stories, framed by neatly-trimmed ivy on the ground floor.

The driveway led up towards a conservatory that was obviously a new addition, not an unusual one for the present-day owners of the island's beautiful old homes. The garage alongside it was of the same vintage as the house and looked as if it had originally been the stables. No cars were visible, so presumably they were tucked away behind the pseudo-wood garage door set in the rose-pink brickwork.

As Liz parked her Figaro, Lana Lorrimer came out of the door of the conservatory to meet her. She was a curvaceous, slightly overweight, blonde in her late forties, carefully made-up, wearing harem pants in green silk and a low-cut black blouse that effectively showcased two of her assets.

"Love the car. Cute. Yours?"

"Mine." Liz got the impression from the eyebrow raised that Mrs. Lorrimer found her ownership of the cute car improbable and possibly suspect. She took out her police ID. "Detective Sergeant Falla, Mrs. Lorrimer. This shouldn't take up too much of your time. I know you had something on this afternoon."

"Something on?" Lana Lorrimer now looked defensive for no immediately apparent reason.

Liz put away her badge, pulled out her notebook and smiled, disarmingly, she hoped. "You couldn't come to the station, so I assumed you might have visitors. Where can we talk?"

"In here."

Lana Lorrimer led the way back into the conservatory, which appeared to be set up for a party or reception of some kind. Amid the palms, ferns and tropical plants were two or three long tables covered in white cloths, each one decorated with an elaborate floral display. On one of them was the tallest fountain Liz had ever seen in a private home, awaiting its chocolate waterfall.

"Looks like you are celebrating something special, Mrs. Lorrimer."

"Oh we are." Lana Lorrimer became animated. "We — that is, the Island Players — are celebrating Hugo's miraculous recovery tonight. But that's why you're here."

"That's why I'm here, and why I need you to confirm what we have been told by —" Liz appeared to consult her notebook, "Mr. Raymond Morris —"

"That he gave me a lift home while my husband talked over some financial stuff with Jim Landers. Yes, he did."

Decision time. To be mean, or not to be mean.

Remembering the raised eyebrow, and abandoning the girls-together approach as unworkable with the lady of the manor, Liz said, "A little more than that,

Mrs. Lorrimer. How generally is it known that you and Mr. Morris are having an affair?"

"Oh my God, what does that have to do with anything?" Lana Lorrimer became both agitated and hostile, her face turning red beneath her tan. "I cannot understand why Raymond felt it necessary to say anything about anything! Apart from the lift, that is."

Reverting again to cheerful, Liz suggested, "I assume, Mrs. Lorrimer, because it would give him an alibi for a longer period of time than just dropping you off here. Obviously, Mr. Morris's version of events would be more than just a car ride. Are you confirming his story?"

"Yes." Lana Lorrimer sank into a massive papasan chair that threatened to engulf her, and she was not a small woman. "Jim Landers knows, but that's all. We take advantage of his meetings with Douglas."

"What's in it for Mr. Landers, Mrs. Lorrimer? How can you be certain he'll keep quiet?"

Lana Lorrimer started to laugh.

"Jim Landers? Jim's only passion is books and all he cares about otherwise is getting on stage, and if he said anything about Raymond and me he'd never act in a Raymond Morris production again. He's one cold fish, so he gets on really well with my husband, who has as little passion in *his* soul as — as — a piece of *wood*."

It was quite an outburst, eyes flashing, bosom quivering, and there was genuine anger in Lana Lorrimer's voice. Liz put her notebook away, waited a moment, and was rewarded with another outpouring, delivered in more measured tones.

"You may be asking yourself why I stick around with a stick. Look around you, Sergeant, and you can see why. If I leave Douglas, I lose all this. Raymond has sacrificed advancement in his career for his love of theatre. He says I am his muse, and in his opinion, and mine, muses do better with smoked salmon and love in the afternoon than sardines on toast in a bed-sit in the evening."

The passion with which Lana Lorrimer talked about her love affair seemed more theatrical than real, unlike the passion with which she spoke about her husband.

"Mrs. Lorrimer — do you have any idea why Hugo Shawcross was attacked? Was there anyone who appeared hostile, or made any verbal threats? He was a newcomer — how was he received by the group?"

"With open arms." Lana Lorrimer laughed. "We were in a rut and we needed a new audience, and Hugo's play would have got us out of our rut and into more money. Even Marie had been won over. Why on earth this happened is beyond me. I can only think that Hugo was followed here by someone or something —" Her voice trailed off.

"What do you mean?"

Lana Lorrimer looked bemused by her own comment. "I had the feeling Hugo was here to get away from something, but I don't know what. Raymond felt the same way."

"What is Mr. Morris's day job, Mrs. Lorrimer?"

"Day job? Oh, he works in Doug's office. He's so good at putting on an act with the clients. Soul-destroying, but necessary. Besides, it has its advantages.

He knows where Doug is most of the time, and he knows — well, he knows what properties are vacant."

On which depressingly practical note from the muse about her grand passion, Liz took her leave.

It was only on her way back to St. Peter Port that Liz remembered something Elodie had said when they were talking about the Island Players, and about Jim Landers's behaviour towards her.

We went out to dinner a couple of times. But he wanted more.

Didn't sound like much of a cold fish to Liz Falla.

The offices of Maxwell and Lorrimer Estate Agents were on a small slice of a street between a large car park and Government House Hotel, one of the premier establishments on the island. Before going in, Al Brown stopped to look at some of the properties in the window. Some were breathtaking and all were top-drawer, ranging from multi-million-pound estates to "little gems" that cost a mere handful of hundred-thousands.

When he opened the door and walked in, he got quite a surprise. Raymond Morris was sitting behind a desk in the front office and, from the look on his face, Al's arrival was a little more fist in the solar plexus than surprise. His white skin went whiter, and he took an intake of breath that rocked his chair. Before he could speak, Al put one finger to his lips, putting him out of his misery, then announced in carrying tones the reason for his appearance.

"I am here to interview Mr. Lorrimer. He's expecting me."

On cue, Douglas Lorrimer appeared at a door at the back of the office.

"Are you the policeman who phoned?"

"I am, sir. Detective Constable Aloisio Brown."

"Come in, come in. Raymond, let me know if Mr. Gupta calls about the Kubla Khan, won't you."

After which cryptic remark and a nod from his wife's lover, Douglas Lorrimer ushered Al into as splendid an office as he had ever entered. The furniture had certainly never seen the inside of an Ikea flatpack, and the wall panelling and flooring were in a matching tone of genuine wood, not some look-alike man-made substitute. There were two paintings on the walls, both of houses — one centuries-old manor, one Frank Lloyd Wright-like construction — that were not paint-by-numbers, run-of-the-mill reproductions. They had verve and style, and Al liked them. Through a large window overlooking the town beyond the buildings that descended towards the harbour, Al could see they were in for a beautiful evening after the rain.

The only other accessory was a dark-haired, middle-aged woman sitting at her own small desk by a computer screen, who stood up as they came in and said to her boss, "Would you like me to make coffee, Mr. Lorrimer?"

"No, Grace, not necessary. This is not a client. Just leave us a moment."

In the manner of an obedient geisha, with eyes down, Grace shuffled past Al into the outer office.

"Sit down, sit down. You've come about where I was when Hugo was attacked, I presume, but I gather Jim Landers has already answered that question."

Small in stature, bristly in manner, surly in speech. Not much he could do about the inches, but Al wondered what Lorrimer's client-face was like. Operating at this level, it had to be very different. He decided to match the manner presented to the insignificant copper.

"But *you* haven't, sir, and I need to hear from you personally that you corroborate Mr. Landers's version of events." Al took out his notebook, and waited, pen poised.

"Version of events? I'm sure he told you what I am going to tell you, that we discussed financial matters — of the Island Players, that is."

"That is what he told me. At his flat on the Strand. For about an hour, would you say?"

"About that. We had a drink, then I drove home."

"And your colleague, Mr. Morris, gave your wife a lift home, I understand."

Al carefully watched the expression on Douglas Lorrimer's face, but found it impossible to read. He looked much as he had since the interview began: impatient and inconvenienced.

"That's right. Then they could chatter on about things that bore the pants off me."

"The arts, do you mean, sir?" Al asked, giving a moment's amused thought to the imagery.

"That's what I mean."

"Have you any theory as to why Mr. Shawcross was attacked?"

"Theory?" Douglas Lorrimer looked as affronted as if he had been asked to attend a *soirée musicale*. "There are all sorts of crazies and unbalanced people attracted to these sorts of groups, aren't there? You read about it in the press all the time, don't you? And now, I have an important meeting at Government House Hotel, if you've finished, Constable."

"About Kubla Khan, sir? Sounds intriguing."

"*The* Kubla Khan." Douglas Lorrimer's expression changed now into one of self-congratulation. "Yes. I am making a move into the more commercial realm, and I am discussing opening a major centre at St. Sampson's, starting with an Indian restaurant — high-end, of course."

"Of course. Will you be calling the centre Xanadu, by any chance?"

Not the least suspicion of a smile crossed the estate agent's face. "We will. I am told that has something to do with pleasure domes, and if the States of Guernsey will co-operate, Mr. Gupta and I are planning to open a casino."

Al Brown looked around. "I understand you are in partnership with Elton Maxwell, sir. Do you share the same office?"

Douglas Lorrimer looked horrified. "Good God, no. Elton generally works from home, but spends a great deal of time out with clients, particularly inter-national financial firms and banks et cetera. Raymond takes care of the more run-of-the-mill stuff. He's particularly good with the distaff side of the *nouveau riche*." It was said without any discernible expression, either of humour or scorn.

At that moment the phone on the massive desk rang, and Douglas Lorrimer picked it up, saying, "That'll be my client. Good day, officer. Ask my secretary to come back, will you, on your way out."

Al Brown let himself out of the office, and passed on her master's instructions to Grace, who slipped by him on her silent feet, eyes averted. Behind him, Al heard Douglas Lorrimer's professional voice, an unsavoury blend of booming volume to suggest command, with underlying tones of glutinous boot-licking.

"Deepak! Are you already there? I'm on my way with a little more good news than I had before — yes — no — yes —"

In the outer office, Raymond Morris greeted Al Brown with the words, "He's lying, of course. It's never going to happen."

It was said in muted tones, heavily laced with distaste and malice.

"The casino?"

"Right. Not where he wants to put it, anyway. There are some palms that will never be greased."

Before he could say anything more, Douglas Lorrimer bustled through without a glance at either minion and was out the door.

Something about Raymond Morris's apparent invisibility left Al Brown with the feeling that Douglas Lorrimer knew exactly what was going on between his wife and his colleague and didn't give a

damn. Just another conquest of the distaff side of the
nouveau riche.

It had been a long meeting at Hospital Lane, going
over the events of the day with Moretti and Al, and
comparing notes. There was now an elaborate official procedure that had to happen with notes gathered and, by the time Liz Falla got back to her flat
on the second floor of one of the eighteenth-century
row houses on the Esplanade, the light was dissolv-
ing into dusk over the islands of Herm and Jethou
beyond the bay. The tide was coming back in, and a
large white heron was fishing from the still-exposed
rocks. She admired him for a moment, the purity of
his outline, like a Japanese print, his utter absorption
in the task, then put on some music: a collection of
twentieth-century string pieces, starting with Bartok.
The disc would finish with Stravinsky. She had been
introduced to this music that had been outside her
realm of experience by a woman she had met on an
earlier case.

   Listen to it a few times. Then it lets you in.
   It had.
   Liz poured herself a glass of red wine, sat down on
her sofa and curled her legs up beneath her, kicking off
her shoes. On the table in front of her was her mobile.
She drank most of the glass of wine, listened to the
Bartok Divertimento, and mulled things over. As the
piece finished, she stopped the disc and picked up her

phone. Her aunt screened most of her calls but, on this occasion, she answered the phone.

"Elodie? It's Liz."

"We must be on the same wavelength. I was just going to phone you."

Elodie sounded rushed, or possibly tense. Hardly surprising, given recent events.

"Something wrong?"

"Not really, but you tell me first what you were phoning about, or were you just — phoning."

"More specific than that. I wanted to ask you if you were planning to go to the Hugo Shawcross shindig tonight."

"You know about that?"

"I was there this afternoon to check on Mrs. Lorrimer's alibi. And that's why I probably shouldn't be making this call. Nothing wrong with her alibi, but I'm probably crossing a line."

"Yes, I'm going. I was asked to bring the wounded hero, but I demurred. The Gastineaus are doing that, and Jim Landers has offered to take me. I wish I could accept his offer, but in the circumstances —"

"You don't want to get his hopes up."

"Right." There was a laugh at the other end of the line. "And I passed on Bob the copper's name to him."

"Thanks. I'll take you, drop you off, and we'll prearrange a pick-up time. No point in saying no, Elodie, because I'll be there, and if I have to come in, I'll be in trouble with my Guvnor."

"No need, Liz, and that's why I was going to call you, to find out if you knew or if this was your doing."

"What was?"

"It's your Guvnor who's giving me a ride, that's what."

Outside the window the heron stretched his wings, took a firm grasp on the fish he held in his beak, and flew away into the evening sky.

Chapter Twenty-Three

A s Elodie Ashton came down the driveway, Moretti could see she was laughing. It disconcerted him, and he was already feeling disconcerted.

"Good evening, Ed. Sorry to keep you waiting, but that was Liz on the phone, offering me a lift to and from the party. A bit like being a teenager again, with anxious parents."

Moretti felt a twinge of anxiety.

"What did she say?"

Moretti opened the door of the Triumph, and Elodie got in. She was dressed casually, not in her best party dress, as he thought she might be, but in slim-fitting jeans with some sort of sparkly belt, and a plain white blouse under a denim jacket. Her curly red hair looked darker at night. The wind was getting up and, as he got into the driver's seat, a strand of hair blew against his face, smelling of mint and lime. But it could have been from one of the ornamental bushes close to the car.

"She said she was watching a heron and listening to Bartok and she'd go and join Dwight and someone called Al for a jam session at the club."

This time he felt a twinge of envy.

"She's good, isn't she — Liz?" Elodie fastened her seatbelt. "At her job, I mean."

"Very."

Moretti started the Triumph and backed down the driveway on to the road. As he moved up through the gears he said, "You two obviously took after different strands of DNA in your family. You couldn't be more dissimilar in looks — colouring, height and so on."

There was silence for a moment, then Elodie said, laughter gone from her voice, "I know. It's a mystery I'll look into one day."

"Care to elaborate?"

"Not much to elaborate, Ed, but here's the thing. I'm a scientist by training, and I work with top scientists in what I do. It's my red hair that's the mystery. All those Norman-French genes, and no one in memory living or dead with red hair. That's the mystery."

"I'm assuming it's a recessive gene, so it's possible, isn't it?"

"Possible, but not probable. Under 2 percent of the population have red hair, higher in the United States."

It had seemed a reasonably harmless topic of conversation, but clearly it was not.

"Sorry."

"Don't be. I've been meaning to deal with this, but haven't felt like doing so yet." Alongside him in the passenger seat he felt Elodie turn towards him. The fragrance of mint and lime was not from the ornamental bushes. "Now you, for instance, take after your Italian father, don't you?"

"So I'm told. But as I grow older, I see my mother in my face."

"And I don't. See mine, I mean. Not a word to Liz about this."

They had arrived just outside the Lorrimers' place, and Moretti stopped the Triumph on the road, from where he could watch her walk up to the house, but not be seen too clearly by any of the guests who were turning into the driveway.

"Take care tonight. No stepping outside for a breath of fresh air. And you're carrying a phone, of course."

"Of course. I've got you on speed-dial."

"If I haven't heard from you by our pre-arranged time I'll be here, knocking at the door. Which I really don't want to do. Some of your fellow thespians have a direct line to my boss."

"You sound just like my niece, only in Liz's version you were the ogre."

They both laughed, and Moretti regretted the journey hadn't taken longer.

As she got out of the car, Elodie called back, "And another thing — I'm the only Ashton alive or dead who can't hold a tune."

Moretti watched her walk across the lawn towards a large conservatory attached to the house, and wished he could join Falla and the others at the Grand Saracen, but he didn't want to risk it. Elodie would only have to make a call if there was an emergency, and if he was playing, he'd never hear it. So, better head for home.

She intrigued him, this solitary, sociable woman with her secrets, and now the mystery of her red hair. If it was a mystery. He had not said too much at the meeting with Falla and Al, but he felt Elodie was at risk because she had been so close to a killer. In fact, she was the reason that Hugo Shawcross had survived, not just because she had applied a tourniquet, but because she had interrupted a murderer who had been unable to finish the job. He had moderated his comments for Falla's sake, but clearly she felt the same way.

What was it Al Brown had said about game-playing and fantasy?

The modus operandi may differ, but the fantasy is always the same.

What was the fantasy? Why Hugo Shawcross? He said he had unleashed the powers of evil, but they had already been unleashed on the hermit of Pleinmont, Gus Dorey, and that was not just the evil act of someone getting his — or her — jollies. That was malice aforethought. And, somewhere in the middle of it all was the half-century-ago relationship between Gus Dorey and Lucy Gastineau, he was sure of it.

Half a century ago, a love affair. Dangerous in those days, before the pill, before the days of safe sex and free love, when making love led to making babies.

Babies.

Moretti heard Falla's voice in his head.

Importance of Being Ernest. Sort of fluffy. Not a great love story or anything.

But a story about an abandoned baby, in a handbag.

The champagne was flowing, as was the chocolate fountain, and in the middle of the conservatory sat the guest of honour in a high-backed rattan chair, a black kerchief around his neck. He had, not surprisingly, lost weight, and was looking frail, with dark circles under his eyes. He was drinking champagne through a straw, with Marie Gastineau hovering protectively at his elbow.

"Greetings, Elodie! Now all the usual suspects are here!"

Lana Lorrimer, swathed in scarlet satin, swam tipsily towards her through the undergrowth holding out a glass of champagne.

From what Elodie could see among the palm trees, most of the usual suspects were indeed there. The group's membership expanded and contracted, but when an event like this was held all the hangers-on turned up, from the occasional scene-shifters and the sporadic program-sellers to the overabundance of women who appeared at audition time. But there were as yet some people missing, most notably Rory and Tanya Gastineau. She could see Ginny talking to Elton Maxwell, and they appeared not to be at each other's throats for once. Misery loving company, she supposed. She had heard on the grapevine that neither of them wanted the show to go on.

She took the proffered glass and gave Lana the customary peck on the cheek usually exchanged by female members of the group. Over Lana's shoulder she saw the beautiful newcomer, Charles Priestley, talking to another newcomer. Good. Jim Landers had got Bob the mole in on the festivities.

"Thanks, Lana. Everything looks wonderful. I must go and have a word with Hugo. How does he seem?"

"Wonderfully brave, a real trouper."

Lana waved her now empty glass in Hugo's direction and made her unsteady way towards Jim Landers and Raymond Morris, who were talking with some earnestness by the chocolate fountain. As Elodie watched, her hostess pushed Jim Landers aside with her hip and a giggle, grabbed a supernaturally large strawberry from the fruit plate and dipped it in chocolate. She then turned and ate it in two bites, all the time her eyes on Raymond Morris, who paid her no attention whatsoever.

"Elodie."

Aaron Gaskell, holding a glass in one hand and a dark red rose in the other, was by her side.

"Aaron, I didn't see you behind the — whatever it is."

"Philodendron, I think. The biggest philodendron in the world. This is for you, courtesy of the smallest rosebush in this monument to grandiosity. You have a buttonhole in that jacket that cries out for a boutonnière. Here, let me."

Elodie shrank back as he touched her jacket, but he took no advantage of the moment, inserting the flower swiftly and deftly.

"Thank you. Now I really must go and say hello to Hugo. Have you spoken to him yet?"

"No. I'll come with you and pay my respects."

They made their way through the throng. The sound level was increasing exponentially with the drink level and, in competition with the muzak, it was difficult to carry on any kind of a conversation anymore. Whether the plant world was responding to stress, or it was just the increasing warmth in the space, the smell of vegetation was growing stronger, it seemed to Elodie. From one corner of the conservatory came shrieks of laughter from Marla Maxwell amidst a cacophony of maidens. En route, they were waylaid by black-and-white-clad servers, offering prawns and pâté and tiny perfect pastries. Elodie took a salmon-filled *bouchée*, popped it into her mouth, and regretted not taking two. Lana always had the very best caterers for her *soirées*.

"Aaaah."

A strangled cry greeted her from the guest of honour, and Elodie flinched. Hugo sounded very much as he had — How many days ago was it? She had forgotten, put it out of her mind — until now. He stretched out his arms towards her and stood up to greet her.

"My saviour!"

His voice was hoarse and weak, but he was talking, and it was good to hear.

Suddenly, Elodie felt close to tears. She had not imagined that seeing Hugo would take her back to that night, and her reaction took her by surprise. She must have shown something of her feelings because, by her side, Aaron Gaskell gently took her by the elbow.

"Hugo, it's wonderful to see you."

What to say in the circumstances was difficult — "how are you" seemed grotesquely inadequate — but she was spared finding the words by Marie Maxwell, who never liked being upstaged.

"*Isn't* he wonderful! And he's even started writing again, haven't you, Hugo?"

Hugo nodded and winced. "Work on Act Two, almost finished," he rasped.

"That's good," said Elodie. "Has Rory confirmed when we can start?"

"I don't see them here," said Aaron Gaskell, looking around. "Or are they concealed behind one of the Lorrimers' giant *arecaceae*?"

Marie did not look amused, but she certainly looked annoyed.

"Yes, it's confirmed, and no, they're not here yet. I imagine Tanya wants to make an entrance."

At that moment the door that led into the house opened, and there stood Rory and Tanya Gastineau. What Rory was wearing was, as usual, somehow rumpled and instantly forgettable, providing an effective foil for his wife. Continuing her Marilyn look-alike theme, her blonde hair skilfully tousled, she was dressed in a gown reminiscent of something out of *Gentlemen Prefer Blondes*, clinging to every curve, shining ivory in the lamplight. She smiled radiantly at the assembled Island Players.

"Sorry we're so late," she said in her little-girl voice. "Rory couldn't decide what to wear."

She giggled, and so did most of the people in the conservatory. Even Rory gave a sheepish grin.

By Elodie's side, Aaron Gaskell observed quietly, "Probably some truth in that. She will have known *exactly* what she was wearing from the moment the email arrived." It was said without malice and some amusement.

Marie Maxwell was not laughing, and neither was her sister. Ginnie Purvis moved away from Elton Maxwell and went over to stand by Jim Landers, who acknowledged her presence with a faint smile and a slight shift of his body away from her.

From her place of honour beside Hugo, Marie called out, "Come in, both of you, and say something to Hugo. *He* is our guest of honour. I'm going to ask Douglas, as our host, to make the toast — Douglas."

Douglas Lorrimer looked as if this had come as an unwelcome surprise. He gestured at one of the servers for a refill of his glass, scowled at his wife who was ineffectively hushing her guests, then silenced everyone with an angry bellow.

"Ladies and gentlemen! Marie has asked me to make the toast and I will not disobey orders." Nervous laughter. "As most of you know, I am not entirely in the pro-performance camp, but suffice to say I am completely in the anti-garrotting camp!"

Stunned silence, as Douglas gave a huge guffaw at his own joke. Unfazed, he went on, "So, Hugo, let's raise our glasses to your return to the land of the living and to the success of your play about the land of the undead!"

Douglas raised his glass, followed by the shell-shocked Island Players, and there were murmurs of "Yes — Hugo — here's to Hugo."

Lana Lorrimer looked as if she were about to cry. Elodie felt a wild desire to laugh.

"Does he always behave like this?" whispered Aaron Gaskell.

"Has been known to, yes. I've never been sure if he lacks a filter, or whether he does it to annoy —"

"Because he knows it teases? His wife, in particular?"

"Possibly."

The moment passed, with everyone returning to their glasses or their flirtations, or their plates of food. A space had been cleared in one corner of the conservatory, and a few of the younger members had started to dance. Elodie wanted to get her mobile out of the little pouch she carried on her belt, but knew that, if she did so, Aaron Gaskell would offer her a lift home.

It was tempting, she had to admit, because she liked him. But she really knew nothing about him — whether there was an ex-wife in the wings, or a current one waiting for him on the mainland, for instance — and she didn't want another Jim Landers episode. Jim was still cool with her after her rejection, and although he was cool with most people, there was something in his attitude towards her that was — well, different — from his usual indifference. Just as she was planning to use a trip to the ladies' room as an excuse to move away, there was a disturbance at the other end of the conservatory, near the door into the main house. Someone was screaming.

"It was you! I thought it was you! You bastard! You creepy-crawly bastard!"

It was Tanya, and she was throwing herself against the tall, slender figure of Charles Priestley, pummelling him with her fists.

The first person to reach her was Bob McMullin, who took her by both arms and pulled her away. Then Rory, who had been talking to Hugo, ran over, followed by Marla Maxwell. Both of them were shouting, but their shouts dissolved into silence as Tanya Gastineau slithered down the body of Bob McMullin and collapsed on the floor in a dead faint.

"Tanya, Tanya."

Rory Gastineau crouched by his wife's side, taking her in his arms. Marla was holding on to Charles Priestley as if he might float away at any time, and her mother was holding on to her daughter as if she might float away with him. Elodie took advantage of the chaos to pull out her phone. Ed Moretti answered immediately.

"Early," he said. "You had enough?"

"Yes. Can you come?"

"I'll be there. Change of plans for me, but I'll explain when I see you."

As she put her mobile away, Elodie saw Aaron Gaskell watching her and then coming towards her. They had been momentarily separated by the onrush of Island Players to get a better look at the action. But he was stopped by Rory getting to his feet, his wife in his arms. He stood there, like Lear with Cordelia, anger and anxiety on his face.

"I'm taking her home," he said. Then he added, "She's pregnant. Tanya's pregnant."

Moretti looked at Elodie as she got into the Triumph.

"Something happened," he said.

"Yes."

"And for me. I've got to go somewhere, and I'll have to drop you at home and leave you. Okay?"

"Not okay. I'll go with you and sit quietly in the car, but I'm not going home, Ed. Not on my own."

What the hell, he thought. *I've found my little lamb lost in the wood, so I might as well be hung. For a sheep as a lamb.*

"Okay," he said.

Part Three

The Closing

Chapter Twenty-Four

"Where are we going?"
"You first. What happened?"

Moretti listened. There was tension in Elodie's voice, but there was precision in her description of the events of the evening, a lack of emotional embroidery and personal comment, much as if she were writing an official report, a reflection perhaps of skills she used in her professional capacity.

"That," she concluded, "is how I saw things." She turned and looked out of the car window into the darkness and up at the night sky. Against the light of a three-quarters moon the clouds were scudding overhead, and they seemed to be the only car on the road. "Where are we going?"

"To Pleinmont. Someone I've been looking for has turned up, and she could take off again."

"She?"

"Yes." He didn't elaborate, but asked, "How did you feel about what happened?"

"Put an interpretation on it, you mean? Well, it was fascinating to see how people reacted to the news of the pregnancy. All the young women — and there were a lot of them — oohed and aahed and clapped, followed by a few others, like Lana Lorrimer, then some of the men. There was the odd, predictable shout of 'Good for you, Rory,' that kind of male chest-thumping. Jim Landers rustled up a chair for Rory and he sat down, still holding Tanya. Marla and Marie and Charles Priestley were all clinging to each other, and —"

"Hold on —" Moretti interrupted her. "How did Priestley look? Angry? Defiant? Shocked?"

"Scared," said Elodie. "That's what struck me. He looked frightened, and I thought he seemed to be looking at someone in the crowd. I know it wasn't me, or Aaron Gaskell, who was near me. I can't be more precise than that, I'm afraid. Then you phoned to say you'd arrived, and I left."

"Last impressions?"

"Of how quickly people get over things. Rory and Tanya went into the house, and the party went on."

"Did anyone leave, apart from you?

"Yes. Aaron Gaskell. But I think his motivation had more to do with me. I think he was about to offer me a lift home and saw you."

"Sorry," said Moretti.

"Don't be."

They had arrived.

* * *

Meg the Gypsy lay curled up on her sofa, holding on to Darcy. She was swathed in a voluminous shawl, with only her mass of wiry grey hair visible above a face gaunt with fatigue. She looked up at Moretti and said, "Vera's son." Beside her, Darcy growled, deep in his throat, but this time he didn't bare his teeth. Maud Cole sat on a rug beside the sofa, her hand on Darcy's collar.

"She came home about an hour ago. Darcy heard her. She's had something to eat and drink, but she's very tired."

"She must be." Moretti came slowly over towards the two women and the dog. "My constable says even Billie didn't know where she was, and she must be 'living rough,' as he put it."

Moretti crouched down beside Maud Cole. "Hello, Meg. Yes, I'm Vera's son, Eduardo. You remember her."

"I remember her. She was kind to me."

"She liked you." *Gently now*, he thought. *The most important thing is she's safe, and Maud Cole may be able to get more out of her than I can.* "Where have you been, Meg? Everyone's been worried about you."

"Around and about. This is Darcy." She stroked Darcy's ear and he closed his eyes.

"Yes. Darcy and I have met. Do you remember the man with the sore hand? He says to thank you, because his hand is now all better."

"Of course it is." She seemed unfazed by Moretti's question, so he decided to press on a little further.

"Someone else hurt him, hurt his hand. You called him 'the other one.' Do you remember who the other one was, Meg?"

She didn't reply immediately, then she said, "I know. But he doesn't know I know. Gus used to tell me, 'Can you keep a secret?' and I used to say, 'Cross my heart and hope to die.'"

She sat up on the sofa, dislodging Darcy's head from her legs, and crossed her heart.

Hope to die.

Maud Cole and Moretti looked at each other, and Moretti knew there was no point in going on. Not even the son of Vera Domaille would be able to get her break her oath of silence to Gus Dorey.

"Darcy and I will keep an eye on her, don't worry — there's someone in your car, looking through the window."

"Yes. She is at risk, just like Meg, until I can find out who 'the other one' is. Meg may tell you, Miss Cole."

In the darkness of the courtyard, Moretti heard Maud Cole sigh.

"I think she would rather go to her grave than betray Gus Dorey."

"Except —" Moretti unlocked the Triumph, and turned back to Maud Cole, who was now waving at Elodie. She smiled at Moretti, but said nothing more. "Gus the hermit went to his grave because of 'the other one.' You might persuade her of that, Miss Cole."

"I'll try. Goodnight, and say hello to Elodie for me."

"You know Miss Cole? I think she now thinks we're an item."

"Heavens. I only know her because of her beautiful work. I bought a shawl from her at a show in the old market — when it was still the old market. *Les Halles*. Such a shame — the disappearance of the market, I mean. We had a long talk about — oh, various things. The woman you are worried about is the one who lives on the property, isn't she. Meg."

"Yes. Do you know her?"

"No. I just know *of* her. One of the things we talked about, Maud Cole and I, was the pleasure of living alone. She mentioned her neighbour. Three solitudes, she called us."

Elodie turned and looked at him as he started the engine, and Moretti wondered if she was thinking what he was thinking. *Not three solitudes. Four.* But what she said was, "Could we stop and look at the sea for a moment? I don't usually have a male escort, and it's not something I often do on my own, and certainly not now."

As Moretti smiled back at her, he felt a very slight tremor shiver through him that did not come from the engine of the Triumph. Later he would remember it, and marvel at the power of matter over mind, desire over reason, the moment at which he should have said, "No." Perhaps he had felt protected by Elodie Ashton's own cloistered nature.

So he said, "Yes. Why not."

It only took about a minute or two to drive to the sea wall at Portelet Harbour, and park the Triumph in the deserted space where the buses turned. Behind them, the Imperial Hotel stood elevated on its rise of land, still glowing with light like a beacon over the water, as it had done for over a century. As they got out of the car, the spray from the sea splashed their faces, and Elodie gasped and shivered, zipping her denim jacket over her shirt.

"Tide's up and you're not dressed for this," Moretti called out, buttoning up his own, heavier jacket.

"Just for a moment."

She moved away from him and went to lean over the low wall, looking in the direction of Rocquaine Bay, stretching to the north.

"Look at the moon on the water." The reflection disappeared almost immediately as a cloud covered its face. Moretti joined her, leaning against the parapet, the spray soaking them both. Suddenly, the clouds cleared and the luminosity returned to the water.

"Up there," she said, pointing towards the north and raising her voice above wind and wave, "the witches lived, up at L'Erée. A colony of them, flying out on their brooms to scare the country folk, so they say."

"So they say — any of your relatives among them?"

"I like to think so."

She turned and laughed at him, as a gust of wind blew her now soaking-wet hair across her face and into his eyes, temporarily blinding him. She staggered with the force of the gust and he put his hands on her shoulders to steady her, her body jolting against his as he did so, dislodging a small, battered rose from the buttonhole of her jacket.

For a moment he felt her resist, and then she didn't.

As he lay sleepless overnight, Moretti settled on a name for the investigation, for the chief officer's benefit. Operation Vampire-Slayer. Op VS for short. It sounded like a video game. In an effort to refocus his attention, Moretti was writing it up on the board in the incident room as Falla walked in the door with Al Brown, the two of them laughing together about something that had happened the night before, something to do with Lonnie and the Latvian girl.

Moretti interrupted their merry mood with a curt remark about private conversations, at which Al looked startled, and Falla mutinous. Bernie Mauger was already there and, as Moretti waited for the rest of his hastily assembled team, he had time to think about why he had jumped all over them. He came to no useful conclusion before the arrival of Rick Le Marchant and Bob McMullin, and turned his attention to the business at hand.

"Falla, Al, Bob, Bernie, Rick, you are what Al and the Met calls an MI Team and I am your Action Manager. It'll keep the chief officer happy." Al smiled, guardedly. "We may need to add Perkins, but I'm hoping to keep it to the six of us. And to the one *Guernsey Press* reporter I spoke to yesterday, who was asking questions about hospital gossip. I am supposedly keeping him in the loop as the price for his silence — for now. I'll just go over last night's events."

As Moretti described in detail Elodie's account of Tanya's hysterical outburst and updated the team on the reappearance of Meg the Gypsy, leaving his companion out of the account, he watched Falla's expressive eyebrows do their familiar disappearing trick beneath the jagged line of her bangs. Then he turned to Bob McMullin.

"Okay, Bob. Have you anything to add to Ms. Ashton's account?"

Bob shrugged his shoulders, and took a notebook out of his pocket. "Not really, but I wrote everything down as soon as I got home."

Bob's account differed little from Elodie's, apart from the conversation he was having with Charles Priestley before Tanya's outburst, which was apparently all about music.

"Music?"

"Yes. Groups we like, that kind of thing. Nothing else. They'd started playing some sort of antediluvian music, which we both hate."

"Antediluvian as in — ?"

"Rolling Stones, that era. Seriously retro stuff."

Feeling seriously retro himself, Moretti turned to Bernie Mauger.

"Bernie, tell the team what you told me before everyone got here. Tell us about Hugo Shawcross."

Bernie surveyed the room with the air of someone who has struck the motherlode.

"Hugo Shawcross doesn't have a police record, which was why we didn't find him on the NPC, but he *does* have a record on the privately kept files of one of the top security companies in the U.K. They handled a complaint about his involvement with the underage daughter of Sir Henry Arnold."

"The politician?" asked Moretti.

"Yes. Member of the Cabinet. They put a tail on Shawcross, and from what I can read between the lines, he was caught in the act, as you might say, and force was used to — dissuade him. That was the word used in the report."

"Why didn't the police handle this? Why a private security firm?"

Bernie Mauger nodded in agreement at Falla's question.

"That's what *I* wondered. Looks like Sir Henry was more bothered about his own reputation being dragged through the mud by the goings-on than about his daughter. Seems there were some kinky stuff involved that the tabloids would have jumped on, according to the report."

"Kinky things?"

"Yes. Black masses and such."

"Wow." Rick Le Marchant's eyes shone. "How did you get access to this info, Bernie?"

Bernie Mauger looked uneasy, and Moretti moved swiftly on.

"We have now interviewed the principle players in this melodrama, with the exception of Charles

Priestley. Al, you and I are going to do that and, while we're doing that, I want you, Falla, to see if you can get anything out of Tanya Gastineau. Clearly, she thinks Charles Priestley is her phone tormentor, and maybe she's now scared enough to talk to you."

"Right, Guv."

Moretti looked at Falla for signs of either hostility or goodwill, but saw neither. He turned to Bob McMullin and Rick Le Marchant.

"The two of you are to pay a visit to Roddy, Tanya Gastineau's groomsman. Horseperson," he added, when he saw mystification on the two faces opposite him. "You'll find all we know about him in Falla's notes, which is very little. Say that we are just doing a background check on the people connected with the Gastineau family. No need to be any more specific than that. And Bob, no mention of last night's episode and nothing about your connection with the Island Players. It's unlikely he knows, yet."

Bob McMullin nodded in agreement.

"Do you think, Guv, that Hugo's past has come back to haunt him?" Al spoke tentatively, testing the waters.

"Looks like it, doesn't it?" Moretti replied, smiling, and the tension in the room eased.

"But that," he added, "is exactly what we are supposed to think. And I don't."

The six people in the incident room looked at him for further enlightenment, but, instead, Moretti moved away from the blackboard, with its graphic images, the backstory to a life and a death, now confirmed a murder, and the Op VS Team started to disperse. All except Al, who was waiting for Moretti, and Falla.

"Guv, can I have a word?"

Al Brown picked up his jacket and followed the rest of the team out of the room.

Moretti waited. He didn't know what he was expecting to hear, but Falla's question took him by surprise.

"Guv, are you dissatisfied with my work on this case?"

"Why would you think that?" was all he could find to say, and "No" seemed an adequate enough reply.

"That's good to know." She was giving him one of those looks from her dark, expressive eyes that he found totally unfathomable. Then she added, "And that's all I need to know. My personal life and your personal life are off-limits, right?"

It was said as a statement, not a question.

"Right."

She slung her bag over her shoulder, and added, "Only, sometimes it's easier said than done."

Moretti felt no need to answer, because he couldn't have agreed more — and that he had just proved by his own childish response to their laughter.

Chapter Twenty-Five

Liz Falla was glad Moretti was not with her in the police car, or she would have found herself doing either good cop or bad cop. The good cop would have asked leading questions like, "So Elodie called you when the fight broke out? You took her with you to question Meg? Then you took her back home so she wasn't on her own?" The bad cop would have lost control, blown a gasket with such remarks as, "Elodie isn't one of your one-night stands. Elodie has been hurt in the past." Or even, "If you hurt Elodie, you'll have me to deal with." As if she was her god-mother's mum.

Both cops would have been disastrous.

She was greeted at the Gastineau front door by a member of the household she had not seen before, but if she had thought about it, must have known existed. A servant. No way Tanya and Rory did the dusting.

She was a solidly built middle-aged woman, wearing an overall and carrying a small dog in her arms that looked like a terrier of some sort. Certainly, it didn't seem to have been chosen as a guard dog, because it was delighted to see Liz, its whole body almost wriggling free of its minder.

"Yes?"

The tone was unfriendly, as the household help struggled to hold on.

Liz held out her police badge, decided to give no explanations, but to sound as if she was expected.

"DS Falla, here to interview Mrs. Gastineau."

"I wasn't told about this."

From the resigned expression on the woman's bleak face that gave the impression of being carved out of island granite, this was not the first time.

"Oh." Liz looked at her watch, tutted, then waited.

"You'd better come in. I can't hold this animal much longer."

Liz crossed the threshold and helpfully closed the door behind her.

"That's quite an armful you've got there. I don't remember seeing him before, or you, Mrs. —?"

"Livingstone. I'm the housekeeper. It's a she, and they just got it. Must have been my day off when you came before. I'll just shut her in the cloakroom and see you through to Mrs. Gastineau. She piddles — the dog, I mean — and she might as well make it the cloakroom as anywhere else. Just a minute."

The housekeeper deposited her burden behind a door in the hallway, and a pathetic whimpering sound emerged under the edge of the door, followed by snuffling.

"Poor little thing. Perhaps we could take it to Mrs. Gastineau? I don't mind."

"Mrs. Gastineau would. She just asked me to take her away, because she keeps chewing the tassels on her slippers. Mr. Gastineau got it as a present for her, but they just don't think, do they. She's called it Honeybun, would you believe."

No comment seemed called-for, or necessary, so Liz followed in the housekeeper's wake.

Tanya Gastineau was lying on a sofa in the room in which she and Moretti had first interviewed her and Rory Gastineau. She was wearing pink from head to toe; a fluffy mohair shawl over what looked like a silk dressing gown and pyjamas, and the puppy-magnet slippers on the floor at her feet. There was a glass of milk on a low table close to her, and a plate of fruit. She looked up as Liz and the housekeeper came in.

"Oh it's you," she said to Liz. "Rory is — indisposed." She gave a sound somewhere between a giggle and a gulp, and Liz hoped her internal celebration at this stroke of luck didn't show on her face.

Tanya without her watchdog, and I don't mean the puppy!

"I'm sorry to hear that, so I'll just have a brief word with you, Mrs. Gastineau."

"Can I get you anything, ma'am?" Mrs. Livingstone managed to sound both curt and deferential.

Tanya sat up and pointed to the table.

"No, but you can take something away. The sight of that milk makes me feel even more like puking."

"Very well. But Mr. Gastineau wants you to —"

"Mr. Gastineau can drink it himself. Hair of the dog that *didn't* bite him."

Tanya gave a short, sharp laugh at her joke. Mrs. Livingstone picked up the glass, checked with Liz that she wanted neither tea nor coffee, and left the room. Liz sat down in a plumply upholstered chair opposite Tanya.

"Congratulations. You and your husband must be very happy at the news," she said.

Tanya swung around and sat up. Her formerly rosy cheeks were now a whitish-yellow, and she had dark circles under her eyes that were partly smudged eyeliner and partly not.

"You'd think, wouldn't you? Rory was over the moon, then last night happens and he's hitting the bottle again."

A tear made its way through one dark circle and ran down her cheek. Clearly, she had been doing a lot of crying, and this time the super-mascara had not stood up to it.

"Last night happens?"

"Well, that's why you're here, isn't it. Me yelling."

"You attacked —" Liz took out her notebook and appeared to check the name, "Charles Priestley."

"*Ooooh* — is that what he calls it? Is he bringing charges?" Tanya now sounded derisive. She pulled a grape off a small bunch on the plate and popped it in her mouth.

"Actually, Mrs. Gastineau, I wondered if *you* might be thinking of charges. Is he the person you suspected of making threatening calls? That's what it sounded like to the witnesses."

Thankfully, Tanya didn't ask who those supposed witnesses were. Instead, she leaned forwards and said, "I think he was. As soon as I heard his voice that night at the Maxwells', I thought it was. But what could I prove? And any time Rory thinks I know any bloke under the age of seventy, he gets —" Here, Tanya paused. Liz waited, and then jumped in.

"Are you saying that your husband gets suspicious? Violent?"

"Rory, violent?" Tanya found this amusing. "Suspicious is what he gets, but violent? No. He gets weepy. God, I hate weepy, and now look at me." She took a tissue out of the dressing-gown pocket and blew her nose.

"Mrs. Gastineau — Tanya — If you know why Charles Priestley is doing this, you will be much safer if you tell me. Particularly now you're pregnant. Is it about who inherits? Because that's what it looks like."

"I wish I knew." Tanya lowered her voice. "I married Rory for all the wrong reasons. Well, one wrong reason and I'll give you one guess." It was clearly a rhetorical statement, because Tanya ploughed rapidly on. "I had no idea, not at the time, not all this first-born stuff and show me the wedding-ring and the piece of paper and all that. And then I found out."

"Found out what?"

"That his family were a bunch of lunatics! They hate me and I hate them."

"Has any family member threatened you directly?"

"Directly?" Tanya snorted. "Directly is not the way they work, that lot. I'm sure someone put that la-di-da weasel up to it, but it could be any of them. Honest, I'd tell you if I knew. The only fun I was having was with the Island Players crowd, and then somebody went for poor little Hugo."

Tanya leaned forward again and lowered her voice. "Between you and me, I think that was all about me and not about vampires and such. But what do I know? I'm just a dumb blonde dolly-bird!"

Tanya threw herself back against the sofa, her movement dislodging a packet of cigarettes from the pocket of her dressing gown. She hastily pushed them back into the pocket and whispered, "Don't tell Rory," like a naughty child.

"But he's right, isn't he?" Liz tried to make her remark sound lighthearted rather than judgmental, watched Tanya's expression become petulant, and moved the conversation along. Healthy pregnancy choices were outside her field of enquiry. "You say your only fun was with the Island Players, but last time I was here you were horseback riding. I don't know much about it, but you looked pretty good to me."

Tanya did not seem cheered by the thought. "Rory says it's now too dangerous and I should stop. It's only an excuse to send Roddy back to Bristol."

A door opening. "So you knew your riding companion in Bristol? As an employer, or a friend. Or both?"

Tanya cheered up a bit. "Both. He worked for daddy, and that's how we met. Daddy had a part interest in a steeple-chaser. Roddy actually asked me to marry him, once."

"And you said 'no.' Why?"

Tanya gave Liz a look that spoke volumes, and took another grape from the bunch on the table.

"Ah. He's got no money."

Another woman who'd chosen smoked salmon over sardines on toast.

"Got it in one. I shall really miss him, and not just because of the riding. Someone to talk to. You know."

Liz looked at the pretty woman sitting opposite her, and wondered. There must have been other choices, other men with enough income to satisfy the needs of this girl-woman who played the baby-doll game so well. Why Rory Gastineau? She went ahead and put her thought into words.

"You must have been beating off men with sticks, Tanya, and surely some of them were well off. Why Mr. Gastineau? What made him a winner?"

Tanya Gastineau looked straight at Liz and said, simply, "Because he was bonkers about me."

As Liz tried to think of a response, Tanya held out her hand towards her in a gesture almost of supplication.

"You wouldn't think it to look at Rory, but when it comes to words, he's like something out of a chick-flick. Looking at *you*, detective, don't tell me you don't know what it's like to have someone head over heels with you, tell you you're everything, the sun, the moon, the stars."

Liz stood up. It seemed like a good time to bring the interview to an end.

All, or nothing at all.

Lost in thought, humming to herself, Liz nearly missed the sound of the car horn just outside the Gastineau grounds. In her rear-view mirror she saw a police car leaving just after her. She pulled over and Bob McMullin and Rick Le Marchant pulled in behind her on the verge of the road. Rick Le Marchant got out of the car on the passenger side and came running towards her.

Le Marchant had been involved in Moretti's enquiries before, and was one of the officers who had been ticked off by Liz Falla's rapid promotion. Theirs was a combative relationship and Liz had once asked her Guvnor why he had chosen "a wet-behind-the-ears dimwit" like Le Marchant over other officers.

"For just those reasons. Bernie Mauger looks like a simple country boy, straight off the farm, and isn't. Le Marchant looks like what he is, and has an endearing way of lulling interviewees into a false sense of security."

Which had, on occasion, proved true. Liz bore that in mind as Le Marchant galloped over the rough turf towards her.

"DS Falla, He's packing up and leaving!"

"Mrs. Gastineau's horseperson?"

"Right. Roddy Bull."

"That's his last name? Bull?"

"Yep. We told him this was a police investigation, and he'd have to stay, and he said we'd have to sort it out with his employer. When I asked him if he meant 'the Gastineaus,' he said, 'Yes, they make the decisions around here, don't they?' Bloody cheek!"

By this time, Bob McMullin had joined Le Marchant, who was breathing heavily and invasively through the car window into Liz's face in his excitement. She got out of the car and turned to Bob McMullin.

"Have you contacted the Guvnor?"

"Yes. He said he'd get back to Hospital Lane as soon as he could, and to warn Bull he could be charged if he left the island. Which we did."

"What was his reaction?"

"Well, he didn't turn around and start unpacking his suitcases, but I think he got the message."

"Was he literally packing his suitcases?"

"Yes. He already had a couple by the door."

"What's he like? Besides cheeky."

Rick Le Marchant answered first.

"Pretty boy. You know the type."

Liz bit her tongue on various possible responses and turned to Bob McMullin who replied, "Bit of a smoothie, yes." Bob McMullin frowned. "But I think he was worried about something. Not just us, but something else."

"As in —?"

Rick Le Marchant got in first again. "As in he can't stand Mr. Gastineau." He seemed to find this comical. "Called him a jealous prat, said he couldn't understand why Tanya Riley — that's what he called her — had chosen such a loser."

"So you got the impression he wasn't at all unhappy to be leaving?"

Bob McMullin looked back at the Gastineau acres.

"I think he couldn't get out of there fast enough. He looked like he was going to bawl when we said he couldn't."

He seemed baffled by what he had observed, but Rick Le Marchant seemed supremely confident about the reason.

"All he was scared of was us."

"You?" Liz tried not to sound incredulous.

"Us. Pretty boy," he repeated. "Got no bal — backbone," he added, giving Liz Falla a look that suggested an intimate knowledge of the workings of pretty boys' minds.

"Sounds more to me like Roddy Bull got to you, Rick, than you got to Roddy Bull." Liz responded, unable to resist the opportunity to put him in his place in the pecking order. "But be sure to put all that useful detail in your report — that stuff about a bull without backbone. Or balls."

On which excellently satisfying exit line, she got back into her car, as her mobile started to ring.

Chapter Twenty-Six

Meadowlands, the house towards which Moretti and Al Brown were heading in the Triumph, had been the home of the same family since the mid-nineteenth century, and Charles Priestley's uncle, retired Colonel Clarence Priestley, was the last surviving member of that family in residence on the island. As they drove, Moretti filled in some of the background for Al.

"I did some checking beforehand. They are an interesting lot, the Priestleys, but not unique. Guernsey has its aristocratic families — the Gastineaus are one of them — and its old island families with names like Dorey, Mauger and Falla. The Priestleys came here in the early eighteenth century, and they almost certainly were attracted by the money to be made from privateering, according to Lydia Machon at the Priaulx. But in the last hundred years or so are much better known as a military family of some distinction."

"They came to plunder, and stayed to stretch their pensions and investments further."

"Something like that."

Moretti looked out of the window of the Triumph at the stretch of wall to their right, a thing of beauty year-round because of the burgeoning bunches of wildflowers growing in the crevices between brick and stone. In the sunlight of autumn slanting between the trees beyond the wall, they glowed like pink, lilac and white jewels. So much had changed, even in his lifetime, like the road names in this part of St. Peter Port. Mount Durand remained the same, but Queen's Road at the top of the Grange had once been la Petite Marche, and Prince Albert Road, where they were heading, was once the much humbler la Pierre Percée. He didn't know how long ago they were rechristened, but his mother always called them by the old names.

"But I think they fell in love with the island."

"Why wouldn't they? What's the estate behind that amazing wall?"

"Government House." Moretti turned the Triumph on to Prince Albert Road. "Here we are."

Meadowlands was a sizeable house, even by Guernsey standards for substantial houses, but it did not have the elegant, spare lines of the island's eighteenth-century mansions. Built of brick overlaid with ivory stucco, it had a complicated structure of many-levelled roofs with two three-storey wings set either side of a lower crenellated section that held the main door. Beyond one of the three-storey wings was another crenellated section, giving the building the appearance of a fortress, or castle.

"Wow. This is different."

"Built to order, I'm told."

Moretti pulled up alongside the front door, and checked his messages before he got out. Nothing yet from Falla, or the other two constables. He was wishing now he had sent Al with McMullin or Le Marchant, particularly since Roddy the Body was an unknown quantity, but he had wanted a show of strength when facing the colonel and his nephew, and Al Brown gave off more powerful vibes of law and order than either of the other two. And he wanted Falla to be the one who interviewed Tanya Gastineau.

Thinking of Falla made him think of non-work-related things, so he stopped thinking of Falla and got out of the car.

The sepulchral sound of the front-door bell clanging through the house beyond the closed door reminded Moretti of a television program about zombies — or the undead — from the seventies, and it was an anticlimax to be greeted by a young woman in a navy-blue dress that looked like a maid's uniform, and not by a ghoulish manservant or a disembodied hand. The maid, if that was what she was, appeared to be chewing gum.

"You're expected," she said, giving Al a speculative glance. "This way."

As they followed in the wake of her bobbing ponytail of multi-coloured hair, she blew an impressive pink bubble that subsided just before she knocked on a massive wooden door to one side of the cavernous hall. Moretti wondered how long it had taken to perfect her timing, or whether it was a natural gift.

The room they entered was like a film set out of *Bowani Junction,* or *The Jewel In The Crown,* by a designer who'd taken leave of his senses, and particularly his sense of proportion. The walls were covered with an armoury of weapons ranging from spears to guns, with the odd scimitar and sword in-between. There was even an animal skin on the floor — mercifully not a lion or tiger, its head snarling up at them, but what looked like it had once been an elegant antelope, or something like it. On the subtle taupe and bronze tones of the animal skin were two large feet encased in felt slippers, and attached to the feet was Colonel Clarence Priestley, wearing a plum-coloured velvet smoking jacket, seated in a vast armchair whose upholstery had seen better days. Behind an impressive set of whiskers his mottled face and small porcine eyes seemed annoyed.

"You're the fellas who've come to harass Charlie," he said. His voice rumbled out in a drawl that still managed to sound threatening.

At least the battle lines were clearly drawn.

Moretti pulled out his police identity badge, Al did the same, and the colonel brushed them away with a flick of his hand as if they were a couple of tsetse flies.

"No need for that. What do you want from the boy?"

"His version, Colonel, of what happened at the Lorrimers' party. Mrs. Gastineau says she lost control because she recognized your nephew's voice as the one on her phone, the person who has been harassing *her* over a period of weeks."

To establish, Colonel Blimp, who might be harassing whom.

At this, the colonel stood up, leaning heavily on both arms of his massive chair.

"Good God, man, this is all pure speculation based on the word of an unbalanced woman of dubious breeding. From what I have heard of her background, this could be an attempt to get money out of us!"

The colonel, it appeared, had done some digging.

But before Moretti could say anything in response, Al Brown had something to say. "That's a very fine sitar, Colonel." He was pointing at the wall just visible behind the armchair. "Looks like a nineteenth-century *gayaki*-style sitar to me. Teak or *tun* wood, do you know, sir?"

Both Moretti and the colonel looked at Al in surprise, and the colonel's face lit up.

"You know something about sitars?"

"Yes, sir. I play a Portuguese guitar, and I'm interested in all stringed instruments, particularly guitars of any kind. May I take a closer look?"

"Please do, young man."

The colonel joined Al as he circled the armchair, shuffling with some difficulty across the uncarpeted section of the floor. Moretti stayed where he was and watched the two men. At some point he had to get things back on track and talk to Charles Priestley, but so far so very good. The colonel was no longer facing the enemy across the pampas, or the veldt, or whatever. At least Al was admitted inside the walls.

"Looks like *tun* to me, sir — it's a sort of mahogany — and the bridge, I think, is possibly camel bone. A gourd, of course, for the *kaddu*, the resonating chamber. All those strings! Most of them to supply that drone sound in the *ragas*. Such skill required. Did you ever hear it played, Colonel?"

"Not this one." The colonel was beaming at Al. "This belonged to my grandfather. He told me stories about the band that played when they played polo in India. 'Often women,' he said, 'playin' the sitars. How those natives could ride their horses! Hell for leather, absolutely no fear whatsoever!'"

Just as Moretti was wondering how he was going to get things back from the polo grounds of nineteenth-century colonial India, the colonel turned away and came back across the room. At one point he stumbled, and Al took his arm. The two made their slow way past Moretti, and it looked for a moment as if the colonel was going to show them the door. Instead, he opened it and shouted in a voice that boomed spectacularly into the hall.

"Charlie! Get down here!"

Colonel Priestley turned and beamed at them both.

"Learned to do that in Africa," he said. "Makin' my voice carry across great distances. Here he is, stupid young fool."

The stupid young fool was making his way down a fine, curving set of stairs that showcased his spectacular good looks. He walked down as if drifting, floating from step to step, his face pale as ivory. The T-shirt and jeans he was wearing seemed like an anachronism in this house, and on him.

"Get in here," said his uncle.

Once back in the room, the colonel reached out for Al's arm, and allowed himself to be helped back to his threadbare throne.

"Tell these officers what you told me."

"It was a joke." Charles Priestley sounded peevish. "I was put up to it."

"By whom?" Moretti was watching the boy's face, remembering what Elodie had said about his expression after Tanya's outburst. He had looked scared, she said. Right now he was looking rebelliously at his uncle, who repeated Moretti's question.

"Tell 'em," he added.

"Marla."

"*Marla?*"

Both Moretti and Al repeated the name, incredulous.

"Why would Marla Maxwell get you to harass her uncle's wife, Charlie?" Moretti shook his head in disbelief. "It makes no sense, and you realise, don't you, that I shall be asking Miss Gastineau if this is true."

"She'll say no, won't she? She'll say she's just jealous of Tanya, and her having a baby."

"And displacing her, is that what you're saying?"

"Yes. She hates her."

It was said melodramatically in Charlie Priestley's melodic voice, and Moretti didn't believe it for a moment. The boy was a terrible liar.

"So you sent threatening messages to Tanya Gastineau on her phone, because Marla Gastineau told you to?"

"Yes."

"I am assuming you did this because you want to impress Marla, be her boyfriend perhaps?"

"Right."

Beside his nephew, the colonel shifted suddenly in his chair, and threw a glance at Moretti he found impossible to read. Al continued the conversation.

"That night at the play-reading, when the lights went out and Marla started to scream — I assume that wasn't you, since you two are in cahoots. Or was it a scheme that misfired? Which was it?"

"That wasn't me! I didn't do it! It was someone else's idea of a joke, because of the play being about vampires and the undead! Not me!"

This time Charlie's indignation sounded genuine, and the colonel patted his arm.

"Calm down, Charlie," he rumbled. "Keep your powder dry."

Charlie subsided on to the broad arm of his uncle's chair, and Moretti took a step closer to him. He was now looking down into Charlie Priestley's clear amethyst-blue eyes, and the boy flinched and turned away.

"Since you two are close, I imagine Marla told you that someone was sending her threatening text messages? And since you are friends, I guess that wasn't you?"

In the thirty seconds or so it took Moretti to ask his question, Charles Priestley's face flooded slowly with colour, the ivory skin suffused with red. His reply was a shake of the head.

"Is that a no, Charlie?"

"Yes," said Charlie, "That's a no."

Moretti and Al exchanged a quick glance to see if each was thinking the same thing. That the negatives and positives in that short statement should be reversed.

No, that's a yes.

"Silly young fool." Colonel Priestley gave his nephew a shove with his shoulder, knocking him off the arm of the chair. He looked up at Moretti. "Will he be charged?"

"We'll need a statement from him, sir, but my feeling is that Mrs. Gastineau won't press charges. But that's up to her."

At the thought of the unbalanced woman of dubious breeding, the colonel snorted and stood up slowly.

"That's all then. Go on, Charlie, get out of my sight."

It was said with affection, more sorrow than anger on his face.

"One last question, Charlie." Moretti chose his moment to ask as the young man walked past him to the door. "Can you think of anyone else who is involved? The person who is behind all this, frightening Marla Gastineau? If it's not you — who?"

It was then he saw in Charlie Priestley's eyes what Elodie had seen at the party. Fear.

"I don't know," he said.

The old man watched Charlie Priestley go out of the room and close the door behind him, then turned to Moretti and Al Brown.

"He's lyin', of course," he said. "Not about who did what, but about the girl."

"Marla Maxwell?" The colonel's porcine little eyes looked both tender and astute, and Moretti reminded himself that pigs were highly intelligent animals, not to be underestimated. "In what way, sir?"

"That boyfriend poppycock." The colonel took Al's arm and led him and Moretti over to a series of portraits on one wall not entirely covered in the instruments of war. With one exception they were all of men, most in some kind of uniform. "My ancestors, gentlemen," he said. "I come from a long line of bachelors. Some were married, or I wouldn't be here, but most were not. I never married, never wanted to. No choice in those days about what I wanted, but there is for Charlie, thank God. Got into a spot of bother about it at school, which is why he's here, to get away from his damn silly parents. This idiocy has nothing to do with that." He turned to face Al, still holding his arm. "D'you see?"

Moretti left it to Al to reply to the question that gave him the answer to one of Charlie Priestley's lies.

"Yes, Colonel, I see," Al said.

And, as he answered, Moretti saw what Colonel Clarence Priestley had seen about Aloisio Brown, and he had not.

Chapter Twenty-Seven

Moretti had gathered his Op VS troops around the largest table in the incident room and ordered in sandwiches and coffee. The air was almost festive as he waited until decisions had been made between ham, cheese, and egg salad on brown or white bread, pickles or no pickles, and black or white coffee. Frowning in the direction of Le Marchant and McMullin as they opened their obtrusively fizzing cans of pop, he took out the notes he had begun compiling in the small hours when sleep eluded him, and began.

"Time for a case review, so let's look at what we've got. A murder, an attempted murder, and threats against two women: Marla Gastineau, and Tanya Gastineau. We have two men who seem scared of something or somebody: Charles Priestley and Roddy Bull. One of those two, Priestley, claims he was put up to harassing one woman, Tanya, by the other, Marla.

Al and I are sure he is lying about that, just as his uncle is sure he is lying about doing it to impress Marla and be her boyfriend. From what the colonel said this afternoon, there are contacts between the two families, so whoever put Priestley up to this is a Gastineau. I'd put money on that. And, although he denied it, I think he also was sending the threatening texts to Marla. So —" Moretti looked around the table at his MI team, "what do those two women have in common?"

"Their sex."

Over the edge of his ham sandwich, Rick Le Marchant gave a lip-curling laugh at his fatuous comment.

"Exactly," said Moretti. "Well done, Rick." Most of the MI Team looked astonished, even Rick looked surprised, and Moretti added, "They are both young women of child-bearing age. For Marie and Elton, Tanya is the enemy. For Ginnie, they are both the enemy."

"But she isn't married." An emboldened Rick added another pearl of wisdom.

With the patience of a kindergarten teacher dealing with a particularly slow pre-schooler, Moretti said, "Not yet. But I gather she has hopes, or so I'm told on good authority. And she is older than Marie, so that puts her second in line, since they are both female. And being older also makes her in a hurry."

On the other side of the table, Falla was watching her Guvnor with interest.

"If it were that simple, we could go in, apply pressure, and extort some truth from weaker suspects like the golden boy, but it isn't. I am now convinced there are two motives here, two strands to what is going on, and how and why one is linked to the other, I cannot quite see yet."

"But why not put more pressure on Priestley?" Bob McMullin asked.

"Because whoever is doing this is more frightening than we are, Bob. I understand you now have a schedule, and start rehearsals this weekend. See what you can do, okay? He might like a shoulder to cry on."

Bob nodded, and Moretti stopped to eat some of his sandwich, and drank some coffee. Liz Falla smoothed out her paper napkin on the table with elaborate care and asked, "Does your good authority have any more to say about Shawcross's role in all this?"

"No." Moretti met his partner's eyes, expecting speculation, and saw instead anxiety. "But I have been rethinking his place in this nasty little drama, and my first priority is to question him again, now that he's able to speak. We know he was fleeing a father's wrath, but why Guernsey? Was that random, or did he have another reason for being here? I may be wrong in assuming the attack on him was to draw our attention away from the real danger to others — that exists, for sure, but maybe Hugo isn't just a red herring."

"If that's the case, sir, doesn't it mean that Ms. Ashton is a target?" Al gave a quick glance at Liz, and went on, "I looked at her statement, and she says she saw no one, but the attacker doesn't know that."

"Yes." Moretti also looked at Liz. "I imagine that's why you asked about Shawcross. See if you can persuade her to move away from the house, move in with you, with her sister, whatever. You may succeed where I have failed, Falla."

Without waiting for her to respond, Moretti continued.

"Loose ends," he said, "let's tie up some loose ends. PC Perkins checked Gus Dorey's mailbox in town and it is empty. We had to get it opened, because the key has disappeared, and the staff has no recollection of anyone coming in and opening it. However, they can't see the box from the front desk, so that proves nothing. I'm thinking of talking to the postman again. Now he's over the shock, he may remember more details of his almost daily chats with Gus Dorey.

"For the night of the attack on Shawcross no one in the Island Players has an alibi worth a damn. I'm not going to check alibis for the death of Gus Dorey, because at the moment it is not a murder, and I want it to stay that way. For the moment."

"Sir." A tentative Bob McMullin spoke up. "What are we doing about the Bristol connection?"

"Absolutely nothing, but it is crucial to this investigation, because that is where the truth lies about whoever killed the hermit, and whoever attacked Shawcross. We now know that Bristol is where Rory Gastineau met his wife, and I suspect he was trying to find out about Gus Dorey and Lucy Gastineau. Not so much a piece of the puzzle that's missing, but a piece that doesn't fit. Yet."

"I don't quite get it, Guv." Bernie Mauger put down the pickle on which he had been crunching, the last vestiges of his meal. "Are you saying that all this vampire stuff is just window dressing? That it's really about Gus Dorey having a kid with a Gastineau?"

"That's just what I'm saying, Bernie. Whoever heard of a vampire biting the *back* of someone's neck? There's something else going on, but it's really all about the hermit. And what *I* don't get is why he was killed when he was. What was the trigger? Because this was not just an act of madness, but a cold, calculated killing. So why then?"

"There are others in danger, Guv — Tanya, for instance." Liz Falla took out her notepad, and flipped through the pages. "Something she said after Bob said he thought Roddy Bull couldn't wait to get out of there." She quelled Rick Le Marchant's attempt to interrupt her with a look. "Here it is. 'Someone to talk to,' she said. Perhaps we should have another chat with Roddy the Body, Guv."

"Good idea. I agree, Tanya's vulnerable, but she has a bodyguard far more effective than Roddy the Body, one who'd give his life for her. Her husband."

"You've left a leading player out of the cast of characters, sir," Al looked ruefully at Moretti, "and she's a slippery character. Meg the gypsy."

Moretti smiled. "I was saving her for last. Meg is the wild card in all this, the most elusive, and the one most at risk."

"More than Ms. Ashton or Mrs. Gastineau?" Bernie Mauger asked.

"Yes." Moretti's face was grim as he looked around the table. "Meg is the only one of this cast of characters who knows who 'the other one' is."

"The 'other one,' sir?"

Rick Le Marchant's enquiry was devoid of levity. The festive air in the incident room was gone, and even PC Le Marchant had divined that much.

"Meg knows who killed her friend, Gus Dorey." Moretti stood up and, as the chairs began to scrape against the floor as the team followed suit, he added, "Unless there are further developments, we meet here again on Monday morning, and I'll assign interviews at that time. But keep your mobiles on, or check them regularly."

As the group began to file out of the room, Moretti called out to Liz Falla.

"Falla, a moment."

She turned and came back, waiting until the last person had left before speaking. She was looking at his face and smiling.

"Why do I have the feeling you are going to spoil my weekend, Guv?"

"Because I am."

It was a relief to be laughing with Falla again, although the laughter only lasted as long as the brief sentence in which he told her what he wanted. She looked at him in disbelief.

"You're joking, Guv," she protested, "You're not serious?"

"I am. Serious, not joking. Come on, let's get out of here."

* * *

Liz Falla had been in Moretti's house before. She knew it had been his family home, that the piano had been his mother's, and that most of the furniture and the prints on the walls had been put there by his parents. On her first visit, the only contribution she had seen that he had made to his surroundings was his really antiquated vintage quad sound system, whose smooth, sweet sound was, in his opinion, unequalled. The first thing she noticed on this visit was a new and up-to-date system, which she knew he had been planning to install, to play the music collection he had acquired in much the same way as she had her Parisian couture.

Liz hung her coat on the ancient coat-stand by the door and said, "Am I right in thinking that, because I'm here, this conversation did not happen?'

"Right." Moretti did not laugh. "We are officially off-duty, Falla, so would you like a beer? I would. How those young men can drink that poison in a can is beyond me, but the sound of those cans opening set me thinking about a decent beer, not necessarily from a can."

"Thanks. I'd love a decent beer. Dark, if you have it."

"I have."

Moretti disappeared into the kitchen and Liz took the opportunity to take another look at the room. The other new acquisition was a small, exquisitely detailed watercolour of island flora, alongside the only other print she knew was not part of his parents' collection. She smiled, thinking of the print's likely connection to an earlier case, and the new painting. Some murderers kept mementos of their terrible crimes; it looked as if detective inspectors kept souvenirs of lost loves. At least, this one did. In his own way, this Guvnor of hers was a hermit also, possibly still in the thrall of a lost wife on the mainland. But whether he was trapped by love, as the hermit of Pleinmont seemed to have been, or by that equally sticky snare, the once bit, twice shy trap, she couldn't guess.

"Here we are." Moretti handed her a tall, foaming glass of something dark and delicious. "Cheers."

They sat opposite each other, an old brass-bound chest that served as a table between them, and Liz raised her glass.

"Cheers. You know how I feel about things that go bump in the night — has all this vampire hogwash got to you? Sorry to sound out of line, Guv, but I'd be a lot more cheery if you have a really good reason for me to be doing what you're asking me to do."

"A really good reason from a really reliable source." Moretti drank some more of his beer, and put down the glass.

"Elodie," he said.

Moretti rethought the events of the previous night, selecting what was essential, filtering out the personal, and a moment best forgotten.

"Where do we go from here?"

She had asked the question once they were back in the car, and Moretti had no intention of enquiring whether she was being literal or figurative. Elodie shivered as she spoke, and Moretti started the engine, turned on the heat, then turned it off.

"I'll have to leave it a bit, but it won't take long. You dropped something."

He pointed to the tiny shape, just visible in a puddle outside the car window.

"A rose. Or it *was* a rose, from Aaron Gaskell. Not important."

"I see."

He doesn't, she thought. But the withered remains of that boutonnière might come in useful. From the tone of his voice when he answered her question, it had.

"I'm taking you home, then coming in to check around and then I'll try again to persuade you to get out of there."

As she swung around in her seat, he put the Triumph into gear and she jolted against him. Perhaps because of the rose lying on the wet pavement, he felt nothing this time. But the brush of her wet hair against this face reminded him to put on the heater.

"Ed, on an island this size I cannot run very far, I certainly can't hide, and I have no intention of leaving Guernsey."

The rest of the drive was in silence. It had started to rain and, as it spattered lightly on the car window, in his head Moretti heard his former sax player, Garth Machin, playing a riff on "It Takes Two to Tango."

Get out of my head, Garth, and stop being so bloody unsubtle, he thought.

The music changed to another tango and another musician, Lonnie playing "Mi Buenos Aires Querido" on his bass, and this time Moretti listened.

After silence, that which comes nearest to expressing the inexpressible is music.

Huxley was right. They drove to Elodie's house in silence, and Moretti listened to Lonnie.

As they pulled into Elodie's driveway and got out of the car, Elodie said, "Yes, I still need you to check around and no, I don't want you to do any arm-twisting."

Moretti looked at her over the top of the Triumph.

"Then you can convince me why you are the last person to involve yourself with anything to do with blood play or the undead."

She didn't reply, but walked ahead of him, let them both into the house, then said, "I'm going to get a towel and dry my hair and change into a sweater. I've no clothing to offer you, so why don't you get us both a Scotch. In the cupboard next to the fridge. Glasses on the sideboard in the sitting room."

Elodie disappeared upstairs and Moretti did as he was told, switching on a small lamp by the sofa in the sitting room. A few minutes later she was back, barefoot, in a voluminous black sweater, rubbing her hair with a white towel. He handed her the Scotch, waited for her to sit down on the sofa on which he had first seen her, and sat down opposite her. She wrapped the towel into a turban around her head and raised her glass.

"*Salut*. Okay, so now I'll tell you. It's a long, complicated, dirty piece of personal laundry that I have never shared with anyone — not even Liz, and I don't want her to know. I am probably crazy to be telling it to a policeman, and if you took it any further I would deny every word."

"That bad?"

"That bad." Elodie took a sip of her Scotch, and a deep breath. "Here we go. As I imagine you know, I was married, once. It was what the tabloids call a love match. We were crazy about each other. My ex-husband was a brilliant medical researcher and pathologist, specializing in heart disease in children. About a decade or so ago, there was a huge scandal, when the parents of a child who had died of congenital heart disease discovered that her body had been returned to them without her heart, which had been kept for research, without their permission. This was just the tip of a gigantic iceberg. Literally thousands of children's hearts had been removed during post mortem examinations, and more than one hospital was implicated. The motivation, of course, was financial: huge donations from pharmaceutical companies to the hospitals involved. My ex was one of the pathologists who did this, and he made no attempt to deny it. He vehemently defended the practice. I can remember exactly what he said. 'The advances we have made in surgery, in understanding, in diagnosis, would not have been possible without this collection.'" Up to this point, Elodie's voice had been even, the tone measured, but now it changed. "It was when he used that word. *Collection.* I remember looking at him and thinking, *I have been blinded by love. I really don't know you at all.*"

Gently, Moretti interrupted. "But he was right, wasn't he, about the advances in medicine? And I have worked with many pathologists, attended more than one post mortem, and if they did not somehow manage to distance themselves, separate themselves from — in your ex's case — those tiny bodies lying on a slab in front of them, they would not survive. Policemen do it too, make jokes or sound cold and unfeeling in the face of tragedy and human suffering."

In response, Elodie held out her glass, and Moretti took it from her, refilled it and handed it back to her. He watched her for a moment, then said, "You implied there was a risk in telling me because of my profession, but I am assuming there was an enquiry, new guidelines set up, and all the shit that happens to appease an outraged public. So I am also assuming there's more."

"There is." She drank no more of the Scotch, but held the refilled glass in front of her, twisting it in the light from the lamp on a side table near the sofa. "Remember I said 'financial motivation'? There was something about my ex's face when he defended the practice, and it looked like fear. Since he didn't seem to have a conscience about it, I wondered what else he hadn't told me. I'm pretty good with computers, and so I hacked into his emails, and some of his other files. Actually, it wasn't that difficult."

Elodie leaned forward and pulled the towel off her hair. Like the whisky in the glass, it shone in the light from the lamp.

"Guess what his email password was, Ed."

She paused, and Moretti took a chance.

"Elodie."

She nodded. "Yes, plus the year we married. As I told you, we loved each other, and that's what he kept saying when I found out the full story. 'But I love you, I love you.'"

"The full story?"

This time she drank some of the Scotch before answering.

"He had a private arrangement of his own with a pharmaceutical company in Europe, and was selling the hearts of children. For profit — obscene, vast amounts of money. I found some of his financial transactions also. And you know what he said when I confronted him? 'For God's sake, Elodie, you're a scientist. Stop being sentimental. They're *dead*.' Then, with that wonderful smile of his he said, 'You're not going to shop me, are you?'"

Elodie leaned back, and closed her eyes.

"So, Detective Inspector Moretti, I have not the least interest in blood plays and the *un*-dead. My ex-husband's *collection* of children's hearts is my alibi, for what it's worth."

Moretti remembered the rose on the sodden pavement, and easily resisted the impulse to go over to her.

"And you didn't shop him."

"No. I let him pay me off, settled for a fortune in his dirty money, came back to the island, and swore never to be sentimental again." She raised her glass to Moretti and said, "And so far so good."

Message taken. "I should go," he said. "I'll check around first."

When he came back downstairs, Elodie was lying on the sofa. He thought she was asleep, but she looked up as he came in.

"Thanks, Ed." She sat up and swung her bare feet back on to the carpet. She had no rings on her fingers, but she had one on her toe, and it looked like a diamond.

Rings on her fingers and bells on her toes, she shall have music wherever she goes.

Absurdly, the old nursery rhyme came into his head, and the thought crossed Moretti's mind that it might once have been on the ring finger of her left hand. A kind of symbolic trampling underfoot of sentimentality, perhaps. The fancy added eroticism to the thought.

"Just a moment more of your time, Detective Inspector," she said. "I have a suggestion to make. About another woman in far more danger than me."

Moretti sat down again, carefully averting his glance from her feet.

Chapter Twenty-Eight

"Rebecca Falla, the wise woman of Icart, that's what your godmother calls her."

"That's what she calls herself. Or that's what her planchette circle calls her. You talked about this after the showdown at the Lorrimers' party?"

"Yes." Moretti returned Liz's direct look with one of his own. "She phoned earlier than I expected, so I took her with me to the farm. Maud Cole had just contacted me about Meg's return. Your aunt already knew Maud Cole, and they had at some point talked about Meg. She also says that, if anyone can get Meg to open up, it's your Aunt Becky, and she thinks they know each other, because your great-aunt knew Gus Dorey."

Liz put down her glass of beer, and sighed. "Now my boss and my godmother conspire to undo all the years of dodging Auntie Becky. What do you want me to do?"

"Go and see her, find out if she does know Meg, and see if she'll take her in for a while."

"Take her in?" Liz looked sceptical. "Why would she do that?"

"Because, according to Elodie, she takes in waifs and strays from time to time — cats, dogs, humans."

Liz looked surprised.

"El must have kept in contact."

"She has. One of life's originals, she finds her. About as unscientific as anyone she has ever met, but at the same time as devoid of sentimentality as anyone she has ever met."

"And that appeals?"

"That appeals."

The thought crossed Liz's mind that her Guvnor knew her godmother better than she did. She stood up.

"Thanks for the beer, Guv. I'll leave you a message after I've seen her."

"Saturday tomorrow, but we should meet, the three of us. I didn't say it this morning, but Al is going to talk to the cleaning staff at Aaron Gaskell's office, see if they have anything more to say, and I'm going to talk to Gord Martel again."

"I've got a rehearsal tonight with Jenemie for a gig next weekend. Besides, I'd rather visit Auntie Becky in daylight."

They both laughed, although both of them knew she was not joking.

* * *

It was dusk by the time Moretti reached Hugo Shaw-cross's house. There was really no way to avoid passing Elodie's place, and he wondered if she might see his Triumph go by. With any luck she would be in her study, catching up with work. She had told him she was taking on something new and was behind schedule.

As he drove past the limestone gateposts, he took a look through the gloaming at the bijou little nest, built on blood money. Of course Elodie should have turned her ex in, and perhaps she would have been freer of him if she had. *Simplistic*, he thought. *Stopping loving someone is not like turning off a tap. As he should know.*

When he got out of the car in Hugo Shawcross's driveway, he saw a face peering out of the window. There was no doorbell, only a knocker, and Moretti called out as he rapped on it.

"Mr. Shawcross, it's Detective Inspector Moretti."

A moment later, the door opened halfway, and Hugo Shawcross looked around it.

"Detective Inspector. You're on your own?"

His voice was still rasping, but possibly the wavering tone had as much to do with fear as damaged vocal cords. Opening his front door must still require a real summoning up of the blood for Gandalf.

"Yes. Seemed best. May I come in?"

"Of course!"

False jollity now, probably at the phrase "seemed best."

Brenda Le Huray's home seemed very much as she had left it. The style of furniture was more likely to be hers than its present occupant, with flowery cretonne covers, frilly lampshades and numerous knickknacks still in place on numerous small, heavily varnished tables. Moretti wiped his feet on a mat that faintly read "Welcome" and followed Hugo through the hallway, past what Brenda Le Huray would probably have called a lounge, to the back of the house. As he did so, a large cat streaked past him into one of the front rooms, from whence came the sound of vigorous scratching as Mrs. Le Huray's cretonne came under attack.

"Stoker, I presume."

"Yes. Don't know what I'd do without him. Very grateful to your detective sergeant. She likes cats?"

"She likes Ms. Ashton. We didn't want her helping out, for obvious reasons."

They were now in a room overlooking the back garden, or what Moretti could see of it through the dusk. Hugo Shawcross had set it up as his study, and in this room the furniture looked functional rather than frilly. Besides a desk of modern design with a laptop on it, the walls were lined with bookshelves, many of which were still empty. In front of the desk was a swivel chair in fake leather, and there was another, similar chair in front of a panel television on a space between the bookshelves.

"A drink, Detective Inspector? Coffee? Something stronger?"

"No thank you, sir." Moretti crossed over to the window. "This room is on the ground floor and you have no covering on your window. Perhaps you should change that."

"Great minds, Inspector!" Again, the mock-jollity. "I've got someone coming in to measure for blinds tomorrow."

"Good. Let's get started." Moretti turned the chair in front of the television screen around to face the one by the desk, and Hugo took the hint, sat down and leaned forward earnestly.

"How can I help you, Inspector? As you know from my statement, I saw nothing of my attacker."

"That's not why I'm here. I want you to tell me why you are in Guernsey — oh, not because of the business with the underage daughter of a cabinet minister, I know about that — but why specifically Guernsey. It wasn't the scenery that brought you here, was it?"

A gobbling noise came out of Hugo, and for a minute Moretti wondered if his shock attack might have been too much for Gandalf's present state of health. The face behind his now re-growing beard went white, then red, then purple.

"I don't see what you ..."

"You do, sir, and I need that information to find out who attacked you, whoever is putting the fear of God in Marla Maxwell and, more significantly, who killed a harmless old man. I think part of the answer lies with you, and this was not a random attack after all. I think you knew that all along, and I'm here on my own because the reason you are in Guernsey may not be illegal, but is so important to you that you are unwilling to share it."

Moretti leaned back, unbuttoned his jacket, rested his head against the high back of the chair, and waited. It didn't take long before it all came tumbling out, interspersed with gulps of brandy that Gandalf had brought out, after asking, from a cabinet in the desk unit.

It was all about books.

Or *a* book.

"I am not a book collector, Detective Inspector, but my field of expertise is folklore and I am particularly interested in vampirology, witchcraft, that sort of thing. I am involved with a research group looking at the *Malleus Maleficarum* ..."

"The Hammer of Witches. I know about this from Sergeant Falla. Go on."

"A few months ago, one of our members came to a meeting with very exciting news. It came from a Canadian newspaper — he has family there — and it was about the discovery at the University of Alberta of an incredibly rare book called *Invectives Against the Sect of the Waldensians*. Written around 1465 by a French monk, the article described it, not inappropriately, as a how-to guide on battling witchcraft. There are only three other known copies in various universities, and this one is thought to be the actual original, beyond price. But what really excited me was that this member of our group said he had spoken about it to a London book dealer, and *he* said he was pretty sure that, years ago, he had sold something similar to a regular customer. The dealer said he was just starting out and was too young and wet behind the ears to realize what he had sold, until this book came to light. Of course, as he said, he could be wrong, but all he could remember about the buyer was that he came from Guernsey. They had talked about the folklore and the superstitions here, which is why he remembered."

Hugo Shawcross took another swig of brandy and coughed.

"Voice tired," he said, putting up an apologetic hand. "Give me a moment."

Moretti waited, then said, "And it would have suited you, I imagine, to leave the country for a while?" Hugo Shawcross nodded, gingerly. "So you came here, joined the Island Players, and started to talk about vampires and similar subjects — or did you know who you were looking for?"

Hugo shook his head vigorously, then winced. "No idea. Saw an ad for the group in the paper, thought it might give me a start. Then all the funny stuff started to happen."

"So you assumed, when you were attacked, that someone thought you were on the trail of something they also wanted? Had you dropped hints about the actual book?"

Hugo nodded. "Only indirectly."

"Can you remember to whom you spoke, and what do you mean by 'indirectly'?"

Hugo looked thoughtful. "Actually, now I come to think of it, I may have said something about it when all the discussion started about vampires and so on, and Marie Gastineau got up on her high horse. But it was all in the context of the power of the written word, and I am pretty sure I never mentioned the title."

"Do you remember who was there?"

"Most of the Island Players la Gastineau calls 'the ones who matter.'" Hugo gave a snort of disdain, and clearly regretted it.

"You say you're pretty sure you didn't mention the title. Why not? Wouldn't that have speeded up your search?"

"Inspector, when there are millions involved, one can't be too careful."

"Millions?"

Hugo nodded again. "Possibly." He examined his empty glass, got up, and refilled it from the bottle of excellent cognac.

Moretti stood up and fastened his jacket.

"There's the motivation for all this, Mr. Shawcross, rather than abstract twaddle about vampires and the undead. Money. I wish you'd said all this earlier, instead of limiting yourself to variations on the theme of 'evil exists.'"

"Oh, but it does." Hugo swung around, moving his whole body to avoid turning his neck. It was now very dark in the room, and he switched on a light on the desk, and turned on his laptop. "Let me show you what I am talking about," he said.

It took Hugo Shawcross only a few moments to find what he was looking for. On the screen appeared a photograph of a battered leather-bound book, looking all of its five-hundred years of age, with what appeared to be studs on the cover. There was an article beneath it.

"There it is," said Hugo, his voice hushed in awe now, rather than discomfort.

"What sort of size and length is it?" Moretti asked.

"Not big. A hundred and fifty pages. You can read the article if you like."

"Give me the gist."

With a sudden burst of energy, Hugo swung around in the chair to face Moretti. Behind him on the laptop the image of the *Invective Against the Sect of the Waldensians* glowed in the bubble of light from the desk lamp.

"The article quotes a professor of mediaeval history at the university saying it is a picture of human beings as agents of the Devil and he doesn't like to touch it, or be near it. When I said 'evil exists,' I wasn't joking, Detective Inspector. Looking for this book nearly cost me my life. I think anyone else doing that should be very, very careful."

Backing out of Gandalf's driveway was a relief and a pleasure, and Moretti took the corner too sharply as he came onto the road, the Triumph brushing against the post holding up the name of Brenda Le Huray's house, "Cosy Corner."

Moretti swore, loudly, to rid himself of the creepy feeling left by the interview. Anything less suitable than Cosy Corner as a name for its present incarnation would be hard to find. His feeling of discomfort was not eased by seeing a car in Elodie's driveway as he drove past. He slowed down and made a mental note of the number. The make of car was easy to remember and Moretti had a suspicion he knew whose it might be.

He drove on until he was out of sight of the house, pulled to the side of the road, and left a message on both Falla's private and police mobiles. Then he looked at his watch, saw it was still quite early, turned the car around and drove back into St. Peter Port.

The first people he saw at Emidio's were Don Taylor and Irene Edwards, sitting in a booth near the window. They were laughing together, and Moretti was about to walk past and not intrude on their privacy when Don looked up.

"Look who's here! We came to get something to eat, and in the hopes you might be playing. Deb said she'd no idea, but that didn't mean anything. Join us."

Irene Edwards seemed as delighted to see him as Don and, a bowl of *stracciatella* later, Moretti was feeling much better. Don and Irene seemed very comfortable with each other, and that too made him feel good. Then Lonnie and Dwight walked in and the miasma that had hung over him since the interview finally dispersed. The four of them went downstairs to the club, where the beautiful Latvian girl was serving a handful of customers, most of whom were there because of her, and not for the décor. She seemed relieved to see their arrival, and waved at Lonnie, who waved back, then turned to Moretti.

"Let's open with 'You Go to My Head.' Marika's favourite. Okay?"

"Okay."

Moretti grinned, sat down and opened the piano. A few minutes later, and all there was in his head and his heart was the music.

Gradually, the Grand Saracen began to fill up, and when they took a break, Moretti saw that Don and Irene were no longer there. They played another set, and then prepared to leave. Or, rather, Moretti and Dwight did. Lonnie was making his way over to the bar. As Moretti passed him, Lonnie called out.

"Hey Ed, nearly forgot. Billie the Bus Bum had a message for someone called Perkins. Copper, he said."

"Where to find Meg? Tell him not to worry. We found her."

"I'll tell him. Only he wants to know, because someone else is looking for her, and he'll get a reward if he knows. A gent, he says. Mind you, you never know with Billie, do you?"

"No," said Moretti. Back in the Triumph he texted Al Brown.

"*Among the hermit's books, was there one called 'Invective against the Sect of the Waldensians'?*"

The miasma returned, as if it had never left.

Chapter Twenty-Nine

The run-through with Jenemie had taken Liz Falla's mind off things, and she had got back to her flat on the Esplanade to find Dwight sitting on the doorstep. Normally the sight of his smiling face would be reason for celebration, but Ed Moretti's two messages had put her mind right back on things temporarily forgotten.

Falla, there's a car in your aunt's driveway I think belongs to Aaron Gaskell. Jaguar. Did you take details when you helped him with his parking problems?

She had, and it was.

She had dismissed Dwight, to his disappointment and her own, phoned her aunt, to Elodie's annoyance, and her own discomfort.

"Are you all right, El?"

"I *was*. I was asleep. Why, what's wrong?"

"Nothing, just checking."

"At this hour?"

"You had a visitor and we wondered …"

"We? Oh."

Click, as the line went dead.

Well, at least Elodie wasn't.

It was so long since Liz visited her great-aunt that she had to check municipal records to make sure of the address, and she still got lost in the winding maze of lanes that ran between Le Gouffre and Le Havre de Bon Repos on the south coast, most of them ending up close to the cliff edge with nowhere further to go. Unless you were a goat, that is, and not driving a Figaro. There were few houses in this area, some crumbling Napoleonic battery sites and watch towers, and, with most of the tourists gone, the only visitors were the flocks of gulls and other seabirds wheeling and screaming overhead. It had been a wet and windy night, and the damp coolness in the air added to the chill Liz felt about this whole expedition.

Just as she was about to give up and make her way back to the main Forest-l'Erée road, she saw a sign on the roadside and turned the Figaro in the direction of the arrow beneath the words, "Planchette, Tarot, Palms Read. Goat's Milk and Cheese."

Auntie Becky, who else.

The cottage had been part of a sixteenth-century farmhouse on the cliffs, probably the cattle byre, and was now all that remained. Built in island granite, it had a wide entrance with double doors, and only one window, beneath a steeply sloping roof on the upper floor facing the road. There was a sturdily constructed picket fence around the cottage to protect the wise woman's fruit and veggies from any marauding goat, and the rest of the land was open, because Becky tried to keep her goats tethered, much as Guernsey cows were. At some point, Liz's Uncle Vern had put in a couple of skylights in the sloping roof and updated the plumbing. That is, he had installed a bathroom. As far as Liz knew, there was still no electricity.

As she pulled the Figaro up close to the front door, Aunt Becky appeared.

"It's you," she called out as Liz opened the car door. "I thought you were my ten o'clock."

Not second sight, then.

"I should be gone by then, Aunt Becky. It's only 9:30."

Rebecca Falla was dressed in black from head to toe, which showed off her wonderfully thick silver-white hair. She always wore it in a beautiful smooth coil around her head, and if there was anything Liz wouldn't mind inheriting from this so-called Becquet ancestor of hers it was that magnificent mane. At this moment in her life, her own was too short to judge. Her aunt had the tall genes of the Falla and Ashton families, her deeply wrinkled face tanned year-round by sun, wind and rain. As befitted a witch, her eyes were green and not brown, and beneath two strong, dark eyebrows they were fixed on her niece with what looked like melancholy.

"Come in," she said. "I am in mourning."

Without waiting to explain, she disappeared back into the house and Liz followed her.

Inside, the cottage was dark, lit only by two oil-lamps in the main space that served as siting-room, consulting room and séance room. The planchette wheel was on a circular central table covered by a crocheted cloth with astrological symbols embroidered in black and silver, and her aunt's crystal ball glowed beneath the light of one of the oil lamps on a spectacularly carved sideboard in a dark wood of some kind.

"Why are you in mourning?"

Her aunt turned back and said, "It's the subsidence."

She had retained into old age the mellifluous voice used to great effect in her métier, but her explanation was as woolly and unclear as many of her divinations, as Liz remembered them. They usually covered a range of possibilities.

"Come. I'll show you."

Liz followed her through into the small kitchen at the back of the cottage. There was a pleasant and un-otherworldly aroma of fresh baking in the air, and cups, saucers and small plates were set on the red-and-white gingham tablecloth over the kitchen table. It looked as if Aunt Becky's ten o'clock was going to have some cake with the clairvoyance. Her aunt opened the back door of the kitchen, and Liz followed her onto the stretch of land behind the cottage, the wind hitting her face with salt spray. It was dotted with tethered goats of various colours chewing away at the rough grass. They looked up, some more interested in their arrival than others.

"There. Take a look. I won't come with you."

Her aunt was pointing at the edge of the cliff, and Liz walked over, moving cautiously between the tethered animals. At some point in her childhood she had been butted by one of her aunt's goats, and it had hurt both her backside and her feelings. The drop was vertiginous, the cliffs high and steep at this point, the sea below churning around rocky outcrops, whipped up by the strong wind. There was always subsidence here, caused by the collapse of one or more of the numerous caves that honeycombed the coastline — many of which could only be reached at low tide, some only by boat.

Then she saw what she had been sent to see. Way below, caught on an outcrop of rock was a large chunk of grass-covered soil, and on it lay the remains of a goat, almost obscured by the clouds of gulls and other seabirds doing what scavengers do. She turned back and looked at her aunt, who was crying.

"I'm so sorry."

"My precious Delilah. Toggenburg-Saanen cross she was. Lovely milker. The earth broke away. I tried to save her, but when I looked over I saw she was dead, strangled by the rope. Hung by the neck until she was dead. Then the earth dropped down the cliff."

"I'm sorry," said Liz, again.

Not entirely devoid of sentimentality, Elodie, Liz thought.

Her aunt moved back into the cottage, and Liz followed her. Sitting at the table in the warm, cosy kitchen was a very thin, very old woman, eating a large slice of cake, and Liz did not have to be clairvoyant to know she was looking at Meg the gypsy.

When she saw Liz come through the door, Meg got up from her chair in distress, still clutching her piece of cake. Becky went over and touched her shoulder.

"This is my niece, Liz. Not to worry, Margie."

"Carrot cake," said Margie to Liz. "My favourite," and went back to the matter in hand.

"How did you know?"

They were now in the front room. Aunt Becky sighed, more irritated now than grieving.

"I didn't, though with your attitude I don't know why I should be honest about that. She comes here, she always has, and there's none that knows it, though with that fancy car of yours outside I'll have to worry about *that* now."

"Becky, did you know Gus Dorey? Elodie says you did."

"Margie's friend. 'course I knew him. I saw it all, in the cards." She indicated the Tarot pack near the planchette wheel. "It's all there, the hermit, the hanged man. Death."

Here we go, thought Liz.

"And the Lovers."

Liz started to pay attention.

"What do you know about that?"

Aunt Becky pulled out a chair and sat down, indicating that Liz should do the same.

"That was long ago, but that is why he died," she said. "That's what Margie says."

"Does she? Who was it that he loved?"

Her aunt stroked the pack of cards and smiled.

"If Margie knows that, she's not saying. But from what I remember at the time, there was talk that he reached above himself, and the girl had to be taken away to the mainland. Most of them come back — after — but this one left here forever."

"Could it have been one of the *messux*?"

"More likely than not."

Confirmation, thought Liz. *But I need more.*

"You say she often comes here, but this time she has a reason. Who is Margie running away from, Becky?"

Becky picked up the Tarot pack, shuffled through them and extracted two cards. She held one out to Liz, who took it.

"The Magician. Is that all she calls him? The Magician? See if you can get a name out of her."

Becky looked doubtful. "I'll try."

There was a knock at the door and Liz stood up.

"That'll be your ten o'clock. Let me know if she says anything, anything at all. I know Uncle Vern gave you a mobile. Do you know how to use it?"

Becky laughed scornfully.

"Yes, but it's no good to me, now it's lost its powers." She grinned, wickedly. "You'll just have to come round again."

As Liz turned to leave, Becky held out the other card.

"There's not just the Magician, she says. This one's with him, sometimes."

Liz took the card.

"The Fool. Is that what she calls him?"

Becky nodded. "I saw it all, you know, in the cards. The Hermit, the hanging. Death."

Just as Liz was toying with saying, "Maybe what you saw was poor little Delilah, hanging over the cliff edge," her aunt added, "Sometimes she calls the Magician this card."

She was holding out the Devil. He was carrying a spear or lance of some kind, and, incongruously, was mounted on a white horse.

"And Margie doesn't call the Fool a 'him.' She calls the Fool a 'her.'"

Chapter Thirty

Gord Martel lived in St. Sampson, where Moretti kept his Centaur. He had agreed to meet Moretti in the pub on the Bridge, an area close to the harbour, because he said the neighbours would talk if a policeman came to the door, and his wife would be upset, and plainclothes or not, they'd know, sooner or later.

If there was any area on the island that could be called industrial, it was St. Sampson, and the pub near the Bridge had no fancy trappings to provide atmosphere for tourists. At this hour on a Saturday morning, there were only one or two customers getting started on their day's drinking, and their well-worn clothes and unshaven faces matched the décor — or lack of it. The barmaid was engrossed in a horrific account of child abuse on the overhead TV by the bar, and barely paid any attention as Moretti came in. He sat by the only attractive feature on the premises, a finely etched glass window overlooking the harbour, and waited for Gord Martel, who came in a few minutes later, greeting the barmaid by name.

"'morning, Avril. My usual, please, and one for my friend."

The postman's usual turned out to be a surprisingly good cup of coffee.

"Well," he said, "let's get on with it, Inspector. I promised the wife I'd lay tiles today and I really don't know what else I can tell you."

"Good coffee," said Moretti, putting down his cup. "It's not so much about that day, Mr. Martel, but about the days before, the days when you and Gus Dorey talked, anything he might have said to you that might help us."

"About what?" Gord Martel looked agitated. "The poor old bugger killed himself."

Shock tactics, thought Moretti.

"No easy way to tell you this, Mr. Martel, but your friend did not kill himself. He was murdered, and can you think of anything he might have said to help us catch his killer."

After a brandy, fetched from the bar and paid for by Moretti, Gord Martel pulled himself together.

"Oh my Lord, Inspector, what a bombshell. Who would do such a thing. Let me think." The postman closed his eyes a moment, then said, "There was the time he said he couldn't lay his hands on stuff."

"Stuff?"

"Yes. Books, he meant. He thought it was his eyes, but I could see he wasn't sure. Mind you, how he would know there was anything missing, I don't know, because he had so many."

"So you wondered if someone was stealing his books?"

"I didn't. He did. I thought he'd just mislaid them. But now you've said this, I wonder."

Moretti thought back to the books around the hermit's body, scattered as if someone was hunting for something. Because books of value hadn't been touched, he had jumped to the conclusion that the hermit's private library was complete.

Moretti brought the interview to a swift end and left the pub. Once back in the Triumph, he checked his messages. There were three.

The first, from Maud Cole, was worrying.

Meg's been gone twenty-four hours.

The second was from Al Brown.

Man of mystery, Aaron Gaskell. Re. book, no, not a title to forget. Can we meet?

The third was from Falla, and it was baffling.

Magician, Fool — two of them?

As he started the car, his mobile rang. It was Falla.

"Don't want to say too much, Guv, but Maud's neighbour is safe as houses. See you at Hospital Lane?"

"My place. I'll text Al and say you'll give him a lift here."

Moretti finished the call and contacted Aloisio Brown.

* * *

"Take-away pizza, not from Emidio's, but not bad. I'm going to make coffee."

They settled around the large, circular kitchen table, pizza in the middle, notebooks in hand, plus Al's iPad. The coffee mugs were china, as were the plates.

"Nice." Al traced the Greek key design on his plate.

"Yes." Moretti cleared a space for his large notepad, turned to a blank page.

"You first, Falla. The Jag — Gaskell's?"

"Yes, but more than that I don't know because El hung up on me." Moretti said nothing, so Liz went crisply through her visit to Rebecca Ashton, omitting such details as Delilah's demise and the arrival of her aunt's ten o'clock, who turned out to be an august member of the States of Guernsey, the island parliament, and not thrilled at crossing paths with her.

"So, two people. A Magician who is also the Devil, and a woman who is a Fool. Al, I think you met the Devil. Or almost." Moretti got up and refilled his mug. Outside the cottage window it looked as if there was a storm brewing. The wind was rising, the sky darkening. He put on the overhead light. "The Devil is good at getting people to do his bidding if there's something in it for them, and I have always thought there were two motivations here. Any ideas about who the Fool might be?"

Liz spoke first. "My money's on Ginny Gastineau," she said.

Moretti nodded. "Mine too." He turned to Liz. "At the party, your godmother said Priestley was looking at someone and he was scared, and she didn't think it was Gaskell. It was probably Ginnie Gastineau, but how she put him up to it we have yet to find out."

"That makes three votes for Ginnie." Al Brown scrolled through his iPad. "And for the Devil I nominate Aaron Gaskell. Before I went to his office today, I talked to Bernie, who's been doing some digging. He's had trouble checking Gaskell's background. He's worked for the same private bank for years, but as for finding any kind of address for him, personal details — nothing. Or virtually nothing. Looks like he's lived in hotels, that kind of accommodation, and he has enough money to do that. He's still working on it, but he hasn't yet found a birth certificate that matches up. Bernie's done this kind of checking a hundred times, and he says it looks like a deliberate attempt to hide. He found no involvement with any acting group of any kind, and all he *has* found is a membership in a book club — not one where you all sit around and read books the members choose, but one where you buy certain books, many of them very pricey, according to Bernie."

"Ah," said Moretti. "Which leads us to the Waldensians and my own cock-up, Al. Someone was looking for just one particular book, and they found it."

When Moretti had finished going through the interview with Hugo Shawcross, Al leaned back in his chair and gave a low whistle.

"The hermit was killed for one book?"

"Looks like it, but that doesn't explain the nonsense with Marla Maxwell, and the threats against Tanya Gastineau. Gandalf was being scared off, but why scare him off *after* the book was stolen?"

"Because he was just what you thought he was, Guv. A red herring."

"Maybe." Moretti turned to Al Brown who was, he noticed, wearing a diamond stud in his ear. Well, it was Saturday, wasn't it. "What do the cleaning staff have to say?"

Al grinned. "I saw you taking in my ear decoration, Guv, and the ladies loved it. They became quite chatty. They say he asks a lot of questions about island people, particularly the old families. His secretary, who's related to one of the cleaning staff, told her it's like — and I quote — working for a zombie. When I asked her what they thought she meant, they said it's like he's not all there, a piece missing, and they don't mean thick as two short planks. To quote again."

"Interesting." Moretti got up and walked over to the window. The first rain drops had started to bead against the glass. "They rehearse tonight, don't they? I think we should make an appearance at some point in the evening."

Liz closed her notepad and looked across the kitchen at Moretti. He was stroking a small sculpture of a black cat on the windowsill, and both the gesture and the carving seemed out of character and out of place. It was more the kind of decoration favoured by her great-aunt.

"A bit dramatic, Guv, don't you think? Mightn't it start something?"

"It might." Her Guvnor seemed angry. "What other option is there? We take Ginnie in for questioning, because a madwoman has identified a Fool involved, from the Tarot, and we think it's her? And we pick up

Aaron Gaskell and tell him he is the Magician? God, Falla, I'd look and sound like something out of a bloody board game."

Al Brown still sat in his chair, watching the two of them with interest. Liz did not appear in the least put out. She was smiling as she picked up her bag and slung it across her shoulders.

"And they'd be Miss Scarlett and Professor Plum, right? Want me to phone Elodie, Guv, and ask her about last night's visit from the chief suspect?"

Moretti was picking up his notepad from the table in which he had taken notes while Liz and Al talked, and Al couldn't see his face.

"If Elodie Ashton wants to live dangerously, she has made it very clear there's nothing we can do. Leave it, Falla."

Liz was still smiling. "When and where shall we three meet again, Guv?"

"Hospital Lane, at seven."

Al Brown was silent in the car, and it was Liz who spoke first.

"Penny for your thoughts."

She heard him laugh in the darkness.

"About what they're worth. Can I buy you a drink?"

"No, but I've got a nice red at my place."

Liz parked the car in the small garage she rented on the road behind the Esplanade, and they walked in the now steady rain to her second-floor flat facing the islands of Herm and Jethou, across the waters of the bay.

"Nice."

Al looked around appreciatively at the little sitting room's cosy, eclectic mix of furnishings, the attractive rug on the floor. Interesting choice — it looked like a Turkoman.

"I like it." Liz poured them both a glass of wine, handed one to Al, who was looking at her collection of CDs. They sat down, facing each other, and there was a moment of awkward silence. Again, it was Liz who bridged the gap.

"So, has coming here solved any problems, Al?"

Al gave the laugh Liz had heard in the car. It was not a happy laugh.

"You guessed, huh? Not one." He took a sip of wine, then said, "No, that's not accurate. I now know I don't want to be a policeman."

"Ouch!" Liz was genuinely taken aback. "Is that the effect we've had on you?"

"Yes." Al drank some wine, and added, "If I don't like working with you and Moretti, I will never like it. I am thinking of going back to school, going into psychology, something like that. It is the only part of this that interests me."

Liz put down her glass of wine. "So, let's psychoanalyze a bit. We all agreed about the Fool. But how about the Magician? See, there's something about Aaron Gaskell that doesn't quite fit to me, and yet there's something nagging me about him, and I don't know what it is." She laughed. "Maybe what I need is hypnosis, not psychoanalysis."

Al got up, and started to walk around the room, stopping to look at a picture on the wall of a woman in a long white dress, walking alone in a forest.

"Douanier Rousseau. Not one I know — is that how you see yourself, Liz? No, don't answer that. About Gaskell. When I met him, I thought of something I read about in one of my courses. The French call it '*la belle indifférence.*' It describes a beautiful, exterior calm that hides an ugly interior of hysteria, hatred, rage. Gaskell fits the bill perfectly."

"Yes, Al, but why?" Liz was now up and pacing. She put her wine glass back on the kitchen counter under the window overlooking the bay, where she had watched a white heron, and worried about Elodie. "Means, yes — anyone can make a garrotte — opportunity, yes. But *why*? What's his motive?"

"Maybe he's mad — no reason. And maybe it's all about the book, after all."

Liz looked sceptical. "Maybe. But I don't think the Guvnor is entirely sold on Gaskell as the Devil, or I think he'd be more concerned about Elodie."

"You think so?" Al smiled at Liz and finished the last of the wine in his glass. "Moretti's a difficult man to read, but I don't think he wants to go in that direction." He got up from the chair and took his empty glass over to the kitchen counter. "I think he'd rather your luscious aunt took up with a good-looking zombie with mucho cash, and a perfect profile."

"Perfect profile. *Perfect profile.* Oh my God, oh my God."

Liz ran across the room and grabbed Al by the

shoulders, so hard he staggered. "You've shaken it loose. Remember the mortuary, seeing the hermit's body?"

"And you said he reminded you of someone, but you couldn't place it. Peculiar, you said. I remember."

"I'd just had to deal with a parking problem, and it was fresh in my mind, but not fresh enough."

"Aaron Gaskell."

They spoke in unison.

Just as Liz picked up her mobile to call Moretti, it rang.

"Guv, I was just going to call you."

Moretti interrupted her.

"Al with you? Get out to the Gastineau place in Forest. I'm on my way there now. Dr. Edwards is already there."

"Another attack?"

Al was picking up her coat and car keys for her as she walked towards the door.

"Two. One dead, one alive."

Chapter Thirty-One

Moretti knelt down on the sodden grass beside Irene Edwards.

Lying there, her blonde hair drenched and darkened, her mouth slightly open, eyelids fluttering, surrounded by wet, drooping Ladies' Tresses, Tanya brought to mind a pre-Raphaelite painting of Ophelia on the riverbank. *Millais*, if he remembered rightly. They had wrapped her in blankets, and someone had fetched a tarp of some kind from the house and propped it up on what looked like tent poles. It flapped loudly in the wind with a sound like gunshots, and they had to shout above the racket.

"Where is her husband?"

"Sedated. He was hysterical, getting in the way. I gave him a needle, and someone took him back inside. Your copper, I believe. He was the one who called first, and he has everyone corralled somewhere. Couldn't move her until we'd stabilized her." Irene Edwards looked up at Moretti through a mass of soaked, dark hair. "Same as last time. Attempted garrotting."

"Bite marks?"

"Yes. Vicious, far worse than on Shawcross. Probably saved her life, because that took time. Let's get her out of here now." Irene Edwards stood up and gestured at the ambulance attendants, who ran over, the stretcher between them. "God, Ed, what in the hell was she doing out here in this weather? An assignation?"

Moretti bent down and extracted a sodden fragment from the grass near the path.

"An assignation, yes, with a bloody cigarette. Cigarettes kill, and this one nearly cost her her life."

As they ran to the ambulance, Irene called out, "I'll stay with her, Ed."

"Glad you were around."

"Me too. Think I'm going to be around for quite a while."

The ambulance doors shut, and they were gone, the tires screaming on the gravel path, as Liz Falla's Figaro hurtled towards Moretti. As Liz and Al got out, Moretti pulled out his mobile.

"Bob? Have you got backup yet? Mauger and Le Marchant, good. Hold them there and don't let anyone go anywhere — yes, that includes using the facilities — no, Falla is coming with me, and La Gastineau will just have to put up with it. Check first there's no way to get out, okay?"

Moretti turned off his mobile and grabbed Falla by the arm, both the gesture and the force behind it coming with the shock of the unfamiliar.

"Jimmy's already with the other victim. He says to be prepared. It's — nasty."

"Sir." Al also put his hand on Liz Falla's arm, his touch protective. "Falla could stay here, couldn't she? With Bob McMullin?"

"No." Moretti spoke quite calmly. He started to walk towards the Figaro. "Falla comes. The case is wrapping up, and Falla is always in at the kill. Aren't you, Falla?"

Liz didn't bother to reply. She took her car keys out of her pocket and got into the driver's seat.

The light from the interior of the little cottage streamed out the open door into the night sky, augmented by SOCO's arc lamps, splintering in the rain. The three stood in the doorway and stayed there, staring.

Blood everywhere. Floor, carpets, walls, ceiling, evidence of the violent struggle that had taken place as Roddy the Body fought for his life. He was a fit young man, and had put up a fight that had knocked lamps from tables, turned over chairs. There was broken glass on the floor. He had even used the two suitcases that McMullin and Le Marchant had talked about to defend himself. Blood-covered, they lay in the centre of the room, one split open. Jimmy Le Poidevin came towards them, his white protective clothing spattered, his face grim.

"Not a pretty sight," he said. "Perkins has already lost his dinner. Steel yourselves." He held out three pairs of latex gloves and covers for their shoes.

Roddy Bull lay face upwards on the floor, with what looked like a second mouth above the neck of his sweater. Moretti knelt down beside him. His eyes were open, staring up at them, and to Moretti they didn't yet seem vacant of life, as if the image of his killer still lived on the retina. Blood had begun to dry around the garrotte that remained in the wound, embedded in the tortured flesh.

"Any bites?"

"None this time. Same double loop, you see."

"Yes. How long ago, would you say?"

"Not long. An hour or two? The photographer's on his way, then we'll move him. Why the hell did this happen?" Jimmy Le Poidevin spoke without his usual bombast, his voice subdued.

"Because his ex-girlfriend confided in him."

Al and Liz were now looking around the wrecked, bloodied mess of a living room, and Moretti bent down to take a closer look at the items pulled from the damaged suitcase.

"Hold on. What have we here?"

Half-hidden by a solitary shoe was a book. As Moretti extricated it, Liz and Al came over to take a look.

"Reading matter for the journey? I don't think so."

"That Waldensian thing?" Al asked.

"No, but just as unlikely a book for Roddy Bull to own. Victorian porn, with some smuttily graphic illustrations." Moretti held it out, and Al took it from him.

"This doesn't fit in with the pattern of the hermit's collection," he said.

Moretti and Falla were looking at each other.

"Remember our Tin Pan Alley conversation, Falla? What was it you said to me?

"It was something Elodie said. 'His only passion is books.'"

"Words, words, words," said Moretti.

As they made for the door, Jimmy Le Poidevin shouted after them, "Wherever he is, the bastard that did this, he'll be easy to spot. He'll be soaked with the dead man's blood."

In the Gastineaus' grand sitting room, they were greeted by Bob McMullin. Behind him, with PC Le Marchant hovering in the background, on various sofas and chairs sat the Island Players — or some of them. They looked like a group assembled for a photograph, or the final unveiling of the murderer in a Golden Age mystery. Some were in shell-shocked silence, some whimpering or openly crying, some chattering nervously to one another, but none were blood-covered.

"Where's Jim Landers?"

It was Raymond Morris who answered Moretti. "How one was expected to have a rehearsal without the leading man, is beyond credulity, but there you are." His outrage did not seem related in any way to the violence outside.

"Raymond, I left him a message."

Marie Maxwell also sounded outraged, sitting with her arms around her daughter, who was sobbing.

"Where's Ginnie Purvis?"

"With PC Mauger, Guv. Under restraint. She tried to resist, and she's quite strong. And she was really wet. I cautioned her."

"Good man."

Bob McMullin looked relieved.

"Who found Mrs. Gastineau?"

"Rory." It was Lana Lorrimer who answered. "He went berserk."

Before Moretti could ask his next question, Liz Falla asked it for him.

"Where's Elodie?"

This time it was Marie Maxwell who answered, huffily.

"Another one who didn't bother to show."

As Liz turned to run, Moretti stopped her.

"No."

"I'm always in at the kill. Guv." Her voice was rough, as she controlled her emotions. "You said it."

"This won't be a kill, Falla. He needs to spill his guts, and I want you here, to get Ginnie Purvis to spill hers. She'll talk to you, I'm sure — remember the bookmarks? And that's an order."

He sat opposite her on the wing chair she had bought in a moment of nostalgia in a local second-hand store, cradling the glass of whiskey he had requested. Jim Landers seemed quite at home.

"Forgive my appearance," he said.

If she had had a spyhole in the front door as her father had suggested, he would never have crossed the threshold. Apart from the overcoat he had put on after whatever it was he had done, he was blood-soaked from head to toe. Even his hair was smeared with it. He had pushed past her into the hallway, and then pushed her ahead of him into her sitting room, pressing the knife he held into her back.

"Sorry about this," he said, in his usual calm, disconnected way, "but it's for your own good. I remember how ably you rejected my advances and, to speak in clichés, resistance is futile."

Elodie tried to copy the cool tone of Jim Landers's voice.

"Is that what this is about?"

"God no!" He laughed, genuinely amused. "This is far bigger than you, although I was disappointed. This is about the story of my life. I want to tell it to you, I always did. Hence the knife, and not my preferred method."

Speak in clichés, think in clichés. Keep him talking.

"Whose blood, Jim?"

"This?" He looked down, as if mildly surprised. "No one you know, don't worry. Some of it is mine. He put up a good fight."

"Why?"

"Ah, that's a good question, but to understand the answer, first I have to tell you the story of my life. Someone to talk to, you know."

And out it came, like a dam burst, a waterfall of childhood memories — of an absent mother, immersed in her own world; a father full of tales of past glories. As long as Jim Landers the child wanted to hear them, he had his father's full attention. Most of them were brutal, and Jim Landers cheerily told them, his amusement as grotesque as the mocking laughter and macabre clown figures on the ghost trains of Elodie's childhood that gave her nightmares.

The wounded self, she thought. *Freud's phrase for the hidden persona of the neglected, abused child.*

At some point in the narrative, he pulled a piece of cord out of his pocket to illustrate his story, putting down his glass to do so, still holding on to the knife.

"The preferred method of garrotting by the Foreign Legion, my father said. *La loupe*, a double loop. The victim pulls on one, only to tighten the other. Once thought of running away from home to join them in the desert. *Marche ou crève*, that's what they had tattooed on their feet. Couldn't have been any worse than boarding school."

Slowly, carefully, she thought. *But at some point, one of us must make a move.* "I asked you 'why,' and you said it was a good question. Why, Jim? What is the answer?"

Jim Landers face glowed. "Because this one acquisition is my chance at deliverance from penury, and I had to make sure no one stood in the way. This chap, for instance." Deadpan, he tugged at his sodden sleeve. "Came into the shop one day, rattling on about some secret Rory's bimbo has told him. No idea what it was, but couldn't risk it, not so close to the financial freedom I'd always wanted."

"Why Hugo, Jim?"

"Apart from being a pompous clot, you mean? Ginnie suggested it."

"*Ginnie*?"

"Yes, she was there when the aforementioned clot held forth about vampires, and evil existing at the first meeting about the new play. He said something about curses and witches and books, and I knew he was on the same track. A man like that would be. Ginnie saw I was upset."

"Upset?"

The understatement was chilling.

"Yes. Ginnie adores me, you see, so I told her about my quest. 'Why don't we hoist him on his own petard!' she said."

"So, the whole vampire thing, the biting and so on, was a red herring?"

Jim Landers giggled, a grotesque little sound. "Very funny, Elodie, very funny." He was instantly serious again. "Bit of a challenge for me, when I tried it. Not as easy as you might think. But Ginnie was a chum, the only person I trusted with my story, and she had her own reasons for being interested in the Pleinmont hermit." Jim Landers's blood-smeared face now radiated delight. "Luck, for once, was on my side. You see, I had already been setting free some of the books. No way they should be owned by a down-and-out in a hovel. Then I read about this rare book in Alberta, that there was possibly another copy somewhere, and Hugo started dropping hints. I had an advantage over him, because I knew where it was likely to be!"

"One book, Jim? One book could change your life? What one book could do that?"

Jim Landers looked impatient. "A book worth millions, of course. Ginnie was thrilled when I found it. Thought we'd be walking off into the sunset together. One day the troglodyte saw me, and so did the old bag who hung around his place. I told Ginnie, and Ginnie helped, so I was happy to go along with her vampire idea, and Hugo had to go, just in case. What the hell she was looking for in that dump, I don't know. Not my business." Landers leaned towards Elodie, lowering his voice theatrically. "Only I'll have to hold on to it for a while till the heat dies down."

"How can you bear to sell something about which you feel such passion?"

Jim Landers looked disapproving. "It is a disgusting book, and I don't want it near my Jane Austens. Like the piece of filth I offered this chap." Another tug at his sleeve.

Inconsequential thoughts began to flit through Elodie's mind.

That lovely fresh sea bass in the fridge. Should I offer him dinner, and is he mad enough to accept? Difficult, while eating, to hold on to any weapon other than cutlery. I'll have to get rid of that chair, but I wasn't that sure about it in the first place. Ginnie, dear God, Ginnie.

Suddenly, Elodie began to feel very angry. She was getting tired of waiting to die, and she'd decided that she had to try to break through that prissy, prudish façade.

"Ginnie had other motives, Jim, you're right. You weren't supposed to be a *chum*, you're supposed to be her stud, mate with her and give her a son as heir to the Gastineau throne. She didn't adore you, she adored your *prick*."

"You dirty-minded bitch!" His voice rose.

"And you didn't kill Hugo, did you? You failed even at that, didn't you? What *would* Daddy have to say about that?"

"I should put a stop to that mouth of yours."

Jim Landers stood up, the garotte in his hand. As he lunged towards her, there was an ear-splitting crash from behind Elodie, as her back door smashed to the floor. The guitar-playing policeman raced past her and had the rope out of Jim Landers's hands with a high kick worthy of a Rockette, then she was in Ed Moretti's arms.

Through the blur of shock she could hear his voice. "Great lock on the front door and a lousy one on the back. Thankfully, I forgot to remind you," he said.

Chapter Thirty-Two

There were four of them in the roundhouse: Moretti, Liz Falla, Al Brown and Aaron Gaskell.

Or Lucas Dorey, as he was now calling himself.

Just before they put on the protective gloves and masks they would need, Liz asked Moretti, "How do you know?"

He smiled at her.

"*The Lady's Not For Burning*. After our last meeting, I went back to Hospital Lane and got Gus Dorey's copy out of storage." Moretti turned to Lucas Dorey. "Your father liked to underline or highlight passages that meant something to him, and all of them were about the love he had for your mother. Two from the play were not about love. One was 'hidden in a cloud of crimson Catherine-wheels,' and the other was 'nest in my flax.' The second is about love if the whole phrase is underlined, and the 'nest in my flax' has been underlined twice. Your father was very deliberate in his highlighting, as Al will tell you."

Al was pulling on the thick gloves as he replied. "'Nest in my flax' is said by the young hero, who falls hopelessly in love with the heroine who is promised to someone else."

Lucas Dorey was looking around him as he spoke.

"Tell me what it is. So I can feel him in here with me."

Al looked at Moretti.

"You'll remember it best," he said, and Moretti turned to Gus Dorey's son.

"'Oh God, God, God, God, God. I can see such trouble. Is life sending a flame to nest in my flax?'"

Moretti wondered if they were all thinking the same thing.

What must it be to feel such a love.

"Let's get started."

They put on the masks and gloves, got up on the sets of steps they had brought with them, and started to cut into Gus Dorey's pink ceiling and, fittingly enough, it was Lucas who found what Gus Dorey had kept hidden from envious eyes. He pulled the papers out from their hiding place, and the late afternoon sun flooded the little space, turning the pink batts into crimson Catherine-wheels.

They stayed with Lucas as he read his father's will, leaving everything to his long-lost son, and looked through the marriage lines that would make any male offspring of his the Gastineau heir. Sitting in his father's chair, he told them what he knew of his past and his quest to discover Gus Dorey. His mother died young, he always thought his name was Gaskell, and he was raised by a distant relative in the Gastineau family whose surname was not Gastineau.

"My mother also called herself Gaskell, but when I started digging, I found she had changed it by deed poll before I was born, and the shortened birth certificate that came in after 1947 made it easier to hide illegitimacy, which made my search more difficult. So I investigated my adoptive father's family, and that is how I came across the Gastineau name. I got my bank to transfer me to Guernsey, but was getting nowhere." He smiled at Moretti. "Then you found him for me."

"Didn't you think of confronting the Gastineaus?" Al asked, and Lucas laughed.

"They had hidden my mother's past with such care, I knew I would get nowhere. I had to find my father, and I had to find out if they were, in fact, married. I work in finance, and I know the power of money. I was sure this was about money.

"I decided that it would be a good idea to hide myself from them too while I was looking. So, I changed my first name to Aaron. Lucas-Lucy. Too alike."

Lucas Gastineau-Dorey raised his face to catch the last rays of the setting sun.

"But they both mean 'Bringer of Light,'" he said. "Illumination."

* * *

"So, the murder of Roddy Bull was just a case of a madman taking precautions," Al said, as he and Moretti and Falla walked back to their cars in a glorious sunset at the end of a beautiful day.

"From what Elodie was told by Jim Landers, yes," replied Falla. "That right, Guv? That's what Elodie told you?" She was giving Moretti one of her unfathomable looks, except he could guess what she was trying to fathom, and that made two of them.

"That's how Landers saw it, but from what Ginnie said to you, she may well have egged Jim on to do it, while she took care of Tanya. What would be the point of killing only Tanya if she had told Roddy Bull about the search in Bristol for evidence of the marriage?"

"Jim Landers thought he was the leader, but he may have been the follower, you think?" Al asked. "Certainly it fits the pattern of his personality, always in someone's shadow, hiding behind his books."

"An easily persuaded follower. Ginnie needed them both out of the way, and at some point she found out that the husband of Lucy Gastineau was probably Gus Dorey. Probably learned that from Rory. Those Gastineaus stick together when there's a threat to the family. We now know that Rory had discovered that much from tracing a Bristol connection."

"But Lucas is a Dorey, descended from a female Gastineau, isn't he?" Al asked. "Couldn't Ginnie have challenged it?"

"Lucas is older than Rory, and she knows the terms of the Gastineau inheritance better than we do, and more than anything else, she wanted to dethrone Marla. Remember, Falla, what she said to you, how she hated both mother and daughter."

Liz thought back to the hour she had spent with Ginnie Purvis, listening to the hatred of all things bright and beautiful spewing from her. "Remember what I said to you, Guv, after we interviewed her? About babes?"

"I remember."

Moretti thought of another quotation underlined in the play that had changed the lives of two young people, and the son they had left behind.

> ... *whenever my thoughts are cold, and I lay them*
> *Against Richard's name, they seem to rest*
> *On the warm ground where summer sits*
> *As golden as a humblebee,*
> *So I did very little but think of you.*

Gus Dorey had altered the name "Richard" in the words he must have heard Lucy Gastineau say, when she played Alizon, opposite his Richard, and he fell in love with her. He had written in her name, three times.

Lucy, Lucy, Lucy.

Curtain Call

"*Curlew*. I like the name."

They had lowered the sails as they approached the coastline, well out from the rocks by Les Sommeilleuses, and dropped anchor where the curve of the land protected them from the wind. Liz had lowered the anchor from the bow, making sure the chain ran freely, sinking into the sandy sea floor.

"Glad you like it. Who knew you were a sailor, Falla."

Seemed strange to call her "Falla" out here, but asking her to crew for him had been enough of a step, and one forced upon him because Don was otherwise occupied — and who could blame him.

"Haven't been one for years. Used to crew for my Uncle Vern."

"The uncle who cries at weddings?"

"Mr. Histrionic, yes. He's a fan of yours."

The *Curlew* bobbed gently in the light breeze on an amazing autumn day that Moretti had described as a gift from the gods. But the birds were not fooled by this return to summer and, overhead, the skies teemed with plovers, waders, birds Moretti didn't recognize, passing over the island on their way south.

"I wanted the name of a bird for the boat, and chose *Curlew* because they stay with us. And I like their cry — can hardly call it a song. Too lonely for that."

Liz looked up at the cliffs that towered above them, the honeycomb of caves where they touched the water.

"There's a cave that sings along here. That's a lonely sound, also."

Moretti took out a foil-wrapped baguette, sliced, stuffed with cheese, olives and prosciutto, and waved it at Falla.

"From Deb. She's cheerful again, now she's convinced Ronnie Marika is a no-go."

"I think Lonnie did that for her." They both laughed. "Pass me a chunk."

Moretti did so.

"By the way, Elodie has given Lucas the push."

"Really." Moretti's face was buried in a large slice of baguette, his voice muffled.

"She says she's not interested in being the mother of his children, just to put Gastineau noses out of joint."

"Ah."

"Tanya lost her baby."

"Yes. And I think Rory will lose Tanya."

"She'll leave him, you mean."

"Yes."

There was a moment's silence between them, and Moretti listened to the waves slapping gently against the side of the *Curlew*. The sound made him think of Dwight playing drums as Falla sang "What's It All About, Alfie?" and that made him think of Aloisio Brown. It was a pity the Fénions were going to lose his talent.

As if reading his thoughts, Falla broke the silence.

"I shall miss Al."

"Me too."

"So it was Ginnie who turned off the lights at the reading, and Priestley who screamed."

"He was terrified of Ginnie, who knew about the school scandal and threatened him with exposure. It involved an underage boy."

"Biggest mystery of all, Guv. Why didn't Lucy fight for Gus Dorey? Bernie says he was a really successful lawyer, specializing in women's rights et cetera. So why not?"

Moretti looked at Liz Falla's cheerful, happy face, lightly smeared with Deb's homemade mayonnaise. She neatly flicked at a drop before it landed on the Guernsey beneath her open windbreaker, and turned to laugh at him as she licked it off her finger. He felt a million years old.

"The Dark Ages, Falla. That's what it was like for women back then. A baby out of wedlock, and you were hidden away until the deed was over. Even girls who were nobodies were sent to another island or to the mainland, and this was a Gastineau."

Jill Downie

"Of course, it could be, you know, that for her this was just a fling, but for Gus Dorey it was — what's that French phrase?"

Liz Falla was wiping her fingers as he answered, but something in his voice made her look up as he replied.

"*Coup de foudre*. I think you could be right. I think they married, legitimizing the baby, and then she gave in to family pressure. There's a possibility it was a shotgun wedding to — as they said in the bad old days — hide her shame. Because of the mess-up at the university, we don't know if she even finished her degree. *Coup de foudre* for one and a fling for the other."

Lucy, Lucy, Lucy.

Overhead the seabirds continued their relentless drive to leave the approaching winter behind them.

Acknowledgements

The idea for this book was born from a conversation with my brother Richard, about his memories of a childhood friend from one of the great Guernsey families: *les messux*. Thank you, Richard! My thanks also go to my stepson, Rob, a plainclothes detective, for information about the mentality of killers, their fantasies and patterns of behaviour; and to my grandson, Colin, for sharing his knowledge of vampire lore. The tragic Guernsey goat story was passed on to me by longtime friend, Jan Howieson, and the incident in the Naval Observation Tower is based on something that happened to my brother Christopher, when we were children.

I am grateful to Mark Waddicor, my contemporary at Bristol University, for checking the e-book versions, and catching problems as they become available in the United Kingdom, and to Hilda Michel, for help with the German. My daughter Helena has patiently guided me as I entered another mysterious world, the world of social media, holding my hand as I once held hers. The rare book discovered at the University of Alberta is a fact; the Guernsey edition is a fiction.

My gratitude goes to my agent, Bill Hanna, the Dundurn team of Diane Young, Editorial Director, Margaret Bryant, Director of Sales and Marketing, designer Laura Boyle, and publicist Jim Hatch, for guiding the Moretti and Falla series through the reefs and shoals of the publishing world. Warm thanks go to my editor, Dominic Farrell, for his attention to detail and his clarity.

And thank you to Elaine Berry, and my Guernsey Ladies' College schoolfriend, Ros Hammarskjold, and her husband, Frank, for their hospitality, and the pleasure of their company every time we visit the island. To my husband, Ian, my first reader, with whom I now share this beautiful island, love always.

Other Moretti and Falla Mysteries

Daggers and Men's Smiles
9781554888689
$11.99

On the English Channel Island of Guernsey, Detective Inspector Ed Moretti and his new partner, Liz Falla, investigate vicious attacks on Epicure Films. The international production company is shooting a movie based on British bad-boy author Gilbert Ensor's best-selling novel about an Italian aristocratic family at the end of the Second World War, using fortifications from the German occupation of Guernsey as locations, and the manor house belonging to the expatriate Vannonis.

When vandalism escalates into murder, Moretti must resist the attractions of Ensor's glamorous American wife, Sydney, consolidate his working relationship with Falla, and establish whether the murders on Guernsey go beyond the island.

Why is the Marchesa Vannoni in Guernsey? What is the significance of the design that appears on the daggers used as murder weapons, as well as on the Vannoni family crest? And what role does the marchesa's statuesque niece, Giulia, who runs the family business, really play?

A Grave Waiting
9781459706361
$11.99

In St. Peter Port Harbour, on the Channel Island of Guernsey, Detective Inspector Ed Moretti and his partner, Detective Sergeant Liz Falla, are called in to investigate the shooting death of arms dealer Bernard Masterson on the *Just Desserts*, his luxury yacht. Why are Masterson, his glamorous partner in crime, Adèle Letourneau, and his thuggish bodyguard here on the island? And how are an ex-Folies Bergère dancer, a former espionage agent, and a wealthy sax-playing financier involved — or are they?

With the knowledge that there's nowhere to hide in a world now as small as his island, and not knowing whom to trust in a mystery involving money and international intrigue, Moretti goes to London in search of answers, returning to Guernsey for a violent showdown on the *Just Desserts*.

Available at your favourite bookseller

DUNDURN

Visit us at
Dundurn.com | @dundurnpress | Facebook.com/dundurnpress
Pinterest.com/dundurnpress